RED RIBBONS

LOUISE PHILLIPS

RED
RIBBONS

still clearer if we knew the style of the real music which went with the plays but is now lost—yet the quality is first of all one of mind or temperament, that of a poet so powerful he can transmute the most abject material into his own magnanimity, as he can the dreariest into his own joy. There is, at this pitch of comedy, a kind of *katharsis* not unlike the tragic. If tragedy converts the dreadful and the pitiable into a variety of pleasure, one might say that comedy—at least the Aristophanic sort—converts the degrading and stultifying and hateful into sheer joy. Indeed it can convert even the dreadful and pitiable—as the Peloponnesian war into the *Lysistrata*—so Plato may well have identified the tragedian and the comedian on something like this ground.

Of a Greek play one may also expect a dramatic structure as severe as some ideal of the Doric order in architecture. To a classical theorist Aristophanes is again disappointing, especially when compared to the elegant carpentry of Menander or Terence. His construction, if one must call it that, is usually episodic and arbitrary, and Aristotle himself has given that kind of construction a very low grade, at least in tragedy. We do not know what he thought of it in comedy, but he perhaps would have allowed a value to it, as he was willing to call Euripides the most tragic of tragedians though the "economics" of his form were poor. A closed and tight construction, even in tragedy, is open to question, as for example what really alienates one at last from most of Ibsen is that not a syllable is free from direct contribution to the total form. And who has a kind word for the "well-made play"?

Aristophanes is a very mixed case. The *Lysistrata* does have a fairly consecutive construction, even a "beginning, middle, and end" in spite of many outriding episodes. But most of his plays are more loosely put together than a Broadway review—loosely, that is, in terms of "serious" dramaturgy. The looseness is necessary to accommodate the essentially wayward movement of the comic mind. If tragedy lives on consequence, comedy lives on inconsequence, so that New Comedy, with its carefully arranged intrigues, tends to be rather serious and a comedy of character rather than of action. If the action of the *Lysistrata*—the organization, the vicissitudes, and the final success of a sex-strike against war—does provide a sort of framing unity and even a gravity, it is worked mainly to yield occasions for a wild variety of episodes, topics, anecdotes, and numbers . . . rather as the plot of the average opera is worked. The scheme, especially the metrical scheme, of many of the numbers was, it appears, traditional, but the tradition seems to have been of a variety show, not at all strict but naturally exploiting familiar topics and manners.

One tends to expect a comedy to maintain a single tone of

humor throughout, rather as one expects a Greek tragedy to begin with lugubriousness and stay with it to the end, or else to become very steadily more and more lugubrious until a climax of unendurability is reached, but Aristophanes varies both frequently and far from the broad style of humor one expects of him. Most of these variations are still easy to follow, but sometimes there is a very quick change to a different vein of wit which can be confusing and hence not funny. After all, the English or American reader is not likely to have the mercuriality of the Athenian mind and may expect a tone to be sustained somewhat longer. Aristophanes will shift, as for example on page 13, from a rollicking grotesque to a very pretty almost childish whimsy and back again. I for one find the bellicose old man's giving orders to his firepot, as a general would to a colonel, not very funny. I might find it delightful in another context or in another work, a more delicate fantasy than this play is as a whole, but the Athenian seems to have been perfectly ready for such changes in manner. Again, there are four songs of so delicate and playful a form of wit that one is baffled to find them in so forcible a work. These songs, which severally make offers of money, dinners, clothing, and wheat, but then make these gifts implicitly unavailable, have a sort of gentle flirtatiousness, a mildness and a Hellenistic grace which is bewildering to the reader fixed for the next High Classical guffaw.

> "All the rich embroideries, the
> scarves, the gold accessories, the
> trailing gowns, the robes I own
> I begrudge to no man: let him take what things he will
> for his daughter or a grown
> daughter who must dress for the procession up Athena's hill.
> Freely of my present stocks
> I invite you all to take.
> There are here no seals nor locks
> very hard to break.
> Search through every bag and box,
> look—you will find nothing there
> if your eyesight isn't fine—
> sharper far than mine!"

Again, the little songs on Melanion and Timon have a casualness and ease about them that one has trouble getting into focus after more violent passages. Most disturbing, however, is the blend of tears and laughter when the women conciliate the old men who are weeping from the intensity of their inward struggle between outraged dignity and need for affection. This moment of almost maudlin sentimentality is the last thing one would expect of Aristophanes, though it is standard in the English music hall and very good Dickens. It is genuinely touching—at least I have to admit I am touched by it—but so disconcerting one is not ready to move even into the bland manner of the passage which follows. Aristophanes is wonderfully skilled in modulating his tones and keys, and with them the feelings of his original audience, but in order to begin to follow him properly we now have to read him with a somewhat forced alertness of response. Besides the finesse of feeling there is a finesse of logic which can escape a mind less infatuated with legalities than the Athenian. For example:

"Cross-examine them! Never believe one word
  they tell you—refute them, confound them!"

or, in its context:

"Such things as that result of course in things like this:"

Can a modern audience catch these absurdities on the wing, so to say? The reader can take his own time and appreciate them, but they were written for an audience whose principal form of entertainment, outside of the theatre, was the court of law.

His variability keeps up to the very end. The last few songs are, in the original, quite conventionally beautiful songs, but one of them is straight poetry and the others, quite as beautiful, are overlaid by a comic Doric accent. And the final twist, more somber than funny, is the last word of the play: *pammachon,* which I have translated perhaps too emphatically as "unvanquished in war." After peace has been made, in the play, and the whole chorus is engaged in jubilant dance and song, we get this final word, like a sudden trumpet or roll of drums, as if to return the audience to the real war still going on. The song is in the Doric or Spartan dialect, so its invocation of the war-goddess of Athens has a strange, perhaps a comic, coloring from the enemy accent, though that accent coheres well enough with what was no doubt the Dorian mode in the music, the proper mode for war-songs. I am not at all certain of the effect Aristophanes intended, but I suspect that with his high comic hand he is throwing away the whole play or reversing its meaning— a form of irony that is inexactly called "romantic." Perhaps the ambiguous ending would conciliate the war-minded among his audience as the rest of the play would cheer the peace-minded? Or is he making a last-minute suggestion that Sparta ally herself with Athens against their old common enemy, Persia?

There are many such problems about the exact effects intended, and I must at times have flatted the original tones abominably in translating. But let me not go into a lament on the difficulties of translation—it is a form of lament which has never been a pleasure to anyone, and the whole question is covered once for all in the Italian formula: *traduttore, traditore.*

Yet a few explanations are due the reader who is unfamiliar with the Greek original and cannot tell how much is being betrayed. I have generalized a number of the jokes, added about three which came of themselves into the English wording, and reduced to common knowledge some of the less familiar references. Otherwise I have made as literal a translation as I could, under verse conditions. In the choric parts and in the long dispute between Lysistrata and the Commissioner and so on I have used rhyme, and this requires a little juggling with the sense and a bit of padding here and there. The original does not rhyme, but I think that to the modern ear rhyme is necessary to mark the measures of the rhythm and heighten the movement. I have used metrical schemes reasonably like those of the original, sometimes very like, but the metric of Greek choruses is usually so complex that when roughly duplicated in English the rhythm turns out languid or irresolute or positively inert. Or so it affects me, and I am fairly sure that stage verse in English, above all if it is comic, should have a very emphatic beat and momentum, at the risk of vulgarity. At the same time I have tried for an effect of rhythmic variety as abundant as that of the original. Tried. But the reader is implored to remember, when my verse fails to remind him, that the *Lysistrata* is a lyric poem in the form of a play.

As to diction, especially in the matter of obscene words, I have kept as closely as I could to basic slang. I have in one instance used the overly dignified word *penis* because I needed two syllables at the time and could tell myself that the passage in which it occurs is mock-tragic. Otherwise I have kept to words of one syllable and the standard usage of the American barroom as I know it.

The reader will perhaps be startled by the use of an American Southern accent when the Spartan characters speak or sing. It happens to be a miraculously good equivalent of the Doric accent as it affected the Attic ear. It was a cooing sort of noise, a little comic and sometimes irritating. It sounded rustic and yet could suggest aggressive pomposity, like certain Texan subvarieties of our Southern norm. In British translations of Greek, the Doric is often represented by a Scots accent or some other diction from the rural areas of the island, but the flavor is largely lost on an American reader and I think none of them gets so exactly the tone and connotation of Doric as a modified Texan does. For the pastorals of Theocritus no doubt a Mississippi accent is indicated, but for the Spartans of Aristophanes I think Texan is the key.

Dudley Fitts has already used the Southern accent for Doric in his translation of the *Lysistrata,* but it so happens, because of my elliptical habits of scholarship, that I do not owe the device to him. I neglected to read his translation before doing this one. I now owe him my confidence, however, that the device is entirely right, and I appeal to his authority.

I used, for the translation, both the Oxford text and the Budé text with French translation. Sometimes, when in a quandary about interpretations, I consulted the English translations by B. B. Rogers and Professor C. T. Murphy, as well as the anonymous prose translation in *The Complete Greek Drama,* edited by Oates and O'Neill.

Aristophanes:
LYSISTRATA

Translated by Donald Sutherland

Characters   *Lysistrata*

               Kalonike   } *Athenian women*

               Myrrhina

               Lampito, a Spartan woman

               Chorus of Old Men

               Chorus of Women

               Athenian Commissioner

               Old Market-Women

               Cinesias, an Athenian, husband of Myrrhina

               Spartan Herald

               Spartan Ambassadors

               Athenian Ambassadors

A street in Athens before daylight.

Lysistrata

If anyone had asked them to a festival
of Aphrodite or of Bacchus or of Pan,
you couldn't get through Athens for the tambourines,
but now there's not one solitary woman here.
Except my next-door neighbor. Here she's coming out.
Hello, Kalonike.

Kalonike

Hello, Lysistrata.
What are you so upset about? Don't scowl so, dear.
You're less attractive when you knit your brows and
glare.

Lysistrata

I know, Kalonike, but I am smoldering
with indignation at the way we women act.
Men think we are so gifted for all sorts of crime
that we will stop at nothing—

Kalonike

Well, we are, by Zeus!

Lysistrata

—but when it comes to an appointment here with me
to plot and plan for something really serious
they lie in bed and do not come.

Kalonike

They'll come, my dear.
You know what trouble women have in going out:
one of us will be wrapped up in her husband still,
another waking up the maid, or with a child
to put to sleep, or give its bath, or feed its pap.

Lysistrata

But they had other more important things to do than
those.

Kalonike

What ever is it, dear Lysistrata?
What have you called us women all together for?

13

How much of a thing is it?

Lysistrata

Very big.

Kalonike

And thick?

Lysistrata

Oh very thick indeed.

Kalonike

Then *how* can we be late?

Lysistrata

That's not the way it is. Or we would all be here.
But it is something I have figured out myself
and turned and tossed upon for many a sleepless night.

Kalonike

It must be something slick you've turned and tossed
upon!

Lysistrata

So slick that the survival of all Greece depends upon the
women.

Kalonike

On the women? In that case
poor Greece has next to nothing to depend upon.

Lysistrata

Since now it's we who must decide affairs of state:
either there is to be no Spartan left alive—

Kalonike

A very good thing too, if none were left, by Zeus!

Lysistrata

—and every living soul in Thebes to be destroyed—

Kalonike

Except the eels! Spare the delicious eels of Thebes!

Lysistrata

—and as for Athens—I can't bring myself to say
the like of that for us. But just think what I mean!
Yet if the women meet here as I told them to
from Sparta, Thebes, and all of their allies,
and we of Athens, all together we'll save Greece.

Kalonike

What reasonable thing could women ever do,
or glorious, we who sit around all prettied up
in flowers and scandalous saffron-yellow gowns,
groomed and draped to the ground in oriental stuffs
and fancy pumps?

Lysistrata
>>>>>And those are just the very things
I count upon to save us—wicked saffron gowns,
perfumes and pumps and rouge and sheer transparent
>>frocks.

Kalonike
But what use can they be?

Lysistrata
>>>>>So no man in our time
will raise a spear against another man again—

Kalonike
I'll get a dress dyed saffron-yellow, come what may!

Lysistrata
—nor touch a shield—

Kalonike
>>>>>I'll slip into the sheerest gown!

Lysistrata
—nor so much as a dagger—

Kalonike
>>>>>I'll buy a pair of pumps!

Lysistrata
So don't you think the women should be here by now?

Kalonike
I don't. They should have *flown* and got here long ago.

Lysistrata
You'll see, my dear. They will, like good Athenians,
do everything too late. But from the coastal towns
no woman is here either, nor from Salamis.

Kalonike
I'm certain those from Salamis have crossed the strait:
they're always straddling *something* at this time of night.

Lysistrata
Not even those I was expecting would be first
to get here, from Acharnae, from so close to town,
not even they are here.

Kalonike
>>>>>But one of them, I know,
is under way, and three sheets to the wind, by now.
But look—some women are approaching over there.

Lysistrata
And over here are some, coming this way—

Kalonike
>>>>>Phew! Phew!

Where are they from?

Lysistrata

Down by the marshes.

Kalonike

Yes, by Zeus!
It smells as if the bottoms had been all churned up!
[*Enter* MYRRHINA, *and others.*

Myrrhina
Hello Lysistrata. Are we a little late?
What's that? Why don't you speak?

Lysistrata

I don't think much of you,
Myrrhina, coming to this business only now.

Myrrhina
Well, I could hardly find my girdle in the dark.
If it's so urgent, tell us what it is. We're here.

Kalonike
Oh no. Let's wait for just a little while until
the delegates from Sparta and from Thebes arrive.

Lysistrata
You show much better judgment.
[*Enter* LAMPITO, *and others.*]

Here comes Lampito!

Lysistrata
Well, darling Lampito! My dearest Spartan friend!
How very sweet, how beautiful you look! That fresh
complexion! How magnificent your figure is!
Enough to crush a bull!

Lampito

Ah shorely think Ah could.
Ah take mah exacise. Ah jump and thump mah butt.

Kalonike
And really, what a handsome set of tits you have!

Lampito
You feel me ovah lahk a cow fo sacrafahce!

Lysistrata
And this other young thing—where ever is *she* from?

Lampito
She's prominent, Ah sweah, in Thebes—a delegate
ample enough.

Lysistrata

By Zeus, she represents Thebes well,
having so trim a ploughland.

Kalonike

Yes, by Zeus, she does!
There's not a weed of all her field she hasn't plucked.

Lysistrata

And who's the other girl?

Lampito

Theah's nothing small, Ah sweah,
or tahght about her folks in Corinth.

Kalonike

No, by Zeus!—
to judge by this side of her, nothing small or tight.

Lampito

But who has called togethah such a regiment
of all us women?

Lysistrata

Here I am. I did.

Lampito

Speak up,
just tell us what you want.

Kalonike

Oh yes, by Zeus, my dear,
do let us know what the important business is!

Lysistrata

Let me explain it, then. And yet ... before I do ...
I have one little question.

Kalonike

Anything you like.

Lysistrata

Don't you all miss the fathers of your little ones,
your husbands who have gone away to war? I'm sure
you all have husbands in the armies far from home.

Kalonike

Mine's been away five months in Thrace—a
general's guard,
posted to see his general does not desert.

Myrrhina

And mine has been away in Pylos seven whole months.

Lampito

And mahn, though he does get back home on leave
sometahms,
no soonah has he come than he is gone again.

Lysistrata

No lovers either. Not a sign of one is left.

For since our eastern allies have deserted us
they haven't sent a single six-inch substitute
to serve as leatherware replacement for our men.
Would you be willing, then, if I thought out a scheme,
to join with me to end the war?

Kalonike

Indeed I would,
even if I had to pawn this very wrap-around
and drink up all the money in one day, I would!

Myrrhina

And so would I, even if I had to see myself
split like a flounder, and give half of me away!

Lampito

And so would Ah! Ah'd climb up Mount Taygetos
if Ah just had a chance of seeing peace from theah!

Lysistrata

Then I will tell you. I may now divulge my plan.
Women of Greece!—if we intend to force the men
to make a peace, we must abstain . . .

Kalonike

From what! Speak out!

Lysistrata

But will you do it?

Kalonike

We will, though death should be the price!

Lysistrata

Well then, we must abstain utterly from the prick.
Why do you turn your backs? Where are you off to now?
And you—why pout and make such faces, shake
    your heads?
Why has your color changed? Why do you shed
    those tears?
Will you do it or will you not? Why hesitate?

Kalonike

I will not do it. Never. Let the war go on!

Myrrhina

Neither will I. By Zeus, no! Let the war go on!

Lysistrata

How can you say so, Madam Flounder, when just now
you were declaiming you would split yourself in half?

Kalonike

Anything else you like, anything! If I must
I'll gladly walk through fire. That, rather than the prick!

Because there's nothing like it, dear Lysistrata.

Lysistrata
How about you?

Myrrhina
          I too would gladly walk through fire.

Lysistrata
Oh the complete depravity of our whole sex!
It is no wonder tragedies are made of us,
we have such unrelenting unity of mind!
But you, my friend from Sparta, dear, if you alone
stand by me, only you, we still might save the cause.
Vote on my side!

Lampito
        They'ah hahd conditions, mahty hahd,
to sleep without so much as the fo'skin of one . . .
but all the same . . . well . . . yes. We need peace
    just as bad.

Lysistrata
Oh dearest friend!—the one real woman of them all!

Kalonike
And if we really should abstain from what you say—
which Heaven forbid!—do you suppose on that account
that peace might come to be?

Lysistrata
             I'm absolutely sure.
If we should sit around, rouged and with skins
    well creamed,
with nothing on but a transparent negligée,
and come up to them with our deltas plucked
    quite smooth,
and, once our men get stiff and want to come to grips,
we do not yield to them at all but just hold off,
they'll make a truce in no time. There's no doubt of that.

Lampito
We say in Spahta that when Menelaos saw
Helen's ba'e apples he just tossed away his swo'd.

Kalonike
And what, please, if our husbands just toss *us* away?

Lysistrata
Well, you have heard the good old saying: Know Thyself.

Kalonike
It isn't worth the candle. I hate cheap substitutes.
But what if they should seize and drag us by brute force

into the bedroom?

Lysistrata

Hang onto the doors!

Kalonike

And if—

they beat us?

Lysistrata

Then you must give in, but nastily,
and do it badly. There's no fun in it by force.
And then, just keep them straining. They will give it up
in no time—don't you worry. For never will a man
enjoy himself unless the woman coincides.

Kalonike

If both of you are for this plan, then so are we.

Lampito

And we of Spahta shall persuade ouah men to keep
the peace sinceahly and with honah in all ways,
but how could anyone pe'suade the vulgah mob
of Athens not to deviate from discipline?

Lysistrata

Don't worry, we'll persuade our men. They'll keep
      the peace.

Lampito

They won't, so long as they have battleships afloat
and endless money sto'ed up in the Pahthenon.

Lysistrata

But that too has been carefully provided for:
we shall take over the Acropolis today.
The oldest women have their orders to do that:
while *we* meet here, *they* go as if to sacrifice
up there, but really seizing the Acropolis.

Lampito

All should go well. What you say theah is very smaht.

Lysistrata

In that case, Lampito, what are we waitng for?
Let's take an oath, to bind us indissolubly.

Lampito

Well, just you show us what the oath is. Then
      we'll sweah.

Lysistrata

You're right. Where is that lady cop?
[*To the armed* LADY COP *looking around for a* LADY COP.]

What do you think

you're looking for? Put down your shield in front of us,
there, on its back, and someone get some scraps of gut.

Kalonike

Lysistrata, what in the world do you intend
to make us take an oath on?

Lysistrata

What? Why, on a shield,
just as they tell me some insurgents in a play
by Aeschylus once did, with a sheep's blood and guts.

Kalonike

Oh, *don't*, Lysistrata, don't swear upon a *shield*,
not if the oath has anything to do with peace!

Lysistrata

Well then, what *will* we swear on? Maybe we
   should get
a white horse somewhere, like the Amazons, and cut
some bits of gut from it.

Kalonike

Where would we get a horse?

Lysistrata

But what kind of an oath *is* suitable for us?

Kalonike

By Zeus, I'll tell you if you like. First we put down
a big black drinking-cup, face up, and then we let
the neck of a good jug of wine bleed into it,
and take a solemn oath to—add no water in.

Lampito

Bah Zeus, Ah jest can't tell you how Ah lahk that oath!

Lysistrata

Someone go get a cup and winejug from inside.

[KALONIKE *goes and is back in a flash.*

Kalonike

My dears, my dearest dears—how's *this* for pottery?
You feel good right away, just laying hold of it.

Lysistrata

Well, set it down, and lay your right hand on this pig.
O goddess of Persuasion, and O Loving-cup,
accept this victim's blood! Be gracious unto us.

Kalonike

It's not anemic, and flows clear. Those are good signs.

Lampito

What an aroma, too! Bah Castah it *is* sweet!

Kalonike

My dears, if you don't mind—I'll be the first to swear.

Lysistrata

By Aphrodite, no! If you had drawn first place
by lot—but now let all lay hands upon the cup.
Yes, Lampito—and now, let one of you repeat
for all of you what I shall say. You will be sworn
by every word she says, and bound to keep this oath:
No lover and no husband and no man on earth—

Kalonike

No lover and no husband and no man on earth—

Lysistrata

shall e'er approach me with his penis up. Repeat.

Kalonike

shall e'er approach me with his penis up. Oh dear,
my knees are buckling under me, Lysistrata!

Lysistrata

and I shall lead an unlaid life alone at home,

Kalonike

and I shall lead an unlaid life alone at home,

Lysistrata

wearing a saffron gown and groomed and beautified

Kalonike

wearing a saffron gown and groomed and beautified

Lysistrata

so that my husband will be all on fire for me

Kalonike

so that my husband will be all on fire for me

Lysistrata

but I will never willingly give in to him

Kalonike

but I will never willingly give in to him

Lysistrata

and if he tries to force me to against my will

Kalonike

and if he tries to force me to against my will

Lysistrata

I'll do it badly and not wiggle in response

Kalonike

I'll do it badly and not wiggle in response

Lysistrata

nor toward the ceiling will I lift my Persian pumps

Kalonike
nor toward the ceiling will I lift my Persian pumps
Lysistrata
nor crouch down as the lions on cheese-graters do
Kalonike
nor crouch down as the lions on cheese-graters do
Lysistrata
and if I keep my promise, may I drink of this—
Kalonike
and if I keep my promise, may I drink of this—
Lysistrata
but if I break it, then may water fill the cup!
Kalonike
but if I break it, then may water fill the cup!
Lysistrata
Do you all swear to this with her?
All
We do, by Zeus!

Lysistrata
I'll consecrate our oath now.
Kalonike
Share alike, my dear,
so we'll be friendly to each other from the start.
Lampito
What was that screaming?
Lysistrata
That's what I was telling you:
the women have already seized the Parthenon
and the Acropolis. But now, dear Lampito,
return to Sparta and set things in order there—
but leave these friends of yours as hostages with us—
And let *us* join the others in the citadel
and help them bar the gates.
Kalonike
But don't you think the men
will rally to the rescue of the citadel,
attacking us at once?
Lysistrata
They don't worry me much:
they'll never bring against us threats or fire enough
to force open the gates, except upon our terms.
Kalonike
Never by Aphrodite! Or we'd lose our name

for being battle-axes and unbearable!

[*Exeunt. The scene changes to the Propylaea of the Acropolis. A* chorus *of very old men struggles slowly in, carrying logs and firepots.*

One Old Man

> Lead on! O Drakës, step by step, although your
>   shoulder's aching
> and under this green olive log's great weight
>   your back be breaking!

Another

> Eh, life is long but always has
>   more surprises for us!
> Now who'd have thought we'd live to hear
>   *this*, O Strymodorus?—
>
> The wives we fed and looked upon
> as helpless liabilities
> now dare to occupy the Parthenon,
> our whole Acropolis, for once they seize
> the Propylaea, straightway
> they lock and bar the gateway.

Chorus

Let's rush to the Acropolis with due precipitation
and lay these logs down circlewise, till presently we
    turn them
into one mighty pyre to make a general cremation
of all the women up there—eh! with our own hands we'll
    burn them,
the leaders and the followers, without discrimination!

An Old Man

> They'll never have the laugh on me!
>   Though I may not look it,
> I rescued the Acropolis
>   when the Spartans took it
> about a hundred years ago.
> We laid a siege that kept their king
> six years unwashed, so when I made him throw
> his armor off, for all his blustering,
> in nothing but his shirt he
> looked very very dirty.

Chorus

How strictly I besieged the man! These gates were all
    invested

with seventeen ranks of armored men all equally
　　ferocious!
Shall women—by Euripides and all the gods detested—
not be restrained—with me on hand—from something
　　so atrocious?
They shall!—or may our trophies won at Marathon
　　be bested!

　　　　But we must go a long way yet
　　　　up that steep and winding road
　　　　before we reach the fortress where we want to
　　　　　　get.
　　　　　　How shall we ever drag this load,
　　　　　　lacking pack-mules, way up there?
I can tell you that my shoulder has caved in
　　beyond repair!
　　　　　　Yet we must trudge ever higher,
　　　　　　ever blowing on the fire,
　　　　so its coals will still be glowing when we get
　　　　　　where we are going
　　　　　　　　Fooh! Fooh!
　　　　　　　　Whoo! I choke!
　　　　　　　　What a smoke!

　　　　　　Lord Herakles! How fierce it flies
　　　　　　out against me from the pot!
and like a rabid bitch it bites me in the eyes!
　　　　　　It's female fire, or it would not
　　　　　　scratch my poor old eyes like this.
Yet undaunted we must onward, up the high
　　Acropolis
　　　　　　where Athena's temple stands
　　　　　　fallen into hostile hands.
O my comrades! shall we ever have a greater
　　need to save her?
　　　　　　　　Fooh! Fooh!
　　　　　　　　Whoo! I choke!
　　　　　　　　What a smoke!

First Old Man
　　Well, thank the gods, I see the fire is yet alive
　　　　and waking!
Second Old Man
　　Why don't we set our lumber down right here in
　　　　handy batches,

then stick a branch of grape-vine in the pot until it
catches

Third Old Man

and hurl ourselves against the gate with battering
and shaking?

First Old Man

and if the women won't unbar at such an ultimatum
we'll set the gate on fire and then the smoke will
suffocate 'em.

Second Old Man

Well, let's put down our load. Fooh fooh, what smoke!
But blow as needed!

Third Old Man

Your ablest generals *these* days would not carry wood
like *we* did.

Second Old Man

At last the lumber ceases grinding my poor back
to pieces!

Third Old Man

These are your orders, Colonel Pot: wake up the coals
and bid them
report here and present to me a torch lit up and flaring.

First Old Man

O Victory, be with us! If you quell the women's daring
we'll raise a splendid trophy of how you and we undid
them!

[A CHORUS *of middle-aged women appears in the offing.*

A Woman

I think that I perceive a smoke in which appears a flurry
of sparks as of a lighted fire. Women, we'll have to hurry!

Chorus of Women

Oh fleetly fly, oh swiftly flit,
my dears, e'er Kalykë be lit
and with Kritylla swallowed up alive
in flames which the gales dreadfully drive
and deadly old men fiercely inflate!
Yet one thing I'm afraid of: will I not arrive
too late?
for filling up my water-jug has been no easy
matter
what with the crowd at the spring in the dusk
and the clamor and pottery clatter.
Pushed as I was, jostled by slave-

women and sluts marked with a brand
yet with my jug firmly in hand
here I have come, hoping to save
    my burning friends and brave,

for certain windy, witless, old,
and wheezy fools, so I was told,
with wood some tons in weight crept up this
    path,
    not having in mind heating a bath
    but uttering threats, vowing they will
consume those nasty women into cinders on grill!
But O Athena! never may I see my friends
    igniting!
Nay!—let them save all the cities of Greece
    and their
        people from folly and fighting!
Goddess whose crest flashes with gold,
they were so bold taking your shine
only for this—Goddess who hold
Athens—for *this* noble design,
braving the flames, calling on you
    to carry water too!

[*One of the old men urinates noisily.*

Chorus of Women

Be still! What was that noise? Aha! Oh, wicked and
    degraded!
Would any good religious men have ever done what
    they did?

Chorus of Men

Just look! It's a surprise-attack! Oh, dear, we're being
    raided
by swarms of them below us when we've got a swarm
    above us!

Chorus of Women

Why panic at the sight of us? This is not many of us.
We number tens of thousands but you've hardly seen a
    fraction.

Chorus of Men

O Phaidrias, shall they talk so big and we not take some
    action?
Oh, should we not be bashing them and splintering our
    lumber?

[*The old men begin to strip for combat.*

Chorus of Women

    Let us, too, set our pitchers down, so they will not
encumber

    our movements if these gentlemen should care to offer
battle.

Chorus of Men

    Oh someone should have clipped their jaws—twice,
thrice, until they rattle—

    (as once the poet put it)—then we wouldn't hear their
prating.

Chorus of Women

    Well, here's your chance. Won't someone hit me? Here
I stand, just waiting!

    No other bitch will ever grab your balls, the way I'll
treat you!

Chorus of Men

    Shut up—or I will drub you so old age will never reach
you!

Chorus of Women

    Won't anyone step and lay one finger on Stratyllis?

Chorus of Men

    And if we pulverize her with our knuckles, will you
kill us?

Chorus of Women

    No, only chew your lungs out and your innards and
your eyes, sir.

Chorus of Men

    How clever is Euripides! There is no poet wiser: he says
indeed that women are the worst of living creatures.

Chorus of Women

    Now is the time, Rhodippe: let us raise our brimming
pitchers.

Chorus of Men

    Why come up here with water, you, the gods' abom-
ination?

Chorus of Women

    And why come here with fire, you tomb? To give
yourself cremation?

Chorus of Men

    To set your friends alight upon a pyre erected for them.

Chorus of Women

    And so we brought our water-jugs. Upon your pyre we'll

pour them.

Chorus of Men

You'll put my fire out?

Chorus of Women

Any time! You'll see there's nothing to it.

Chorus of Men

I think I'll grill you right away, with just this torch to
do it!

Chorus of Women

Have you some dusting-powder? Here's your wedding-
bath all ready.

Chorus of Men

You'll bathe me, garbage that you are?

Chorus of Women

Yes, bridegroom, just hold steady!

Chorus of Men

Friends, you have heard her insolence—

Chorus of Women

I'm free-born, not your slave, sir.

Chorus of Men

I'll have this noise of yours restrained—

Chorus of Women

Court's out—so be less grave, sir.

Chorus of Men

Why don't you set her hair on fire?

Chorus of Women

Oh, Water, be of service!

Chorus of Men

Oh woe is me!

Chorus of Women

Was it too hot?

Chorus of Men

Oh, stop! What *is* this? Hot? Oh no!

Chorus of Women

I'm watering you to make you grow.

Chorus of Men

I'm withered from this chill I got!

Chorus of Women

You've got a fire, so warm yourself. You're trembling:
are you nervous?

[*Enter a* COMMISSIONER, *escorted by four Scythian policemen with bows and quivers slung on their backs.*

Commissioner

Has the extravagance of women broken out
into full fury, with their banging tambourines
and constant wailings for their oriental gods,
and on the rooftops their Adonis festival,
which I could hear myself from the Assembly once?
For while Demostratos—that numbskull—had the floor,
urging an expedition against Sicily,
his wife was dancing and we heard her crying out
"Weep for Adonis!"—so the expedition failed
with such an omen. When the same Demostratos
was urging that we levy troops from our allies
his wife was on the roof again, a little drunk:
"Weep for Adonis! Beat your breast!" says she. At that,
he gets more bellicose, that god-Damn-ox-tratos.
To this has the incontinence of women come!

Chorus of Men

You haven't *yet* heard how outrageous they can be!
With other acts of violence, these women here
have showered us from their jugs, so now we are reduced
to shaking out our shirts as if we'd pissed in them.

Commissioner

Well, by the God of Waters, what do you expect?
When we ourselves conspire with them in waywardness
and give them good examples of perversity
such wicked notions naturally sprout in them.
We go into a shop and say something like this:
"Goldsmith, about that necklace you repaired: last night
my wife was dancing, when the peg that bolts the catch
fell from its hole. I have to sail for Salamis,
but if you have the time, by all means try to come
towards evening, and put in the peg she needs."
Another man says to a cobbler who is young
and has no child's play of a prick, "Cobbler," he says,
"her sandal-strap is pinching my wife's little toe,
which is quite delicate. So please come by at noon
and stretch it for her so it has a wider play."
Such things as that result of course in things like this:
when I, as a Commissioner, have made a deal
to fit the fleet with oars and need the money now,
I'm locked out by these women from the very gates.
But it's no use just standing here. Bring on the bars,
so I can keep these women in their proper place.

What are *you* gaping at, you poor unfortunate?
Where are *you* looking? Only seeing if a bar
is open yet downtown? Come, drive these crowbars in
under the gates on that side, pry away, and I
will pry away on this.
[LYSISTRATA *comes out.*

Lysistrata

No need to pry at all.
I'm coming out, of my own will. What use are bars?
It isn't bolts and bars we need so much as brains.

Commissioner

Really, you dirty slut? Where is that officer?
Arrest her, and tie both her hands behind her back.

Lysistrata

By Artemis, just let him lift a hand at me
and, public officer or not, you'll hear him howl.

Commissioner

You let her scare you? Grab her round the middle, you.
Then *you* go help him and between you get her tied.
[KALONIKE *comes out.*

Kalonike

By Artemis, if you just lay one hand on her
I have a mind to trample the shit out of you.

Commissioner

It's out already! Look! Now where's the other one?
Tie up *that* woman first. She babbles, with it all.
[MYRRHINA *comes out.*

Myrrhina

By Hecatë, if you just lay a hand on her
you'll soon ask for a cup—to get your swellings down!
[*The policeman dashes behind the* COMMISSIONER *and
clings to him for protection.*

Commissioner

What happened? Where's that bowman, now? Hold onto
her! [*He moves quickly away downhill.*]
I'll see that none of you can get away through here!

Lysistrata

By Artemis, you come near her and I'll bereave
your head of every hair! You'll weep for each one, too.

Commissioner

What a calamity! This one has failed me too.
But never must we let ourselves be overcome
by women. All together now, O Scythians!—

let's march against them in formation!

Lysistrata

You'll find out
that inside there we have four companies
of fighting women perfectly equipped for war.

Commissioner

Charge! Turn their flanks, O Scythians! and tie their
hands!

Lysistrata

O allies—comrades—women! Sally forth and fight!
O vegetable vendors, O green-grocery-
grain-garlic-bread-bean-dealers and inn-keepers all!

[*A group of fierce* OLD MARKET-WOMEN, *carrying baskets
of vegetables, spindles, etc. emerges. There is a volley
of vegetables. The Scythians are soon routed.*

Come pull them, push them, smite them, smash them
into bits!
Rail and abuse them in the strongest words you know!
Halt, Halt! Retire in order! We'll forego the spoils!

Commissioner

[*Tragically, like say Xerxes.*] Oh what reverses have my
bowmen undergone!

Lysistrata

But what did you imagine? Did you think you came
against a pack of slaves? Perhaps you didn't know
that women can be resolute?

Commissioner

I know they can—
above all when they spot a bar across the way.

Chorus of Men

Commissioner of Athens, you are spending words
unduly,
to argue with these animals, who only roar the louder,
or don't you know they showered us so coldly and so
cruelly,
and in our undershirts at that, and furnished us no
powder?

Chorus of Women

But beating up your neighbor is inevitably bringing
a beating on yourself, sir, with your own eyes black and
bloody.
I'd rather sit securely like a little girl demurely
not stirring up a single straw nor harming anybody,

So long as no one robs my hive and rouses me to
>   stinging.

Chorus of Men

How shall we ever tame these brutes? We cannot tolerate
the situation further, so we must investigate
>   this occurrence and find
>   with what purpose in mind
they profane the Acropolis, seize it, and lock
the approach to this huge and prohibited rock,
>   to our holiest ground!

Cross-examine them! Never believe one word
>   they tell you—refute them, confound them!
We must get to the bottom of things like this
>   and the circumstances around them.

Commissioner

Yes indeed! and I want to know first one thing:
>   just *why* you committed this treason,
barricading the fortress with locks and bars—
>   I insist on knowing the reason.

Lysistrata

To protect all the money up there from you—
>   you'll have nothing to fight for without it.

Commissioner

You think it is *money* we're fighting for?

Lysistrata

All the troubles we have are about it.
It was so Peisander and those in power
>   of his kind could embezzle the treasure
that they cooked up emergencies all the time.
>   Well, let them, if such is their pleasure,
but they'll never get into this money again,
>   though you men should elect them to spend it.

Commissioner

And just what will *you* do with it?

Lysistrata

>   Can you ask?
>   Of course we shall superintend it.

Commissioner

You will superintend the treasury, *you!?*

Lysistrata

And why should it strike you so funny?
when we manage our houses in everything

                    and it's we who look after your money.
Commissioner
    But it's not the same thing!
Lysistrata
                                   Why not?
Commissioner
                                        It's war,
    and *this* money must pay the expenses.
Lysistrata
    To begin with, you needn't be waging war.
Commissioner
                    To survive, we don't need our defenses?
Lysistrata
    You'll survive: we shall save you.
Commissioner
                                   Who? You?
Lysistrata
                                        Yes, we.
Commissioner
    You absolutely disgust me.
Lysistrata
    You may like it or not, but you *shall* be saved.
Commissioner
    I protest!
Lysistrata
                    If you care to, but, trust me,
    this has got to be done all the same.
Commissioner
                                   It has?
    It's illegal, unjust, and outrageous!
Lysistrata
    We must save you, sir.
Commissioner
                    Yes? And if I refuse?
Lysistrata
                    You will much the more grimly engage us.
Commissioner
    And whence does it happen that war and peace are fit
        matters for women to mention?
Lysistrata
    I will gladly explain—
Commissioner
                    And be quick, or else

you'll be howling!

Lysistrata

Now, just pay attention
and keep your hands to yourself, if you can!

Commissioner

But I can't. You can't think how I suffer
from holding them back in my anger!

An Old Woman

Sir—
if you don't you will have it much rougher.

Commissioner

You may croak that remark to yourself, you hag?
Will *you* do the explaining?

Lysistrata

I'll do it.
Heretofore we women in time of war
have endured very patiently through it,
putting up with whatever you men might do,
for never a peep would you let us
deliver on your unstatesmanly acts
no matter how much they upset us,
but we knew very well, while we sat at home,
when you'd handled a big issue poorly,
and we'd ask you then, with a pretty smile
though our heart would be grieving us sorely,
"And what were the terms for a truce, my dear,
you drew up in assembly this morning?"
"And what's it to you?" says our husband, "Shut up!"
—so, as ever, at this gentle warning
I of course would discreetly shut up.

Kalonike

Not me!
You can bet I would never be quiet!

Commissioner

I'll bet, if you weren't, you were beaten up.

Lysistrata

I'd shut up, and I do not deny it,
but when plan after plan was decided on,
so bad we could scarcely believe it,
I would say, "This last is so mindless, dear,
I cannot think how you achieve it!"
And then he would say, with a dirty look,
"Just you think what your spindle is for, dear,

or your head will be spinning for days on end—
>   let the *men* attend to the war, dear."

Commissioner

By Zeus, *he* had the right idea!

Lysistrata

>   You fool!
Right ideas were quite out of the question,
when your reckless policies failed, and yet
>   we never could make a suggestion.
And lately we heard you say so yourselves:
>   in the streets there'd be someone lamenting:
"There's not one man in the country now!"
>   —and we heard many others assenting.
After that, we conferred through our deputies
>   and agreed, having briefly debated,
to act in common to save all Greece
>   at once—for why should we have waited?
So now, when we women are talking sense,
>   if you'll only agree to be quiet
and to listen to us as we did to you,
>   you'll be very much edified by it.

Commissioner

You will edify *us!* I protest!

Lysistrata

>   Shut up!

Commissioner

I'm to shut up and listen, you scum, you?!
Sooner death! And a veil on your head at that!

Lysistrata

>   We'll fix that. It may really become you:
do accept this veil as a present from me.
Drape it modestly—so—round your head, do you see?
And now—*not* a word more, sir.

Kalonike

Do accept this dear little wool-basket, too!
Hitch your girdle and card! Here are beans you
>   may chew
the way all of the nicest Athenians do—
and the *women* will see to the war, sir!

Chorus of Women

Oh women, set your jugs aside and keep a closer
>   distance:

our friends may need from us as well some resolute
assistance.

Since never shall I weary of the stepping of the
dance
nor will my knees of treading, for these ladies I'll
advance
anywhere they may lead,
and they're daring indeed,
they have wit, a fine figure, and boldness of heart,
they are prudent and charming, efficient and smart,
patriotic and brave!

But, O manliest grandmothers, onward now!
And you matronly nettles, don't waver!
but continue to bristle and rage, my dears,
for you've still got the wind in your favor!

[*The* CHORUS OF WOMEN *and the* OLD MARKET-WOMEN *join.*

Lysistrata
But if only the spirit of tender Love
and the power of sweet Aphrodite
were to breathe down over our breasts and thighs
an attraction both melting and mighty,
and infuse a pleasanter rigor in men,
raising only their cudgels of passion,
then I think we'd be known throughout all of Greece
as makers of peace and good fashion.

Commissioner
Having done just what?

Lysistrata
Well, first of all
we shall certainly make it unlawful
to go madly to market in armor.

Old Market-Woman
Yes!
By dear Aphrodite, it's awful!

Lysistrata
For now, in the midst of the pottery-stalls
and the greens and the beans and the garlic,
men go charging all over the market-place
in full armor and beetling and warlike.

Commissioner
They must do as their valor impels them to!

Lysistrata

        But it makes a man only look funny
   to be wearing a shield with a Gorgon's head
      and be wanting sardines for less money.

Old Market-Women

   Well, I saw a huge cavalry captain once
      on a stallion that scarcely could hold him,
   pouring into his helmet of bronze a pint
      of pea-soup an old woman had sold him,
   and a Thracian who, brandishing shield and spear
      like some savage Euripides staged once,
   when he'd frightened a vendor of figs to death,
      gobbled up all her ripest and aged ones.

Commissioner

   And how, on the international scale,
      can you straighten out the enormous
   confusion among all the states of Greece?

Lysistrata

      Very easily.

Commissioner

          How? Do inform us.

Lysistrata

   When our skein's in a tangle we take it thus
      on our spindles, or haven't you seen us?—
   one on this side and one on the other side,
      and we work out the tangles between us.
   And that is the way we'll undo this war,
      by exchanging ambassadors, whether
   you like it or not, one from either side,
      and we'll work out the tangles together.

Commissioner

   Do you really think that with wools and skeins
      and just being able to spin you
   can end these momentous affairs, you fools?

Lysistrata

      With any intelligence in you
   you statesmen would govern as we work wool,
      and in everything Athens would profit.

Commissioner

   How so? Do tell.

Lysistrata

          First, you take raw fleece
   and you wash the beshittedness off it:

just so, you should first lay the city out
      on a washboard and beat out the rotters
and pluck out the sharpers like burrs, and when
      you find tight knots of schemers and plotters
who are out for key offices, card them loose,
      but best tear off their heads in addition.
Then into one basket together card
      all those of a good disposition
be they citizens, resident aliens, friends,
      an ally or an absolute stranger,
even people in debt to the commonwealth,
      you can mix them all in with no danger.
And the cities which Athens has colonized—
      by Zeus, you should try to conceive them
as so many shreddings and tufts of wool
      that are scattered about and not leave them
to lie around loose, but from all of them
      draw the threads in here, and collect them
into one big ball and then weave a coat
      for the people, to warm and protect them.

Commissioner
Now, isn't this awful? They treat the state
      like wool to be beaten and carded,
who have nothing at all to do with war!

Lysistrata
      Yes we do, you damnable hard-head!
We have none of your honors but we have more
      then double your sufferings by it.
First of all, we bear sons whom you send to war.

Commissioner
      Don't bring up our old sorrows! Be quiet!

Lysistrata
And now, when we ought to enjoy ourselves,
      making much of our prime and our beauty,
we are sleeping alone because all the men
      are away on their soldierly duty.
But never mind *us*—when young girls grow old
      in their bedrooms with no men to share them.

Commissioner
You seem to forget that men, too, grow old.

Lysistrata
      By Zeus, but you cannot compare them!
When a man gets back, though he be quite gray,

he can wed a young girl in a minute,
but the season of woman is very short:
she must take what she can while she's in it.
And you know she must, for when it's past,
although you're not awfully astute, you're
aware that no man will marry her then
and she sits staring into the future.

Commissioner

But he who can raise an erection still—

Lysistrata

Is there some good reason you don't drop dead?
We'll sell you a coffin if you but will.
Here's a string of onions to crown your head
and I'll make a honey-cake large and round
you can feed to Cerberus underground!

First Old-Market-Woman

Accept these few fillets of leek from me!

Second Old-Market-Woman

Let me offer you these for your garland, sir!

Lysistrata

What now? Do you want something else you see?
Listen! Charon's calling his passenger—
will you catch the ferry or still delay
when his other dead want to sail away?

Commissioner

Is it not downright monstrous to treat *me* like this?
By Zeus, I'll go right now to the Commissioners
and show myself in evidence, just as I am!

[*He begins to withdraw with dignity and his four Scythian policemen.*

Lysistrata

Will you accuse us of not giving you a wake?
But your departed spirit will receive from us
burnt offerings in due form, two days from now at dawn!

[LYSISTRATA *with the other women goes into the Acropolis.
The* COMMISSIONER *etc. have left. The male chorus and
the mixed female chorus are alone.*

Chorus of Men

No man now dare fall to drowsing, if he wishes to stay
free!
Men, let's strip and gird ourselves for this eventuality!

To me this all begins to have a smell

of bigger things and larger things as well:
most of all I sniff a tyranny afoot. I'm much afraid
   certain secret agents of the Spartans may have
      come,
   meeting under cover here, in Cleisthenes's
      home,
instigating those damned women by deceit to
   make a raid
   upon our treasury and that great sum
   the city paid my pension from.

Sinister events already!—think of lecturing the state,
women as they are, and prattling on of things like shields
   of bronze,
even trying hard to get us reconciled to those we hate—
those of Sparta, to be trusted like a lean wolf when it
   yawns!
All of this is just a pretext, men, for a dictatorship—
but to me they shall not dictate! Watch and ward! A
   sword I'll hide
underneath a branch of myrtle; through the agora I'll slip,
following Aristogeiton, backing the tyrannicide!
[*The* OLD MEN *pair off to imitate the gestures of the famous group statue of the tyrannicides Harmodius and
Aristogeiton.*
   Thus I'll take my stand beside him! Now my rage is
   goaded raw
   I'm as like as not to clip this damned old woman on the
   jaw!

Chorus of Women
   Your own mother will not know you when you come
   home, if you do!
   Let us first, though, lay our things down, O my dear old
   friends and true.

      For now, O fellow-citizens, we would
      consider what will do our city good.
   Well I may, because it bred me up in wealth and
      elegance:
      letting me at seven help with the embroidering
      of Athena's mantle, and at ten with offering
   cakes and flowers. When I was grown and beautiful I
   had my chance

> to bear her baskets, at my neck a string
> of figs, and proud as anything.

Must I not, then, give my city any good advice I can?
Need you hold the fact against me that I was not born
  a man,
when I offer better methods than the present ones, and
  when
I've a share in this economy, for I contribute men?
But, you sad old codgers, *yours* is forfeited on many
  scores:
you have drawn upon our treasure dating from the
  Persian wars,
what they call grampatrimony, and you've paid no taxes
  back.
Worse, you've run it nearly bankrupt, and the prospect's
  pretty black.
Have you anything to answer? Say you were within the
  law
and I'll take this rawhide boot and clip you one across
  the jaw!

Chorus of Men

> Greater insolence than ever!—
> that's the method that she calls
> "better"—if you would believe her.

But this threat must be prevented! Every man with both
  balls
must make ready—take our shirts off, for a man must reek
  of male
outright—not wrapped up in leafage like an omelet for
  sale!

> Forward and barefoot: we'll do it again
> to the death, just as when we resisted
> tyranny out at Leipsydrion, when
> we really existed!

> Now or never we must grow
> young again and, sprouting wings
> over all our bodies, throw
> off this heaviness age brings!

For if any of us give them even just a little hold

nothing will be safe from their tenacious grasp. They are
    so bold
they will soon build ships of war and, with exorbitant
    intent,
send such navies out against us as Queen Artemisia sent.
But if they attack with horse, our knights we might as
    well delete:
nothing rides so well as woman, with so marvelous a seat,
never slipping at the gallop. Just look at those Amazons
in that picture in the Stoa, from their horses bringing
    bronze
axes down on men. We'd better grab *these* members of
    the sex
one and all, arrest them, get some wooden collars on their
    necks!

Chorus of Women

By the gods, if you chagrin me
or annoy me, if you dare,
I'll turn loose the sow that's in me
till you rouse the town to help you with the way I've
    done your hair!
Let us too make ready, women, and our garments
    quickly doff
so we'll smell like women angered fit to bite our fingers
    off!

Now I am ready: let one of the men
come against me, and *he'll* never hanker
after black bean or garlic again:
no woman smells ranker!

Say a single unkind word,
I'll pursue you till you drop,
as the beetle did the bird.
My revenge will never stop!

Yet you will not worry me so long as Lampito's alive
and my noble friends in Thebes and other cities still
    survive.
You'll not overpower us, even passing seven decrees or
    eight,
you, poor brutes, whom everyone and everybody's
    neighbors hate.
Only yesterday I gave a party, honoring Hecatë,

but when I invited in the neighbor's child to come and
> play,
such a pretty thing from Thebes, as nice and quiet as
> you please,
just an eel, they said she couldn't, on account of your
> decrees.
You'll go on forever passing such decrees without a check
till somebody takes you firmly by the leg and breaks your
> neck!

[LYSISTRATA *comes out. The* CHORUS OF WOMEN *addresses
her in the manner of tragedy.*

Oh Queen of this our enterprise and all our hopes,
wherefore in baleful brooding hast thou issued forth?

Lysistrata

The deeds of wicked women and the female mind
discourage me and set me pacing up and down.

Chorus of Women

What's that? What's that you say?

Lysistrata

The truth, alas, the truth!

Chorus of Women

What is it that's so dreadful? Tell it to your friends.

Lysistrata

A shameful thing to tell and heavy not to tell.

Chorus of Women

Oh, never hide from me misfortune that is ours!

Lysistrata

To put it briefly as I can, we are in heat.

Chorus of Women

Oh Zeus!

Lysistrata

Why call on Zeus? This is the way things are.
At least it seems I am no longer capable
of keeping them from men. They are deserting me.
This morning I caught one of them digging away
to make a tunnel to Pan's grotto down the slope,
another letting herself down the parapet
with rope and pulley, and another climbing down
its sheerest face, and yesterday was one I found
sitting upon a sparrow with a mind to fly
down to some well-equipped whoremaster's place in
> town.
Just as she swooped I pulled her backward by the hair.

They think of every far-fetched excuse they can
for going home. And here comes one deserter now.
You there, where are you running?

First Woman

I want to go home,
because I left some fine Milesian wools at home
that must be riddled now with moths.

Lysistrata

Oh, damn your moths!
Go back inside.

First Woman

But I shall come back right away,
just time enough to stretch them out upon my bed.

Lysistrata

Stretch nothing out, and don't you go away at all.

First Woman

But shall I let my wools be ruined?

Lysistrata

If you must.

Second Woman

Oh miserable me! I sorrow for the flax
I left at home unbeaten and unstripped!

Lysistrata

One more—
wanting to leave for stalks of flax she hasn't stripped.
Come back here!

Second Woman

But, by Artemis, I only want
to strip my flax. Then I'll come right back here again.

Lysistrata

Strip me no strippings! If you start this kind of thing
some other woman soon will want to do the same.

Third Woman

O lady Artemis, hold back this birth until
I can get safe to some unconsecrated place!

Lysistrata

What is this raving?

Third Woman

I'm about to have a child.

Lysistrata

But you weren't pregnant yesterday.

Third Woman

I am today.

Oh, send me home this instant, dear Lysistrata,
so I can find a midwife.

Lysistrata

What strange tale is this?
What is this hard thing you have here?

Third Woman

The child is male.

Lysistrata

By Aphrodite, no! You obviously have
some hollow thing of bronze. I'll find out what it is.
You silly thing!—you have Athena's helmet here—
and claiming to be pregnant!

Third Woman

So I am, by Zeus!

Lysistrata

In that case, what's the helmet for?

Third Woman

So if the pains
came on me while I'm still up here, I might give birth
inside the helmet, as I've seen the pigeons do.

Lysistrata

What an excuse! The case is obvious. Wait here.
I want to show this bouncing baby helmet off.

[*She passes the huge helmet around the* CHORUS OF
WOMEN.

Second Woman

But I can't even sleep in the Acropolis,
not for an instant since I saw the sacred snake!

Fourth Woman

The owls are what are killing *me*. How can I sleep
with their eternal whit-to-whoo-to-whit-to-whoo?

Lysistrata

You're crazy! Will you stop this hocus-pocus now?
No doubt you miss your husbands: don't you think that
      they
are missing us as much? I'm sure the nights they pass
are just as hard. But, gallant comrades, do bear up,
and face these gruelling hardships yet a little while.
There is an oracle that says we'll win, if we
only will stick together. Here's the oracle.

Chorus of Women

Oh, read us what it says!

Lysistrata

Keep silence, then, and hear:

"Now when to one high place are gathered the fluttering
swallows,
Fleeing the Hawk and the Cock however hotly it
follows,
Then will their miseries end, and that which is over be
under:
Thundering Zeus will decide.

A Woman

Will *we* lie on top now, I wonder?

Lysistrata

But if the Swallows go fighting each other and springing
and winging
Out of the holy and high sanctuary, then people will
never
Say there was any more dissolute bitch of a bird
whatsoever.

A Woman

The oracle is clear, by Zeus!

Lysistrata

By *all* the gods!

So let us not renounce the hardships we endure.
But let us go back in. Indeed, my dearest friends,
it would be shameful to betray the oracle.

[*Exeunt into the Acropolis.*

Chorus of Men

Let me tell you a story I heard one day
  when I was a child:
There was once a young fellow Melanion by name
who refused to get married and ran away
    to the wild.
    To the mountains he came
    and inhabited there
      in a grove
    and hunted the hare
    both early and late
    with nets that he wove
    and also a hound
and he never came home again, such was his hate,
    all women he found
    so nasty, and we

quite wisely agree.

Let us kiss you, dear old dears!

Chorus of Women

With no onions, you'll shed tears!

Chorus of Men

I mean, lift my leg and *kick*.

Chorus of Women

My, you wear your thicket thick!

Chorus of Men

Great Myronides was rough
at the front and black enough
in the ass to scare his foes.
Just ask anyone who knows:
it's with hair that wars are won—
take for instance Phormion.

Chorus of Women

Let me tell you a story in answer to
Melanion's case.
There is now a man, Timon, who wanders around
in the wilderness, hiding his face from view
in a place
where the brambles abound
so he looks like a chip
off a Fur-
y, curling his lip.
Now Timon retired
in hatred and pure
contempt of all men
and he cursed them in words that were truly inspired
again and again
but women he found
delightful and sound.

Would you like your jaw repaired?

Chorus of Men

Thank you, no. You've got me scared.

Chorus of Women

Let me jump and kick it though.

Chorus of Men

You will let your man-sack show.

Chorus of Women

All the same you wouldn't see,

old and gray as I may be,
any superfluity
　　of unbarbered hair on me;
　　it is plucked and more, you scamp,
　　since I singe it with a lamp!

[*Enter* LYSISTRATA *on the wall.*

Lysistrata
Women, O women, come here quickly, here to me!

Women
Whatever is it? Tell me! What's the shouting for?

Lysistrata
I see a man approaching, shaken and possessed,
seized and inspired by Aphrodite's power.
O thou, of Cyprus, Paphos, and Cythera, queen!
continue straight along this way you have begun!

A Woman
Whoever he is, where is he?

Lysistrata
　　　　　　　　　　Near Demeter's shrine.

A Woman
Why yes, by Zeus, he is. Who ever can he be?

Lysistrata
Well, look at him. Do any of you know him?

Myrrhina
　　　　　　　　　　　　　　　　Yes.
I do. He's my own husband, too, Cinesias.

Lysistrata
Then it's your duty now to turn him on a spit,
cajole him and make love to him and not make love,
to offer everything, short of those things of which
the wine-cup knows.

Myrrhina
　　　　　　　　I'll do it, don't you fear.

Lysistrata
　　　　　　　　　　　　　　　　And I
will help you tantalize him. I will stay up here
and help you roast him slowly. But now, disappear!

[*Enter* CINESIAS.

Cinesias
Oh how unfortunate I am, gripped by what spasms,
stretched tight like being tortured on a wheel!

Lysistrata
Who's there? Who has got this far past the sentries?

Cinesias

I.

Lysistrata
 A man?
Cinesias
    A man for sure.
Lysistrata
        Then clear away from here.
Cinesias
 Who're you to throw me out?
Lysistrata
            The lookout for the day.
Cinesias
 Then, for the gods' sake, call Myrrhina out for me.
Lysistrata
 You don't say! Call Myrrhina out! And who are you?
Cinesias
 Her husband. I'm Cinesias Paionides.
Lysistrata
 Well, my dear man, hello! Your name is not unknown
 among us here and not without a certain fame,
 because your wife has it forever on her lips.
 She can't pick up an egg or quince but she must say:
 Cinesias would enjoy it so!
Cinesias
        How wonderful!
Lysistrata
 By Aphrodite, yes. And if we chance to talk
 of husbands, your wife interrupts and says the rest
 are nothing much compared to her Cinesias.
Cinesias
 Go call her.
Lysistrata
        Will you give me something if I do?
Cinesias
 Indeed I will, by Zeus, if it is what you want.
 I can but offer what I have, and I have this.
Lysistrata
 Wait there. I will go down and call her.
Cinesias
            Hurry up!
 because I find no charm whatever left in life
 since she departed from the house. I get depressed

whenever I go into it, and everything
seems lonely to me now, and when I eat my food
I find no taste in it at all—because I'm stiff.

Myrrhina

[*Offstage.*] I love him, how I love him! But he doesn't want
my love! [*on wall*] So what's the use of calling me to
him?

Cinesias

My sweet little Myrrhina, why do you act like that?
Come down here.

Myrrhina

                    There? By Zeus, I certainly will not.

Cinesias

Won't you come down, Myrrhina, when I'm calling you?

Myrrhina

Not when you call me without needing anything.

Cinesias

Not needing anything? I'm desperate with need.

Myrrhina

I'm going now.

Cinesias

                    Oh no! No, don't go yet! At least
you'll listen to the baby. Call your mammy, you.

Baby

Mammy mammy mammy!

Cinesias

What's wrong with you? Have you no pity on your child
when it is six days now since he was washed or nursed?

Myrrhina

Oh, *I* have pity. But his father takes no care
of him.

Cinesias

Come down, you flighty creature, for the child.

Myrrhina

Oh, what it is to be a mother! I'll come down,
for what else can I do? [MYRRHINA *exits to reenter
below.*]

Cinesias

                    It seems to me she's grown
much younger, and her eyes have a more tender look.
Even her being angry with me and her scorn
are just the things that pain me with the more desire.

Myrrhina

Come let me kiss you, dear sweet little baby mine,
with such a horrid father. Mammy loves you, though.

Cinesias

But why are you so mean? Why do you listen to
those other women, giving me such pain?—And you,
you're suffering yourself.

Myrrhina

Take your hands off of me!

Cinesias

But everything we have at home, my things and yours,
you're letting go to pieces.

Myrrhina

Little do I care!

Cinesias

Little you care even if your weaving's pecked apart
and carried off by chickens?

Myrrhina

[*Bravely.*]

Little I care, by Zeus!

Cinesias

You have neglected Aphrodite's rituals
for such a long time now. Won't you come back again?

Myrrhina

Not I, unless you men negotiate a truce
and make an end of war.

Cinesias

Well, if it's so decreed,
we will do even that.

Myrrhina

Well, if it's so decreed,
I will come home again. Not now. I've sworn I won't.

Cinesias

All right, all right. But now lie down with me once more.

Myrrhina

No! No!—yet I don't say I'm not in love with you.

Cinesias

You love me? Then why not lie down, Myrrhina dear?

Myrrhina

Don't be ridiculous! Not right before the child!

Cinesias

By Zeus, of course not. Manes, carry him back home.
There now. You see the baby isn't in your way.
Won't you lie down?

Myrrhina

But *where,* you rogue, just where
is one to do it?

Cinesias

Where? Pan's grotto's a fine place.

Myrrhina

But how could I come back to the Acropolis
in proper purity?

Cinesias

Well, there's a spring below
the grotto—you can very nicely bathe in that.

[*Ekkyklema or inset-scene with grotto.*

Myrrhina

And then I'm under oath. What if I break my vows?

Cinesias

Let me bear all the blame. Don't worry about your oath.

Myrrhina

Wait here, and I'll go get a cot for us.

Cinesias

No no,
the ground will do.

Myrrhina

No, by Apollo! Though you *are*
so horrid, I can't have you lying on the ground. [*Leaves.*]

Cinesias

You know, the woman loves me—*that's* as plain as day.

Myrrhina

There. Get yourself in bed and I'll take off my clothes.
Oh, what a nuisance! I must go and get a mat.

Cinesias

What for? I don't need one.

Myrrhina

Oh yes, by Artemis!
On the bare cords? How ghastly!

Cinesias

Let me kiss you now.

Myrrhina

Oh, very well.

Cinesias

Wow! Hurry, hurry and come back

[MYRRHINA *leaves. A long wait.*

Myrrhina

Here is the mat. Lie down now, while I get undressed.

Oh, what a nuisance! You don't have a pillow, dear.

Cinesias

But I don't need one, not one bit!

Myrrhina

      By Zeus, *I* do! [*Leaves.*]

Cinesias

Poor prick, the service around here is terrible!

Myrrhina

Sit up, my dear, jump up! Now I've got everything.

Cinesias

Indeed you have. And now, my golden girl, come here.

Myrrhina

I'm just untying my brassiere. Now don't forget:
about that treaty—you won't disappoint me, dear?

Cinesias

By Zeus, no! On my life!

Myrrhina

     You have no blanket, dear.

Cinesias

By Zeus, I do not need one. I just want to screw.

Myrrhina

Don't worry, dear, you will. I'll be back right away.
[*Leaves.*]

Cinesias

This number, with her bedding, means to murder me.

Myrrhina

Now raise yourself upright.

Cinesias

     But *this* is upright now!

Myrrhina

Wouldn't you like some perfume?

Cinesias

     By Apollo, no!

Myrrhina

By Aphrodite, yes! You must—like it or not. [*Leaves.*]

Cinesias

Lord Zeus! Just let the perfume spill! That's all I ask!

Myrrhina

Hold out your hand. Take some of this and rub it on.

Cinesias

This perfume, by Apollo, isn't sweet at all.
It smells a bit of stalling—not of wedding nights!

Myrrhina
I brought the *Rhodian* perfume! How absurd of me!
Cinesias
It's fine! Let's keep it.
Myrrhina
                    You *will* have your little joke.
[*Leaves.*
Cinesias
Just let me at the man who first distilled perfumes!
Myrrhina
Try this, in the long vial.
Cinesias
                    I've got one like it, dear.
But don't be tedious. Lie down. And please don't bring
anything more.
Myrrhina
[*Going*] That's what I'll do, by Artemis!
I'm taking off my shoes. But dearest, don't forget
you're going to vote for peace.
Cinesias
                    I will consider it.

She has destroyed me, murdered me, that woman has!
On top of which she's got me skinned and gone away!
                    What shall I do? Oh, whom shall I screw,
                    cheated of dear Myrrhina, the first
                    beauty of all, a creature divine?
                    How shall I tend this infant of mine?
                    Find me a pimp: it has to be nursed!

Chorus of Men
[*In tragic style, as if to Prometheus or Andromeda bound.*]
                    In what dire woe, how heavy-hearted
                    I see thee languishing, outsmarted!
                        I pity thee, alas I do.
                    What kidney could endure such pain,
                    what spirit could, what balls, what back,
                    what loins, what sacroiliac,
                    If they came under such a strain
                    and never had a morning screw?

Cinesias
O Zeus! the twinges! Oh, the twitches!
Chorus of Men
                    And this is what she did to you,

that vilest, hatefullest of bitches!

Cinesias

Oh nay, by Zeus, she's dear and sweet!

Chorus of Men

How can she be? She's vile, O Zeus, she's vile!
Oh treat her, Zeus, like so much wheat—
O God of Weather, hear my prayer—
and raise a whirlwind's mighty blast
to roll her up into a pile
and carry her into the sky
far up and up and then at last
drop her and land her suddenly
astride that pointed penis there!

[*The ekkylema turns, closing the inset-scene. Enter, from opposite sides, a* SPARTAN *and an Athenian official.*

Spartan

Wheah is the Senate-house of the Athenians?
Ah wish to see the chaihman. Ah have news fo him.

Athenian

And who are you? Are you a Satyr or a man?

Spartan

Ah am a herald, mah young friend, yes, by the gods,
and Ah have come from Sparta to negotiate.

Athenian

And yet you come here with a spear under your arm?

Spartan

Not Ah, bah Zeus, not Ah!

Athenian

Why do you turn around?
Why throw your cloak out so in front? Has the long trip
given you a swelling?

Spartan

Ah do think the man is queah!

Athenian

But you have an erection, oh you reprobate!

Spartan

Bah Zeus, Ah've no sech thing! And don't you fool
around!

Athenian

And what have you got there?

Spartan

A Spahtan scroll-stick, suh.

Athenian
> Well, if it is, *this* is a Spartan scroll-stick, too.
> But look, I know what's up: you can tell *me* the truth.
> Just how are things with you in Sparta: tell me that.

Spartan
> Theah is uprising in all Spahta. Ouah allies
> are all erect as well. We need ouah milkin'-pails.

Athenian
> From where has this great scourge of frenzy fallen on
> you?
> From Pan?

Spartan
> No, Ah think Lampito began it all,
> and then, the othah women throughout Spahta joined
> togethah, just lahk at a signal fo a race,
> and fought theah husbands off and drove them from
> theah cunts.

Athenian
> So, how're you getting on?

Spartan
> We suffah. Through the town
> we walk bent ovah as if we were carrying
> lamps in the wind. The women will not let us touch
> even theah berries, till we all with one acco'd
> have made a peace among the cities of all Greece.

Athenian
> This is an international conspiracy
> launched by the women! Now I comprehend it all!
> Return at once to Sparta. Tell them they must send
> ambassadors fully empowered to make peace.
> And our Assembly will elect ambassadors
> from our side, when I say so, showing them this prick.

Spartan
> Ah'll run! Ah'll flah! Fo all you say is excellent!

Chorus of Men
> No wild beast is more impossible than woman is to fight,
> nor is fire, nor has the panther such unbridled appetite!

Chorus of Women
> Well you know it, yet you go on warring with me
> without end,
> when you might, you cross-grained creature, have me
> as a trusty friend.

Chorus of Men

Listen: I will never cease from hating women till I die!

Chorus of Women

Any time you like. But meanwhile is there any reason why

I should let you stand there naked, looking so ridiculous?

I am only coming near you, now, to slip your coat on, thus.

Chorus of Men

That was very civil of you, very kind to treat me so,

when in such uncivil rage I took it off a while ago.

Chorus of Women

Now you're looking like a man again, and not ridiculous.

If you hadn't hurt my feelings, I would not have made a fuss,

I would even have removed that little beast that's in your eye.

Chorus of Men

That is what was hurting me! Well, won't you take my ring to pry

back my eyelid? Rake the beast out. When you have it, let me see,

for some time now it's been at my eye and irritating me.

Chorus of Women

Very well, I will—though you were *born* an irritable man.

What a monster of a gnat, by Zeus! Look at it if you can.

Don't you see it? It's a native of great marshes, can't you tell?

Chorus of Men

Much obliged, by Zeus! The brute's been digging at me like a well!

So that now you have removed it, streams of tears come welling out.

Chorus of Women

I will dry them. You're the meanest man alive, beyond a doubt,

yet I will, and kiss you, too.

Chorus of Men

Don't kiss me!

Chorus of Women

If you will or not!

Chorus of Men

Damn you! Oh, what wheedling flatterers you all are,

born and bred!
That old proverb is quite right and not inelegantly said:
"There's no living *with* the bitches and, without them,
    even *less*"—
so I might as well make peace with you, and from now
    on, I guess,
I'll do nothing mean to you, and from you, suffer nothing
    wrong.
So let's draw our ranks together now and start a little
    song:

For a change, we're not preparing
any mean remark or daring
aimed at any man in town,
but the very opposite: we plan to do and say
only good to everyone,
when the ills we have already are sufficient
    anyway.
Any man or woman who
wants a little money, oh
say three minas, maybe two,
kindly let us know.
What we have is right in here.
(Notice we have purses, too!)
And if ever peace appear,
he who takes our loan today
    never need repay.

We are having guests for supper,
allies asked in by our upper
classes to improve the town.
There's pea-soup, and I had killed a sucking-pig
    of mine:
I shall see it is well done,
so you will be tasting something very succulent
    and fine.
Come to see us, then, tonight
early, just as soon as you
have a bath and dress up right:
bring your children, too.
Enter boldly, never mind
asking anyone in sight.
Go straight in and you will find

you are quite at home there, but
all the doors are shut.

And here come the Spartan ambassadors,
                  dragging beards that are really the biggest I
have ever beheld, and around their thighs
                  they are wearing some sort of a pig-sty.

Oh men of Sparta, let me bid you welcome first,
and then you tell us how you are and why you
    come.

Spartan
What need is theah to speak to you in many words?
Fo you may see youahself in what a fix we come.

Chorus of Men
Too bad! Your situation has become
terribly hard and seems to be at fever-pitch.

Spartan
Unutterably so! And what is theah to say?
Let someone bring us peace on any tuhms he will!

Chorus of Men
And here I see some natives of Athenian soil,
holding their cloaks far off their bellies, like the best
wrestlers, who sicken at the touch of cloth. It seems
that overtraining may bring on this strange disease.

Athenian
Will someone tell us where to find Lysistrata?
We're men, and here we are, in this capacity.

Chorus of Men
This symptom and that other one sound much alike.
Toward morning I expect convulsions do occur?

Athenian
By Zeus, we are exhausted with just doing that,
so, if somebody doesn't reconcile us quick,
there's nothing for it: we'll be screwing Cleisthenes.

Chorus of Men
Be careful—put your cloaks on, or you might be seen
by some young blade who knocks the phalluses off
    herms.

Athenian
By Zeus, an excellent idea!

Spartan
[*Having overheard.*] Yes, bah the gods!

It altogethah is. Quick, let's put on our cloaks.
[*Both groups cover quick and then recognize each other
with full diplomatic pomp.*

Athenian

Greetings, O men of Sparta! [*To his group.*] We have
been disgraced!

Spartan

[*To one of his group.*] Mah dearest fellah, what a dreadful thing fo *us*,
if these Athenians had seen ouah wo'st defeat!

Athenian

Come now, O Spartans: one must specify each point.
Why have you come here?

Athenian

To negotiate a peace.

Spartan

We ah ambassadahs.

Athenian

Well put. And so are we.
Therefore, why do we not call in Lysistrata,
she who alone might get us to agree on terms?

Spartan

Call her or any man, even a Lysistratus!

Chorus of Men

But you will have no need, it seems, to call her now,
for here she is. She heard you and is coming out.

Chorus of Men and Chorus of Women

All hail, O manliest woman of all!
It is time for you now to be turning
into something still better, more dreadful, mean,
unapproachable, charming, discerning,
for here are the foremost nations of Greece,
bewitched by your spells like a lover,
who have come to you, bringing you all their claims,
and to *you* turning everything over.

Lysistrata

The work's not difficult, if one can catch them now
while they're excited and not making passes at
each other. I will soon find out. Where's *HARMONY*?
[*A naked maid, perhaps wearing a large ribbon reading
HARMONY, appears from inside.*
Go take the Spartans first, and lead them over here,
not with a rough hand nor an overbearing one,

nor, as our husbands used to do this, clumsily,
but like a woman, in our most familiar style:
If he won't give his hand, then lead him by the prick.
And now, go bring me those Athenians as well,
leading them by whatever they will offer you.
O men of Sparta, stand right here, close by my side,
and *you* stand over there, and listen to my words.
I am a woman, yes, but there is mind in me.
In native judgment I am not so badly off,
and, having heard my father and my elders talk
often enough, I have some cultivation, too.
And so, I want to take and scold you, on both sides,
as you deserve, for though you use a lustral urn
in common at the altars, like blood-relatives,
when at Olympia, Delphi, or Thermopylae—
how many others I might name if I took time!—
yet, with barbarian hords of enemies at hand,
it is Greek men, it is Greek cities, you destroy.
That is one argument so far, and it is done.

Athenian
My prick is skinned alive—that's what's destroying *me*.

Lysistrata
Now, men of Sparta—for I shall address you first—
do you not know that once one of your kings came here
and as a suppliant of the Athenians
sat by our altars, death-pale in his purple robe,
and begged us for an army? For Messenë then
oppressed you, and an earthquake from the gods as well.
Then Cimon went, taking four thousand infantry,
and saved the whole of Lacedaemon for your state.
That is the way Athenians once treated you;
you ravage their land now, which once received you well.

Athenian
By Zeus, these men are in the wrong, Lysistrata!

Spartan
[*With his eyes on* HARMONY.] We'ah wrong . . . What an
unutterably lovely ass!

Lysistrata
Do you suppose I'm letting you Athenians off?
Do you not know that once the Spartans in their turn,
when you were wearing the hide-skirts of slavery,
came with their spears and slew many Thessalians,
many companions and allies of Hippias?

They were the only ones who fought for you that day,
freed you from tyranny and, for the skirt of hide,
gave back your people the wool mantle of free men.

Spartan

Ah nevah saw a woman broadah—in her views.

Athenian

And I have never seen a lovelier little nook.

Lysistrata

So why, when you have done each other so much good,
go on fighting with no end of malevolence?
Why don't you make a peace? Tell me, what's in your
        way?

Spartan

Whah, *we* ah willin', if *they* will give up to us
that very temptin' cuhve.   [*Of* HARMONY, *as hereafter.*]

Lysistrata

                        What curve, my friend?

Spartan

                                                The bay
of Pylos, which we've wanted and felt out so long.

Athenian

No, by Poseidon, you will not get into that!

Lysistrata

Good friend, do let them have it.

Athenian

                                        No! What other town
can we manipulate so well?

Lysistrata

                                Ask them for one.

Athenian

Damn, let me think! Now first suppose you cede to us
that bristling tip of land, Echinos, behind which
the gulf of Malia recedes, and those long walls,
the legs on which Megara reaches to the sea.

Spartan

No, mah deah man, not *everything*, bah Castah, no!

Lysistrata

Oh, give them up. Why quarrel for a pair of legs?

Athenian

I'd like to strip and get to plowing right away.

Spartan

And *Ah* would lahk to push manuah, still earliah.

Lysistrata

When you have made a peace, then you will do all that.
But if you want to do it, first deliberate,
go and inform your allies and consult with them.

Athenian

Oh, damn our allies, my good woman! We are stiff.
Will all of our allies not stand resolved with us—
namely, to screw?

Spartan

And so will ouahs, Ah'll guarantee.

Athenian

Our mercenaries, even, will agree with us.

Lysistrata

Excellent. Now to get you washed and purified
so you may enter the Acropolis, where we
women will entertain you out of our supplies.
You will exchange your pledges there and vows for
peace.
And after that each one of you will take his wife,
departing then for home.

Athenian

Let's go in right away.

Spartan

Lead on, ma'am, anywheah you lahk.

Athenian

Yes, and be quick.

[*Exeunt into Acropolis.*

Chorus of Men and Chorus of Women

All the rich embroideries, the
scarves, the gold accessories, the
trailing gowns, the robes I own
I begrudge to no man: let him take what things he
will
for his children or a grown
daughter who must dress for the procession up
Athena's hill.

Freely of my present stocks
I invite you all to take.
There are here no seals nor locks
very hard to break.
Search through every bag and box,
look—you will find nothing there

if your eyesight isn't fine—
sharper far than mine!

Are there any of you needing
food for all the slaves you're feeding,
all your little children, too?
I have wheat in tiny grains for you, the finest sort,
and I also offer you
plenty of the handsome strapping grains that slaves
get by the quart.
So let any of the poor
visit me with bag or sack
which my slave will fill with more
wheat than they can pack,
giving each his ample share.
Might I add that at my door
I have watch-dogs?—so beware.
Come too close by day or night,
you will find they bite.

[*Voice of drunken* ATHENIANS *from inside.*

First Athenian

Open the door! [*Shoves the porter aside.*]
And will you get out of my way?

[*A second drunken* ATHENIAN *follows. The first sees the chorus.*

What are you sitting *there* for? Shall I, with this torch,
burn you alive? [*Drops character.*]
How vulgar! Oh, how commonplace!
I can not do it!

[*Starts back in. The second* ATHENIAN *stops him and remonstrates with him in a whisper. The first turns and addresses the audience.*

Well, if it really must be done
to please you, we shall face it and go through with it.

Chorus of Men and Chorus of Women

And *we* shall face it and go through with it with you.

First Athenian

[*In character again, extravagantly.*]
Clear out of here! Or you'll be wailing for your hair!

[CHORUS OF WOMEN *scours away in mock terror.*

Clear out of here! so that the Spartans can come out
and have no trouble leaving, after they have dined.

[CHORUS OF MEN *scours away in mock terror.*

Second Athenian

    I never saw a drinking-party like this one:
    even the Spartans were quite charming, and of course
    we make the cleverest company, when in our cups.

First Athenian

    You're right, because when sober we are not quite sane.

    If I can only talk the Athenians into it,
    we'll always go on any embassy quite drunk,
    for now, going to Sparta sober, we're so quick
    to look around and see what trouble we can make
    that we don't listen to a single word they say—
    instead we think we hear them say what they do not—
    and none of our reports on anything agree.
    But just now everything was pleasant. If a man
    got singing words belonging to another song,
    we all applauded and swore falsely it was fine!
    But here are those same people coming back again
    to the same spot! Go and be damned, the pack of you!

[*The* CHORUS, *having thrown off their masks, put on other
cloaks, and rushed back on stage, stay put.*]

Second Athenian

    Yes, damn them, Zeus! Just when the party's coming out!

[*The party comes rolling out.*]

Spartan

[*To another.*]

    Mah very chahmin friend, will you take up youah flutes?
    Ah'll dance the dipody and sing a lovely song
    of us and the Athenians, of both at once!

First Athenian

[*As pleasantly as he can.*]

    Oh yes, take up your little reeds, by all the gods:
    I very much enjoy seeing you people dance.

Spartan

           Memory, come,
        come inspiah thah young
        votaries to song,
        come inspiah theah dance!

[*Other* SPARTANS *join in.*]

        Bring thah daughtah, bring the sweet
           Muse, fo well she knows
        us and the Athenians,
           how at Ahtemisium

they in godlike onslaught rose
hahd against the Puhsian fleet,
    drove it to defeat!
Well she knows the Spartan waws,
    how Leonidas
    in the deadly pass
    led us on lahk baws
whettin' shahp theah tusks, how sweat
on ouah cheeks in thick foam flowahed,
off ouah legs how thick it showahed,
    fo the Puhsians men were mo'
    than the sands along the sho'.
Goddess, huntress, Ahtemis,
slayeh of the beasts, descend:
vuhgin goddess, come to this
feast of truce to bind us fast
so ouah peace may nevah end.
Now let friendship, love, and wealth
come with ouah acco'd at last.
May we stop ouah villainous
wahly foxy stealth!
    Come, O huntress, heah to us,
    heah, O vuhgin, neah to us!

Lysistrata

Come, now that all the rest has been so well arranged,
you Spartans take these women home; these others, you.
Let husband stand beside his wife, and let each wife
stand by her husband: then, when we have danced a
    dance
to thank the gods for our good fortune, let's take care
hereafter not to make the same mistakes again.

Athenian

Bring on the chorus! Invite the three Graces to follow,
and then call on Artemis, call her twin brother,
the leader of choruses, healer Apollo!

Chorus

[*Joins.*] Pray for their friendliest favor, the one and the
    other.
Call Dionysus, his tender eyes casting
flame in the midst of his Maenads ecstatic with dancing.
    Call upon Zeus, the resplendent in fire,
    call on his wife, rich in honor and ire,
call on the powers who possess everlasting

memory, call them to aid,
call them to witness the kindly, entrancing
peace Aphrodite has made!

> Alalai!
> Bound, and leap high! Alalai!
> Cry, as for victory, cry
> Alalai!

Lysistrata

Sing us a new song, Spartans, capping our new song.

Spartans

Leave thah favohed mountain's height,
Spahtan Muse, come celebrate
Amyclae's lord with us and great
Athena housed in bronze;
praise Tyndareus' paih of sons,
gods who pass the days in spoht
wheah the cold Eurotas runs.

[*General dancing.*]

Now to tread the dance,
now to tread it light,
praising Spahta, wheah you find
love of singing quickened bah the pounding beat of
dancing feet,
when ouah guhls lahk foals cavoht
wheah the cold Eurotas runs,
when they fleetly bound and prance
till theah haih unfilleted shakes in the wind,
as of Maenads brandishin'
ahvied wands and revelin',
Leda's daughtah, puah and faiah,
leads the holy dances theah.

Full Chorus

[*As everyone leaves dancing.*]

So come bind up youah haih with youah hand,
with youah feet make a bound
lahk a deeah; for the chorus clap out
an encouragin' sound,
singin' praise of the temple of bronze
housin' her we adaw:
sing the praise of Athena: the goddess unvanquished
in waw!

II

Aristophanic Comedy: The Conscience of a Conservative
by Robert W. Corrigan

The Greek comic poet Aristophanes (*ca.* 450–387 B.C.) was certainly one of the giants of the classical theatre; but on rereading his plays today, he seems more like an early-day version of a Barry Goldwater, who had the quick and contentious mind of William Buckley and the raucous sense of humor and comic invention of Al Capp, and whose program was, in effect, to urge the Greeks to repeal the second half of the fifth century. Actually comedy, because of its central concern with society's need and ability to maintain and preserve itself, is by nature conservative, and Aristophanes and all other writers of comedy tend more or less to be conservatives. Tragedy has always dealt with that rebellious spirit in man which resists the limitations of being human, including the limits imposed on him by society. It focuses on man's heroic capacity to suffer in his rebellion, and celebrates the essential nobility of the rebellious spirit. But while tragedy celebrates the hero's capacity to suffer, and thereby to earn a new and deeper knowledge of himself and his universe, comedy tends to be more concerned with the fact that, for all our individual defeats, life does nonetheless continue on its merry way. Or, as Christopher Fry once put it, "comedy senses and reaches out to that . . . angle of experience where the dark is distilled into light, . . . where our tragic fate finds itself with perfect pitch, and goes straight to the key which creation was composed in." Comedy, then, celebrates man's capacity to endure; such capacity is ultimately conserving in spirit and quality.

This in large measure explains why love is always central to comedy. The basic comic plot can be reduced to the following elements: 1) boy meets girl; 2) boy falls

in love with girl; 3) there is an obstacle to the fulfilling
of that love (this obstacle is usually parental); 4) the
obstacle is overcome and there is a reorganization of society. The persisting regularity of this pattern has led
Ben Lehmann to observe, quite correctly I think, in his
essay "Comedy and Laughter," that the "obstacles to the
hero's desire, then, form the action of comedy, and the
overcoming of them the comic resolution." But it must be
noted that the reconciliation at the end of comedy always
involves the preserving of the social context. Opposition,
frustration, malice, lust, prejudice, and greed can and do
inhabit the world of comedy, but these divisive powers
are always overcome and then assimilated into the lovers'
happy world. Comedy always ends in fusion and with a
sense of social union. To quote Lehmann once again:
"The vision of comedy fixes its eye on separateness, on
diversity, even on oppositions, but it insists at last on to-
getherness for lovers and on the restored social fabric, on
solidarity for the group."

As a satirist, rather than a writer of comedies,[1] Aristophanes has plenty of sex in his plays, but no love. First
and foremost, the writer of satire must have the gift of
turning our eyes inward in hilarious scorn of ourselves.
But his purpose is always corrective. In showing us the
immensity of our follies, the satirist is either seeking to
restore values and patterns of behavior that he believes
have been lost, forgotten, or debased, or he is urging us
to discover new ideals and ways of living. Therefore, all
of his jibes—no matter how bitter—are ultimately directed
at the restoration or preservation of the social order.

In each of his plays, Aristophanes is attacking the manifestations of political, social, and moral corruption that
he believed were the direct result of the Athenians' shift
away from an agricultural to an artisan and mercantile
economy, their adoption of a more imperialist "foreign
policy," and their willingness to accept the validity of new
forms of thought and art. All his life, Aristophanes shared
the attitudes of the rapidly disappearing landed aristoc-

[1] It should be understood that for the Greeks in the fifth century,
any play with an invented plot and subject matter drawn from
contemporary life was called a "comedy," and therefore was
presented during the afternoon portion of the Dionysian Festivals.

racy, whose religion, morality, ideals, and patterns of social organization were based upon an agricultural economy and a closed, heroic view of society. He resisted all that was modern. He condemned the innovators or any who would seek to change or reform the traditional ways of doing things because they were old or outmoded. Euripides, Socrates, the Sophists, the orators, the early scientists Empedocles and Pythagoras were all characterized in Aristophanes' plays as charlatans and subversives who were destroying the national fiber and upsetting the traional patterns of government, thought, art, and everyday behavior. The Delian League (the classical Greek equivalent to the United Nations) was a striking instance of government waste and a good example of the evils of the new policy of Greek "internationalism." The increased number of people depending upon the government for support was seen by Aristophanes as a maneuver on the part of the central government to gain greater power, as well as another symptom that the old value that each man should earn his own way was rapidly breaking down. One could continue this list of his grievances at some length, but each item would be much the same.

To be sure, Aristophanes had a point and his position was not without justification. He lived and wrote in one of the most turbulent periods in the world's history. It was a time of war, expansion, and rapid, radical change, and the breakdown of the traditional ways of doing things can be seen in every aspect of Greek life, from architecture to the worship of Zeus. As a larger and more centralized government became necessary, it was easier for the demagogues to gain power and widespread graft soon came to be commonplace. New religions from foreign lands, and especially from the Orient, were introduced into the country by the merchants, traders, soldiers, and slaves, with the result that new moralities did begin to emerge. As the Athenian people began to produce a great deal more than they consumed, the acquiring and accumulating of wealth (not to mention the social problems that the acquisition of capital wealth creates) tended to become the central concern of more and more people. Aristophanes, then, lived in a volatile atmosphere and he was deeply disturbed by the many changes that were taking place and the effects they were having on Athe-

nian life. He was determined, like so many of our South-
erners today—although for different reasons—to do all he
could to resist this erosion of the time-honored Greek traditions. He would fight till the death for the old order;
and he did.

To those who might consider this evaluation of Aristophanes' position to be either erroneous or too harsh, I
call their attention specifically to the plays in this volume.
In *The Birds*, probably the greatest of Aristophanes' three
"Utopia" plays, the ideal society (Cloud-Cuckoo-Land)
will be established by the farmers, who will then run
their brave new world like a large farm. Certainly, this
solution is exaggerated and fanciful, but there is little
doubt that Aristophanes did believe that things would be
much better in Athens if the old values—as embodied and
propounded by Pithetaerus—were restored to their former
position of dominance. For all of its delightful (and sometimes scatalogical) grotesquerie, *Peace* celebrates the same
values. Only the farmers, of all the people in Greece, are
shown to be strong enough and capable of working together long enough to pull Peace out of her underground
prison so she can once again rule the earth. Not only do
the farmers save Greece from the horrors of war, but Try-
gaeus—who is clearly Aristophanes' mouthpiece—states ex-
plicitly that peace is the opportunity for the farmers to
work in their fields. In *The Plutus* the solution to all the
misuse of wealth in the world is to give Plutus, the god of
wealth, to the honest, hardworking farmers. They will
solve all of the problems: no more corruption, no injustice,
no more crime. If only it were so, even in fourth-century
Greece. Finally, behind all the sexual fun of *Lysistrata*,
Aristophanes is really trying to solve the question of Pan-
hellenic unity and the problems of war. After the women
have overcome the old men who were guarding the treasury on the Acropolis, Lysistrata begins the long *agon* (the
most significant one in the play) with the Commissioner.
As her arguments become increasingly persuasive, she
finally gets to the central issue: "How can we have
peace?" I should like to quote this passage at some length,
because I believe it makes my point so clearly.

   Commissioner
      And how, on the international scale, can you
         straighten out the enormous

confusion among all the states of Greece?

Lysistrata

Very easily.

Commissioner

How? Do inform us.

Lysistrata

When our skein's in a tangle we take it thus
　　　on our spindles, or haven't you seen us?—
One on this side and one on the other side,
　　　and we work out the tangles between us,
And that is the way we'll undo this war,
　　　by exchanging ambassadors, whether
You like it or not, one from either side,
　　　and we'll work out the tangles together.

Commissioner

Do you really think that with wools and skeins ·
　　　and just being able to skein you
can end these momentous affairs, you fools?

Lysistrata

With any intelligence in you
　　　you statesmen would govern as we work wool,
and in everything Athens would profit.

Commissioner

How so? Do tell.

Lysistrata

First, you take raw fleece
　　　and you wash the beshittedness off it:
just so, you should first lay the city out
　　　on a washboard and beat out the rotters
and pluck out the sharpers like burrs, and when
　　　you find tight knots of schemers and plotters
who are out for key offices, card them loose,
　　　but best tear off their heads in addition.
Then into one basket together card
　　　all those of a good disposition
be they citizens, resident aliens, friends,
　　　an ally or an absolute stranger,
even people in debt to the commonwealth,
　　　you can mix them all in with no danger.
And the cities which Athens has colonized—
　　　by Zeus, you should try to conceive them
as so many shreddings and tufts of wool
　　　that are scattered about and not leave them

> to lie around loose, but from all of them
>   draw the threads in here, and collect them
> into one big ball and then weave a coat
>   for the people, to warm and protect them.
>
> *Commissioner*
> Now isn't this awful? They treat the state like wool
>   to be beaten and carded,
> who have nothing at all to do with war!

Lysistrata's arguments make such very good sense. She's so logical, and therein lies the play's great appeal. But such a solution to the problems of achieving world peace is too simple; it assumes that the tightly wound and complex strands of world affairs can be worked like a skein of wool. It also assumes that, once the skein has been untangled, it will stay that way. It is this desire for a simple solution to complex problems, and more important, the belief that the use of time-tested patterns of the past makes such solutions possible, that prompted me to link Aristophanes with Mr. Goldwater at the beginning of this introduction.

For better or worse, Aristophanes failed in his attempts to change the patterns of Greek history. Quite predictably, the Greeks did not follow his advice and go back to the good old days. Nor have his condemnations of Euripides and Socrates held up; as a teacher of literature and philosophy, Aristophanes was a failure. But in one very important area of the history of ideas he has had a profound and lasting influence: namely, in the judging of poetry. Quite correctly, Aristophanes can be called the "father" of Greek literary criticism, and his belief that the chief function of poetry is to teach morality is an idea that is still very much with us. Euripides is condemned in nearly all of the plays because Aristophanes believed that the tragedian's poetry corrupted the youth of Athens, poisoned patriotic spirit, and advanced the cause of immorality everywhere. Aeschylus is set up as the model for tragedy in *The Frogs* not because of his ability with language (even Aristophanes admitted that Euripides was the best versifier of all writers of tragedy), but because his plays—like "all genuine poetry"—helped to make us better human beings. Aristophanes was the first Greek writer to insist that the basic aim of the arts and all culture should be education. Plato developed this idea more fully in *The Republic* and *The Laws,* and it was finally developed in its fullest (although somewhat compromised) form in Horace's *Art of Poetry* in the dictum that art should both delight and teach. The idea was militantly reasserted in the eighteenth and nineteenth centuries by Lessing, Herder, and the Schlegels in their criticism of Greek drama; and it is fascinating to note that even Nietzsche's description of the decay of Greek tragedy is nearly identical to the one put forth by Aristophanes more than 2,000 years earlier. And this view has lost none of its virulence today—ranging in scope and significance from the controversy over awarding the Bollingen Prize to Ezra Pound to local obscenity trials.

I have no intention of getting involved in this argument here, but finally I believe Aristophanes must be seen as a romantic reactionary, who refused to give up what was already lost. Instead of welcoming the new, he mourned the loss of the old. History has shown that he (and all like him) was wrong in his moral objections to change. The traditional code is never the *only* morality; there is always the possibility of another sanction. The fact that men oppose traditional values and appeal to other and new authorities does not make them troublemakers, or immoral. What Aristophanes either did not see or refused to recognize, is the fact that as long as a new idea of what is right is held with conviction and is not just an isolated sentiment, it may be fully as moral as obedience to established laws or customs.

However, thus far I have presented only one side of the case. Aristophanes may have been a reactionary but he was certainly no weepy sentimentalist. As I said earlier, he lived in a volatile atmosphere when life was wide open, and so too are his plays. All of his work has an extravagant power and a quality of overriding buoyancy and verve. This almost animal exuberance and vitality is probably best seen in the free use of sex in his plays. We sense neither neurotic lust nor puritanical guilt in his use of it, and this probably explains (differences in taste and dramatic conventions notwithstanding) why his blatant sexuality is still so inoffensive when it is read or produced on our stages today. But no matter what he took for his subject, he had the capacity as a writer to take any idea and push it as far as it would go, and then he gave it one more push. In our day he is probably best compared to such comedians as Mort Sahl, Dick Gregory, Lenny Bruce, or Shelly Berman. (The only writer in the theatre today who even approaches Aristophanes is the Swiss playwright, Friederich Duerrenmatt, whose grotesque ironies and biting satire, in such plays as *The Visit, Romulus The Great,* and *The Physicists,* have a certain resemblance to the Athenian's wit.) However, with these modern satirists, unlike Aristophanes, it is difficult—except on the issue of civil rights—to know exactly what they are for. But their techniques are much the same.

Actually, a fuller understanding of the Aristophanic techniques is the key to our enjoyment of his plays. Rather than having a comic action, Aristophanes' plays are built upon the comic conceit (the sex-strike in *Lysistrata* or Socrates in the balloon in *The Clouds*), which acts like a mousetrap to create the world of the play for us. To be sure, all of the plays share certain structural characteristics that make it possible for us to talk of an "Aristophanic structure," and such giants of classical scholarship as Gilbert Murray, F. M. Cornford, and Jane Harrison have shown that his structure originated in the rituals of the Dionysian worship. But such discussions, while undoubtedly true, tend to be misleading for they force upon early Greek comedy a terminology of dramatic criticism that is, for the most part, either inappropriate or irrelevant. There is not really very much plot to most of Aristophanes' plays (certainly not in the sense that there are plots in the comedies of Shakespeare, Moliere, Congreve, or Shaw), only a series of episodes that serve as the occasions for his wit and satiric thrusts. His plays move from moment to moment and have a sense of spontaneity rather than structure. Such an episodic structure (if the term must be used) not only gives freedom to the ranging and wayward movements of Aristophanes' comic mind, but it also sets up the audience for the rapid-fire potshots that he takes at every kind of subject. Like our own late George S. Kaufman, or more recently Bob Hope, Aristophanes was a master of the phraseology and attitude of the wisecrack. But the basic strategy of the wisecrack is to keep the audience with you. This becomes almost impossible if the audience becomes too involved in the workings of a plot.

Aristophanes was not a subtle writer, and his plays—

more than most—are a theatrical rather than a literary experience. He has little interest in the more refined phases of human absurdity, and everything in his comedy is dependent upon the immediacy of the theatrical effect. His satiric wit is, of all forms of wit, the most ephemeral. The basic comic gesture is universal in its appeal, but the particularities of the form are based on immediate, topical references—usually the absurdities of current political or social behavior—and these are almost impossible to translate or pass on to future generations. In tone, Aristophanic comedy is much like that of the newspaper cartoons of a Herblock, Bill Maudlin, the early Al Capp, or Jules Pfeiffer; in technique, it is like the gridiron dinner show or the topical review.

Almost, that is! But one important ingredient is still missing. Aristophanes wrote in verse, and it is clear that music and dance played an all-important role in the productions of classical Greek comedy. For this reason we will completely miss the essential quality of an Aristophanic play if we do not think of it as a comic musical revue. The two most significant and highly praised recent revivals of his plays were successful because they accented this musical base. The well-known Greek director, Karolos Kouns, won the first prize and world-wide acclaim at the International Theatre Festival in Paris in 1962 with a production of *The Birds*. Not only did he modernize the dialogue, but he had new music composed by Manos Hadjadakis (the composer of *Never on Sunday*) and the production was choreographed by the eminent Greek dancer, Zouzou Nicoloudi. More recently (1964), in our own country, Herbert Blau had a similar success with the same play at the Actor's Workshop in San Francisco, when he presented it in a jazz version. These two productions provide sufficient proof that Aristophanes can continue to live in the theatre (and not just as a museum piece in the library or the classroom) if we understand the dynamics and techniques of his plays.

But for all of Aristophanes' vitality, what is known as Greek "Old Comedy" went into a decline shortly after the turn of the fourth century, and this decline is probably best described as a process of diminution, which was finally completed in the drama of Menander. The fact that the decline had begun can easily be seen in Aristophanes' last

preserved play, *The Plutus*, which was first performed
sometime during the years 390–388 B.C. We can still discover traces of the old Aristophanes: his bias toward the
farmers, the episodic structure, the open stagecraft and
the presentational style of musical comedy, and the too-
simple solution. Yet everything is different. The bite is
gone. The comedy is generalized. Instead of dealing with
the particular behavior of specific people, we find a
gentle mockery of the manners of people in general. The
episodes seem unrelated; each of them deals with human
foibles, but they lack a cumulative force. The whole play
is probably best summed up by Browning in his "Aristophanes' Apology."

> Aristophanes
> Surmounts his rivals now as heretofore,
> Though stinted to mere sober prosy verse—
> "Manners and Men," so squeamish gets the world!
> No more "Step forward, strip for anapaests!"
> No calling naughty people by their names.[2]

MENANDER AND GREEK NEW COMEDY

By the time of Menander (*ca.* 342–291 B.C.) and Greek
New Comedy, the vitality of the early Aristophanes
had completely disappeared from comic drama, and the
younger writer had assumed a position of dominance that
was virtually undisputed until the beginning of the Renaissance. This phenomenon is one of the strange quirks in
the history of literary criticism and taste. Today—even
after we finally have an almost complete text of one of
his plays—Menander, at best, seems second-rate. To compare his comedies with those of Jonson and Shakespeare,
Wycherley and Congreve, or Shaw and Moliere is hardly
worth the effort. Yet he was praised by all the classical
authors, including Virgil, and that most judicious of critics,
Quintillian, considered him the finest writer of comedy in
classical literature. Menander can rightly be called the
"father" of that staple of the theatre in all ages, the domestic comedy of manners, but his significance for us today

[2] I am indebted to my colleague, Lionel Casson, for bringing my
attention to Browning's poem in his fine book *Masters of
Ancient Comedy* (N. Y.: Macmillan Co., 1960).

is largely historical. His drama is the only existing link between the last works of Aristophanes and Euripides and the early plays of Plautus; and *The Grouch,* in particular, is significant because it illustrates how the highly complex but logical plot came to replace the bizarre and improbable situation as the source of a comic action. According to Plutarch, Menander considered a play practically finished once he had completed the scenario and had only the dialogue left to write. If this is true, it probably explains why his plots have a repetitious quality that can only remind us of the worst of film and television drama; all of his characters are types; his vaunted insight into human nature is unimpressive and certainly superficial by today's standards; and his language, while graceful, is more decorative than meaningful. It is clear—at least on the basis of existing records—that by the end of the fourth century the Greek theatre had become little more than a commodity theatre that catered to its audience's need for diversion.

The final question to be asked here is "What happened?" Why, in less than a century, had the scope of comedy been so drastically reduced? Obviously, we cannot know for certain, but it is very likely related to the Greeks' loss of political freedom. This had been coming for some time, and with the fall of Athens to Sparta in 404 B.C. the end was in sight. Then in 338 B.C. Athens was conquered by the Macedonians and all public occasions (including the theatre) were rigidly censored. Comedy has never flourished under a dictatorship. Audiences who do come to the theatre in such times want to escape the problems of life, and more important, dictators have never tolerated comedy. S. N. Behrman put it best when he wrote: "Dictators are terribly afraid of comedy and its laughter. For laughter is the most humanizing—as well as the most critical—agency in the world. The ability to laugh at its own pretensions and shortcomings is the true mark of the civilized nation, as it is of the civilized man." One need only remember what happened to the German theatre under Hitler to see the truth of these remarks. Moreover, we should realize that in recent times, even in our own country, there are some things we can no longer make fun of and laugh about. One of the most significant documents on the subject of comedy and freedom that I know of is an essay entitled "It's Hideously True" by the cartoonist Al Capp. It was published as an article in 1952 in *Life* magazine, and in it Mr. Capp explained why he finally decided to have L'l Abner marry Daisy Mae. Admittedly, this was at the time when Senator McCarthy was at the height of his power and an almost hysterical fear was sweeping the nation. But Capp, who had thrived for twenty years kidding hell out of all the lunacies of American life, suddenly discovered that there were some things he no longer had the freedom to kid. (As he put it, "We lost our fifth freedom, the freedom to laugh at ourselves.") When the comic writer loses this freedom, he invariably turns from broad, topical satire on a national level to the more gentle forms of humor found in domestic life. (It's significant, I think, that "Blondie" is the most popular comic strip in America.) And if this restricting atmosphere continues, the comic must eventually turn in upon himself, and he becomes the butt of his own humor. This is what probably happened to classical comedy, and the decline in Aristophanes' comic power is probably more a matter of political freedom than it is of artistry. Aristophanes was the Will Rogers of the classical Greek theatre; unfortunately, he wasn't able to be its Jack Benny as well.

Aristophanes:
THE BIRDS

Acting Edition by Walter Kerr

Characters *Pithetaerus, The Footloose*

Euelpides, The Footsore

Trochilus, The Butler Bird

Epops, King of the Birds

Procne, The Nightingale, wife to Epops

Leader of the Chorus

The Priest-Bird

The Poet

The Prophet

The Real-Estate Man

The Inspector

The Lawyer

A First Messenger

A Second Messenger

Iris, The Swift, a small-time Goddess

A Herald

Prometheus

Hercules

A Barbarian God

Neptune

A Chorus of Birds

A *rugged mountain-top some distance from Athens, about 414* B.C. *Limitless sky in the background. The rock formations should afford six or seven varied entrances, at different heights, with stair-like formation to connect the acting levels. At one side a little bridge between two pinnacles. A high point of the stage at downstage Right is so arranged as to be useful to Pithetaerus as a sort of pulpit.*

Various gnarled and barren trees, especially on the upper reaches of the stage, including one tree which is practical for a perch and may occasionally be used by one of the Birds.

At downstage Left, there is a gap in the rock formation which seems to lead downward and which is used for any ascent from the earth.

In a crevice somewhere upstage is concealed Procne's nest, if possible behind a movable scrim which is identical with the other rock surfaces when not lighted from within. Some rock formations can jut forward so that concealment is possible on one side or on both sides.

The small birds carried by Pithetaerus and Euelpides are so constructed as to fit over one arm, like a sleeve. Their heads can then be manipulated by the actors' fingers.

Act One

[PITHETAERUS *and* EUELPIDES *appear down Left, as though climbing from the earth below.* PITHETAERUS *carries a crow in his arms,* EUELPIDES *a jay. Both are exhausted from the long climb. Before they can relax, however,* EUELPIDES' *jay begins pecking its head vigorously toward Center.*

Euelpides

[*Listening to his jay.*] Straight ahead, you say? To the tree over there?

[*The jay nods excitedly and* EUELPIDES *starts Center. As* PITHETAERUS *follows him, his own crow begins wagging its head violently in another direction.*

Pithetaerus

Oh, this damn pigeon! [*To the bird.*]
What do you say now? Go two miles *back?*

[PITHETAERUS *howls with disgust and collapses on a rock, near Left.* EUELPIDES *comes to him, shaking his finger at the crow.*

Euelpides

Listen, bird. You're supposed to be guiding us. But all we do is go backwards and sideways. We haven't got that kind of time.

[*The crow bites his shaking finger and he leaps away, nursing it.*

Pithetaerus

To think that I—a mature man!—should travel a hundred miles with a bird giving me directions!

[*His crow sets up a violent jerking and* EUELPIDES *comes in warily to listen.*

Euelpides

[*Interpreting.*] He says it isn't far as the crow flies.

[PITHETAERUS *looks at the crow in disgust, begins slapping its head vigorously; the crow bites him.*

Euelpides

[*Surveying the rocky terrain.*] Personally, I'm worn down to my toenails.

Pithetaerus

If I only knew where we were—

Euelpides

[*Wistfully.*] Suppose we could ever find our way home again?

Pithetaerus

No.

Euelpides

Oh, dear.

Pithetaerus

[*Sudden renewal of determination.*] And if I could I wouldn't want to!

Euelpides
Oh, dear.

Pithetaerus
[*On his feet again, looking around.*] I wonder what road this is.

Euelpides
Oh, dear. [*Helpfully.*] It's the Oh Dear Road. [PITHE-TAERUS *swats him one, he dodges; he then takes it out on his jay, swatting the bird as he continues.*] A lot of good you are! [*Calling to* PITHETAERUS, *who is wandering about the stage.*] I told you we couldn't trust that bird-seller. Telling us these fellows would just naturally lead us to the King of the Birds! [*Sits down, Center, despond-ently.*] I don't think they ever heard of the King of the Birds. And if they did, I'll bet they're disloyal. [*Jay opens his mouth.*] Don't open your face like that! You look any-thing but attractive. [*Jay's head begins jutting toward Right.*] Where? Where? Over there? [*His eyes glued to the jay, he quickly rises and moves in the indicated direction.*] All right. All right. I'm going. Keep showing me. [*He walks smack into a wall of rock, rebounds, turns on the jay.*] That's rock! Oh, you knew that! That's what you had in mind! [*Begins to throttle his jay.* PITHE-TAERUS, *who has been wandering up Center, peering off at the highest point of the rocks with his back to us, now seems to be engaged in some excitement with his bird.*] Find something? What's your bird doing?

Pithetaerus
[*In a rage.*] Biting my damn fingers off!

Euelpides
Any road up there?

Pithetaerus
Nothing. No road anywhere.

Euelpides
Oh, dear. I haven't got a nerve left. I've used up every single nerve trying to go to the birds, and now they're all gone. [*He shudders violently.*] See? [*Turns to the audience, comes down toward them.*] I suppose you wonder what we're doing here? I wonder, too. [*Keeping up a direct conversation with the audience, he now goes to Left where they have come up, and hauls over a couple of heavy sacks filled with equipment. He drags*

*these across stage, with great effort, and deposits them
at extreme downstage Right, meanwhile continuing the
conversation.*] You probably think we're crazy. We are.
We come of very good families. Legitimate. We were
very respected people back home. Athens. Very fine city.
You probably think we were thrown out. [*Shakes his
head.*] Just got up and left. Walked out. Still walking. We don't hate Athens. Fine city. Rich, too. Everybody equal. Every man has absolute freedom to pay
taxes. Every man has a constitutional right to ruin himself. [*These are read as though they were virtues; now
his face falls.*] Of course, the town's full of lawyers.
Always suing everybody. Government men, too. And
inspectors. Always inspectors!

[PITHETAERUS *has momentarily abandoned his search above
to listen to these last remarks; now he adds his own
complaints, coming down to* EUELPIDES *and sitting down
while* EUELPIDES *continues doing all the work.*

Pithetaerus

Tell 'em about the real estate. Tell 'em about the long-
haired poets!

Euelpides

He's right. The city's infested. A lot of prophets, too.
Always predicting what's going to happen the day after
tomorrow. Very wearing.

Pithetaerus

Bores, bores, bores!

Euelpides

That's why we left.

Pithetaerus

Get away from the bores, get a little peace!

Euelpides

That's why we're looking for the King of the Birds. [*His
work finished, coming down to the audience again.*] If
anybody should know of a nice quiet place where a
couple of men could settle—with no bores—it should be
the King of the Birds. Birds get around.

[PITHETAERUS *suddenly jumps up, attending to his crow.*

Pithetaerus

My bird's doing something!

Euelpides

I'll bet I know what.

Pithetaerus

[*Excited, moving anxiously wherever the bird indicates, but never more than a few steps in any one direction.*] No—no—watch!

Euelpides

[*Indifferently and sadly, to the audience, playing against* PITHETAERUS' *excitement.*] So we started off with a stewpot, a knife and a fork—a few myrtle berries—and, now you know.

Pithetaerus

Here! Look!

Euelpides

[*To his jay, laconically.*] Has that other bird really got anything?

[*The jay shakes his head slowly, with contempt.*

Pithetaerus

It's behaving like there were other birds around somewhere!

[*Now* EUELPIDES' *bird becomes agitated.*

Euelpides

Mine's doing it, too! Where? Where? [*He runs agitatedly wherever his bird indicates, so that both* PITHETAERUS *and* EUELPIDES *are scurrying hither and thither independently. Suddenly they cross each other unexpectedly, so that* EUELPIDES *gives a little scream of fright, then calms down as he sees it is* PITHETAERUS.] Oh, it's you.

Pithetaerus

Yes, dammit, it's me! Look for some birds!

Euelpides

Maybe we could scare them up if we made some noise.

Pithetaerus

[*Indicating rock Right Center.*] That's right. Here—kick your leg against that rock.

Euelpides

[*Responds automatically, about to do it, then considers.*] Wouldn't it be louder if we used your head?

Pithetaerus

[*Roaring.*] Kick your leg against that rock!

Euelpides

[*Resignedly.*] All right. [*Braces himself and does it; lets out a great series of yowls.*

Pithetaerus

[*Listening to the yowls with approval.*] That's fine. That ought to do it. [*Motioning* EUELPIDES *to join him.*] Ready, now. They'll be coming.

[*Together they move warily, expectantly among the rocks Up Right. Coming on from Up Left, we see* TROCHILUS, *the Butler Bird, entering matter-of-factly, nose in air. He turns around a rock unexpectedly and comes face to face with* PITHETAERUS *and* EUELPIDES. ALL *leap into the air in terror of each other, screaming and chattering, and dive for hiding places.* PITHETAERUS *and* EUELPIDES *hide in the rock formation at Right,* TROCHILUS *high on the rock formation at Left.*]

Euelpides

Mercy have Apollo. I mean, Apollo have mercy. [*His teeth chatter.*]

Pithetaerus

[*Peeping over a ledge, trembling.*] What a beak!

Trochilus

[*Waveringly, from his hiding place.*] Men! Bird-catchers!

Pithetaerus

[*Trying to get up nerve, his voice faltering.*] H-ho there! D-d-don't be frightened of us!

Trochilus

[*Adopting the same bravura, calling across.*] F-f-frightened of you? F-f-frightened of men? [*Bats his wings at them.*] Y-y-you're done for!

Euelpides

[*Helpfully.*] Oh—we're not men! [*To himself.*] No. Never say that.

Trochilus

[*Relaxing.*] You're not? What are you, then?

Euelpides

[*Indicating* PITHETAERUS.] Well, I don't know about him, but I'm a bird. An African bird. The—the Fearling.

Trochilus

Never heard of him. [*Becoming braver, taking command.*] And what kind of a bird is that bird? Huh?

Pithetaerus

[*Half-rising from behind ledge.*] Why, I'm a—[*Pauses to consider, then with some self-disgust.*]—a Crapple, if you must know.

Euelpides
One of the yellow-bellied school.

Pithetaerus
[*Regaining confidence.*] Now, see here. You're a bit of a fright yourself. What are you?

Trochilus
[*Coming down the rock, manservant style.*] I am a butler bird. Butler to Epops, King of the Birds.

Euelpides
[*Excited.*] He's our man—! [TROCHILUS' *head whips around, alert.*] I mean, bird.

Trochilus
Choose your language.

Pithetaerus
[*Tentatively coming down from the rock formation.*] Would you—do us the kindness to call your master?

Trochilus
I'm sorry. He has just fallen asleep after a dainty supper of berries and a few choice grubs. I picked the grubs myself.

Euelpides
[*Relaxed now, assuming an air.*] Wake him up. Tell him we're here.

Trochilus
He will be angry.

Pithetaerus
[*Taking a deep breath.*] We'll risk it.

Trochilus
Very well. [*Starts to go, Left above, pauses to check.*] The Fearling, and the—

Pithetaerus
[*Obligingly.*] Crapple.

Trochilus
Crapple. I think I understand.

[TROCHILUS *goes, Up Left.* PITHETAERUS *and* EUELPIDES *follow him a step or two, completely off the rock formation; then* PITHETAERUS *turns on* EUELPIDES *and kicks him to Down Right.*

Pithetaerus
You mouse! You flyspeck! What were you so frightened about? You were so frightened you made me frightened. What was the matter with you?

Euelpides

I was frightened.

Pithetaerus

Where's your jay? You were so frightened, you big coward, you let your jay go!

Euelpides

Where's your crow?

Pithetaerus

[*Realizing he no longer has his crow.*] I gave him his freedom.

Euelpides

That was decent of you.

[*There is a sudden loud whirr and* EPOPS *rises to the top of a rock at the highest stage point, Up Center.* PITHETAERUS *and* EUELPIDES *realize that something has happened. Slowly they turn to face* EPOPS, *above. When they have finally turned full face to him, they collapse in a trembling heap together, and scurry on hands and knees for the shelter of a downstage Right rock.*

Epops

[*In a great voice.*] Who wants me?

Euelpides

[*Terrified, trying to laugh it off.*] I can't imagine. [*To* PITHETAERUS.] Did you see anybody?

Epops

Does someone dare to laugh at the King of the Birds?

Euelpides

No—no—just a little giddy—[*Shoving* PITHETAERUS, *as though to start him running out of this place.*] Giddyap.

[PITHETAERUS *collapses into* EUELPIDES' *arms;* EUELPIDES *is struggling to hold him up during the ensuing conversation.*

Epops

You must know, strangers, that I once was a man.

Euelpides

[*Looking down at* PITHETAERUS.] We all were.

Epops

Born of woman, married to a wife, I was unfaithful to my dear Procne. Now I am changed by Apollo into a bird, and Procne is the nightingale, and I am faithful at last.

Euelpides

[*To the audience.*] We're certainly getting the exposition out.

Epops

Who are you?

Euelpides

Mortals. Haven't had any affairs with nightingales.

Epops

From what country?

Euelpides

The land of democracy, where everyone is equal.

Epops

[*Suddenly suspicious.*] You're not government men?

Euelpides

Anti-government men.

Epops

[*Relaxing, moving gracefully across bridge at Left so that he can see them better from across the stage.*] They're getting around to that, are they?

Euelpides

Not fast enough. That's why we came.

Epops

Why have you come?

[PITHETAERUS, *in* EUELPIDES' *arms, begins to stir.*

Pithetaerus

What? What?

Euelpides

He wants to know why we came.

Pithetaerus

Tell him.

Euelpides

If you can lie down somewhere else, I will. [*Drops* PITHETAERUS *with a thud and goes to Center, speaking up to* EPOPS *on the bridge at mid-Left.* PITHETAERUS *crawls to a small rock and sits down.*] We came to see you.

Epops

Why me?

Euelpides

[*Taking on graces and airs, in the manner of a rather florid ambassador.*] Because formerly you were a man, as we are. Formerly you had debts, as we do. And formerly you did not want to pay them, as we don't. Furthermore, now that you're a bird, you must have flown everywhere. And while you were flying all over the world, you must have seen—somewhere—some little town, where a man can sit back, stretch out, drop a berry into his mouth—[*Pantomimes what he describes.*]

Pithetaerus

[*Chiming in.*]—and not be bothered with bores!

Epops

Are you looking for a city greater than your own?

Euelpides

No, not a greater one. Just one more pleasant to live in.

Pithetaerus

[*Nodding.*] No bores.

Epops

What sort of city would please you?

Euelpides

I'll tell you. A city where the following would be the most important business transacted—Some friend would come banging on your door at a reasonable hour in the morning, and say: [*Dramatizing, in a harsh voice.*] "Get up! Get your wife and children! Get over to my house. Sit down at my table and eat till you bust. And if you don't, I'll be mad at you!" I have something like that in mind.

Epops

I see. Sort of—roughing it?

Euelpides

Yes.

Epops

[*To* PITHETAERUS.] And you?

Pithetaerus

My tastes are similar.

Epops

I see. As a matter of fact, there is a city like that. It's on the Red Sea.

Pithetaerus

[*Rising, asserting himself now.*] No, no! No sea ports. Let a ship dock, and there'll be a process server on it. Someplace remote. Uninhabited. Inaccessible. [*Has been envisioning such a place as he speaks; suddenly there is a gleam in his eye.*] Wait a minute. Now, wait a minute!

Euelpides
[*Resignedly.*] You have an idea.

Pithetaerus
Yes!

Euelpides
The last idea you had was using birds for guides. I hate to bring it up.

Pithetaerus
[*Excited.*] No, listen, now. Listen! [*Grabs* EUELPIDES *by the shoulders and sits him down between himself and* EPOPS, *who moves slightly down on his rock perch.*]

Euelpides
It isn't as though I had a choice. [*To the audience.*] You do. You can go home anytime.

Pithetaerus
[*Striding around, his eyes ablaze as he works out his plan.*] Sh-h-h-h!

Euelpides
[*Relaying it unnecessarily to the audience.*] Sh-h-h-h!

Pithetaerus
[*Ready to talk now, becoming momentously confidential with* EPOPS.] Tell me. What is it like to live with the birds themselves?

Epops
What?

Pithetaerus
You ought to know. What's the life like?

Epops
[*Rising and moving on the bridge as he considers.*] Why, it's not a bad sort of life. Of course, you have no money.

Euelpides
I'm as good as a bird now.
[PITHETAERUS *kicks him.*

Epops
And, naturally, you have none of the problems that go with money.

Euelpides
That's logical.
[PITHETAERUS *kicks him.*

Epops
The food is nice. White sesame, myrtle, poppies, mint—

Euelpides
Worms.

[PITHETAERUS *about to kick him,* EUELPIDES *quickly walks, without making himself erect, from one rock to another.*

Pithetaerus

[*Grandiosely.*] I am beginning to conceive a great plan. [*To* EPOPS, *moving up the rocks at Right toward him.*] All you have to do is take my advice.

Epops

Take your advice? How?

Pithetaerus

[*After a significant pause.*] Found a city!

Epops

A city for birds? What kind of city could we have?

Pithetaerus

[*Dragging* EPOPS *to high point Up Center.*] Oh, come on, come on! Don't be a fool. Here. Look down.

[EPOPS *bends over the high point and looks down, then waits for* PITHETAERUS *to say something more; he doesn't.*

Epops

I'm looking.

Pithetaerus

Now look up.

Epops

[*Repeats business.*] I'm looking.

Pithetaerus

Turn your head around. [EPOPS *does, twisting his head.*] Well! What do you find?

Epops

That my neck is getting stiff.

Pithetaerus

No, no! What do you *see?*

Epops

The same old clouds and sky.

Pithetaerus

[*As though it were quite simple.*] That's it! The land of the birds!

Epops

I knew that.

Euelpides

[*Still below, indifferent.*] *I* knew that. He gets excited about nothing.

Pithetaerus

But you can turn it into a city!

Epops
[*Incredulously.*] A city in the air?

Pithetaerus
Surround it with walls and fortify it!

Euelpides
[*To audience.*] He's going to surround space.

Epops
What for?

Pithetaerus
To seize all the power of the universe—for yourself. For the birds. [*Offhand.*] And, of course, we'll have a little share in it, too. [*The salesman again.*] You can reign over mankind as you now do over grasshoppers! You can rule the gods!

Epops
How?

Pithetaerus
By starving them into submission.

Epops
I don't follow you.

Euelpides
You're not the first.

Pithetaerus
Now, listen! When men are on their last legs, when they're desperate—what is the only thing that can help them?

Epops
The gods.

Pithetaerus
And how do they get the gods to help them?

Epops
[*Indicating a small altar-like rock downstage Left of Center.*] By offering sacrifice. They put a goat or an ox in the sacrificial fire.

Pithetaerus
[*Moving downstage with* EPOPS *and dramatizing what he says.*] And the smoke rises up through the air until it reaches the heavens. The gods notice it, and come to the rescue. Is that right? [EPOPS *nods.*] Listen carefully. In the practical business affairs of earth, suppose I am a man living in this country. [*Marks out an area on the ground with his foot;* EUELPIDES *jumps up and puts his foot in the area, helpfully.*] But I want to go to that

country over there on business. [*Indicates an area some distance toward Right.*] Between the two countries is a middle country which I must pass through. [EUELPIDES *starts to travel toward the second area through middle area, but* PITHETAERUS *stops him midway.*] Now, when I want to pass through it, what do I have to do?

Epops

Pay tribute.

Pithetaerus

Precisely! [EUELPIDES *reaches for his purse, but it is empty; shrugs, goes away and sits down, Left.*] Now here is all that smoke going through *your* country for nothing. But if you build a wall and fortify it, you can demand that men acknowledge you as rulers of the universe and pay you a tribute. Otherwise, *you don't let the smoke through!* [*He pauses for* EPOPS *and* EUELPIDES *to grasp and admire this notion.*] In addition, with no smoke coming up, the gods starve to death. You rule the universe!

Epops

[*His imagination fired, darting about the stage.*] By snares! By networks! By cages! That's the cleverest idea I've ever heard. I've been wanting to get back at that Apollo. [*Faces them.*] If I can get the approval of the other birds, I'll do it.

Pithetaerus

Will you explain the matter to them?

Epops

No, *you* will. You're a splendid talker.

Euelpides

Splendid.

Pithetaerus

How will you get them all together?

Epops

No trouble at all. I shall awaken dear Procne, my nightingale. Once they hear our voices, they will come to us hot on the wing!

Pithetaerus

Then hurry, my dear fellow, hurry. Wake up Procne! [*Begin MUSIC.* EPOPS *waves them aside as he goes to the nest in the rocks.* PITHETAERUS *and* EUELPIDES *scurry downstage Left of Center and conceal themselves, watching.* EPOPS *makes several birdlike sounds and the nest door slowly opens, or unfolds.* PROCNE *is discovered asleep. Slowly she wakes. Moving from the nest, she dances drowsily, waking herself, as* EPOPS *speaks softly.*

Epops
Chase off drowsy sleep, my mate!
Shake off thy slumbers, and clear and strong
Let loose thy flood of glorious song.
With the liquid note of thy tawny throat
Through the leafy curls of the woodbine sweet
Send thy pure sound to the heavenly seat
Of Phoebus, lord of the golden lair,
Who lists to thy wild plaint echoing there.
Draw answering strains from Phoebus' lyre
Till he stirs the dance of the aerial choir
And calls from the blessed lips on high
Of a thousand birds, divine reply
To the tones of thy witching melody . . .

Euelpides
[*As* PROCNE *now stands erect, ready to call.*] Oh, by Zeus, what a sweet little bird. I'm charmed, charmed.

Pithetaerus
Sh-h!

Euelpides
What's the matter?

Pithetaerus
The King is ready. Procne is ready. They're going to call the birds!
[*During the ensuing passage* PROCNE *takes the lead, moving in dance rhythm to each promontory on the set and singing a birdlike strain.* EPOPS, *also in dance rhythms, moves to each position after her, keeping on a lower level.*

Procne
Apopopoi popoi popopopoi popoi!

Epops
Come hither any bird with plumage like my own,
Come hither ye that fatten on the acres newly sown,
On the acres by the farmer newly sown.
And the myriad tribes that feed on the barley, and the
seed
The tribes that lightly fly, giving out a gentle cry—

Procne
[*On another promontory.*] Tio, tio, tio, tio tiotinx!

Epops

> And ye who in the gardens pleasant harvest glean
> Lurking in the branches of the ivy ever green
> And ye who top the mountains with gay and airy flight,
> Come hither one and all, come flying to our call—

Procne

> Trioto, trioto, totobrinx!

Birds

> [*Off faintly.*] Trioto, trioto, totobrinx!

[*Faintly a whirring of wings begins off, and the stage begins to darken as though from a sky filled with approaching birds.*

Epops

> Ye that snap up the gnats, shrilly voiced,
> Mid the deep water-glens of the fens,
> And the bird with the gay mottled plumes, come away—

Procne

> Francolin! Francolin!

Epops

> Come away!

Birds

> [*Off louder.*] Tio tio, tio, tiotinx

Pithetaerus

> See any birds yet?

Euelpides

> No, but I've got my eyes open.

Pithetaerus

> That's your mouth, stupid.

[EPOPS *and* PROCNE *now take up a kingly position together on the rock tower at Right and remain still.* EPOPS *speaks climactically, as the music and the offstage whirring become louder.*

Epops

[*Majestically.*]

> Ye with the halcyons flitting delightedly
> Over the surge of the infinite sea,
> Come to the great Revolution awaiting us,
> Hither, come hither, come hither to me.

[*Now the* BIRDS *begin to arrive. Some flutter in from one upstage promontory, others swoop in from another. They whirr down the formations, crossing one another in spectacular dance movement.*

Epops

All the feathered airy nation—
Birds of every size and station
Come in a flurry, with a hurry-scurry—

Euelpides

How they thicken, how they muster!

Pithetaerus

How they clutter, how they cluster!

Euelpides

How they ramble here and thither,
How they scramble altogether.
There's a marsh bird—

Pithetaerus

—a flamingo—

Euelpides

Thyme-finch—

Pithetaerus

—ring-dove next, and then
Rock-dove, stock-dove,
cuckoo, falcon,
Fiery crest and willow wren.

Euelpides

Oho for the birds, oho, oho!
Oho for the blackbirds, ho!

The Birds

[*In final ecstatic movement.*] Toro toro toro torotinx
Kikkabau! Kikkibau! Toro toro toro toro lililinx!

[*With the last phrase the birds suddenly become still,
perched about the stage in a great arc facing* EPOPS *at
Right.* PITHETAERUS *and* EUELPIDES *are crouching on our
side of a rock Left of Center. The* CHORUS LEADER *steps
forward.*

Leader

We have answered the call of the King of the Birds.
We await his pleasure and attend his words.

Epops

An envoy, queer and shrewd,
Begs to address the multitude
Submitting to their decision
A surprising proposition—

Birds

[*Chattily pleasant, among themselves.*]

News amazing! News auspicious! News delightful, we
agree.

Epops

Birds—two men of subtlest genius
Have proposed a plan to me.

Birds

[*Suddenly ruffled, stirring.*] Who? What? When?

Leader

[*Sternly.*] Say that again.

Epops

[*Indicating* PITHETAERUS *and* EUELPIDES, *who now make
bold to arise from behind their rock and present themselves modestly.*]

Here, I say, have come two humans
Traveling to the birds from man;
And they bring with them the kernel
Of a most stupendous plan.

Birds

[*Aroused, now; shocked, angry.*] You have made the greatest error, since our life up here began!

Epops

Now, you mustn't be so nervous—

Euelpides

[*A little worried.*] Everybody's *nervous!*

Birds

[*Rising to full height, awesomely.*] Explain your conduct,
if you can!

Epops

[*Patiently, indicating them.*] I've received two men—

[PITHETAERUS *is about to step forward and introduce himself, grandly.*

Birds

[*Shrill, terrifying, ruffling feathers.*] Among us? Have you
really, truly dared?

Epops

Yes, and I shall introduce them—

Euelpides

[*Trembling.*] I hate to say it, but I'm getting scared!

Birds

[*A great blast.*] Out! Out upon you!

[PITHETAERUS *and* EUELPIDES, *shaken by the impact, scurry
to extreme down Right and take shelter behind a ledge,*

as the BIRDS *turn from* EPOPS *and gather in quick, violent consultation at Left.*

We are cheated and betrayed, we have suffered shame
    and wrong!
Our comrade and our King, who has fed with us so long,
Has broken every oath, and his holy plighted troth,
And the old social customs of our clan!
He has led us unawares into wiles and into snares—
He has given us as prey, all helpless and forlorn
To those who were our foes from the time that they
    were born,
To vile and abominable man!

Leader

[*Rising high among the choral group.*]
    For the bird our Chief, hereafter he must answer to the
        state!
    With respect to these intruders, I propose, without
        debate,
    Bit by bit to tear and rend them—
[*The* BIRDS *begin to sharpen their claws and make greedy, slavering sounds.*

Pithetaerus

Here's a horrid mess.

Euelpides

It's all your fault, your fault, you and your cleverness!
Why didn't you leave me home?

Pithetaerus

I wanted a companion.

Euelpides

Your companion is going to melt into tears.

Pithetaerus

Don't be silly. How're you going to cry with your eyes
pecked out?

[EUELPIDES *begins to bawl, loudly.*

Birds

[*Thunderously, a climax to* EUELPIDES' *cry.*] Form in rank!
Form in rank! [BIRDS *begin to take military formation at Left.*]
    Then move forward and outflank them. Let us see them
        overpowered,
    Hacked, demolished, and devoured! [*Despairing panto-mime by* PITHETAERUS *and* EUELPIDES.]

Both, both of them shall die
And their bodies shall supply
Rare, dainty morsels for our beaks—
Where's the Captain? What detains him?
We are ready to proceed!
On the right there, call the Captain!
Let him form his troop and lead!

[*The* CAPTAIN, *a very shabby-looking bird, hurries in and proceeds to meet troops at Left.*

Pithetaerus

He's a seedy-looking Captain.

Captain

[*Glancing back, huffily.*] I was moulting.

[*Gives signal to* BIRDS, *who drop to crouched formation as though ready to spring into air and fly directly at the humans across stage.*

Euelpides

[*As* CAPTAIN *pantomimes instructions to the crouched and waiting* BIRDS.]

They're coming! They're coming! [*Shakes hands with* PITHETAERUS, *quickly.*]

Goodbye. [*Starts directly toward* BIRDS.]

Pithetaerus

[*Grabbing him.*] Where do you think you're going?

Euelpides

I'm going to give myself up.

Pithetaerus

[*Shaking him and roaring.*] Stand up and fight! Here!

[*Digs into their equipment and hands him a fork.*

Euelpides

Somehow I'm not hungry.

Pithetaerus

Use it for a sword!

Euelpides

No. When my eyes are pecked out, I won't be able to see who I'm stabbing. I might stab myself.

Pithetaerus

[*Throwing him a stewpot.*] Here! Shield your eyes!

Euelpides

[*Delighted, trying it on.*] Oh, that's nice! Want a test match?

[*Begins to feint at* PITHETAERUS, *who slaps him away and digs out a pot and a ladle for his own weapons. At the*

same time the CAPTAIN *leaps back from his pantomimed instructions to the* BIRDS *and shouts.*

Captain
Ready, Birds! Present your beaks! In double time,
charge and attack!

Leader
Pounce upon them—

Captain
—smash the potlid—

Leader
Clapperclaw them—

Captain
—tear and hack!

[*The* BIRDS *leap and dart forward and there ensues a slash-
ing duel between the* BIRDS *and* PITHETAERUS *and* EUEL-
PIDES. *The* BIRDS *keep up a great chattering racket
throughout. Momentarily* PITHETAERUS *and* EUELPIDES
disappear in a melee of surrounding BIRDS, *then appear
dueling each other. Recognizing their mistake, they
separate and take on half the* BIRDS *each. The* BIRDS
force them back to the rock towers, PITHETAERUS *at
Right and* EUELPIDES *at Left. The two men climb their
towers, dueling, the* BIRDS *pursuing, clawing at them.
When both are about to be overcome,* EPOPS *decides to
reassert himself, takes Center.*

Epops
Cease! Most unworthy creatures, scandal of the feathered race;
Must I see my friends and yours massacred before my
face?

[THE BIRDS *pause where they are, but do not release their
hold on the humans.*

Captain
Friends? They're *men*. Men invented the slingshot.

Euelpides
I hope they'll mark my grave.

Epops
But they have abandoned other men, and come to give
us advice.

Leader
Take advice—from an enemy?

Epops
How else do you suppose men learned to build strong

walls and make new weapons—if not from their enemies? We always learn from the enemy.

Leader

Who are these men?

Captain

Why have they come to us?

Epops

Because they love you, and wish to share your life—to
dwell and remain with you always.

Leader

Are they mad?

Epops

The sanest men in the world.

Euelpides

[*Signaling* EPOPS *with his finger.*] Don't overdo it.

Leader

Clever men, eh?

Epops

Cleverness itself! Men of the world, cunning, ingenious,
sly—[*Searching for a perfect phrase.*]

Pithetaerus

[*Prompting in a loud whisper.*] Brave. Brave.

Epops

And brave. They have wonderful plans!

Leader

Plans?

Epops

To make us the rulers of the universe! All power, above
and below, shall be ours!

[*Chattering noises among the* BIRDS, *to each other;* LEADER
listens and considers.

Leader

Well. I should like to hear this.

Pithetaerus

[*Confident now, adopting an attitude.*] Well. You won't
hear it from me.

Birds

What's this? What's this?

Pithetaerus

[*Moving away toward Right, stubborn.*] Not a word. I'm
a clam.

Euelpides

[*Helpless.*] He's changed his mind. He wants to be a clam.

Epops

You must speak!

Pithetaerus

[*Turning, in full command.*] Not until we reach an agreement! No more pecking, no more clawing, no more biting! Is it agreed?

Leader

[*After a glance around at the* BIRDS, *whose heads bob up and down in encouragement.*] It is agreed.

Birds

We swear it. [*Raising one wing each.*]

Leader

You have my word. And if I break my word—[*Glancing directly out front.*]—may the audience speak unkindly of me in the lobby.

Pithetaerus

Very well.

Leader

[*Coming directly downstage now and speaking confidentially to the audience.*] On the other hand, if I keep my word, mention my performance to your friends. [*Turns immediately and rejoins* BIRDS *as* EPOPS *speaks.*]

Epops

Birds! Gather yourselves and listen!

[*In a quick flurry the* BIRDS *dart to seated positions at Right extending to Center, facing the rock tower at Left. As they speak,* PITHETAERUS *mounts the tower slowly.*

Birds

Full of wiles, full of guiles, at all times, in all ways

Are the children of men. Still—we'll hear what he says.

Epops

[*To* PITHETAERUS.] Speak!

Pithetaerus

[*Surveys the group with slow deliberation, waiting for absolute silence; finally he speaks softly, for impressive effect.*] I am bursting to speak. [*Pause while he straightens to full height.*] I have already mixed the dough of my address and I am ready to knead it.

[*Flurry of wings from the* BIRDS *as though in applause.*

Euelpides

A very pretty image.

Pithetaerus

[*Takes a deep breath, begins to open his mouth and raise his arm in gesture; then halts.*] Water, please.

Euelpides

These long pauses are hard on the throat.

[LEADER *scurries to the tower, taps a rock nearby and water gushes forth.* PITHETAERUS *drinks, wipes his mouth, faces his assembly again.*

Pithetaerus

I shall say what I have to say in a few, well-chosen words. [EUELPIDES *yawns loudly*; PITHETAERUS *hurls a rock at him*; EUELPIDES *ducks.*] Birds. My heart bleeds for you. You—who were formerly Emperors!

A Bird

[*To another near him, chattily.*] Did you ever hear that?

Leader

Emperors? Over whom?

Pithetaerus

Over all that exists! Over me. Over that man.

[*Indicates* EUELPIDES, *who rises and bows.*] Over Zeus himself! You belong to a race older than Saturn—older than the Titans—older than the very Earth!

[EUELPIDES *applauds, vociferously*; PITHETAERUS *throws another rock at him.*

Birds

Than the Earth itself! We never heard that before.

Pithetaerus

[*Warmed up now, the thoroughgoing demagogue.*]

You never heard that before because you haven't read your Aesop! Aesop clearly tells us—and I quote—that the lark—and the lark is a bird—existed before the earth itself!

[*Having reached a climax, he turns to drink.*

Euelpides

[*The unwelcome question.*] Where does Aesop say that?

Pithetaerus

[*Stares at him hard, then dismisses it, speaking with casual rapidity as he takes up a cup and prepares to get more water.*] Oh, in that little story about how the lark's father died and went unburied for five days, and finally had to be buried in the lark's head. You know that.

Euelpides

No. I didn't. Now that I do, it doesn't seem to explain anything.

Pithetaerus

[*Hurling the cup at him in sudden fury and then plunging directly into his speech.*] It explains this: if the lark had to bury its own father in its own head, that can only have been because there was no earth in which to bury him. Ergo, the lark existed before the earth. Aesop. [*Pronounces his source with finality; the* BIRDS *buzz buzz excitedly among themselves.*] Furthermore. The birds existed before the gods!

A Bird

[*To another, chattily.*] Do you think he's going too far?

Pithetaerus

[*Thundering.*] The gods stole their power from the birds!

Another Bird

[*Replying confidentially to the first.*] Too far.

Pithetaerus

They derive their very authority from the birds! Else why should they carry on their sceptres—the symbol of their authority—a hawk? Why should Zeus always be seen with an eagle on his head?

Leader

[*Interested.*] Why, indeed?

Euelpides

And so uncomfortable, too.

Pithetaerus

Why should Victory be winged? Why Cupid? And my friends, I ask you to consider the rooster.

Euelpides

[*Willing.*] All right.

Pithetaerus

Just consider the rooster.

Euelpides

All right.

Pithetaerus

[*After a quick, disgusted glance at Euelpides.*] What creature, in all the universe, wears a crown that will not come off?

Euelpides

[*After a moment's consideration.*] The rooster.

Pithetaerus

[*To Euelpides, annoyed.*] That was a rhetorical question.

Euelpides

That was a rhetorical answer.

Pithetaerus

[*Whipping back into his tirade.*] All other crowns must be put on and taken off. Only a bird has a natural crown! Consider further. This Great King of old, this rooster, even now is so powerful, so great, so feared by men that the moment he crows at daybreak, they all jump out of bed. [*Pause for effect.*] What effect does the call of the rooster have?

Euelpides

Scares the hell out of me.

Pithetaerus

It makes blacksmiths, potters, tanners, shoemakers, corn-dealers, lyre-makers, and armorers all put on their shoes and go to work even before it is daylight! This is the power of the bird! [*Quick change to pathos.*] And yet—how are birds treated today? Stones are thrown at you. Men set snares for you—twigs and nets of all kinds. You are caught. Caught. Sold in heaps for a banquet. The buyer fingers you over to be sure you are fat enough. [BIRDS *shudder, emit little cries as* PITHETAERUS *pictures the full horror of their existence in juicy tones.*] If only—if only they would serve you up simply roasted. But no! What do they do? They grate cheese into a mixture of oil and vinegar—they add to this a greasy sauce—and they pour it scalding over your backs for all the world as though you were diseased meat! Oh!

[*He cries out, unable to bear it; the* BIRDS *echo him, take up his wail.*

Birds

Oh Oh!
Sad and dismal is the story
We have heard this stranger tell
Of our fathers' ancient glory
Ere the fated empire fell. [*On their knees to* PITHE-
    TAERUS.]
From the depths of degradation
A benignant happy fate
Sends you to restore our nation,
To redeem and save our state!

Pithetaerus

Birds! The hour has come! Your power must be re-
claimed—from men, and from the gods above!

Euelpides

[*Frowning.*] I just can't see Zeus turning things over to a
woodpecker.

Leader

But how shall we do this?

Birds

Tell us how!

Pithetaerus

[*During this he descends slowly and actually mingles
with the* BIRDS, *dramatizing it for them in gestures and
whipping up their enthusiasm.*

Very well.

First I propose that the Air you enclose

And the space twixt the Earth and the Sky,

Encircling it all with a brick-built wall

Like Babylon's, solid and high.

As soon as the building is brought to an end

A herald or envoy to Zeus we shall send

To require his immediate and prompt abdication;

If he refuses, or shows hesitation

Or evades the demand, we shall further proceed

With legitimate warfare, avowed and decreed:

[*In the manner of a proclamation.*] "Hereafter no god,
neither Zeus nor any of the others residing in heaven,
may pass through our aerial domain for the purpose of
impromptu lovemaking down below. Permission must
first be granted by the Birds, and a small fee paid.
Otherwise—back to Olympus!" [BIRDS *chatter approval;
he resumes his description.*]

Another ambassador also will go

To the earth, and tell those below

That in future:

[*Again the style of proclamation.*] "Every man wishing to
beg favors of the gods, and therefore offering sacrifice to
the aforesaid gods, must first of all make an appropriate
sacrifice to the Birds. For instance—if an ox is to be
sacrificed to Zeus, the Birds must first be appeased by
the sacrifice of one male mosquito!"

[BIRDS *lick their chops in anticipation.*

Leader

And what if they will not obey?

Euelpides

What if Zeus lets loose with thunder and lightning?

Leader

What if men ignore us?

Pithetaerus

Then you will swoop onto their fields and eat up all their seed. [EUELIPIDES *pantomimes this helpfully.*] Nothing will grow. Nor will Zeus be offered any oxen. You will fly to the pastures and peck out their eyes.

Leader

And if they obey us, what do we promise in return?

Pithetaerus

To defend their fields from insects and pests, as Zeus never did. Never more will they fear the beetle or roach. You will guide their sailing vessels, flying back to warn of an oncoming storm, and showing them favorable winds.

Euelpides

[*Starting to go.*] I'm leaving. I'm going into the shipping business.

[PITHETAERUS *collars him, holds him steady, as the* BIRDS *rise and then kneel in homage, with a burst of triumphant confidence.*

Birds

All honor to you, oh man! [PITHETAERUS *takes a self-satisfied stance, and* EUELPIDES *leaps to the fore to share in the praise.*]
We thought thee at first of our foemen the worst
And lo! we have found thee the wisest
And best of our friends. Our nation intends
To do whatsoever this great man advisest.
A spirit so lofty and rare
Thy words have within us excited
That we lift up our souls and we swear
That if thou wilt with us be united
In bonds that are holy and true
And honest and just and sincere—
If our hearts are attuned to one song,
We will march on the gods without fear!
Now whatever by muscle and strength can be done,
We birds will assuredly do;

But whatever by prudence and skill must be won,
We leave altogether to you.

Epops

[*To* PITHETAERUS.] Come. Come with me and we shall
lay our plans.

Pithetaerus

Very well. [*To* EUELPIDES, *who has started off with*
EPOPS *too willingly.*] Bring the luggage. [EUELPIDES
*wearily goes back for their belongings and drags them
forward. Meanwhile* EPOPS *has leaped to a great
promontory as though to fly off when* PITHETAERUS
intervenes.] Hi! Wait! Come back here! How are we
going to keep up with you? We haven't got wings.

Epops

[*Considering.*] That's true.

Euelpides

[*Tugging at* PITHETAERUS' *sleeve, confidentially.*] I remember something else from Aesop. When the fox made
an alliance with the eagle, he got the worst of it.

[PITHETAERUS *pushes him away and his load throws him
off balance.*

Epops

Never fear. You shall eat of a certain root, and wings
will grow on your shoulders.

Leader

[*To* EPOPS.] As you take them to dine, send us Procne. We
wish to sing of our new-found happiness.

Epops

[*Turns on promontory and chants.*] Procne! Nightingale!
Come forth!

[PROCNE *darts onto stage from between rocks at upstage
Left.*

Leader

Oh, nightingale—who are all melody—help us to show
our joy!

[PROCNE *dances to Center.*

Euelpides

[*As* PITHETAERUS *follows* EPOPS *off Left, dragging after
them and looking back at* PROCNE.] Oh, that nice
nightingale! [PITHETAERUS *reappears to collar him.*]
How I should like to kiss her!

Pithetaerus

You fool. She has two sharp points on her beak.

Euelpides

[*Sighing, lovelorn.*] I've got around worse.

[PITHETAERUS *pulls him off with a great jerk, Left. Only* PROCNE *and the* BIRDS, *with their* LEADER, *are left. They now dance the following passage as they speak or sing it.*

Birds

[*Addressing* PROCNE, *who dances.*]

Oh darling, oh tawny-throat!
Love, whom I love the best,
Dearer than all the rest.
Playmate and partner in all my soft lays,
Thou art come! Thou art come!
Thou art sweet to my gaze
And sweeter thy note—nightingale, nightingale!

Procne

Oh woodland muse—

Birds

Tio, tio, tio, tiotinx!

Procne

Of varied plume, with whose dear aid
On the mountain top, and the sylvan glade—

Birds

Tio, tio, tiotinx!

Procne

I, sitting aloft on a leafy ash, full oft—

Birds

Tio, tio, tio, tiotinx!

Procne

Pour forth a warbling note from my little tawny throat,
Pour festive choral dances to the mountain mother's
    praise,
And to Pan the holy music of his own immortal lays,

Birds

Totototototototototinx,
Tio, tio, tio, tio, tiotinx!

Procne

[*Moving down toward the audience and speaking softly to it.*]

You men who are dimly existing below,
Who perish and fade as the leaf—
Pale, woebegone, shadowlike, spiritless—
Frail castings in clay who are gone in a **day**
Like a dream full of sorrow and sighing,

Come listen with care to the birds of the air,
The ageless, the deathless, who flying
In joy and the freshness of air, are wont
To muse on wisdom undying.

Birds

[*All speaking to the audience.*]

Yes, take us for gods, as is proper and fit,
And Muses prophetic you'll have at your call,
Spring, winter, summer, and autumn and all.
And we won't run away from your worship and sit
Up above in the clouds, very stately and grand,
The way that old Zeus does. But, always at hand,
Health and wealth we'll bestow, as the formula runs,
On yourselves and your sons and the sons of your sons.
And happiness, plenty, and peace shall belong
To you all, and the revel, the dance, and the song
And laughter, and youth, we'll supply.
We'll never forsake you.

One Bird

[*A trifle giddy with it all.*] You'll be quiet overburdened
with pleasures and joys!

Birds

So happy and blest we will make you.

Leader

Is there anyone amongst you, O spectators, who would
lead
With the birds a life of pleasure?

Captain

Let him come to us
with speed!

Birds

Truly to be clad in feather is the very best of things.

[*With increasing lightness as they continue to face the
audience but move to exit positions.*]

Only fancy, dear spectators, had you each a brace of
wings,
Never need you, tired and hungry, at our lengthy
chorus stay.
You would lightly, when we bored you, spread your
wings and fly away!
Back returning, after luncheon, to enjoy our comic play.

[BIRDS *disappear, slipping away behind various sections
of rock. A moment later* PITHETAERUS *and* EUELPIDES

enter from upstage Left, now equipped with great flop-
ping wings which they are unable to manage properly.
They test them awkwardly, absorbed, finally managing
to bang them into one another. With this, PITHETAERUS
pauses and really looks at Euelpides. He bursts out
laughing.

Euelpides

What are you laughing at?

Pithetaerus

You. You look like a goose in a paint-bucket.

Euelpides

You look like a blackbird in need of a shave.

Pithetaerus

Just think. They're our feathers. All our own.

Euelpides

D'you suppose we can fly?

Pithetaerus

[*Pointing to a high rock.*] Go up there and jump off.

Euelpides

[*Sizing it up skeptically.*] No, I think I have a loose feather
back here. [*Turning around and backing into* PITHE-
TAERUS.] Would you see if I have a loose feather?

Pithetaerus

[*Roaring.*] Would you get that thing out of my eye?
[*In trying to disentangle himself from one of* EUELPIDES'
wings, he becomes enmeshed in the other and, as EUEL-
PIDES *starts to turn around, there is a pantomimed*
melee in which each fights his way, through the other's
wings. This concludes with PITHETAERUS' *booting* EUEL-
PIDES *clear across the stage.*

Euelpides

[*Looking up from his prone position on the ground.*]
Did I fly?
[EPOPS *appears.*]

Pithetaerus

Hi, King-ol Look. The wings are very nice. But how
do we fly?

Epops

You must go slowly at first, like the newborn bird fresh
from the egg. One step at a time. [EPOPS *does one, to*
show them how. PITHETAERUS *does his best to imitate*
it. EUELPIDES *does a very cautious one, barely taking*
himself off the ground.] Now another. [*They try again.*]

And another. [*There ensues a* DANCE *in which* EPOPS *leads the two men in a series of leaps and bounds, he expertly, they clumsily. At conclusion:*] That will be enough for today.

Euelpides

Same time tomorrow?

Pithetaerus

Now. We have work to do.

Epops

What first?

Pithetaerus

Have the birds begun the city?

Epops

They are already hard at work. [*We hear* SOUNDS *of hammering and building offstage.*] You hear? [*Several* BIRDS *cross through carrying sticks and straw.*] You see [*During remainder of scene occasional* BIRDS *go through in this manner.*]

Pithetaerus

Then we must give our city a name.

Euelpides

Yes. We must have an address.

Epops

What shall we call it?

Euelpides

How about The New Athens?

Pithetaerus

Not a word about Athens, city of pests!

Euelpides

How about Athens-on-the-Incline?

Pithetaerus

Quiet!

Euelpides

How about Sparta?

Pithetaerus

You! Into the air with you. Help the workers who are building the wall. Carry up rubble. Strip yourself to mix the mortar. Take up the hod. Tumble down the ladder. Post sentinels. [EUELPIDES *has started in a different direction with each command, and is now turning every way in a daze.*] Keep the fires burning! Go round the walls. Ring bells. Despatch two heralds. One to the gods above. The other to mankind. And don't stop till you're finished! [EUELPIDES *finally falls out of sight beyond some rocks. At intervals during the following dialogue he reappears, rushing messengers in various directions, pushing* BIRDS *carrying hods, etc. Turns to* EPOPS.] Now. Do you have a priest-bird? To offer sacrifice.

Epops

Surely we're not going to offer sacrifice to the gods! We've just declared war!

Pithetaerus

To the bird-gods—the new gods!

Epops

Ah! I will call him. [EPOPS *leaps to a high rock and emits a bird call to summon the* PRIEST-BIRD. *Then he whirls round to* PITHETAERUS.] But how can we offer sacrifice when we haven't named the city?

Pithetaerus

I have named it.

Epops

You have a name?

Pithetaerus

Just thought of it.

Epops

What? What is the name?

Pithetaerus

Cloud Cuckoo-land!

Epops

[*Ravished.*] Cloud Cuckoo-land! Brilliant! Brilliant! [*To* PRIEST-BIRD, *as he enters.*] Here! Do as he tells you! [*To* PITHETAERUS.] I shall announce to the others our glorious name!

[EPOPS *exits, as* PITHETAERUS *turns to* PRIEST-BIRD.

Pithetaerus

You are a priest-bird?

Priest

As my father before me, and his father before him, and his father before—

[*This may go on forever.*

Pithetaerus

All right, all right. Do you know how to offer sacrifice?

Priest

[*Says nothing but immediately crosses to Center, kneels,*

throws back his wings.] I begin. [*Throws open his arms, then stops.*] Where's the sacrifice?

Pithetaerus

Oh.

[PITHETAERUS *looks around, goes through the business of spotting a gnat flying through the air, pursuing and catching it; he then delicately deposits it before the priest.*

Priest

[*Peers at gnat dubiously, shrugs, and raises his arms again.*] Oh, birds who preside over the earth, and oh, god and goddess birds who preside over heaven—

Pithetaerus

[*Getting into the act, kneeling down.*] Oh hawk—oh, god of the storks!—

Priest

[*After a disdainful glance at* PITHETAERUS, *forces himself to continue, more fulsome.*] Oh, swan of Delos, oh mother of the quails, oh goldfinch—

Pithetaerus

Goldfinch?

Priest

[*Paying no attention.*] Oh, ostrich, mother of the gods and mankind—

Pithetaerus

[*Going along with it.*] Oh, ostrich—

Priest

Grant health and safety to the Cloud Cuckoo-landers, as well as to all who pay us tribute—

Pithetaerus

Yes, put them in.

Priest

Oh, heroes—oh, sons of heroes—oh, sons of the sons of—

Pithetaerus

[*Quickly.*] Don't get off on that again.

Priest

Oh, porphyrion—

Pithetaerus

[*Competing with him now.*] Oh, pelican—

Priest

Oh, spoonbill—

Pithetaerus

Oh—

Priest

[*Before* PITHETAERUS *can get one in.*] Oh, redbreast—

Pithetaerus

Oh—

Priest

[*Beating him to it again.*] Oh, grouse—[*Hereafter intoning more rapidly so that* PITHETAERUS *cannot do much more than get his mouth open for each phrase;* PITHETAERUS *becomes increasingly disgusted.*] Oh, peacock—oh, horned-owl—oh, heron—oh, stormy petrel—oh, woodpecker—oh, titmouse—

Pithetaerus

Oh, hell. [*Jumping up.*] That'll be enough now. Out of here, out of here. You'll drive me crazy. Next you'll be inviting the vultures. Can't you see there isn't enough sacrifice for more than one small bluebird? Out, out, I'll finish it myself. [*As he is hustling the* PRIEST-BIRD *off the stage,* EUELPIDES *is making the last of his flying trips through, urging a* BIRD *before him.* PITHETAERUS *grabs him and drags him downstage to position for sacrifice, as the* BIRD *scurries on off.*] Here. Don't say anything. Just assist me. [PITHETAERUS *gets down on his knees again,* EUELPIDES *mimics him, puzzled.* PITHETAERUS *spreads his arms.*] We will address our sacrifice to *all* winged things—

[*Climbing up from the earth below,* A POET—*dressed in rags, and with long flowing hair—appears.*

Poet

Hello! Anyone here?

Euelpides

[*In an "oh-oh" tone of voice.*] Here comes the first pest!

Poet

[*In overecstatic admiration of the view.*] Oh, Muse! Oh, come, my Muse! Teach me to sing of happy, happy Cloud Cuckoo-land!

Pithetaerus

What have we got here? Where'd you come from? Who are you?

Poet

I am, a poet—a warbler—whose language is sweeter than honey. An eager, meagre servant of the Muses. As Homer says.

Pithetaerus

You certainly wear your hair long.

Poet

It flows as my songs do. Ah, I have worn myself out in the serivce of the Muses. As Homer says.

Pithetaerus

Worn your cloak out, too, I see. What ill wind blew you up here?

Poet

[*Taking out a great sheaf of papers.*] I have heard of your city, and I have composed a few small verses in its honor. They are small, but splendid.

Pithetaerus

I see. And when did you compose them? How long since?

Poet

Oh, I've been working at them a long time. Yes, a long, long time.

Pithetaerus

That's interesting, considering I've just founded the place. Just named it, like a little baby, two minutes ago.

Poet

Ah, but, you reckon without the Muses, and how quickly they spread the word! [*Declamatory.*]
"Fleet, fleet as twinkling horses' feet
The airy, fairy rumor of the Muses
Sped to me."
[*Dropping tone.*] I went right to work.

Pithetaerus

And why did you put yourself to such trouble?

Poet

For beauty's sake. Beauty alone. The soul. [*Putting out his hand, with pretended indifference.*] Of course, if you want to give me a little something to keep body and soul together—

Pithetaerus

As Homer says.

Poet

Yes. I find it a little chilly walking the mountains in these old things—
[*Indicating his ragged clothes and bravely smiling. Then, by way of suggestion, his teeth begin to chatter.*

Euelpides

Poor fellow. Give him something.

Pithetaerus

You think we ought to be charitable, do you?

Euelpides

[*Nodding.*] The generous man shares his benefits.

Pithetaerus

[*Putting his arm around* EUELPIDES.] I have misjudged
you. You have a kind heart. [*Rips* EUELPIDES' *fur jacket
off and presents it to the* POET.] Here. Take this fur.
Maybe your teeth won't chatter so much.

Poet

My Muse thanks you.

Pithetaerus

It was nothing.

Euelpides

It was a fur jacket.

[EUELPIDES' *teeth start to chatter.*

Poet

Do you remember those lovely lines from Pindar?

Pithetaerus

Which ones?

Poet

"Out among the Scythians yonder
See poor Straton wander, wander—
Poor, poor Straton, not possessed
Of a warmly woven under-vest.
What matter his jacket of fur if below
There's no soft tunic for him to show?
[*Quietly.*] Get it?

[PITHETAERUS *starts toward* EUELPIDES, *as though to
relieve him of something else—he hasn't much else on—
but* EUELPIDES *backs away protesting.*

Euelpides

I don't remember those lines! Don't remember 'em!

[*But* PITHETAERUS *has snatched off another piece of*
EUELPIDES' *clothing, leaving him in the absolute mini-
mum.*

Pithetaerus

[*Tossing the garment to* POET]: Now here and get out. I
can't spare another thing.

Euelpides

Not decently.

Poet

I shall go, I shall go. And I shall sing your praises for-
ever. [*Quoting, as he skips about the stage toward an
exit.*]
"Oh Muse, on your golden throne
Prepare me a solemn ditty.
To the mighty, to the flighty,
To the cloudy, quivering, shivering,
To the snowy, to the blowy lovely city.
Cloud Cuckoo-land! Cloud Cuckoo-land!
Tra la la la la la la la la!
[POET *has danced off.*

Pithetaerus

What's he talking about—snowy, blowy? We gave him
the clothes off your backs! How d'you suppose that
plague found his way up here already? [EUELPIDES *is
about to reply, but his chattering teeth prevent him.*]
What are you muttering about? [EUELPIDES *tries help-
lessly to speak but again breaks down into chattering.*]
Come back to the sacrifice. And don't say a word.
[EUELPIDES *motions that he can't, pointing to his chattering teeth;* PITHETAERUS' *arms are spread again.*] Oh,
snowbird—! [EUELPIDES *worse than ever at this.*] Oh,
penguin—[EUELPIDES *shivering all over.*] Oh, gull of the
frosty mountains—!
[EUELPIDES *in a state of collapse. A* PROPHET *has climbed
into view from the earth below.*

Prophet

Cease! Do not continue the sacrifice!

Pithetaerus

Why not?

Prophet

All the signs are against it!

Pithetaerus

Who are you?

Prophet

I—am a prophet, and the author of several prophetic
books.

[*The* PROPHET *might well speak in a voice resembling that
of some contemporary radio or television oracle.*

Pithetaerus

Beat it.

Prophet

Fool! Would you fly in the face of destiny? There is a prophecy in my book—[*Opens a huge volume he carries.*] —which applies exactly to Cloud Cuckoo-land.

Pithetaerus

This is a fine time to tell me! Why didn't you mention it while I was on earth below, before I got everything started?

Prophet

[*Wisely.*] The time was not propitious. However, since hearing of the foundation of Cloud Cuckoo-land, Apollo has appeared to me in a dream. He has interpreted the prophecy in my book. Which I shall now interpret for you.

Pithetaerus

[*Wearily.*] All right. Interpret.

Prophet

[*Reading portentously.*] "When the wolves and the white crows shall dwell together between the spoon and the great bowl. . . ."

Pithetaerus

Now, see here. What has all this kitchenware got to do with me?

Prophet

The great bowl stands for Cloud Cuckoo-land—when you know how to interpret it. It continues: "Before a sacrifice can be offered, those who would offer it must first give to the prophet who reveals these words a new pair of sandals."

[EUELPIDES *just sits down and takes off his shoes.*

Pithetaerus

It says sandals, does it?

Prophet

[*Smugly.*] Look at the book. [*Reading again.*] "Besides this he must be given a goblet of wine and a good share of the entrails of the victim sacrificed."

[EUELPIDES *peers at the gnat, wondering how this is to be done.*

Pithetaerus

It says entrails, does it?

Prophet

Look at the book. "If you do as I command, you shall be

an eagle among the clouds. If not, you shall be neither turtle-dove, nor eagle, nor woodpecker."

Pithetaerus
It says all that, does it?

Prophet
Look at the book.

Pithetaerus
You know, that's funny. Apollo appeared to me in a dream, too. He told me how to interpret another passage.

Prophet
He did?

Pithetaerus
Yes. [*Snatching the book.*] Ah, here it is. [*Obviously improvising.*] "If an imposter comes without invitation to annoy you during the sacrifice and to demand a share of the victim, give to this man a sharp blow on the head."

Prophet
Ridiculous!

Pithetaerus
Look at the book.

[*Shoves the book under* PROPHET's *nose,* PROPHET *incredulously peers at it, and* PITHETAERUS *claps it shut on his nose. As* PROPHET *dances away in pain,* PITHE-TAERUS *batters him with it soundly, driving him to a high rock from which he leaps;* PITHETAERUS *hurls the book down after him, and we hear a faraway howl.*

Euelpides
[*Holding up his sandals.*] All right to put these back on?

Pithetaerus
[*Dusting off his hands, coming down.*] Yes.

Euelpides
My Muse thanks you. [EUELPIDES *sneezes while putting them on and thereafter developes a cold, which affects his voice. Meantime,* A REAL ESTATE MAN, *equipped with curious measuring instruments, has climbed from the earth below.* PITHETAERUS *lets out a mighty roar on seeing him, which frightens* EUELPIDES.] What? What?

Pithetaerus
Another one!

Real Estate Man

[*Briskly and efficiently striding Center with his instruments.* ADDITIONAL SUGGESTION: *though this business
was not used in the original production, the* REAL ESTATE
MAN *may have a fleet of assistants who immediately
begin to tape and mark out the space on stage, planting
signs reading "Lot One," "Lot Two," "Dead End"—
at a high peak—and so on.*] Good morning. Good morning. Nice development you have here.

Pithetaerus

What are you after? Who are you?

Real Estate Man

I am going to survey the plains of the air for you. Then
we'll subdivide.

Pithetaerus

What are those things?

Real Estate Man

Tools. For measuring the air.

Pithetaerus

You can measure the air, can you?

Real Estate Man

Oh, yes. With this bent ruler I draw a line from top to
bottom. From one of its points I describe a circle with
the compass. Then I take the hypotenuse. Follow me?

Pithetaerus

Not at all.

Real Estate Man

[*Patronizing throughout.*] Well, we can't all understand
these things. Next, with a straight ruler I inscribe a
square within the circle. Its center will be the market-
place, into which all the straight streets will lead. They
will converge to a center like a star, which, although
only orbicular, sends forth its rays in a straight line
from all sides. Better now?

Pithetaerus

Come here. I want to talk with you.

[*Draws him downstage, confidentially.*

Real Estate Man

[*Beaming.*] Yes?

Pithetaerus

You don't know this, but I'm a friend of yours.

Real Estate Man

Oh, that's nice.

Pithetaerus

Don't let on, but I'm going to slip you a piece of advice.

Real Estate Man

Oh, fine. What's that?

Pithetaerus

Run. Run like hell.

Real Estate Man

Good heavens! Have I an enemy here?

Pithetaerus

Yes.

Real Estate Man

Someone in the city?

Pithetaerus

Yes. Someone very important. In fact, he's had a law passed.

Real Estate Man

What's that?

Pithetaerus

"All quacks, profiteers, and other pests are to be swept from the borders."

Real Estate Man

[*Thinking it over a moment.*] Oh. Then I'd better be going. [*Starts, hesitates.*] Tell me one thing. Who is this person I have to fear?

Pithetaerus

[*Beckons to him, very confidential, heads together.*] Me.

Real Estate Man

Oh, I see! You're joking! [*Laughs heartily.* PITHETAERUS *joins in the laugh, and, as though slapping him jovially, gives him a smart blow.* REAL ESTATE MAN *sobers at this.*] You *are* joking?

Pithetaerus

[*Hitting him harder and laughing.*] Yes, yes!

Real Estate Man

[*Reeling from blows, suspiciously.*] You're *not* joking!

[*In a roar of laughter,* PITHETAERUS *pummels him severely, driving him across the stage. But before he can get him off, they pass* A TAX INSPECTOR *who has just come up from earth, equipped with notebook and tax forms.* PITHETAERUS *doubles back in a non-stop movement, grabbing the* TAX INSPECTOR *by the seat of the pants.*

Pithetaerus

Here, now! This is the way out!

Inspector

[*Routine formality.*] You will please declare your personal property.

Pithetaerus

Who sent you?

Inspector

Government. Tax inspector.

Pithetaerus

Haven't got any personal property. We've just started to build.

Inspector

Very well. I'll have to leave an estimated bill, based upon what we happen to need at the moment.

[*Having scribbled on form, rips it off and hands it to* PITHETAERUS.

Pithetaerus

[*Tearing it up matter-of-factly.*] Very well. And I'm going to make an estimated payment, based upon how I happen to feel at the moment—[*Hits him with a stewpot which* EUELPIDES *has casually handed him, then trips him up.*]

Inspector

You'll go to court—you'll go to court!

[*A* LAWYER *has arrived from earth during this melee and is already tacking a list of printed regulations to a place on the rocks.* PITHETAERUS *sees him.*

Pithetaerus

Here! What are you putting up there?

Lawyer

The new laws for the community. "If a Cloud Cuckoolander should commit libel against Athens or any Athenian—"

Pithetaerus

[*Tearing down list to look at it.*] We don't need any lawyers up here!

Lawyer

Have to have lawyers. Don't want to spend all our time in jail, do we?

Pithetaerus

[*Reading.*] "The Cloud Cuckoo-landers shall adopt the same weights and measure as now prevail in—"

Lawyer

The standard weights and measures, of course.

Pithetaerus

No, we have new measures up here. Like this.

[*Pushes him backward over* EUELPIDES, *who has prepared himself. At same time* INSPECTOR *has pulled himself together and from now on both* PITHETAERUS *and* EUEL-PIDES *are very busy handling the reappearing pests, no sooner laying hands on one than another pops up, until the stage is a swirl of confused activity.*

Inspector

You are now liable to penalty of ten thousand—

[*As* PITHETAERUS *is getting hold of him,* POET *has reappeared.*

Poet

Tralalalalalalalalala! My Muses are back. They say I should also have a crown.

[EUELPIDES *claps the stewpot over his head.*

Lawyer

[*Reading from list.*] "Should anyone drive away the magistrates and not receive them, according to the decree duly posted—"

Euelpides

[*Calling off to* THE BIRDS, *desperate.*] Help! Help! We have vermin!

[PROPHET *has also reappeared.*

Prophet

I came to tell you that your doom is sealed. I have just had another chat with Apollo—

[PITHETAERUS *and* EUELPIDES *cannot keep up with all of them and are losing the battle. The combined nuisances are surrounding them, successfully bending their ears, forcing them into a tight knot down Center.*

Real Estate Man

What I forgot to mention is that there is a great profit in this for you, personally—

Inspector

Of course, if you would like to offer a small bribe—

Prophet

The signs are all very unfavorable—

[PITHETAERUS *and* EUELPIDES *have slumped exhausted down Center as* POET, PROPHET, REAL ESTATE MAN, TAX INSPECTOR, *and* LAWYER *bend over them, all talking at*

once, ad lib in a great yammering babble PITHETAERUS
and EUELPIDES *are holding their ears, rocking back and
forth.*

By this time BIRDS *have begun to appear over the rocks,
some of them carrying a great net. They steal downstage
behind the group and, at a signal, throw the net over the
yammering nuisances.* PITHETAERUS *and* EUELPIDES *immediately duck out from under and the net is drawn
tight about the others.*

Prophet

[*A continuation of his previous line, with net business
timed between.*] I was so right.

Poet

Whither has joy flown? Oh darkest day!

Inspector

[*Inside net.*] Get me a lawyer!

Lawyer

[*Right next to him, inside net.*] I'm a lawyer.

Pithetaerus

There! Now we'll put them all in a man-cage. We'll
hang them from the ceiling of Cloud Cuckoo-land, and
there they can sing to us all day! Take them away!

[PITHETAERUS *and* EUELPIDES *supervise the* BIRDS *as they
drag them out of sight beyond rocks and the* CHORUS OF
BIRDS *takes over.*

Chorus

[*A great burst.*]
Hear ye!
Henceforth—our worth,
Our right, our might,
Shall be shown,
Acknowledged, known.
Mankind shall raise
Prayers, vows, praise
To the Birds alone! [*Change of tone, lighter.*]
Oh, the happy clan of birds
Clad in feather,
Needing not a woolen vest in
Wintry weather—

[PITETAERUS *and* EUELPIDES *returning, dusting off their
hands. The* CHORUS OF BIRDS *are distributing themselves
in happy, comfortable, languorous positions, and* PITHE-
TAERUS *and* EUELPIDES *come down front, stretch out,*

entirely comfortable at last. BIRDS *bring them fruit and wine, dropping grapes into their mouths—in all, the picture of sybaritic luxury.*

Heeding not the warm far-flashing
Summer ray,
For within the leafy bosoms
Of the flowery meads we stay,
When the Chirruper in ecstasy is shrilling forth his tune,
Maddened with the sunshine and the raptures of the
    noon.
And we winter in the caverns' hollow spaces.
In spring we crop the flowers of the myrtles white and
    tender,
Dainties that are fashioned in the gardens of the graces.
[*Climax of luxurious passage.*
Oh, many a herb and many a berry
Serves to feast and make us merry! [*Pause.*]
It's a nice life. [*Real break from choral quality to conversational prose tone.*] And now, just before the intermission, one word to the critics. If the reviews are good tomorrow, we are prepared to do several nice things for you. We will build nests in your chimneys and sing for you sweetly from time to time. When we die, we will leave you our claws, for use on other occasions. As you sit down to dinner, we may even fly in with some plovers' eggs, if you happen to like them. [*Slight pause.*] On the other hand. Should the reviews be bad tomorrow—and should the critics thereafter just happen to be walking down a public street—well—let them wear hats. [*Portentous, with a slight upward glance.*]
Let them wear hats!

                                            CURTAIN

Act Two

[*The scene as before.* PITHETAERUS *discovered asleep on the stage. He wakes up, stretches, yawns, then gets up, pleasantly drowsy. He comes directly downstage and speaks in an easy conversational tone.*

Pithetaerus

[*To audience.*] Well, friends. We've got the sacrifice over
with and those pests out of the way. So far, so good.
Now we'll have to make preparations for a splendid
banquet to celebrate the building of the city. Just as
soon as it's built. That reminds me. I haven't had any
report on how it's coming. There ought to be a messenger, bringing me news. There always is a messenger in
these plays. It's not right to have no messenger. Probably produced this thing on a low budget. Still, maybe
one will be coming along. We'll have a look. [*Goes to
high point, looks off.*] Ah, yes. Swift as lightning, he
comes!

[*As* PITHETAERUS *turns to greet him, the* MESSENGER *speeds
in at a terrific rate, passing* PITHETAERUS *altogether and
exiting opposite.* PITHETAERUS *looks after him, pokes his
way down near where* MESSENGER *has gone off. At this
moment* MESSENGER *whizzes past him again from opposite direction, and off.* PITHETAERUS *has nearly had his
nose clipped off in the process. He now considers a moment, starts toward second exit, but pauses a moment to pick up a rock and weigh it in his hand, then
climbs to a point above exit prepared to drop rock on
returning* MESSENGER'S *head.* MESSENGER *whizzes in
again,* PITHETAERUS *hurls the rock down onto his own
foot. His yowl stops the* MESSENGER, *who turns, but who
continues his running motions even as he speaks.*

Messenger

Where is he? Where, where? Oh, where? Where is he?

Pithetaerus

Who, dammit?

Messenger

Our leader. Pithetaerus. Where is he?

Pithetaerus

Here, you idiot!

[*Grabs him to stop his legs from running motions.*

Messenger

[*Stepping back, military, breathing hard.*] You—are—Pithetaerus?

Pithetaerus

Yes, dammit!

Messenger

[*A military step forward, with a salute, still breathing hard.*]

I have a message for you, sir.

Pithetaerus

That's what I thought. Well, well, what is it? [MESSEN-GER *opens mouth to deliver message, then faints dead away on the floor.*] Oh, these bit players! Here! Here! Come to! [*Slapping* MESSENGER *vigorously.* MESSENGER *comes to, dazed, and* PITHETAERUS *lifts him to his feet.* MESSENGER *immediately begins running again.*] Here, stop! [*Grabs* MESSENGER.] Now. What's the message?

Messenger

The wall is finished.

Pithetaerus

[*Dismissing him, as though finished.*] Good.

Messenger

[*Holding his ground.*] And a most amazing, magnificent work it is!

Pithetaerus

[*Turning back, a gesture of dismissal.*] Fine, fine.

Messenger

[*Obviously has a set-speech of a part and is going to deliver it, no matter what.*] Big enough for two chariots to pass on it, driven by steeds as big as the Trojan horse. [*Becoming increasingly declamatory, with gestures.*]

Pithetaerus

That's wonderful. Good-bye.

Messenger

The height—I measured it myself—is exactly a hundred fathoms.

Pithetaerus

[*Being drawn into it now.*] Is that so? Who could have built such a wall?

Messenger

[*Making the most of his opportunity, taking over the stage, walking away from* PITHETAERUS *toward audience.*] The Birds! Nobody else, no foreigners, Egyptian bricklayers, workmen or mason. But they themselves—alone—by their own efforts—

Pithetaerus

[*Aware of what he is doing, mockingly helpful.*] Unaided.

Messenger

[*Striding off to another part of stage, forcing* PITHETAERUS *to follow him.*] The Birds, I say, completed everything.

I was as surprised as you are. But I was there. An eye-witness.

Pithetaerus

[*Same tone, more mocking.*] You saw it.

Messenger

[*Striding off again.*] I saw it.

There came a body of thirty thousand Cranes
With stones from Africa—
I won't be positive. There might have been more.

Pithetaerus

[*Irritated, shouting, hoping he'll get on with it and get off.*]
All right! There were more.

Messenger

With stones from Africa in their craws and gizzards,
Which the Sandpipers and Stone-chatterers
Worked into shape and finished.
The Mudlarks, too, were busy in their department
Mixing the mortar, while the Water Birds
As fast as it was wanted, brought water
To a temper and loosen it.

Pithetaerus

[*Fascinated by his spiel.*] Who were the masons? Who did
you get to carry it?

Messenger

Carry? Why, the carrion crows, of course. [*Laughs loudly
at the audience, announcing this as a joke.* PITHETAERUS
hits him a quieting slap.]

Pithetaerus

I'll tell the jokes. How did you fill the hods? How did
they manage that?

Messenger

Oh, capitally, I promise you! [*Demonstrating the follow-
ing movements ludicrously with his hands and feet.*]
There were the Geese, all barefoot,
Trampling the mortar, and when all was ready
They handed it into the hods—so cleverly—
With their flat feet!

[*He is making a production number out of this.* PITHE-
TAERUS *says nothing so he repeats the business without
the lines.*]

Pithetaerus

All right, you do that very well. Go on.

Messenger

You should have been there. It was a sight to see them.
Trains of Ducks, clambering the ladders—[*Demonstrating again.*]
With their little duck legs, like bricklayer's prentices,
All dapper and handy, with their little trowels. [*Shows how they trowel with their beaks.*]

Pithetaerus

[*Nailing him down.*] Could you finish this standing still?
What of the woodwork? Who were the carpenters?

Messenger

The woodpeckers, of course! And there they were
Laboring upon the gates, driving and banging
With their hard hatchet beaks, and such a din,
Such a clatter as they made, hammering and hacking,
In a perpetual peal, pelting away,
Like shipwrights, hard at work in the docks.

Pithetaerus

You had a lot to say once you got started, didn't you?

Messenger

[*Exuberantly, for climactic effect.*]
And now their work is finished, gates and all,
Staples and bolts, and bars and everything.
The sentries at their posts, patrols appointed,
Watchmen in the towers, the beacons
Prepared for lightning, all their signals set—
[*Immediate drop to conversational tone.*] And now if you'll
excuse me, I have to wash my hands. [*Drops off the stage and goes up the aisle of the theatre to the men's washroom. At same time* EPOPS *and the* BIRD CHORUS *begin to appear over the rocks.*]

Epops

Well! What do you say to us? Aren't you astonished at
how quick we've been? The city completed and ready?

Pithetaerus

By the gods, yes. It's simply not to be believed. [*A stir is heard offstage.*] What's that?

Leader

A messenger is coming.

Pithetaerus

Not another! Well, somebody's got to help me this time!

[SECOND MESSENGER *darts in, as first one did.* PITHETAERUS *immediately blocks off second exit, causing* MESSENGER *to turn and head for another, but the* BIRDS *leap to positions blocking him off one place and another until he is surrounded and crowded in down Center, still running in a static position, facing front. On a signal,* PITHETAERUS *and surrounding* BIRDS *grab him to stop him.*

Second Messenger

Alas, alas, alas, alas, alas!

Pithetaerus

Is that the whole message?

Second Messenger

Terrible news?

Chorus

What? What news? What's the matter?

Pithetaerus

[*To* CHORUS.] Sh-h-h! Be quiet! [*In shushing them,* PITHETAERUS *has momentarily loosed his hold on* SECOND MESSENGER, *who promptly starts running again.* PITHETAERUS *tackles him in a flying dive.* MESSENGER *goes down and out.* PITHETAERUS *is bending over him.*] What news? [*No response from* SECOND MESSENGER.] Now, *he's* out. Here! Here! Answer me!

[*Begins the slapping business. At same time a* ROPE *dangles down from the city above and, as* BIRDS *clear a space,* EUELPIDES *slides down it.*

Euelpides

Ho there! Look out below!

Pithetaerus

What are you doing?

Epops

He's come from the city.

Euelpides

I still don't trust these wings.

Pithetaerus

Get down out of there!

Euelpides

Did you get the message?

Pithetaerus

No, dammit!

[*To* EPOPS, *as he glances at knocked-out* SECOND MESSENGER.] Put it on order right away—stronger messengers!

Leader

Tell us! What is this terrible news?

Euelpides

[*Dropping to the stage floor.*] A horrible outrage. Horrible!

Pithetaerus

Well, get on with it!

Euelpides

Here's what happened—

[*The* SECOND MESSENGER *has been coming to, unnoticed.*] The gods have heard about our intention, and Zeus has already—

Second Messenger

[*Quickly jumping in, attempting to give the message himself, overlapping* EUELPIDES.] The thing is that Zeus has already heard what we plan to do—

[*Both* EUELPIDES *and* SECOND MESSENGER *continue explaining but since they are both talking at once, we cannot understand a word they are saying.*

Pithetaerus

Silence! Shut up! One at a time!

Euelpides

[*To* SECOND MESSENGER, *quarrelsome.*] You lie down.

Second Messenger

But I was sent here to—

Euelpides

I started to tell this story.

Second Messenger

I got here first!

Euelpides

[*Shouting.*] You had your chance! You didn't—

Second Messenger

But they're *my* lines!

Euelpides

I slid all the way down here, getting several rope burns—

[*By now they are shouting at each other at the same time and they begin to rough it up.* PITHETAERUS *pulls them apart.*

Pithetaerus

Here! Here!

Second Messenger

I was sent here to relay this information—

Pithetaerus

Look. You've run a long way. Don't you want to wash your hands?

Second Messenger

[*Reflective pause.*] As a matter of fact, I do.

Pithetaerus

[*Pointing down aisle to men's room.*] Right there.

Second Messenger

Oh. Thank you.

[*Leaps off stage as original* MESSENGER *has done; at same time* FIRST MESSENGER *reappears from men's room and they pass each other midway down the aisle, shake hands, and go their ways,* SECOND MESSENGER *to the men's room,* FIRST MESSENGER *up onto the stage.*

Pithetaerus

[*Seeing original* MESSENGER *coming.*] Now before *he* gets up here with *his* big mouth, will you tell us the news?

Euelpides

A god has penetrated the city.

Chorus

What? A sacrilege, on the day our city was built! Oh, horrible! Let terror strike.

Euelpides

[*Shrugging his shoulders.*] Got through somehow.

Leader

Who was on guard?

Euelpides

The jays.

Leader

Death to the jays!

Euelpides

But it's one of those minor gods with little wings. That made it tougher.

Epops

Where is this god now?

Euelpides

We don't know. Flying around somewhere. Liable to turn up any minute.

Pithetaerus

[*To* LEADER.] Despatch thirty thousand hawks of the legion of Mounted Archers!

Leader

[*Hustling some* BIRDS *off and calling offstage to others, bawling orders. A few birds remain, gathered about* EPOPS.] All hook-clawed birds into the air! Kestrels, buzzards, vultures, great-horned owls! Cleave the air till it resounds with the flapping of wings. Look everywhere!

Chorus

To arms, all, with beak and talon!

War, a terrible war, is breaking out between us and the gods!

Leader

Look everywhere!

[*A conventional puff of smoke at opposite side of stage.*

Euelpides

Look right there.

[*All huddle at opposite side, staring toward the rock from which the smoke puff has come.* IRIS *appears through the cloud, an unlikely looking goddess with small wings. She stands looking at them, then speaks in a flat, nasal voice.*

Iris

Hello.

Pithetaerus

Halt! Don't stir. Not a beat of your wing. Who are you? Where do you come from?

Iris

Me? I come from Olympus, my abode.

Pithetaerus

Who are you?

Iris

I yam swift Iris.

Pithetaerus

Call the buzzards and let them seize her!

Iris

Say, I handled plenty a buzzards who tried to do that.

Pithetaerus

Woe to you!

Iris

Woe to you, too. What's up?

Leader

By which gate did you pass through the wall, wretched goddess?

Iris

I didn't see no gate. I was just out for a short flap.

Pithetaerus

Fine, innocent airs she gives herself! [*Mockingly.*] You applied to the Pelicans, I suppose? The captain of the Cormorants let you in?

Iris

Well, I seen a nice Captain, but I let it pass.

Pithetaerus

So, you confess! You came without permission! You didn't get a passport. Nobody put a label on you!

Iris

[*Instinctively starts to reach with her hand, stops.*] Is that what that was?

Pithetaerus

Without permission from anybody, you ramble and fly through the air—the air that belongs to us!

Iris

To you?

Chorus

To us!

Iris

Where do you think us gods are gonna take our exercise?

Pithetaerus

I don't know and I don't care. But I'll tell you this—let us catch you once more flying through this territory and you're done for. You'll be put to death!

Chorus

To death!

Iris

Listen. I'm immortal.

Pithetaerus

Don't try to wriggle out of it, now. Mortal or immortal, you'll be put to death. We can't have the whole universe obeying us and you lackadaisical gods floating around where you please.

Iris

[*Snaps her fingers.*] Almost forgot. Had an errand to do.
[*Starts to promenade across the stage, heading for earth.*

Pithetaerus

Wait a minute, here! What errand?

Iris

Zeus sent me. I'm supposed to go down to earth and tell mankind to sacrifice an ox. Zeus wants a little heady smoke coming up. Helps his sinus.

Pithetaerus

Sacrifice to him?

Iris

Who else? Zeus, he's my father. He's a deity.

Pithetaerus

Zeus a deity?

[*Laughs mockingly.* BIRDS *join him in a great hollow cackling.*

Iris

Best deity going.

Pithetaerus

[*Roaring.*] Silence! Remember—once for all—that We, the Birds, are the only Deities, from this time forth!

Iris

Huh?

Pithetaerus

Man henceforth will sacrifice to us and not to Zeus, by Zeus!

Iris

[*Suddenly going into grand tragic style, beating her breast, clinging dramatically to rocks, writhing on the floor, etc.*]
Oh, fool, fool, fool! Stir not the mighty wrath
Of angry gods, lest Justice, with the spade
Of vengeful Jove, demolish all thy race,
And fiery vapor, with lightning strokes,
Incinerate thy city and thyself!

Pithetaerus

[*Matter-of-fact tones.*] Now, listen, girl. Never mind the oratory. You can save that speech for some tragedy or other. And if Zeus keeps troubling me, I'll be doing some incinerating myself. [*Slowing down his rate, half-abstracted as he looks at her.*] I'll send eagles carrying fire up into his halls of state, and he'll find out. [*Slower still.*] And as for you, unless you learn to mind your manners— [*Suddenly.*] Say, are you doing anything tonight?

Iris

What are you suggesting?

Pithetaerus

Well, I'm building a little nest up here—

Iris

[*Backing away from him.*] I'll tell my father, I'll tell my father—

Pithetaerus

[*Giving it up.*] Oh, bother. Scuttle away. Convey your person elsewhere. Be brisk. Leave a vacancy. Brush off. [*She has backed away but not gone. He shouts.*] Well?

Iris

[*Terrified, as she runs off.*] Daddy! Zeus! Daddy!

Chorus

Never again shall the Zeus-born gods
Never again shall they pass this way!
Never again through this realm of ours
Shall men send up to the heavenly powers
The smoke of beasts which on earth they slay!
We, too, shall slay! Slay!

Pithetaerus

Now whatever's happened to that Herald we sent down
to earth, to tell the people? [*To* EUELPIDES.] You sent
him, didn't you?

Euelpides

I did.

Pithetaerus

Why can't we keep these actors around here?

[HERALD *enters on the double, late, obviously having missed
his cue, and still fixing his costume.*

Euelpides

He's in.

Herald

[*Stentorian tones.*] Oh, Pithetaerus—!

Pithetaerus

High time.

Herald

Oh, thou wisest, thou best—oh, thou wisest *and* best—
thou wisest, deepest, happiest of mankind—happiest,
deepest, wisest—

Pithetaerus

Did he play the priest in the first act?

Herald

Most glorious Pithetaerus, most—

[*Snapping his fingers, looking off.*] Prompter! Prompter!

Prompter's Voice

[*Off.*] Revered of men—

Herald

Revered of men, most—[*Thinks a moment, then speaks
confidentially to* PITHETAERUS.] Let me try it again.
[*Takes a step back as though entering anew, begins from
the beginning.*] Oh Pithetaerus—!

Pithetaerus

No, you don't! Suppose we get on with the message?

Herald

[*Hurt.*] All right. But I knew it. [*Stentorian again.*] All men on earth have been notified, and all are filled with admiration for your wisdom. They acknowledge your leadership, and that of the Birds, and have sent you this golden crown. [*Holds out his hands in motion of giving crown, but they are empty.*]

Pithetaerus

Yes?

Herald

[*Noticing he has no crown.*] Oh, dammit! [*Goes to the wings.*] Where's that crown? Somebody was supposed to hand it to me!

Prompter's Voice

[*Off.*] You were supposed to pick it up!

Herald

[*Shouting off, beginning an ad-lib quarrel, both talking at once.*] When an actor has to make an entrance, he can't be worrying about props!

[*There is an almost out-of-sight scuffle between the* HER-ALD *and some member of the stage crew, whose hands only are seen, over the crown.* PITHETAERUS *wearily breaks it, brings* HERALD *back to position, plants him there, thrusts the crown into his hands, deliberately takes it out again, doing the whole business himself to make sure it gets done, and crams it on his own head in disgust.*]

Pithetaerus

Now will you get on with the message?

Herald

[*Pulling himself together.*] All right. [*In a sudden confidence to* PITHETAERUS.] Do you get stage fright? I do.

Pithetaerus

[*Roaring.*] Get on with it!

Herald

[*Opens his mouth to speak, then breaks down completely, a nervous shambles.*] I'm sorry. I'll have to turn in my part. I'm a wreck.

[*He leaves.*]

Pithetaerus

Does anybody know his lines?

Messenger

[*Hopping to his feet.*] Yes, sir. I do!

Pithetaerus

I'd hoped it would be anybody but you. All right.

Messenger

[*Quickly taking* HERALD's *place.*] I, who have just returned from earth—[*Aside to* PITHETAERUS.] I haven't, of course. I'm saying *his* lines. [*Back into speech.*]—bring you this message. All men accept your reign and themselves wish to become birds. More than ten thousand have followed me here and now await your pleasure. They have gone bird-mad. [HERALD *sticks his head in from the wings.*]

Herald

[*To* MESSENGER.] I hate you.

[PITHETAERUS *makes a threatening gesture and* HERALD *disappears again. We begin to see the hands and heads of people climbing up from earth.* PITHETAERUS *is immediately aware of them and he goes to the earth-entrance and is busy counting heads as the* MESSENGER *completes his speech.*

Messenger

They wish to be supplied with feathers and hooked claws, in honor of their masters. Will you oblige them?

Pithetaerus

Ah, yes. Yes, indeed. Quick! There's no time for idling.

[*Men are arriving from earth:* PITHETAERUS *gives directions to* EUELPIDES *and various* BIRDS.] Go and fill every hamper, every basket you can find with wings. Bring them to me, and I will welcome our new subjects!

Chorus

[*As a bustle ensues.*]

Shortly shall our noble town
Be populous and gay,
High in honor and renown.

Pithetaerus

[*Impatiently.*] If I get those wings, it may.

[EUELPIDES *rushes in with a basketful, which* PITHETAERUS *snatches and, as* MEN *pass by him single file, he doles out wings to each of them. They are affixing their new wings as they file across stage to a promontory and leap off, one by one, rapidly.* EUELPIDES *helps* PITHETAERUS *as* BIRDS *bring several more baskets.*

Chorus

[*During this business.*]

Now rush them forth, in yellow, red, and blue
Feathers of every form and size and hue.

Pithetaerus

Give me a hand, can't you?

[EUELPIDES *offers his hand matter-of-factly and gets slapped for it.*

Chorus

Where in all this earthly range
He that wishes for a change
   Can he find a seat,
Joyous and secure as this,
Filled with happiness and bliss,
   Such a fair retreat?

Pithetaerus

[*Busy distributing wings, to* EUELPIDES.] Ask that chorus if it has to be so loud, will you?

[EUELPIDES *goes to chorus to shush them but before he can say anything they double their volume in à great blast which shakes* PITHETAERUS *and nearly blows* EUELPIDES *down.*

Chorus

Here is Wisdom and Wit and each exquisite Grace
And here the unruffled, benevolent face
Of Quiet, and loving desire.

Pithetaerus

[*Shouting.*] It is my desire that you *keep* quiet so I won't be so ruffled!

Chorus

[*Wounded.*] Don't you *like* choruses?

Pithetaerus

[*To* EUELPIDES, *at the baskets.*] Back to business here.

[*As thy turn back to the oncoming line of men, the* POET *of Act One bursts from the line.*

Poet

Wings! Give me wings!

Pithetaerus

Ye gods, you're back.

Poet

On the lightest of wings I shall soar up on high
And lightly from measure to measure I'll fly.

Pithetaerus

You want wings, do you?

Poet

Let me live and let me sing
Like a bird upon the wing.

Pithetaerus

Oh, stop that! Talk prose! What do you want wings for?

Poet

I wish to make a tour among the clouds, collecting images
and metaphors and things of that description.

Pithetaerus

Oh, you pick all your poems out of the clouds, eh?

Poet

Oh, yes. All modern poetry is very cloudy. Our most
brilliant poems now are those that flap their wings in
empty space and are clothed in mist. What we want is a
dense obscurity. Listen. I'll give you a sample.

Pithetaerus

[*Picking up a pair of wings to hit him with.*] No, you won't.

Poet

Now this one is *all* air. Listen

"Shadowy visions of
Wing-spreading, air-treading
Taper-necked birds . . ."

[*Changing his tactic,* PITHETAERUS *begins to tickle poet
with wings.* POET *giggles wildly then turns on* PITHE-
TAERUS *reprovingly.*]

You're not listening. [*Dancing now.*]

"Bounding along on the path to the seas,
Fain I would float on the streams and the breeze—

[*Behind* POET'S *back,* PITHETAERUS *signals to several* BIRDS,
who get a blanket and begin to steal up behind POET.]

First do I stray on a southerly way,
Then to the northward my body I bear,
Cutting a harborless furrow of air,
The air I'll cleave, I'll cleave the sky—

[PITHETAERUS *pushes him over into blanket and they toss
him in the air several times.*

Pithetaerus

[*As they let him down.*] How do you like cleaving the air?

Poet

If this is how you treat people—

Pithetaerus

Off with him! Out!

[BIRDS *start dragging him out.*

Poet

But where are my wings? Wings! I want wings!

[BIRDS *get* POET *off, and the remaining* MEN *have now jumped off.*

Pithetaerus

Now! Prepare for the feast! Bring me food to roast, and a spit, and the makings of a fire. Oh, dear, I have to do everything.

[*As* EUELPIDES *and* BIRDS *have scattered in all directions to get supplies, leaving the stage clear, a sneaky, shadowy figure, his cloak about his face and carrying an umbrella, has darted on, looked about the stage suspiciously, checking every nook and corner for someone who may be following him. This is* PROMETHEUS. PITHETAERUS *has spotted him, watched him with open-mouthed curiosity, but said nothing. Finally* PROMETHEUS *comes directly down to* PITHETAERUS.

Prometheus

Is there a god following me?

Pithetaerus

Not that I know of. What are you all muffled up about?

Prometheus

If only Zeus doesn't see me. That Zeus, always looking. Where is Pithetaerus?

Pithetaerus

I am Pithetaerus.

Prometheus

Oh, are you? Good boy.

[*Taps him approvingly, darts upstage to look around again.*

Pithetaerus

Who are you?

Prometheus

[*Coming back to him.*] What time is it?

Pithetaerus

Time? Oh, about noon. Who are you?

Prometheus

Only noon? Is that all it is?

Pithetaerus

How should I know? Who are you?

Prometheus

[*After more darting away.*] What's Zeus doing? Is he behind the clouds or is he peeping?

Pithetaerus

[*To audience.*] I don't know about you, but I'm getting
bored. [*Shouting at* PROMETHEUS.] WHO ARE YOU?

Prometheus

[*Coming back to him, mysteriously.*] I shall reveal myself.

Pithetaerus

Well, take your time. Don't rush. [PROMETHEUS *throws
the cloak back from his face.* PITHETAERUS *throws open
his arms and greets him loudly and delightedly.*] Prometheus! My old friend Prometheus!

Prometheus

[*In a panic.*] Shh! Not so loud.

Pithetaerus

Why, what's the matter, Prometheus?

Prometheus

Shh! Don't mention my name. If Zeus hears you, I'm
in for it. He mustn't know I'm here.

Pithetaerus

Very well.

Prometheus

Here. If you don't mind. Hold the umbrella over me.
Then he can't see us.

Pithetaerus

Right. Right.

[*They sit down on edge of stage, umbrella over them, speak
quietly.*

Prometheus

Zeus never liked me, you know.

Pithetaerus

No.

Prometheus

Ever since I stole that fire from him. Gave it to men.
My name has been mud. I still get in up there, but he
doesn't trust me.

Pithetaerus

Of course.

Prometheus

Well. Let me tell you. I've got all the news from Olympus.

Pithetaerus

Ah?

Prometheus

Just listen.

Pithetaerus
I'm listening.

Prometheus
Zeus is ruined.

Pithetaerus
[*Delighted.*] Ah! Since when?

Prometheus
Since you went to work down here. Built your city.
They can't get a message through! Not a thing comes
up. No smoke. No incense. Absolutely nothing. They're
all on a strict diet up there. The whole bunch. You've
done it. [*Shakes* PITHETAERUS' *hand.*]

Pithetaerus
Good!

Prometheus
More than that. Mutiny.

Pithetaerus
Mutiny up there? [PROMETHEUS *nods knowingly.*] Who?

Prometheus
The new gods. Especially those barbarian gods they took
in recently. Hell to pay. Zeus can't meet his commit-
ments. They're furious. Open rebellion. All starving to
death. Unless Zeus can get the air lanes open—get traffic
started again—he'll be out on his ear. Don't say I told you.

Pithetaerus
Not a word. But what's Zeus going to do?

Prometheus
That's it. That's what I came for. Zeus is sending a committee. Committee of gods. Ought to be here any minute. I ought to get out of here before they come. One of
the barbarian gods is with 'em. Checking up. Anyway.
They're going to come to you and sue for peace. Here's
the thing. Don't you do it. Don't you agree to a thing
unless Zeus acknowledges the rule of the birds. *And*—
are you listening? [PITHETAERUS *nods eagerly.*] Don't
stop there. To protect yourself—ask for one of the goddesses in marriage. That'll make it stick. Protect your
line.

Pithetaerus
Oh.

Prometheus
Any particular goddess you like?

Pithetaerus

Why, yes. Yes! There was a little thing in here today. Iris, her name was.

Prometheus

Fine. Ask for Iris. [*Getting up.*] Well, I've got to get out of here. Hell to pay. I only came for a minute. Let you know. But you can count on me. I'm a friend. Steady to the human interest. Always was.

Pithetaerus

I never eat a roast without thinking of you.

Prometheus

I hate these gods, you know.

Pithetaerus

Yes, I know.

Prometheus

I'm a regular scourge to them, a regular scourge. Well, bye-bye. Give me the umbrella. If anyone asks, you haven't seen me.

Pithetaerus

Right.

Prometheus

[*At the exit.*] Courage.

[*As* PROMETHEUS *goes,* PITHETAERUS *begins hopping around excitedly.*

Pithetaerus

Oh, my goodness, I've got to hurry! [*As* EPOPS *and other* BIRDS *scurry in, carrying an open-fire spit with a pig already on it, together with all the necessary utensils— oversize forks, spoons, salt-cellars, etc.*] Here! Good!

[*The spit is mounted downstage, a fire is built under it, and several* BIRDS *remain nearby to help* PITHETAERUS *as he needs things for the cooking.*

Epops

We have done your bidding, brave leader. Here is food and a fire and everything you need for a banquet.

Pithetaerus

Fine, fine. Now you must all disappear. I have very important visitors coming. The moment is at hand when our fate will be decided.

Epops

I can bring you armies of birds for support.

Pithetaerus

No, no, no. I must handle this alone. They mustn't think

we expect them. Give everything away. I won't even
pretend to notice them. [*As* EUELPIDES *runs on.*] Here.
Help me here. [*Showing him how to turn spit.*] Epops,
you stand by in the rocks and when the meeting is over
you can spread the word.

Epops

As you say, oh leader!

[EPOPS *disappears.* EUELPIDES *is savoring the roasting pig
with a loud "Mmmm!" but* PITHETAERUS *slaps him away.*

Pithetaerus

Keep your nose out of that. You'll sniff up all the smell.
I'm going to win a war with that smell.

Euelpides

We got another war? Where's that fork?

[*Snatches up a fork to defend himself with, when there is
a sudden smoke puff high up on the rocks.* PITHETAERUS
*glances at it, then, with a great show of indifference,
resumes his work with the roast.* NEPTUNE, HERCULES,
and A BARBARIAN GOD *come through the smoke, cough-
ing, sneezing, and flailing with their cloaks to drive the
smoke away.*

Neptune

[*Who carries his tined fork and is a pompous, exceedingly
dignified god.*] This damn smoke. I wish they'd cut that
stuff out. [*Pulling himself together.*] On your dignity,
gods. This is Cloud Cuckoo-land, whither we come as
ambassadors. [*Noticing* BARBARIAN GOD, *whose cloak is
dragging sadly and whose general appearance is sloppy
indeed.*] You! Barbarian God! Look at your cloak. What
a mess. Throw it over your shoulder. [BARBARIAN GOD
does, striking NEPTUNE *full in the face with it.* NEPTUNE
seizes him, forcibly straightens his costume. BARBARIAN
GOD *maintains an unrelievedly stupid, open-mouthed,
deadpan expression.*] What's the matter with you? You
are the most uncouth god I ever saw.

Barbarian God

[*Low, moronic speaking voice.*] Leave me alone. Leave me
alone.

Neptune

[*Looking at him.*] Oh, democracy! Whither are you leading us?

Hercules

[*Bright-faced, simpleminded type.*] Come on. Let's be ambassadors.

Neptune

You will please wait, my dear nephew Hercules, until you have been instructed. Or did you have some plan of your own?

Hercules

[*Pointing to* PITHETAERUS, *below.*] Certainly. There's the fellow. Let me go strangle him to death.

Neptune

My dear nephew, may I remind you that we are ambassadors of peace.

Hercules

Sure. When I strangle him, we got peace. What do you want?

Barbarian God

I wanna go back where I came from.

Neptune

[*Curious.*] How is it he hasn't noticed our smoke? I hate to put up with that for nothing. [*Clears his throat loudly.*]

Pithetaerus

[*Feigning not to notice gods above, now giving directions to* EUELPIDES *and* BIRD *servants who assist him, running for equipment, etc.*] Hand me the grater! Get some spice for the sauce. Where's the cheese? [NEPTUNE *clears his throat again.*] And blow up the fire a little bit. More charcoal.

[NEPTUNE *now strides downstage, without going too close to* PITHETAERUS. EUELPIDES *is backing in his direction at the moment and turns toward him just as* NEPTUNE *happens to lower his tined fork.* EUELPIDES *whips out his own fork and takes a dueling stance.* HERCULES *lifts* EUELPIDES *bodily out of the way, throws him to one side.*]

Neptune

Mortal! We three who greet you are gods.

Pithetaerus

[*Not looking up from his work, waving them away.*] Busy just now. Busy just now. Mixing my sauce. [*To servant bird.*] Where are the pickles? Bring me some pickles.

Hercules

[*Sniffing and moving closer.*] That sauce smells nice.

Pithetaerus

[*Offhand, still not looking up.*] Yes. It's my own recipe.

Hercules

Uh—what you roasting there?

Pithetaerus

Pig.

Euelpides

[*Passing, thinking he means him, startled.*] Who?

Pithetaerus

Later we'll have some nice plump fowl. [*To those around him.*] Salt, please! Get me salt!

Hercules

I thought you liked birds. Didn't think you'd roast 'em.

Pithetaerus

[*Salting the roast.*] Oh, there were some birds who wouldn't join the party. Politically unreliable. [*A servant bird is passing and* PITHETAERUS *salts its tail, too, just for the hell of it.*] Thyme, please. Wild thyme!

Neptune

[*Impatient and offended.*] Are you going to cook the whole meal before you acknowledge us?

Pithetaerus

What? [*Looking up now, feigning recognition.*] What's that? Neptune! Well, for heaven's sake! Welcome! Didn't see you.

Neptune

Well. Now that I have your ear—we have been sent by the gods to sue for peace.

Pithetaerus

[*Wandering back to his roast, absorbed.*] Yes, yes. Mustn't let this get too done. There's no more olive oil. More olive oil, please.

Hercules

Oh, you gotta have olive oil. Plenty of olive oil.

Neptune

[*Turning on his heel and stalking away.*] I told Zeus I didn't want this job. [*Turing back and rapping the floor with his staff.*] Sir! Sir!

Pithetaerus

What? Oh, yes. Excuse me. [*Wiping his hands on his apron, he casually shifts places with* HERCULES *in such a way that* HERCULES *will be placed directly over the roasting pig, inhaling the aroma.* PITHETAERUS *then crosses to* NEPTUNE.] Wouldn't want to spoil a tasty snack like that. Personally, I'm hungry.

[*Watches for effect of this on* NEPTUNE, *who swallows hard, then continues.*

Neptune

What we have come to say is this. We do not wish to fight you. We are eager to be your friends, to be of service. I am sure we can negotiate. Now on our part we are willing to supply you constantly with warm weather. Further, to see that you always have rainwater in your pools. On these points I am prepared to bargain.

Pithetaerus

Well, now, we're just as interested in peace as you are. We have no plans for aggression, and are also ready to bargain. We have just one condition. Zeus must give up. We take the sceptre. Now if you three will simply agree to this, I shall invite you all to dinner.

Hercules

[*Who is nearly fainting with rapture over the aroma from the roast, speaks quickly.*] I agree.

Neptune

You jackass! [*Strides to him quickly and pulls him away from the roast.*] When are you going to stop being a fathead? Just because you're a fool and a glutton, do you want to dethrone your own father?

Hercules

[*Wistfully.*] He'd be mad, wouldn't he?

Pithetaerus

Now, that's not true at all. You're not facing the facts. The gods would be even *more* powerful if they turned things over to the birds.

Euelpides

[*Quietly to* PITHETAERUS, *in passing.*] I hope you can sell this one.

Pithetaerus

How are things now? You gods are stuck up there, behind all those clouds. You don't see *half* of what's going on down below. Men are doing all kinds of things when your back is turned, especially on cloudy days. But if you put us in charge, we'll watch out for you. Birds get around. Let's say some man down on earth has promised

to offer a sacrifice if he gets a certain favor. Well, he gets
the favor and then he forgets all about the sacrifice.
We'll keep track of him and, if he doesn't pay up, peck
his eyes out. Or at least we'll pick up double the amount
of the sacrifice out of his farmyard for you!

[*During this speech he has maneuvered* NEPTUNE *directly
over the roast, and* NEPTUNE *is reacting, too.*

Neptune

[*Considering.*] Of course, there's something in what you
    say—

Hercules

See? I ain't such a fathead.

Pithetaerus

[*Going to* BARBARIAN GOD, *who has been standing just
where he entered, looking stupidly into space, doing
nothing.*] How do *you* feel about that?

Barbarian God

Oh, if it ain't one damn thing it's another.

Pithetaerus

[*To* NEPTUNE.] See? He agrees, too!

Neptune

[*Looking at* BARBARIAN GOD *dubiously.*] I'm not sure I can
    accept that as an official vote. [*Anxious to settle now
    himself, but worried.*] Oh, Barbarian God, what is your
    considered opinion?

Barbarian God

When do we eat?

Pithetaerus

There you are! Now what do you say?

Neptune

Since I am outvoted, two to one—

Euelpides

[*Looking at* BARBARIAN GOD.] Does he get a whole vote?

Pithetaerus

Shh! Shh!

Neptune

I consent as well. You shall receive the sceptre.

[*With a loud "AHHHH!" from* HERCULES, *all three* GODS
*start immediately for the spit, drooling. Just as they get
there,* PITHETAERUS *speaks.*

Pithetaerus

Oh, I almost forgot. [*They turn to him warily.*] There is
one other condition.

[GODS *exchange glances.*

Neptune

And that is?

Pithetaerus

I must have Iris in marriage. Zeus can have all the others. I only want Iris. [*Pause.*]

Neptune

[*Pointedly.*] Then you *don't* want peace.

Pithetaerus

Just little Iris.

Neptune

[*Imposingly.*] The gods do not marry beneath them! Come, we must go!

[*Signals other two* GODS *and they start away.*

Pithetaerus

All right, all right. Doesn't matter to me. [*He goes back to the spit, indifferently.*] How's that gravy coming? That's fine, stir it good. [GODS *are slowing down in their exit, looking back yearningly over their shoulders.*] My, it seems to be turning out just right. Did you ever smell anything like that? [*To* EUELPIDES *and bird servants.*] Mmmm, mmm, here, taste.

[*The* GODS *have tried to force themselves to go, but cannot; they look back to the others relishing a sip of the gravy.*

Hercules

[*Throwing down his club.*] I don't want to go to no war about no woman!

Neptune

It *is* annoying. I never cared much for Iris, anyway. But what can we do?

Hercules

We can give in.

Neptune

I'm sorry. It's impossible.

Hercules

You go back. I'm giving in. [*Starting back toward spit.*]

Neptune

[*Grabbing him.*] Listen, you blockhead. Don't you see? It's not simply a matter of Zeus losing everything. You'd lose everything, too. You're his son and heir.

Hercules

Oh.

Pithetaerus

[*Has been listening and intervenes between* NEPTUNE *and* HERCULES.] No, you don't. No, you don't. Don't let him take you in with *that* story, friend. Come here. I want a word with you. [*Draws him aside.*] As far as Zeus goes, you may be his son, but you're not his heir.

Hercules

What do you mean?

Pithetaerus

I hate to be the one to break it to you. You should have been told. It's been all over Olympus for years.

Hercules

What has?

Pithetaerus

I'm sorry, but you're illegitimate.

Hercules

What!

Pithetaerus

That's the way it is. You won't get a thing.

Neptune

Here, what are you telling my feebleminded nephew?

Hercules

He says I'm a—[*Bursts into tears.*]

Pithetaerus

I was simply mentioning his origins.

Hercules

[*Weeping.*] Uncle Neptune, is it true?

Neptune

[*Turns away, bites his lip, braces himself.*] Well, Hercules. You're a big boy now. It's time you knew.

[HERCULES *bawls louder.*

Euelpides

[*To* BARBARIAN GOD.] Poor fellow. He didn't know.

Barbarian God

What's it to him?

Neptune

Now, now, nephew. Zeus will leave you something in his will.

Pithetaerus

I'll give you something right now. Roast pig!

Hercules

[*Through tears.*] I always knew there was something about me.

Pithetaerus

Be on my side. I will make you a king and will feed you on bird's milk and honey.

Hercules

Take me! I wasn't wanted!

[EUELPIDES *comforts* HERCULES.

Pithetaerus

Neptune! I've got his vote!

Neptune

You haven't got mine.

Pithetaerus

Then it still depends on old stupid here. [*Turns to* BARBARIAN GOD.] What do you say?

Barbarian God

Old Stupid votes yes.

Pithetaerus

We've done it!

Hercules

[*To his uncle.*] And you never told me.

Neptune

All right, all right. I give in. Peace is made.

Pithetaerus

And just to think—we have the wedding feast all ready!

Hercules

[*To* NEPTUNE.] You go get Iris. I'll keep an eye on the roast.

Neptune

No, you're too fat now.

Pithetaerus

I have it. [*Getting* HERCULES' *arm.*] You hurry up to Olympus and bring them the news. *That'll* make them respect you! [HERCULES *brightens up.*] Bring me the sceptre—and bring me Iris. [*To* EUELPIDES, *as* HERCULES *nods and goes.*] Go get the Birds. Spread the glad tidings. [*To* NEPTUNE.] You. You turn the roast. And don't burn it!

Neptune

[*Offended.*] I am not the god of the kitchen.

Pithetaerus

You're taking orders from me now. Remember that! [*Resignedly* NEPTUNE *goes to the spit and tries to turn the roast with his tines, aloofly.* EUELPIDES *has rushed in again with* EPOPS.] Oh, Bird-King! The treaty's concluded! The universe is ours!

[*The full* CHORUS OF BIRDS *is in by now.*

Chorus

> Oh, all-successful, more than tongue can tell!
> Oh, this thrice-blessed, winged race of birds
> To have a leader who does so excel
> In wisdom and in courage and in power
> No man has ever matched him!

[PITHETAERUS *has been benevolently patting various of the kneeling birds, who bow low before him. He goes off. The* CHORUS *changes to a rapid, suspenseful rhythm, as the lights change to a mood of revelry.*]

> There lies a region out of sight
> Far within the realm of night
> Far from torch and candlelight—
> There in feasts of meal and wine,
> Men and demigods may join,
> There they banquet, there they dine—

[*The dancing and reveling among the birds has begun.* PROCNE *appears and she and* EPOPS *dance.* EUELPIDES *from time to time pursues* PROCNE, *but is always intertercepted by* EPOPS.]

> Whilst the light of day prevails
> Honoring the man—the only man—who never fails!

[*The revelry reaches a climax, the music stops at a high point, and the* BIRDS *make a royal path.*]

> Stand aside and clear the ground,
> Spreading in a circle round
> With a worthy welcoming
> To salute our noble King!

[HERALD *enters above.*

Herald

> Pithetaerus—the King! [*Coming off his perch, to the others.*]
> And I remembered every word of it.

Chorus

[*As* PITHETAERUS *enters, now clad in dazzling robes, which look quite pretentious on him.*]

> Mark his entrance,
> Dazzling all eyes, resplendent as a Star.
> Outshining all the golden lights, that beam
> From heaven, even as a summer Sun
> Blazing at noon!

[IRIS *enters, dressed to kill.*]

> Now to join him by his side

Comes his happy, lovely bride.
Oh, the fair delightful face!
What a figure! What a grace!
What a presence! What a carriage!

[IRIS *trips over her own train.*]

What a noble worthy marriage.

[BIRDS *have formed a crossed-sword effect as of a military marriage and* PITHETAERUS *assists* IRIS *down the path. Leaving it, they go into a little dance of their own.*]

Let the Birds rejoice and sing
At the wedding of their King,
Happy to congratulate
Such a blessing to the State.

[THUNDER AND LIGHTNING. *Above,* HERCULES *enters to present* PITHETAERUS *with the thunderbolt of Zeus.* NEPTUNE *and the* BARBARIAN GOD *join him for the ceremony. The thunderbolt is presented to* PITHETAERUS.]

Pithetaerus

I accept this token of heavenly love. [*To the* BIRDS.]
Your music and verse I applaud and admire
But rouse your invention and, raising it higher,
Describe me this terrible engine of Zeus—
—Now mine—
The thunder of earth and the thunder above.

Chorus

Let us sing of the trophies he brings us from heaven,
The earth-crashing thunders, deadly and dire,
And the lightning's angry flashes of fire—

[PITHETAERUS *is wielding the thunderbolt majestically and lightning and thunder ensues, frightening him.*]

Blaze of the lightning, so terribly beautiful,
Golden and grand!
Fire-flashing javelin, glittering now in
Our leader's right hand!

[PITHETAERUS *quickly gets it into his right hand, a little late.*]

Earth-crashing thunder, the hoarsely resounding,
The bringer of showers!

[PITHETAERUS *gives the thunderbolt another good shake, just to reassert himself; it brings on such a blast that he quickly and gingerly tosses the thunderbolt away; it is caught accidentally by* EUELPIDES, *who dances uncomfortably about with it and tosses it away himself;*]

it is now caught by the HERALD, *who matter-of-factly
takes it, as though it were nothing but a prop, and
drags it off after him.*]

He is our Master, he that is shaking the
Earth with his almighty powers!

Pithetaerus

Now follow on, dear feathered tribes,
To see us wed, to see us wed
Mount up to Zeus' golden floor
But watch your head, yes, watch your head!

[BIRDS *are forming an exit processional as* PITHETAERUS
turns to IRIS.]

And oh, my darling, reach thine hand
And take my wing and dance with me,
And I will lightly bear thee up
And carry thee, and carry thee.

[*He picks her up—it requires a mighty effort—and begins
to ascend the rocks with her. In the original production,
these two were blocked out for a moment during the
processional and a dummy, identically dressed, was
substituted for* IRIS, *so that on the last line below* PITHE-
TAERUS *could mightily seem to hoist* IRIS *by one hand
over his head and carry her off. Where this business is
impractical, it is possible to extend the earlier business
of his trying to pick her up, whereupon an escort of*
BIRDS *takes over for him, raising her up and bearing her
off as though on a litter, with* PITHETAERUS *following
in state.*

Chorus

Raise the joyous paean-cry,
Raise the song of Victory.
Iô Paean, alalalai,
Mightiest of powers, to thee!

[*The* BIRDS *dance off, higher and higher, on the rocks as
the lights fade, until only* PROCNE'S *silhouette is visible,
and she, too, disappears.*

III

Introduction
by Sheila D'Atri

The Grouch or the *Dyskolos* was produced in the winter of 316 B.C. when it won first prize at the Athenian festival of the Lenaea. At the time, Menander was in his mid-twenties and five years earlier had won his first victory with the *Orge* (*Anger*). Although he was later admired as the greatest and most popular writer of New Comedy, only a few other plays among over one hundred ascribed to him captured the first prize. He was born in the year 342/1 and grew up at a time when Athens was dominated by Macedon. The year that the *Orge* was produced, a revolt inspired by Athens was crushed in both land and sea battles. In the New Comedy of Menander and his contemporaries, freedom of expression was limited in comparison to the outspoken political and personal attacks with which we are familiar from the comedies of Aristophanes at the end of the fifth century.

In a form of drama which has been called a comedy of manners, Menander was particularly adept at revealing character through dialogue and at coining memorable aphorisms within the dramatic context, much as Shakespeare did with Polonius and Claudius. When contemporary political or philosophical questions arise within the context of the plays, they are of general topical interest, but they are not presented didactically and are always subordinate to the characterization and the demands of the dramatic structure. Therefore, although at the time the *Dyskolos* was written there was considerable discussion about the abuse of religious practices, when Knemon raves against hypocrisy and extravagance, we must keep in mind that the speaker of these lines is a self-denying misanthropic miser whose own religious observances are grudging. The *Dyskolos* is a play which revolves around its title character, Knemon, the "dyskolos" (literally "dyspeptic") or "bad-tempered, intractable" old man. In antiquity, the play had the alternative title "The Misanthrope," a name often given to fourth-century comedies.

161

We are first introduced to Knemon indirectly, through the eyes of a slave he has terrified. He is described as a lonely figure on a barren rural hillside, gathering wild pears and reacting with violent fury when approached. The slave's terror at this meeting raises Knemon to an almost demonic force. This aspect of the old man is reinforced by his comments in his opening speech: he envies Perseus, not for his heroic qualities, but for his ability to fly away from people and turn them to stone with the Medusa's head. The imagery suggests that his aversion to other people borders on the pathological. At first, he is completely unapproachable and unyielding, but little by little, cracks appear in the armor. In a weak moment during Act III, he complains of the "eremia"—the emptiness of his life. His isolation is a prison even though it is self-imposed. The audience also begins to get an impression of a creature whose bark is bigger than his bite when he threatens to force his old female slave Simiche to go down into the well. She is frightened, but in actuality, Knemon descends himself.

The demonic force we see in Knemon at the beginning of the play is paralleled by the fierce and farcical behavior of the slave Getas and the cook Sikon at the end. The musical accompaniment lightens the atmosphere and lessens the impression of willful cruelty towards a sick old man. Knemon's discomforts are turned into ritual as Getas and Sikon force him to dance and badger him into joining the others who are sacrificing and celebrating in the shrine of Pan and the Nymphs. This way, the front-center of the stage becomes unified with the doings behind the entrance to the cave at the rear-center. As Sikon and Getas pester him with his earlier responses, they force him to achieve at least a partial integration into a normal social world. Adding to the atmosphere produced by the music and ritual is the change of role slowly taking place in the tormentors. Sikon, the crudest character in the play, delivers lyrics in the most elevated mode as he describes the party in the cave.

Although most of the *Dyskolos* is written in iambic trimeters, the meter most approximating normal speech, Menander diverges in two places—during Knemon's "apologia," or defense of his way of life after his rescue, and in the scene at the end, played to the accompaniment of the flute. Getas and Sikon torment him in his misery as the characters disguised as woodland creatures at the end of the *The Merry Wives of Windsor* torment Falstaff.

Things even out. The request for a little stew-pot comes back to haunt Knemon, as they ask for huge and expensive paraphernalia. He is too weak to protest effectively and finally yields, just as, when he renounced his property, he gave away everything to his daughter and stepson. It is made clear that Knemon's self-sacrificing personality has been as hard on him as on anyone else.

It is as if the demonic hold has been broken in the course of Knemon's fall into the well, especially in his recognition of the existence of altruism and the need for human interaction. Although at the end he is still a loner and does not want to join the sacrificers, yet he must celebrate, finally realizing that human beings cannot stand completely alone and that he was rescued by a stepson who had never received any good from him and expected nothing in return.

Menander allows Knemon to reveal himself directly in action and in a few very defining speeches, such as at his entrance when he describes a hostility of mythological proportions as he wishes for a Medusa's head. He slowly becomes less of an ogre. In his next monologue, he complains of irreligious sacrifice in terms that are familiar in the writings of the peripatetic philosophers of the late fourth century, complaining about those who give to the god only the inedible parts of the sacrificial animal—the gall and the tail, claiming that the old-fashioned kind of sacrifice is the only true one—of barley cakes, where the meal is totally given up to the gods. Menander has told us earlier that Knemon only greets the god Pan because he is afraid of retribution. He shows no religious interest himself, but clearly he begrudges luxury. The young lover Sos-tratos was rightly advised to take off his fancy cloak and do some farm work. Indulgence disgusts Knemon and self-denial character-izes his way of life. Although his holdings are not small, he works his farmlands without help and with only the barest of tools. The rotten piece of rope that broke as the bucket was lowered into the well may have been his only rope, carefully saved. When he is desperate to find his mattock, we can guess that it is his only one. He works constantly, granting himself no pleasures (except perhaps for hot water), and expects the worst of everyone. Moreover (and Menander handles this motif with the greatest subtlety), Knemon sees himself as a victim, of people individually and of the whole world. When strangers come by and ask a question or (even worse) ask to borrow something, he abusively beats them with poles and leather straps and hurls pieces of sod and stones and even the sour wild pears that he has been at great pains to gather. He calls the in-truders man-eating animals, thinking that he is being tormented and that all he asks is to be left alone.

In a culture that prized hospitality (*xenia*) and where inhospitality was seen as a fundamentally irreligious act against Zeus Xenios, Knemon can be seen as a damned soul in need of rescue from him-self. In the literary tradition, hospitality and transgressions against it are an important theme in tragedy, comedy and satyr play, with an-cestral roots in the *Odyssey*. The Cyclops' eating his guests and Circe's turning them into animals are primordial terrors, and it is images like these that Knemon recalls when he threatens to bite Getas' head off and gobble him down, and when he expresses a wish to turn people into stone statues. When Knemon says that he has no salt and can't lend any, this can be read also as an extreme of inhospitality, in that salt was basic to a household and salt was particularly mentioned to establish the depth of his refusal.

The *Dyskolos* can therefore be read as a kind of rescue drama in which the central character is literally rescued from a well into which he has fallen (to retrieve his broken-down possessions), and figuratively rescued from the inhuman aspect of himself. Pan, in the prologue, characterized him as an *apanthropos anthropos*—more than a misanthrope—an inhuman human being, a living contradiction in terms. Instead of being granted the power to turn people into inanimate objects, Knemon, a human figure lacking a vital aspect of the human anima or spirit, gained it within himself through the working of the god.

The young man in love, named Sostratos, is eager and impetuous, and he doesn't know what hit him. He has been picked by the god Pan as a reward to Knemon's daughter for her goodness and piety. Sostratos' speech stands in contrast to that of the hardworking Gorgias, who is deliberate and full of homilies, and who "talks like a book."

As for the female characters, Simiche is not to be played seriously. She is a perfect parody of a tragic messenger bearing a tale of woe. Old women are frequently treated harshly in the comedies, but this one is hardly real—her presence jolts the action and changes the mood. The other women in the play reveal themselves, as the men reveal their attitudes to them. Sostratos in contemptuous of his mother's habit of sacrificing, but he has no idea that his mother's dream was sent by Pan and is part of the god's plan for his own future. This dream will bring together all the participants and fulfill his fondest wishes. Getas has an impudent manner towards his mistress, but Sostratos' mother knows that she is in charge, ignores the raillery and demands that the job be done. The daughter is innocent and unspoiled and represents a sort of idealized heroine. She is not given any name in the papyrus; she is only identified by the label of "Knemon's daughter." When she first appears, she is concerned about her old nurse, in a manner that is gracious, poised and noble. It has been noted that in her entrance with the water jug, Menander was creating a deliberate parody of the highborn but ignoble-looking Electra of Euripides. Even Knemon enjoys her company, talks to her and really loves her. This capacity for love, which is made clear from the beginning, perhaps contains the germ of Knemon's salvation.

Generally, I have followed the Oxford text edited by F.H. Sandbach, although I have occasionally used E.W. Handley's edition for the apportionment of lines as well as for his very valuable commentary.

Postscript of Papyri

The recovery of an almost complete text of the *Dyskolos* in 1958 from the sands of Egypt represents a major chapter in an ongoing modern miracle. However, we still have no clue as to the exact place and circumstances of the discovery of Papyrus Bodmer IV, which was written in the last half of the third century A.D. and contains the text of the play, a verse synopsis attributed to Aristophanes of Byzantium, and a cast of characters. This text has been matched with approximately forty lines which were previously known from quotations by ancient authors, and since 1958, four more fragments of 5–9 lines each from two other papyrus finds have been added.

The *Dyskolos* is the only example of Greek New Comedy which is virtually complete. The two most significant lacunae consist of a few missing lines easily bridged by stage directions. In the first instance, when Sikon is alone on stage as Knemon is being rescued from the well, four lines are missing and two are damaged between l. 650-656. In all probability, he is reporting and interpreting noises heard offstage. The second instance occurs at the beginning of Knemon's defense of his way of life at l. 703-710. By l. 711, the meter has changed to the trochaic tetrameters which are used until the end of Act IV. One fragment quoted by an ancient author fits very well here, "I was in the habit of inflicting drudgery on myself."

Other plays of Menander survive in part. Papyri found in 1905 contain half of *The Arbitration* and significant parts of *The Shorn Girl* and *The Samian Woman*. Since the discovery of the *Dyskolos*, Acts I and II and the beginning of Act III of *The Shield* have been published (in 1969). Parts of *The Hated Man*, found on the back of papyri containing a deed and a table of fractions, were published in 1965 and 1968. An excellent introduction to the papyri is *Greek Papyri, An Introduction* by Eric Turner, Princeton 1968.

Invenias etiam disiecti membra poetae.

Menander:
THE GROUCH

Translated by Sheila D'Atri

Characters   *The god* **Pan**, *prologue speaker*

Chaireas, *parasite, or friend of Sostratos*

Sostratos, *a young man who has fallen in love*

Pyrrhias, *a slave belonging to the family of Sostratos*

Knemon, *the "dyskolos," the dyspeptic grouch*

An unmarried **Daughter of Knemon** (*no name given in the papyrus*)

Daos, *a slave belonging to Gorgias*

Gorgias, *a farmer, half-brother of Knemon's daughter by the same mother*

Sikon, *a cook*

Getas, *a slave belonging to the family of Sostratos*

The **Mother of Sostratos**

Simiche, *an old woman, Knemon's slave and nurse to his daughter*

Kallipides, *the father of Sostratos*

*The non-speaking roles include the people going with Sostratos'
mother to Pan's shrine. These are Plangon, Sostratos' sister, a
female piper named Parthenis, two slaves named Donax and
Syrus, Myrrhine the wife of Knemon and mother of Gorgias and
the daughter, another piper who appears at l. 880, and a sheep
brought for the sacrifice. The chorus of revellers, a staple of
New Comedy, makes its appearance here between the acts as
worshippers of Pan.*

*The action takes place in Phyle, a village about thirteen miles
from Athens which was famous for a shrine to Pan and the
Nymphs. The actual shrine was on the side of a steep cliff, but in
the theater, it is represented by the opening to a cave in the center
of the stage. On the left is a farmhouse belonging to Knemon,
the dyspeptic misanthrope, and on the right is another farmhouse
belonging to Gorgias and his mother. The spring of the Nymphs
is inside the shrine, and it is there that the sacrifices take place.
The audience cannot see inside, so these actions will be reported.
Next to one of the doors, along the country lane that goes by the
houses, is an altar to Apollo Agyieus, Apollo as the god of streets
and roads. The audience cannot see the well and dung-heap
situated behind Knemon's house on the lands farmed by Knemon
and Gorgias, but these will be imagined by the audience as they
are pointed out. The ridge where Knemon is first seen picking
wild pears is just offstage to the left. Farther away, on the right,
is the large farm owned by Kallipides, the father of Sostratos.
The place has an air of desolation, is hilly, rocky, and very
difficult to farm, and is mostly good for the hunting. At the
outset, in the early morning, the god Pan comes out of his shrine
to deliver the explanatory prologue to the audience.*

Prologue

Pan

Let your imaginative forces work
to make this place appear as Phyle—
an Attic village where the celebrated shrine
from which I come belongs to those
who have the strength to farm the rocks.
The field here on my right belongs to Knemon,
a human lacking in humanity,
bilious towards everyone, detesting crowds,
—"crowds" do I say?—He's lived a lengthy time
and hardly ever said a gracious word
to anyone. He's never first to say "hello"   10
with one exception, and that's me,
his neighbor, Pan. He doesn't like it,
but he must. (I'm dangerous when crossed.)
This Knemon once was married to a widow
whose husband had just died and left her
with a tiny son. Yoked in one harness,
they lived by fighting through the days
and taking up the greater part of night
existing wretchedly. And then a daughter came,
and things got worse. When misery   20
was all there was, and life was harsh
and full of toil, she left and joined her son.
Here, in this neighborhood, he owned a little place,
where now he is his mother's sole support
(with barely enough). One loyal slave,
long in the family, is all the help they have.
This boy's quite grown by now—
His mind's advanced beyond his years—
Experience in living brought him up.

The old man and his daughter live alone   30
with an old female servant. Carrying wood,
digging, he works all the time.
Beginning with his wife and the neighbors—
all the way to Cholargos, down there,
he hates every one of them. The girl
is innocent in all her ways—
not one thing ugly about her.
With pious care she tends the Nymphs
who share my shrine, and as she honors us
so are we moved to care for her.
There's a boy whose father farms a wealthy place,   40
worth many talents, right in this vicinity.
The city's where he lives, but now he's here
to hunt, and just by chance he's in this place
with his companion in the chase.
I've inspired him, made him mad for the girl:
that's the essence. If you want the rest
watch if you wish—and you ought to wish it!
That youth I told you of is coming near,
intent on telling to his friend
these matters that we all might hear.

Act One

[PAN *goes back to his shrine.* SOSTRATOS *and a hunting
companion, named* CHAIREAS, *and called a parasite in the list of
personae in the papyrus, come on stage from the farm belonging to*
SOSTRATOS' *father.*]

Chaireas

What are you saying? You saw a free-born girl   50

putting garlands on the local Nymphs—
and right away you're in love?

Sostratos

Right away.

Chaireas

That's fast. When you started out today
did you plan to fall in love?

Sostratos

You're mocking me,
but I am really wretched, Chaireas.

Chaireas

It's not that I don't believe you.

Sostratos

That's why I'm taking you into my heart.
I also think of you as practical.

Chaireas

That's the way I am, Sostratos.
Suppose a hetaira has captured a friend.
Right away I grab her, get drunk,
burn down the house! Don't listen to reason!   60
Before you discover who she is,
you've got to try your luck.
Slow-going makes you burn for a girl,
and a quick start means a quick finish.
But if you mean marriage with a free-born female,
then I'm a different sort of friend.
I make inquiries about her family,
finances and style. It's permanent
arrangements that we're talking here.
I leave a future record for my friend.

Sostratos

That's well and good,
but not very pleasing.

Chaireas

But even in your case we should
give the facts a thorough hearing. 70

Sostratos

At dawn I sent out Pyrrhias
from home, but not to hunt—

Chaireas

To whom?

Sostratos

To her father. To meet with
the person in charge, whoever he is.

Chaireas

Herakles! What are you saying?

Sostratos

I made a mistake. Missions like these
aren't for slaves. It isn't easy
to know what succeeds, when someone's in love.
It's been quite some time since he's been gone,
and I've been wondering—I said to him—
"Get right back home, and tell me here, 80
where I am waiting, what I want to know."

[*They are suddenly interrupted by a terrified* PYRRHIAS *dashing
onto the stage from the left. He is out of breath and dazed as if he
has just encountered a malevolent spirit of superhuman force.*]

Pyrrhias

Make room! Watch out! Get off the road!
A crazy man is chasing me—he's mad!

Sostratos

What's this all about, my lad?

Pyrrhias

Save yourselves!

Sostratos

What's this?

Pyrrhias

I'm pelted with clods, with sod, with stones.
I'm dead.

Sostratos

Pelted? Where to now, you miserable wretch?

Pyrrhias

[*Trying to escape across to the right.*]
Is he still coming after me?

Sostratos

[*Holding him back.*]
By Zeus, he's not!

Pyrrhias

He was, I thought.

Sostratos

What are you saying?

Pyrrhias

Let's clear out of here, I'm begging!

Sostratos

Where?

Pyrrhias

Away from his door, as far as we're able.
Some son of Distress, a man possessed
by blackness of bile and dreadful demons
lives there. You sent me to a man
who is big trouble. I've broken my toes   90
falling over all those rocks.

Sostratos

Has he been drinking, coming here like this?

Chaireas

His wits are wandering, that's clear.

Pyrrhias

By Zeus, I swear it, Sostratos,
I'd rather die! Watch out somehow.

I can't go on; I'm out of breath.
I knocked on the door and asked for the master,
A beaten-down old woman came—
she stood right here, as I am now—
and showed me where upon the hill   100
that blighted man, that pillory,
was there collecting sour pears.

[PYRRHIAS *is frantic. His encounter with the old man has made him
sound like an incompetent fool.* CHAIREAS *and* SOSTRATOS *find
the story hard to believe since they have not yet seen* KNEMON.]

Chaireas

[*Sarcastically.*]

What excitement!

Pyrrhias

What's that, you lucky dog? But as for me,
I took some steps upon his bit of land,
and while a good way off, in friendly fashion,
put out my hand in greeting as I spoke.
"I've come on business, sir," I said.
"On your behalf, I've hurried here."
Right away, he says, "Damn you, are you   110
spying on my place?" Then he
picked up some sod and threw it in my face.

Chaireas

[*Incredulously.*]

Go to hell!

Pyrrhias

[*Continuing*]

While this was going on, I shut my eyes,
and said, "I hope Poseidon gets you,"
when next he grabbed a pointed pole
and really cleaned me up with it.
He said, "What business could there be,"

of some concern to you and me?"
"Can't you find a public road?" he screamed.

Chaireas

Without a doubt, you're describing
a farmer who's out of his mind.

Pyrrhias

Here's how it ends: I ran away
and he chased me first around the hill,
at least two miles, and then below
into these bushes, throwing clods and stones   120
and then the pears, when nothing else was there.
A rotten business, an absolutely
damned old man. I beg you, find another place.

Sostratos

That's the way that cowards talk.

Pyrrhias

You've no idea what path you walk.
He'll gobble us up.

Chaireas

Perhaps at this moment he's suffering.
It seems to me now, Sostratos, that we
can wait awhile. For you should know,
in business, it's more practical
to wait until the moment's opportune.

Pyrrhias

Very sensible.

Chaireas

Poor farmers are prickly. He's not alone;
it's all of them. At dawn, tomorrow,   130
since I know the house, I'll go alone.
And now it's best you wait at home.
That's the way to play it.

[Having decided to his own satisfaction what would be best,
CHAIREAS *departs without waiting for an answer.* SOSTRATOS *then
turns his attention to his slave after deciding that* CHAIREAS *is of no
use to him.]*

Pyrrhias

[Happy to have CHAIREAS *take care of things.]*

    That's what we should do.

Sostratos

[Thinking CHAIREAS *has failed him.]*

    That's an excuse he's gladly seized upon.

    It was immediately clear

    he didn't want to come with me,

    and didn't approve of my marriage plans.

[Turning furiously to PYRRHIAS.]

    And as for you, you lowest of the low,   140

    I hope the gods destroy you.

Pyrrhias

[Innocently.]

    How have I injured you, Sostratos?

Sostratos

    It's clear you've caused some damage to his place,

    or stole—

Pyrrhias

    I stole?

Sostratos

    Why would someone beat you up

    if you did nothing wrong?

Pyrrhias

    He's here, that man himself! O best of masters,

    now I'll take me off, and you can talk to him.

*[*PYRRHIAS *makes his escape.* SOSTRATOS, *on stage alone, starts
his monologue. As he is speaking, he notices* KNEMON *appear at
the left, coming from the ridge. By the time his speech is finished,*

SOSTRATOS *has moved as far away as he can from* KNEMON'S
house, while KNEMON *is standing in the middle of the stage, ready
to begin his comments to the spectators.*]

Sostratos

[*To himself and answering the absent* PYRRHIAS.]

> I can't! I never can persuade a soul
> no matter what I talk about.
> And how can I address a man like him?
> That's no philanthropist I'm looking at.
> By Zeus, he's serious! I'll slip aside
> a little from the door. That's better.
> How he shouts, while walking all alone!   150
> He must be mad, it seems to me—
> I'm frightened, by Apollo and the gods.
> (Shouldn't a person tell the truth?)

Knemon

> Well, didn't Perseus have double-luck?
> First, the wings—he never had to meet
> with people walking on the ground.
> And then he had some sort of property
> which turned the mob of nuisances to stone.
> That's what I want! They'd be plentiful
> everywhere—human statues made of stone.   160
> By Asclepius, my life is now
> unliveable. They're talking,
> trespassing, crossing my land.
> I suppose, by Zeus, I waste my time
> standing by the side of the road!
> I don't work that bit of field:
> those people coming by have chased me off,
> and now they follow me up to the hill-tops.
> A multi-multitudinous mob!
> Good grief! Another one of them

is standing right beside our door!

Sostratos

[*Aside*.]

Will he really strike at me?

Knemon

[*Aside*.]

A quiet place is nowhere to be found.
You can't even plan to hang yourself in peace.   170

Sostratos

[*Aside*.]

Can it be me enraging him?

[*To* KNEMON.]

I'm waiting here for someone, sir—
it was agreed—

Knemon

[*Ignoring him*.]

What did I say? Is this the stoa
or the local shrine for rendezvous?
Whenever there's a man you wish to see,
arrange to meet them all beside my door.
Certainly, construct an assembly-room,
if that's what you have in mind!
Why not a council-chamber? I'm accursed!
The evil is abusive insolence,
as it appears to me.

Sostratos

I can't be casual about this job.
Real effort is required here.
That's clear, but shall I go for Getas,   180
who's my father's slave? By the gods, I will!
He's hot stuff, with lots of experience
in all sorts of things. He'll beat off his bile.
I don't approve of long delays:

why, even in a single day,
lots could happen. Oh, there's noise at the door!

The Girl

Alas, for all my sufferings;
and what shall I do now? My nurse,   190
while lifting up the jar,
dropped the well-ropes in the well.

Sostratos

[*Aside, thinking only of the appeal of his beloved.*]

O Father Zeus, Apollo the healer,
beloved Dioskuri—unbeatable beauty!

The Girl

Father gave me orders coming in
to make the water hot.

Sostratos

[*Overwhelmed by her.*]

Amazing!

The Girl

If he discovers this, he'll treat her
like a criminal. I have no time to talk.
O dearest Nymphs, you've got to take it on—
But I'm ashamed to go inside
if there are people making sacrifice—

Sostratos

Just give it to me and right away
I'll dip the jug and bring it up.   200

The Girl

Yes, by the gods, and quickly too!

Sostratos

[*To himself as he goes to the shrine.*]

She's a natural aristocrat
although her look is countrified.
O gods deserving deepest reverence,

what can save me now?

The Girl

Dear me, who's banging at the door?

Can that be father coming out?

I'll catch some blows if he catches me out.

Daos

[*Speaking to* GORGIAS' MOTHER *inside as he comes on stage from the other house.*]

I'm slaving and serving forever here

while he's out there digging alone.

I've got to go and help him out.

O cursed Poverty! How have we happened   210

on such an intimate relationship?

Why has your constant presence

settled in our house?

Sostratos

[*Returning.*]

Take the jar.

The Girl

[*From the door of her house.*]

Bring it here.

Daos

Whatever is this man after?

Sostratos

Be well! Take care of your father.

[*To himself.*]

O my! O Sostratos, stop complaining.

It will be all right.

Daos

[*Aside.*]

What will be all right?

Sostratos

[*Still to himself.*]

    Don't worry, do as you planned—get Getas—
    tell him everything and bring him back.

[*He goes off stage.*]

Daos

[*Alone.*]

    Is something ugly going on?
    I'm not the least bit pleased.
    When a boy is waiting on a girl,
    corruption's close. But, Knemon, as for you—   220
    I hope the gods destroy you totally.
    You've left that innocent and harmless girl
    alone in this deserted place,
    with no protection anywhere.
    That's why he came by? Finding out
    he slipped away and thought he'd try his luck.
    Fast as I can, I'll let her brother know.
    We'll watch out on her behalf.
    I believe I will start on it now—
    for here's a group of followers of Pan.   230
    I see they're looking somewhat drunk
    so I think I'm better off away.

[*The crowd of revellers comes on stage, singing a light-hearted paean to* PAN *and providing the choral performance sung between the acts.*]

Act Two

[DAOS *and* GORGIAS *are alone on stage.* GORGIAS, *hearing about*
SOSTRATOS' *arrival at the farm, criticizes* DAOS *for not dealing more*
forcefully with the situation.]

Gorgias
Was this an insignificant affair
that you could handle carelessly?
Daos
How is that?
Gorgias
You should have told him, whoever he was,
as soon as you saw him come forward,
by Zeus, that you'd better never,
ever see him again acting like that.
But you kept off, as if this business
was somebody else's concern.
It isn't possible to run away
from family responsibility.
My sister's our concern although her father   240
wishes it were otherwise. Don't imitate
dyspeptic dispositions.
If she falls victim to some shame,
disgrace would also come to me.
From the outside, no one ever knows
who is to blame. They only see results.
[*They walk toward* KNEMON's *house.*]
Daos
Gorgias, my friend, I'm afraid
of that old man. If he catches me
near his door, he'll hang me on the spot.

Gorgias

He's certainly intractable,
always adversative. How could someone
force him to improve or use persuasion?   250
The law prevents our use of force,
And persuasion's ruled out by his nature.

Daos

Hold on a bit—we haven't come in vain—
Just as I said, he's turning back again.

Gorgias

The one in the fancy cloak?
Have you been speaking of HIM?

Daos

He's the one.

Gorgias

[*To* DAOS.]

I can see from his looks
he's a villain.

[SOSTRATOS, *wearing an obviously expensive cloak, comes on
stage from the right. Preoccupied with gathering his courage to
approach* KNEMON, *he does not notice* GORGIAS *and* DAOS *and
speaks in an aside to the audience.*]

Sostratos

I couldn't find Getas, he wasn't in.
My mother's off to sacrifice
to some divinity—I don't know who—   260
every day she's doing some such thing.
She circles round the entire district
making sacrifice; now Getas is sent
to contract for a cook. I said good-bye
to sacrifice, and here I am again.
I think I'll get rid of this going around
and do my talking for myself.

I'll knock at the door, although it may be,
I'll never take counsel again.

Gorgias

[*Just before* SOSTRATOS *can knock.*]
My lad, would you please wait a while?
I've something serious to say.   270

Sostratos

My pleasure, certainly.

Gorgias

For humankind, I do believe,
for those with luck and those unfortunate,
change and limitation is the rule.
The one with luck remains as such,
flourishing throughout his life,
as long as fortune can be borne
without injustice. But when THAT's there
and leading him by all the goods he owns,
it's then, I think, all changes for the worse.
Yet, as for those who do not have enough,   280
in difficulty, doing nothing wrong,
bearing up with all nobility,
perhaps, in time, they'll find some credit
and share in better expectations.
What am I trying to say?
Although you're rich, don't trust in it,
and don't despise us just because we're poor.
Let anyone who's watching see
you're worth enduring fortune.

Sostratos

Does my behavior appear out of place?

Gorgias

I believe you're eager for some disgrace—
planning to persuade a free-born girl   290

to fall, or else you're waiting
for an opportune time
for an action worth multiple deaths.

Sostratos

[*Genuinely shocked.*]

  By Apollo!

Gorgias

  Certainly, it isn't just
  that at your ease you work your wickedness
  on us who have no leisure for such things.
  Know then, that a poor man harmed
  is the most ferocious of all.
  At first he's piteous, then it's outrage
  he's suffered, not merely injustice.

Sostratos

  May all go well for you, dear boy,
  but let me explain.

Daos

[*To* GORGIAS.]

  Great going sir! Lots of luck to you!   300

Sostratos

[*To* DAOS.]

  As for you, babbler, stifle yourself—
  In this place, I saw a certain girl.
  I love her. If you call that injury—
  then perhaps I'm in the wrong.
  Can anyone say more? Except it's not
  for her I've come—I want to see her father.
  I'm free-born and sufficiently rich
  to marry her without a dowry.
  I pledge to love her perpetually.
  If I have come with malice on my mind,   310
  or wished to plot intrigues in secrecy,

[*Pointing to the statue of* PAN *on stage.*]
>   may this Pan, together with the Nymphs,
>   strike me dead beside the house.
>   I'm really disturbed, I hope you know,
>   if that's the way I seem to you.

Gorgias
>   Maybe I've spoken more than I should—
>   don't get yourself upset—you've changed my mind.
>   Now I'm your friend. I'm no stranger,
>   but her brother (we have the same mother).
>   Best of men, that's why I've spoken this way.

Sostratos
>   And now, by Zeus, you'll be useful!   320

Gorgias
>   What do you mean useful?

Sostratos
>   I see you have a noble character.

Gorgias
>   I don't want to send you off empty.
>   No pretexts—but the plain truth.
>   The father of this girl—he's just—
>   like no one else. There never was
>   a man like him, and no one living's like him now.

Sostratos
>   That vicious man? I've seen him here.

Gorgias
>   An absolute excess of abuse!
>   His holdings (not so small—two talents worth)
>   he farms alone, without a laborer   330
>   to share the work: no household slave
>   or paid employee from the neighborhood,
>   no neighbor either, just himself alone.
>   Happiness to him is seeing no one near.

Mostly he works with his daughter around.
To her alone he cares to speak,
but not to any other easily.
He says he'll never let her marry
until he finds a bridegroom just like him.

Sostratos

What you mean is never.

Gorgias

And that's why, my good friend,
if you take pains to work at this,
you'll work in vain. Leave it to us   340
who have no choice, to bear with him.

Sostratos

By the gods, have you never loved someone?

Gorgias

It's not for me, my friend.

Sostratos

How's that? Who's preventing you?

Gorgias

Calculating the troubles I have
gives me no time to rest.

Sostratos

You've never been, I think. Your speech
shows no experience in things like this.
You exhort me to withdraw.
The decision is no longer mine—
It is the god's.

Gorgias

Although you're doing us no harm,
you're only needlessly distressed.

Sostratos

Not if I can win the girl!

Gorgias

But you won't. Follow me. Attempt to ask.   350
He's farming near us in a wooded glen.

Sostratos

How will it go?

Gorgias

I'll throw in a word about a marriage
to the girl. (That's a thing I'd gladly see!)
Right away he'll start complaining
about everyone, criticizing
the way they live. When he gets sight of you
looking luxurious, he won't even look!

Sostratos

Now—is he there?

Gorgias

No, but in a little while,
it's out he'll come on his accustomed path.

Sostratos

Are you saying he'll bring the girl along?   360

Gorgias

It may work out that way.

Sostratos

Go ahead, I'm ready.

Gorgias

The way you talk!

Sostratos

I'm begging you, be on my side!

Gorgias

But in what way?

Sostratos

What way? Let's go ahead to where you said.

Daos

What now? While we are working

do you plan to hang around
wearing that fancy cloak?

Sostratos

Why shouldn't I?

Daos

He'll pelt you with pieces of sod
and call you a lazy pest. You must
dig along with us. Maybe then he might
perhaps hold off and hear a word,
thinking you lead a poor farmer's life.

Sostratos

I'm ready to do as I'm told. Go on!   370

[SOSTRATOS *takes off the cloak, and can now work unencumbered
in only a short tunic.*]

Gorgias

Why do you force yourself
to suffer such distress?

Daos

[*Aside.*]

What I wish is that today
we get a much as possible
accomplished. Maybe at the same time,
he'll break his back and stop annoying us.

Sostratos

Bring out the two-pronged hoe!

Daos

Go on, take mine. Meanwhile I'll rebuild the wall.
That also must be done.

Sostratos

Hand it over—you've saved me!

Daos

I'm setting out, my man, you follow there.

[DAOS *exits to the fields at the left.*]

Sostratos

> So that's the way it is. I must die trying,   380
> or win her and remain alive.

Gorgias

> If you are speaking as you're thinking,
> I wish you luck.

Sostratos

> Great honored gods! If you believe
> those things you said would turn me off,
> you're wrong—I'm doubly keen.
> If this girl hasn't been reared
> among women, and knows nothing
> of the evils of this life,
> and hasn't been terrified
> by the imaginings of some aunt or nurse,
> but with freedom of spirit, somehow,
> by a harsh father detesting wicked ways—
> Isn't she a specially lucky find?
> But—this hoe must weigh two hundred pounds!   390
> It's killing me! Can't soften now—
> now that I've set myself to work at it.

[GORGIAS *and* SOSTRATOS *exit to the left. Just afterwards,* SIKON *comes on stage from the right with a sheep.*]

Sikon

> A sheep like this one doesn't come along
> every day. Damn it to hell!
> If I carry it up in the air,
> it grabs a branch in its mouth
> and gobbles the fig-leaves from the tree.
> I've got to drag it off by force.
> If you set it on the ground, it won't move.
> The opposite takes place. I am the cook—
> and I'm the one in shreds,

dragged along the road by it.
Happily, here's the temple to the Nymphs,   400
where we will sacrifice. Greetings Pan!
Hey boy! You—Getas—why are you hanging behind?

[GETAS *enters, loaded down with cushions and cookery.*]

Getas

Those damnable women loaded me up
with enough for four donkeys.

Sikon

It looks like a mob is arriving—
That's a lot of bedding you're bearing!

Getas

What now?

Sikon

Lean those things over there.

Getas

O.K. If she should see
Paianian Pan in her sleep,
that's where we'd go, I know—
right for the sacrifice!

Sikon

Who saw something asleep?

Getas

Hey man, don't beat on me.   410

Sikon

Tell me anyway, Getas, who?

Getas

My mistress.

Sikon

But what, by the gods?

Getas

You'll destroy me! It seemed that Pan—

Sikon

[*Pointing to the statue on stage.*]

    This one over here?

Getas

    This one.

Sikon

    What was he doing?

Getas

    —The master, Sostratos—

Sikon

    A really refined young man!

Getas

    —Was shackling him all around.

Sikon

    By Apollo!

Getas

    Then giving him a leather vest

    and a two-pronged hoe, he ordered him to dig

    in some neighbor's land.

Sikon

    Unbelievable!

Getas

    Because of this we sacrifice,

    to turn the nightmare into something good.

Sikon

    Now I've got it! Pick up that stuff again,   420

    and carry it inside. We've got to have

    the cushions set up right

    and everything else in order.

    Nothing should get in the way

    when they're ready to sacrifice.

    Here's to luck! And lift your eyebrows up,

you triple-miserable wretch.
Today I'll gorge you to your taste!

Getas

I've always been quick to praise your craft.
But YOU, I don't trust.

[They go off into the shrine and then the chorus enters with another song.]

Act Three

[KNEMON *comes out of his house, calling back to* SIMICHE *inside.*
He is getting ready to start some farm work, but his plans are
immediately interrupted by the arrival of SOSTRATOS' MOTHER
and the contingent of sacrificers.]

Knemon

>Old woman, once you bar the door,
>don't open it for anyone
>until I come again. By then
>I think it should be quite dark.

Mother of Sostratos

>Plangon—go faster—our sacrifice   430
>ought to be finished by now!

Knemon

[*Unseen and unheard by the others.*]

>What rotten business is this?
>A crowd! Why don't you go where the crows
>can pick your bones?

Mother

[*To the* FLUTE-GIRL.]

>Parthenis! Pipe Pan's melody!
>They say that no one should approach
>this god in silence.

Getas

[*Impudently, as he emerges from the shrine.*]

>By Zeus—you got here safely enough!
>Herakles! How wearing! We've been sitting
>forever and hanging around.

Mother

>Has all been set in order for us?

Getas

> Yes, by Zeus—at least the sheep—
> It almost died waiting.

Mother

> You wretch—it won't wait around
> till you've the time. The rest of you go in—   440
> make ready the basket, the lustral water,
> the sacrificial cakes. Why are you gaping?
> Have you been struck by thunder?

[GETAS *sees* KNEMON *looking furious.*]

Knemon

> Damn you pests to deepest hell!
> They're forcing laziness on me—
> I just can't leave an unprotected house!
> These Nymphs are a curse across my door—
> I think I'll build another house,
> tearing this one down.
> Look how those burglars sacrifice!
> They're bringing bedding and bottles of wine—
> not goods for the gods—but good for them!
> What's holy is incense and barley-cake.   450
> This, when set upon the fire,
> the god takes totally. The other things—
> the inedible gall and the tail—
> that's what they offer to the gods
> while they gulp down the rest.
> Old woman—quickly—open the doors!
> I think we should work on the inside chores.

[SIMICHE *finally responds to his knocking and lets him in. Just after,* GETAS *emerges from the shrine while shouting insults to the* WOMEN *inside.*]

Getas

> The little stew-pot you say you forgot?

You're sleeping it off! What can be done?
I think we've got to trouble the neighbors
of the god.

[*He knocks on* KNEMON's *door calling for* SERVANTS.]

    Slave! By the gods!
Nowhere is there a more miserable   460
mob of serving-girls. Hey, slaves!
It's only screwing that they understand!
My fine fellows! And if someone sees,
why, then they slander someone else. Slave!
What the hell is this? Servants!
No one is in. Oh! Someone's racing up!

[KNEMON *appears at the door.*]

Knemon
    Why are you attached to my door?
Tell me, you miserable boor.

Getas
    Don't bite off my head!

Knemon
    I'll do just that, by Zeus,
and then I'll devour you alive.

Getas
    You won't—by the gods!

Knemon
    Is there some sort of legal covenant
binding me to you, you god-forsaken pest?   470

Getas
    No bond. I haven't come with witnesses
to ask that a debt be repaid.
I'm only requesting a small stew-pot.

Knemon
    Stew-pot?

Getas

Stew-pot.

Knemon

You whipping-post, do you suppose
I make it a habit to sacrifice cows?

Getas

[*Aside*.]

I don't think you'd offer a snail.

[*To* KNEMON.]

I hope you prosper, my good man.
The women suggested I knock and ask
so that's what I did. There isn't any.
When I return, that's the statement I'll make.
O honored gods, this man's a grey-haired snake.   480

[GETAS *returns to the shrine.*]

Knemon

[*Alone*.]

Man-killing beasts! As if I were a friend—
no one hesitates to knock. If I should catch
a man advancing to this door of ours,
if I don't make a warning out of him
to everyone around, then think of me
as just one of the crowd! I don't know
who he was, but this time he lucked out.

[KNEMON *returns inside his house and* SIKON *emerges from the
shrine. He begins by speaking to* GETAS *who is inside.*]

Sikon

Damn you to hell! So he was abusive?
Probably you were foul-mouthed first.
Some people don't understand how to ask—
but I invented the art!
I supply for tens of thousands in this town.   490
You've got to be a bit of a flatterer—

if an older man opens the door,
I call him "Father" or "Pop;"
an older woman I call "Mother;"
if it's a woman of middle-age,
it's "Sister" or "Milady;"
if one of the younger slaves, "My good man."
But you can go hang yourself—
stupidly, you say "Boy" or "Slave,"
where I say "Papa, a word with you, please."

[*He knocks and* KNEMON *appears.*]

Knemon

Are YOU back?   500

Sikon

How's that?

Knemon

You're provoking me purposely.
Didn't I say "keep away from my door?"
Woman, hand me the whip!

Sikon

Never! Let me go.

Knemon

[*Beating him with the whip.*]
Let go?

Sikon

My good man, truly, by the gods!

Knemon

Get back here.

Sikon

May Poseidon grant you—

Knemon

Still chattering?

Sikon

I came to request an earthen casserole.

Knemon

> I have no earthen casserole,
> nor do I possess an axe, nor salt,
> nor vinegar—only nothing!
> I've stated it simply to everyone near—
> Don't approach!

Sikon

> You never said it to me.

Knemon

> Now I'm saying it.

Sikon

> Yes, with brute force! Couldn't you tell me   510
> where one might go to ask for one?

Knemon

> Didn't I say? Will you still jabber at me?

Sikon

> A grand farewell.

Knemon

> I don't want any "farewell" from you.

Sikon

> Fare badly then.

Knemon

> O what incurable ills!

Sikon

> He's furrowed me into strips of sod!
> So that's what you get for polite requests!
> Some difference, by Zeus!
> Should one approach another door?
> If they're all so ready with fighting-gloves here,
> It would be difficult. Maybe it's best
> to roast all the meat. That's how it appears.
> Anyway, I've got a pan.   520
> Good-bye to Phyle—I'll use what's at hand.

[*He returns to the shrine. Shortly afterwards, an exhausted*
SOSTRATOS *enters.*]

Sostratos

Whoever is lacking in troubles,
Let him go hunting in Phyle.
O multiple miseries,
since I have a back and neck and hips—
to put it briefly—my whole body hurts.
I fell into this job like a strong young man;
lifting the hoe like a laborer,
I struck it deep. I laid it on
with diligence, but not for long—
then I'd turn and look, in case it was the time
for the old man to come with the girl,   530
and then, by Zeus, I took hold of my hip,
secretly at first, and after quite a while,
my spine was bent. I was quietly
turning to timber. The sun was burning,
and Gorgias, looking over, saw me
bending slightly up like a swing-beam
and then going heavily down
with all my body in it.
"Young fellow," he said, "That man,
it seems, will not come now." I answered,
"So what should we do? Keep watch tomorrow   540
and let today go by?" Then Daos came
as my successor to the spade.
The first assault is done. I've come here,
though I can't say why, by the gods.
On its own accord, this business
drags me to this place.

[GETAS *appears at the door of the shrine, trying to get the smoke out
of his eyes. He shouts back inside at* SIKON.]

Getas

> What's the trouble now? Do you think,
> my man, I've sixty hands? I kindle the coal,
> cut up the guts, wash, and carry to and fro
> and at the same time I'm kneading the dough.
> I hand this implement around and then—
> I'm blinded by the smoke. At times like these,
> I think I'm the donkey at the feast.

550

Sostratos

> Slave! Getas!

Getas

> Someone's calling me?

Sostratos

> I am.

Getas

[*Still blinded.*]

> And who are you?

Sostratos

> You don't see me?

Getas

> I see you now—Master!

Sostratos

> Tell me what you are doing here.

Getas

> What? We've just made the sacrifice
> and now we're preparing the morning meal.

Sostratos

> Is Mother here?

Getas

> For quite some time.

Sostratos

> And Father?

Getas

We expect him. You can go inside.

Sostratos

After I've run a little errand.
Somehow, the timing's fine for sacrifice.
I'll invite this young man, going just as I am,
in the offerings, then in the future,
they'll be more useful allies of ours
regarding the marriage.   560

Getas

What are you saying? You're planning to go
and invite some people to share the meal?
For my sake, let there be three thousand!
I've known it for a long time—
I won't get a taste of anything. Hardly!
Bring everyone. You've sacrificed
a lovely victim—really worth seeing.
As for these women—they're sophisticates—
but would they give me something? No.
By Demeter, not even a bit of coarse salt!   570

Sostratos

Getas, today it will go well—
I'll prophecy myself, O Pan—
and always pray while passing you.
I'll be a friend to all mankind.

Simiche

[*Dashing tragically out of the house.*]
O woe is me! O woe is me! O woe is me!

Getas

Go to Hell! That's the old man's woman coming up.

Simiche

What will become of me?
Wanting to get the pail from the well,

without the master finding out,
(if only I could have managed it,
to lift it out myself),
I attached the two-pronged hoe
to a weak and rotten piece of rope.   580
It broke on me immediately.

Getas

[*Gloating.*]

That's really good!

Simiche

Unhappy me—I've heaved the hoe
into the well with the pail.

Getas

Now all that's left for you to do
is just to throw yourself in too.

Simiche

It just so happens he's getting ready
to move some dung that's lying around.
For quite a while he's been searching and shouting,
dashing about and—banging the door!

[*She runs off an* KNEMON *emerges in a fury.*]

Getas

[*To* SIMICHE.]

Get moving—you miserable old woman—
move! He'll kill you. No, protect yourself.

Knemon

Where's the thief?

Simiche

Master, it fell against my will.

Knemon

Just start walking inside.

Simiche

Tell me, what will you do?   590

Knemon

I'll tie you to the rope and let you down.

Simiche

Please, no. Oh, misery.

Getas

That's the best use for this same rope—

by the gods!—if it's totally rotten.

Simiche

I'll call on Daos from the neighbor's house.

Knemon

[*Stopping her*.]

You'll call Daos? Damn you,

you've destroyed me. Go faster—inside!

[SIMICHE *goes into the house*.]

I'm miserable with this emptiness—

like no other. I'll descend into the well.

What else is there for me to do?

Getas

[*To* KNEMON.]

We'll get a hook and a rope.   600

Knemon

May the gods destroy you utterly

and horribly, if you speak to me.

Getas

It would only be right! He's jumped in again.

What a confounded wretch he is!

The sort of life he leads! A tried and true

example of an Attic farmer

in battle with the rocks that yield

only thyme and sage. He brings in pain

but reaps no good from it.

But here's my master coming

and bringing his guests along.

They're just local workers! How odd!
Why is he bringing them here?   610
How have they become familiar?

Sostratos

[*Enters talking to* GORGIAS.]

I can't allow you to do otherwise.

Gorgias

We have all we need.

Sostratos

Herakles! Who could refuse completely
to share a meal with a celebrating friend,
for I am your friend, you should know that's true—
Long before I ever saw you, I was.
Daos, take these things, and then come in.

Gorgias

I can't leave my Mother alone at home.

[*Then, to* DAOS.]

Take care of what she needs; I'll be there soon.

[SOSTRATOS *and* GORGIAS *go into the shrine together while* DAOS
takes the hoe, the shovel and other tools and goes into GORGIAS'
*house. When the stage is empty, the chorus of revellers enters for
another performance.*]

Act Four

[*For the second time,* SIMICHE *rushes desperately out of* KNEMON's
house in parody of a tragic messenger.]

Simiche

Who'll rescue us? O wretched me! Who'll rescue us?   620

Sikon

[*Emerging from the shrine.*]

Lord Herakles!

[*To* SIMICHE.]

Let us get on with our libations
in the name of the gods and divinities.
You are abusive, you beat us up—
You—go howl! What a crazy house!

Simiche

My master's in the well.

Sikon

How's that?

Simiche

I'll tell you how—he descended
to retrieve the hoe and pail,
when suddenly he slipped on the rim,
and that's how he fell in.

Sikon

Not that horrible old man?

Simiche

That's the one.

Sikon

By heavens, he's done well for himself!
My dear old woman—now you've got a job to do.   630

Simiche

But how?

Sikon

A mortar or stone or something like that—
hurl it at him from above.

Simiche

[*Pleading.*]

My dear man, go down . . .

Sikon

By Poseidon, I would pay
if I fight with a dog in the well
as the story goes. Never!

Simiche

[*Moving away from him towards* GORGIAS' *house.*]

Gorgias, where on earth are you?

Gorgias

[*Hearing her and coming out of the shrine.*]

Where am I? What is it, Simiche?

Simiche

What? I'll say it again.
The master's in the well.

Gorgias

[*Calling into the shrine.*]

Sostratos, come out.

[*To* SIMICHE.]

You lead the way inside. Go quickly now.

[*After the three of them go into* KNEMON'S *house,* SIKON *speaks.*]

Sikon

There really are gods, by Dionysus!
You wouldn't offer a small stew-pot   640
to the worshippers, you sacrilege.
You grudge everything. Go fall in the well
and drink it down. Then you won't have
water either to offer anyone.
Now the Nymphs have taken revenge
on him, as he deserves.
No one escapes unharmed, if he harms a cook—
Somehow our art is sacrosanct.
You can do what you want to the waiters.

[*He hears noises from behind the house.*]

What's that? He didn't die?

A girl is wailing "Dearest Papa."
I don't care . . . but it's clear they're hauling him up.   650
[*He imagines the scene.*]
    Just look at him, can you believe it
by the gods! Soaked and shivering—elegant!
[*Pointing to the emblem of Apollo Agyieus by the door.*]
    By this Apollo here, I'd like to see it!
[*Calling to the* WOMEN *in the shrine.*]
    You women, pour your libations   660
for these rescuers. Pray that they
save the old man—scarcely.
Let him be maimed and lame—
No longer will this neighbor be the greatest pain
to the ever-present worshippers.
I care how it goes—whenever someone cares to pay.
[SIKON *joins his customers in the shrine as* SOSTRATOS *emerges.*]

Sostratos
[*To the audience.*]
    By Demeter, by Asclepius,
by the gods, never in my life
have I witnessed a more opportune
near-drowning. What a lovely time!
As fast as we got in, Gorgias jumped down   670
into the well, while I and the girl
did nothing from above.
What could we possibly do?
Except that she was broken up
and tore her hair and beat her breast.
I was precious—just like a nurse,
by the gods! I stood there and told her
not to act that way. I begged her,
looking at her as an image
of perfect design. The stricken man

was no concern of mine, except
for all that heaving on the rope.   680
What a pain! By Zeus, I nearly destroyed him—
Looking at my girl, I dropped the rope
three times. Gorgias was a true Atlas.
He kept it up and brought him up,
and when the old man got out, I came here.
I could hardly keep myself in check.
I was just THIS close to kissing her.
I love her dreadfully. I'm preparing—
Oh, they're making noise at the door.   690

[*The door of* KNEMON'S *house opens and* KNEMON *emerges, lying
on a wheeled bed like a wounded tragic hero.* HIS DAUGHTER *and*
GORGIAS *are in attendance.*]

Sostratos

[*Continuing.*]

O Savior Zeus, how odd!

Gorgias

[*To* KNEMON.]

Knemon, tell me what you want.

Knemon

What's the use of talking? I feel awful.

Gorgias

Bear up!

Knemon

I've borne enough. No longer
will Knemon ever bother you.

Gorgias

That's the evil of isolation,
don't you see? You've come within a hair
of dying recently. Someone should
look after you at your time of life.

Knemon

Although I know I'm done for,
call your mother, Gorgias.

Gorgias

Right away.

[*Aside.*]

Troubles alone can teach us   700
as it seems to me.

Knemon

[*Without responding to him.*]

Daughter, would you give me your hand
and help me to stand?

Sostratos

[*Rushing over, in envy of their close contact.*]

[*Aside.*]

Lucky man!

Knemon

[*To* SOSTRATOS.]

Why are you standing over there,
you miserable specimen?

[SOSTRATOS *doesn't answer. Then, to* MYRRHINE *and* GORGIAS.]

I wanted hard work, Myrrhine.
Gorgias, I chose this way of life.   710
No one could have changed my mind, believe me.

[*To all assembled, as an explanation of his life.*]

Perhaps I was mistaken, but I thought
that I alone of everyone
could be sufficient to myself,
needing no one else.
But now I see how fierce and unexpected
the end of life can be. I've discovered
what I never realized before:
we must have someone close at hand—

an ally always ready with assistance.
But—by Hephaistos—I was so far gone
from looking at the lives men lead
and the way they make their calculations
to profit themselves. I didn't believe   720
that anyone could be an altruist.
That's what got in my way.
But one man—Gorgias—has proved the reverse,
having done what only the noblest would do.
I never allowed him to come to my door
or gave him help of any sort,
never addressed him, spoke kindly—
but he saved me anyway.
Someone else would have said, and rightly so,
"You never let me come, so I'm not coming now.
You never were of any use,
and that's how I'll reciprocate."

[*To* GORGIAS, *personally, noticing his discomfort.*]
What is it, my boy? If I should die
(and I think I will—I'm feeling terrible)   730
or whether I escape with my life,
in either case, I make you my son.
All that I happen to have, consider your own.
I hand my daughter over to you—
provide her with a husband. If I were well,
I'd never find one on my own—
there isn't anyone who'd please me.
But as for me, if I should live,
allow me to live as I wish,
while you take care of all the other things.
You're sensible—with the help of the gods,
you're her proper guardian.
Divide my property and offer half

as dowry for her. Manage the rest
for me and your mother.
[*Getting tired, to* HIS DAUGHTER.]
Daughter, help me lie down. I don't believe   740
a man should speak beyond necessity—
except, my child, I want you to know
a few things about me and my habits.
If all the others were like me,
there wouldn't be any law-courts,
and no one would send anyone to jail.
There'd be no war—each man would hold
a moderate share and be content.
If instead, you'd rather follow present paths,
then that's what you should do.
This harsh, dyspeptic aged man won't bother you.

Gorgias

All these things I take with thanks,
but, with your help, as soon as possible,
a husband must be found, if you agree.

Knemon

I told you what I thought.
Now, by the gods, don't bother me.   750

Gorgias

[*Pointing to* SOSTRATOS.]
It just so happens that he wants . . .

Knemon

Never, by the gods!

Gorgias

[*Continuing.*]
He's someone asking for the girl.

Knemon

I don't care about any such things.

Gorgias

He helped save you.

Knemon

Who's that?

Gorgias

[*Bringing* SOSTRATOS *forward.*]

This man here.

Knemon

[*To* SOSTRATOS.]

You, come here.

[KNEMON *looks at him and speaks to* GORGIAS.]

He's sunburned. Is he a farmer?

Gorgias

He is, father—not one of those

who puts on airs and ambles lazily around.

[KNEMON *nods in agreement, and then has had enough.*]

Knemon

Wheel me back inside.

Gorgias

[*To* SIMICHE *at the door.*]

Take care of him.

[KNEMON *goes into his house.* MYRRHINE *and* THE GIRL *follow.*]

Sostratos

[*To* GORGIAS.]

For the rest, you've got to pledge your sister to me.   760

Gorgias

These things should be referred to your father.

Sostratos

Father won't say otherwise.

Gorgias

Therefore, I certainly give her to you

in view of all the gods. It's fitting, Sostratos—

you've approached this business without disguise

and honestly. You thought it worth your while
to work at anything to make this marriage work.
You're delicate and yet you took up the hoe;
you dug and wore yourself out.
In such a manner, a man reveals himself—
when he is prosperous but makes himself
the equal of a man who's poor.
With inner strength, your sort will bear
a change of fortune. You've given sufficient proof   770
of character. Only remain as you are.

Sostratos

[*Eagerly.*]

I'll do better yet.

[*Hesitating.*]

And yet to praise
myself perhaps reveals vulgarity.

[*Noticing* KALLIPIDES *coming on stage at the right.*]

My father's coming just in time, I see.

Gorgias

[*Surprised.*]

Your father is Kallipides?

Sostratos

Very much indeed!

Gorgias

By Zeus, he's rich!

Sostratos

And rightly so—he's an unbeatable farmer.

Kallipides

[*Approaching.*]

Looks like I've been left behind. Probably
they ate up the sheep and returned to the farm.

Gorgias

[*To* SOSTRATOS.]

By Poseidon, he has hunger pains!
Should we wait or tell him now?

Sostratos

First let him eat. Later he'll be milder.

Kallipides

[*To* SOSTRATOS.]

What's this, Sostratos? Have you eaten?

Sostratos

Yes, but yours is set aside—go on.   780

Kallipides

I'm on my way in.

[*He goes into the shrine.*]

Gorgias

Go in and talk to him now if you wish—
just you and your father alone.

Sostratos

You'll wait in the house, won't you?

Gorgias

I'm not coming out.

Sostratos

I'll leave in a little and call you over.

[SOSTRATOS *goes into the shrine and* GORGIAS *joins the rest of his family in* KNEMON'S *house. When the stage is empty, the chorus of revellers returns with its paean before the final act.*]

Act Five

[*When the stage is empty,* KALLIPIDES *and* SOSTRATOS *come out of
the shrine. They are in the middle of a disagreement.*]

Sostratos

It's not everything I wanted, father.

I didn't expect this from you.

Kallipides

What? Didn't I give way?

I said that you could have the girl you love.

I wish it and I say it's got to be.

Sostratos

That's not how it seems to me.

Kallipides

I realize that when you're young,

a marriage turns out to be strong

when a man is moved by love.   790

Sostratos

So I can have this young man's sister

and consider him worthy of us?

How can you say he can't have mine?

Kallipides

What you say is disgraceful.

I don't want a beggarly bridegroom and bride.

One or the other is enough for us.

Sostratos

You're talking money—an uncertain matter.

If you knew that it would remain with you

until the end of time—protect it

and don't hand it over to a soul.

But where you lack control, and all you have

depends on luck and not on you—

why should you grudge—O Father!—anyone?   800
For Lady Luck could take it all away
and give your holdings over
by some mischance to an undeserving man.
That's why I say, as long as you master it
you must use it with nobility.
Be of help to all, and through your actions,
make as many well-provided as you can.
Good deeds don't die. Then, if Fortune trips you up,
these same resources will return to you.   810
A visible friend preferable by far
to secret wealth you've buried in the ground.

Kallipides

You know how it is, Sostratos—
what I've amassed, I haven't hidden for myself—
How could that be? It's yours.
You've passed your judgment on a man
and want to secure him as a friend?
Why are you giving me maxims?
Go ahead, Sostratos—offer and share.
I'm completely persuaded by you.

Sostratos

You're willing?

Kallipides

I'm willing, believe me.
Don't bother yourself about it.

Sostratos

Now I'll call Gorgias.   820

[*He calls over towards* KNEMON'S *house and* GORGIAS *comes out.*]

Gorgias

I heard you both, since I was by the door—
all the things you said from the start.
What then? I consider you my friend,

Sostratos, and I'm extremely fond of you,
but I don't want more than I can manage.
By Zeus, I couldn't do it if I wished.

Sostratos

I don't know what you're saying.

Gorgias

I give you my sister as your wife,
but to take yours—that would be very fine for me!

Sostratos

What do you mean by "fine?"

Gorgias

It wouldn't be pleasant for me
to luxuriate in someone else's labors,   830
but just in what I've accomplished myself.

Sostratos

You're talking nonsense, Gorgias.
How can you judge yourself
unworthy of this marriage?

Gorgias

I've judged myself worthy of her,
but it isn't right to take a lot
if you only have a little.

Kallipides

By Zeus, how you act the aristocrat!

Gorgias

How?

Kallipides

By not wishing to appear indulged.
You've seen me persuaded; it's your turn to yield.
Your manner convinced me double-fold;
now don't you be brainless as well as poor.
Marriage will bring you real security.   840

[*After a pause*, GORGIAS *agrees*.]

Gorgias

You've won. What remains is for us to get engaged.

Kallipides

I pledge my daughter now to you
young man, to produce lawful offspring.
Three talents as dowry, I offer with her.

Gorgias

And I 've one talent for my sister.

Kallipides

Have you? You shouldn't give too much.

Gorgias

But I have it.

Kallipides

Keep possession of your total holdings,
Gorgias. Now bring your mother
and your sister here to join our women.

Gorgias

That's what I should do.

Sostratos

Let's all stay here and celebrate tonight.   850
Tomorrow is the time for marrying.
Gorgias, bring the old man here.
His needs will be better cared for by us.

Gorgias

He won't want to come, Sostratos.

Sostratos

Change his mind.

Gorgias

If I could.

Sostratos

[*To* KALLIPIDES.]

Father, it's time for a fine round of drinks
and an all-night feast for the women.

Kallipides

    The reverse, I think—the women will drink

    while we'll be the ones awake at night.

    I'll go and get things ready for you.   860

[KALLIPIDES *goes into the shrine*.]

Sostratos

    Do it, please.

[*To the audience*.]

    No problem should cause a thinking man

    to ever fall victim to despair—

    Application and care can conquer all!

    I'm the perfect example!

    In just one day I prevailed,

    arranging a marriage for myself

    which no one thought anyone could.

[GORGIAS *comes out of* KNEMON'S *house with* HIS SISTER *and* MOTHER.]

Gorgias

[*To* THE WOMEN.]

    Come forward quickly, will you please.

Sostratos

[*To* MYRRHINE *and* THE GIRL.]

    Come this way.

[*To* HIS MOTHER *at the entrance to the shrine*.]

    Mother, receive these women.

[*To* GORGIAS.]

    Knemon hasn't come yet?

Gorgias

    He begged me to take the old lady—

    so he'd be left alone at last.

Sostratos

    You can't win against him!   870

Gorgias

That's the way he is.

Sostratos

But you should enjoy yourself—let's go in.

Gorgias

Sostratos, I'm embarrassed
to be together with women . . .

Sostratos

Isn't that foolish? Won't you go in?
Now you must take all of us as family.

[GORGIAS *hesitantly agrees and they go into the shrine together.*
Immediately afterwards, SIMICHE *comes out of* KNEMON'S *house*
while talking to KNEMON *in a mixture of sympathy and*
disapproval.]

Simiche

I'm going off, by Artemis.
You can just lie there alone.
You make yourself miserable.
They wanted to take you to visit the god,
and you said no. Something bad will happen—
by Demeter and the maiden,
even worse than now. (May all go well!)

[SIMICHE *walks over to the shrine and goes inside, just as* GETAS *is*
coming out, telling someone that he will check up on KNEMON. *At*
this point, a piper starts to play, and the following scene is
performed with the music in the background. The atmosphere
becomes less realistic as KNEMON *is tormented into celebrating with*
the others. The music helps to create an atmosphere of fantasy, so
that KNEMON'S *miseries at the hands of* GETAS *and* SIKON *seem less*
like cruelty and more like ritual. PAN *will not be denied.*]

Getas

[*Speaking back into the shrine*.]

   I'll go there and see how he is.

[*The music begins*.]

   Why are you piping for me, you wretch?   880

   I have no leisure yet.

   I've been sent to the sick man over there—

   Hold off a bit!

Simiche

[*To* GETAS *at the entrance*.]

   Let someone else sit with him, inside.

   I want to chat with my lady,

   before she leaves as a bride,

   to talk to her before we're separated.

Getas

   That's smart of you—now carry on

   I'll see to him while you are gone.

[*As* SIMICHE *goes into the shrine*, GETAS *calls to* SIKON.]

   Hey, Sikon, cook, come over here

   and hear what I have to say—

   I think we'll have some fun today.   890

[SIKON *comes out of the shrine*.]

Sikon

   You are calling me?

Getas

   Indeed. Would you like some just revenge

   for what you suffered recently?

Sikon

   What I suffered was just?

   Go screw yourself, you talk like a fool.

Getas

   The nasty old man is sleeping alone.

Sikon

So how's he getting on?

Getas

Not outstandingly devastated.

Sikon

Couldn't he stand up and clout us?

Getas

I don't even suppose he could stand.

Sikon

This matter you've mentioned is quite a delight.

I'll go in with some request—

and he'll go out of his mind.

Getas

First, let's see what some deviltry brings—

let's drag him outside and put him down here

then beat on his door and request a few things.

We'll burn him up—it will be such a pleasure.   900

Sikon

What frightens me is Gorgias.

If he finds out, he'll clean the floor with us.

Getas

There's such a lot of noise inside the shrine.

No one will notice—there's too much wine.

We'll civilize him into this family—

If he continues as he is,

We'd all suffer unbearably.

Sikon

There's nothing more that you could say!

Getas

Only watch out so nobody sees

as you bring him up to the front. Lead the way!

Sikon

I beg you, for a little, wait around—

you can't just disappear from sight—
and, by the gods! don't make a sound.

Getas

I'm not making noise, by Gaia! Go right!

[*They arrive at* KNEMON'S *house, look inside, and then* SIKON *goes
in and carries* KNEMON *out to the center of the stage*.]

Sikon

[*To* GETAS.]

Look at him!

Getas

The time is now. That's where to put him.
I'll go first—you watch the rhythm.   910

[*To non-existent domestic slaves*.]

Slave, little slave, fine slaves, little slaves!

Knemon

[*Waking up*.]

Oh my, I'm dying.

Getas

[*Calling louder*.]

Fine slaves, O slave, little slave, slave, slaves!

Knemon

[*In greater agony this time*.]

Oh my, I'm dying.

Getas

Hello! Who's this fellow? Is this where you live?

Knemon

No doubt about it. What do you want?

Getas

Giant bowls and casseroles.

Knemon

Who can help me to stand?

Getas

You have them, you truly have all at hand—

seven stools and twelve tables belong to you—
slaves, pass the word to the inside crew.
I'm in a hurry too.

Knemon

There isn't any.

Getas

[*Incredulously.*]

There isn't?

Knemon

[*Angry.*]

Haven't you heard me ten thousand times?

Getas

I'll make my escape.

[*He runs off and motions to* SIKON *to take over.*]

Knemon

[*Aside.*]

Oh, misery! How did I get to be
brought to this spot? Who put me
down in front of my house?   920

Sikon

[*To* GETAS.]

You go off, I'm on.
Slave, little slave, O women, men, doorman!

Knemon

My man, are you mad? You'll bring down the door.

Sikon

Could you supply . . . nine coverlets?

Knemon

How could I?

Sikon

. . . and a woven Oriental hanging,
in length, one hundred feet.

Knemon

A strap! If only I could beat . . .
Old woman! Where's the old woman?

Sikon

Should I go off to another door?

Knemon

Anywhere else! Old woman! Simiche!

[*To* SIKON.]

May all the gods destroy you
for all the harm you're doing me.

[SIKON *runs off and* GETAS *returns.*]

What do YOU want?

Getas

I want a huge bronze mixing bowl.

Knemon

Who can help me to stand?

[SIKON *returns.*]

Sikon

You have, you truly have the hanging, daddy.   930

Knemon

I don't, by Zeus!

Getas

No mixing bowl?

Knemon

I'll kill Simiche.

Sikon

Sit down and don't mutter.
You run from the crowd, hate the ladies,
and won't allow yourself to join the others
at the sacrifice. You've got to bear these
indignities—no one's here to help.
Bite your lip and listen
to one thing after another:

when your women came to the cave,
hugs and handshakes greeted your wife
and daughter. Their manner of life
was not unappealing. I was near
preparing the entertainment for the men ...   940
Don't you hear me? Don't go to sleep.

Getas

No indeed!

Knemon

Oh me!

Sikon

What then? You don't want to be there?
We were hurrying—here's what follows—
I readied the table and spread the pillows—
do you hear? The cushions and tables were set—
I just happen to be a cook, don't forget.

Getas

[*Aside.*]

He's such a dainty fellow!

Sikon

[*Continuing.*]

Somebody tilted the old Bacchic wine
into a deep bellied cup.
With Naiad springs he mixed it up
and toasted the men in a round.
Another saluted the women in line:
they drank it up like sandy ground ...
You understand?
A serving girl was turning tipsy,   950
and shaded the flush on her blushing young face.
She started to pace in a rhythmic trance,
but hesitating, modestly.
Another maiden took her hand

and joined her in the dance.

Getas

[*Jumping up to dance and grabbing* KNEMON.]

Oh, you've suffered frightfully,
so dance now, join the chorus.

Knemon

What do you wretches want with me?

Getas

You country boor, come dance with us.

Knemon

Stop, by the gods!

Getas

Then let us bring you in.

Knemon

What can I do?

Getas

[*Starting to force him to dance again.*]

Then it's dancing for you!

Knemon

Take me in—better there than here.

Getas

Now you're talking sensibly.
We win! O lovely victory!
Slave, O Donax, Sikon, Syrus!
Bring him in along with us.   960

[DONAX *and* SYRUS, *two slaves without speaking parts, pick*
KNEMON *up from the ground and start to carry him into the shrine.*
Before they go in, GETAS *says to* KNEMON.]

Just watch yourself, 'cause if we catch
you giving trouble again,
we won't react so moderately—
we'll really deal with you then!

[*To* THE SERVANTS.]

Someone bring us garlands and a torch.

Sikon

[*To* GETAS, *handing him a garland from the altar of Apollo.*]

Take this one here.

[SIKON, SYRUS *and* DONAX *bring* KNEMON *into the shrine as* GETAS *speaks the epilogue to the audience.*]

Getas

Proceed. Now you've seen us triumphant
over this troublesome old man.
Your warm applause now, if you please,
dear lads and boys and men. May laughter-loving Victory,
noble-born and maidenly, favor us forever.

Bibliography

Arnott, G. "Menander: Discoveries Since the Dyskolos." *Arethusa,* III 1 (1950), p. 59f.

Arnott, G. *Menander, Plautus and Terence.* Greece and Rome: New Surveys in the Classics. Oxford: Clarendon, 1975.

Arnott, Peter. *Greek Scenic Conventions in the Fifth Century B.C.* Oxford: Clarendon, 1962.

Bieber, M. *The History of the Greek and Roman Theater.* Princeton University Press, 1961.

Blundell, John. "Menander and the Monologue." *Hypomnemata,* 59 Vandenhoeck & Ruprecht in Gottingen, 1980.

Fantham, Elaine. "Sex, Status and Survival in Hellenistic Athens: A Study of Women in New Comedy." *Phoenix,* XXIX (1975), p. 44-74.

Flury, Peter. *Liebe und Liebessprache bei Menander, Plautus und Terence.* Heidelberg, 1968.

Gaiser, K. "Die Plautinische Bacchides und Menanders Dis Exapaton." *Philologus,* 114 (1970), p. 51f.

Goldberg, Sander. "Plautus' Epidicus and the Case of the Missing Original." *TAPA* 108, (1978), p. 81-91.

Goldberg, Sander. *The Making of Menander's Comedy.* Univ. of California Press, 1980.

Gomme, W. and F. H. Sandbach. *Menander: A Commentary.* Oxford Univ. Press, 1973.

Handley, E. W. *Menander and Plautus: A Study in Comparison.* London: University College, 1968.

Hunter, R. L. *The New Comedy of Greece and Rome.* Cambridge University Press, 1985.

Katsouris, A. *Tragic Patterns in Menander.* Athens, 1975.

Ludwig, W. "The Originality of Terence and his Greek Models." *GRBS* IX, (1968), p. 168-182.

MacCary, W. "Menander's Soldiers: Their Names, Roles and Masks." *AJP* 93, (1972), p. 283f.

Menander. *New Fragments of the Misoumenos of Menander*. Ed. Eric Turner. Univ. of London, 1965.

Menander. *The Dyskolos of Menander*. Ed. E.W. Handley. Harvard Univ. Press, 1965.

Pickard-Cambridge, Arthur. *The Dramatic Festivals of Athens*, ed. 2. Revised J. Gould and D.H. Lewis. Oxford: Clarendon, 1968.

Post, L. *From Homer to Menander*. (Sather Classical Lectures 23.), 1953.

Sandbach, F. H. "Menander's Manipulation of Language for Comic Purposes." *Entretiens Hardt* XVI, (1970), p. 113-143.

Sandbach, F. H. *The Comic Theater of Greece and Rome*. N.Y.: W. W. Norton, 1977.

Webster, T. B. L. *Studies in Later Greek Comedy*. Stanford, 1969.

Webster, T. B. L. *An Introduction to Menander*. Manchester Univ. Press, 1974.

Webster, T. B. L. *Studies in Menander*. Manchester Univ. Press, 1960.

IV

Plautus and Farce
by Robert W. Corrigan

FANTASY AND FARCE

When reading the plays of Plautus, one very quickly becomes conscious of what a remarkable sense of the theatre that early Roman playwright had. He seems to have known every theatrical trick, and what's more, he knew how to use them. There is something in his work which would be sure to appeal to every level of sophistication and every social class. As could be expected, much has been written about Plautus and his theatre (unquestionably the best book being George Duckworth's *The Nature of Roman Comedy*, Princeton: Princeton University Press, 1952), and there isn't much we don't know about his sources, his techniques, and the conventions of the theatre of his time. But somehow this isn't enough. None of the magistral studies ever seems to get to the heart of things. Everyone admits that Plautus was a great farceur, and after describing the external characteristics and so-called conventions of farce—usually in a deprecatory manner—the subject is dropped. Q.E.D. But this is the key subject; this is what Plautus was really up to and, if one is ever to understand the spirit which courses through the plays of Plautus, he must also understand something about the nature of farce. Now, farce isn't quite a dirty word in critical parlance, but it certainly hasn't been given very much attention by our serious critics and theorists. At least not until Eric Bentley turned his fine mind to the subject; and as so often is the case, Bentley is right. Attention must be paid!

Farce, like a curse, is the expression of repressed wishes. We in the United States lack the colorful curses of Europe, particularly those of the staunchly Catholic countries such as Spain and Italy. When a Spaniard says, "I'll defecate in your mother's milk" or calls another a "son of a whore," he is in effect committing murder. (Indeed, after he says such things, he may actually be murdered in return.) All such phrases are expressions of the wish to destroy the existence of a person. Farce works in much the same way. As Bentley points out in his *The Life of Drama*, farces are much like dreams in that they "show the disguised fulfillment of repressed wishes." I believe Professor Bentley is right in this, but I believe it would be more fruitful to use a less limiting and more inclusive idea—namely, fantasy. Dreams certainly are assertions on the part of the unconscious to express many things which our consciousness represses. But farce also concerns itself with the materials and images of our conscious fantasies. We know that fantasy and repression are inextricably linked in a dynamic tension, and the rhythm of farce is— to use a forced image—that of the cat of fantasy chasing its tail of repression. And our pleasure in witnessing farce is that our wildest fantasies can be acted out, without— as Bentley reminds us—our having to suffer the consequences. In technique it is like psychiatric therapy: the doctor urges the patient to tell all of his fantasies within the safe confines of the office, so he will not feel so compelled to act them out in more destructive ways elsewhere.

This relationship leads us to one of the central misunderstandings about farce. Just as so many discussions of psychoanalysis are invariably reduced to the psychopathology of sex, so, too, the literature on farce—such as it is—is invariably concerned with farce as an expression of our sexual fantasies. Hence "bedroom" is the adjective most commonly associated with this whole form of drama. There is certainly some justification for this, but when we read (or even better, see) Plautus' plays, we become increasingly conscious of the fact that, although sex is present, so too are many other subjects. Think of Molière's one-act farces, or Chekhov's riotous early plays. Or think of the best known of our modern farceurs: Chaplin, Buster Keaton, the Marx Brothers, Abbott and Costello, Laurel and Hardy. Sex and slapstick have always been combined, but never exclusively, except in the old-time burlesque routines. Farce's spirit of violence and rebellion is also directed to other situations and standards of value such as wealth, social class, life in the city, and even the arts.

The essential condition for the creation of farce is the

existence of strong publicly shared values and standards of behavior. The last really big-hit bedroom farce on Broadway was *The Seven Year Itch*, and I believe it is significant that it was first produced in 1952. The sexual taboos and rigid standards of sexual behavior have been dissolving (or at least are changing profoundly) so rapidly in the past couple of decades, that the old-fashioned bedroom farce has just about disappeared. The *Up in Mabel's Room* and *Getting Gertie's Garter* of my youth just don't make it today, and even such a blatantly lewd piece as the more recent *Pajama Tops* was most successful in the boondocks and to my knowledge was never brought into New York. The sex farce undoubtedly still has some appeal, but usually to less sophisticated and more parochial audiences. (In this regard, it is worth noting that many so-called bedroom comedies can do very badly in New York, and still be counted upon to make money in community theatres around the country.) The Hollywood film is still a pretty hospitable medium for the sex farce, as *The Apartment* and *Some Like It Hot* will attest, but even here things seem to be changing.

Eric Bentley is certainly correct in his explanation of why bedroom farce appeals to audiences. He writes:

> Farce in general offers a special opportunity: shielded by delicious darkness and seated in warm security, we enjoy the privilege of being totally passive while on stage our most treasured, unmentionable wishes are fulfilled before our eyes by the most violently active human beings that ever sprang from the human imagination. In that application of the formula which is bedroom farce, we savor the adventure of adultery, ingeniously exaggerated in the highest degree, and all without taking the responsibility or suffering the guilt. Our wives may be with us leading the laughter.[1]

But as more liberal sexual attitudes develop, farce has tended to move to other realms.

Not too long ago I was talking to some of my students about the subject of farce, and I discovered that they did not find the bedroom variety very funny. Sex, they said,

[1] *The Life of the Drama* (New York: Atheneum Publishers, 1964), p. 229.

was increasingly a take it or leave it matter for most of their generation, and they were neither outraged nor titillated by it when it was represented in the theatre. They even went on to admit that they had actually acted out most of their sexual fantasies—or at least all of those which, with even a modicum of taste, could ever be presented on the stage. Money, business, bureaucratic power, IBM-ization, and the system—these, they insisted, were the widely held values of our time, and hence the more appropriate subject matter for farce. One then thinks of the popularity of *How To Succeed in Business Without Really Trying* and *Dr. Strangelove, A Hard Day's Night* and the films featuring Jean-Paul Belmondo, or such farcical contemporary novels as *Up the Down Staircase* and *Catch-22*. Perhaps the younger generation is right.

The real point, however, is that farce can and does have many masks. The theatre of Plautus is one of the first in the Western world to reveal this fact. Sex and the family, money and social caste, accomplishment and pride, are just some of the materials that this first farceur used. He seemed, instinctively, to understand the cathartic nature of fantasy. He also knew—and equally as well—that fantasy is both preceded and followed by repression.

THE TEMPO OF FARCE

Whenever stage directors talk about the problems of producing farce, inevitably the first matter mentioned is the question of pace. Farce, they say, must be played at breakneck speed. So everything is speeded up, only to discover, more often than not, that what has been created is not art at all—only confusion. This chaos usually stems from the director's failure to understand the inner dynamics of farce. But directors are not the only guilty parties; the critics and scholars have been just as far off the mark, and nowhere is this fact more apparent than in the studies of Roman comedy.

Even those critics well-disposed to Plautus cannot help but approach his plays with an air of slight superiority. We must like Plautus, they imply, because it is our cultural duty to do so; but they then go on to admit in confidential tones that his plays are really pretty thin. This prejudice against farce in general and Plautus in particular is inevitably revealed when the critics begin discussing the tempo of his plays. Farce, they say, deals with "amusing confusions rather than psychological complications." They go on to say that there is no real conflict in farce and the characters have little stature and practically no significance. Being only a drama of situation, it is peopled with passive characters who in no way determine the course of events. Finally, they argue that, since the characters lack complexity and the situations exist only to be superficially exploited, these situations have no other meaning than confusion and embarrassment for their own sake. Hence the conclusion: if a situation has no intrinsic meaning, then the playwright must depend upon variety, novelty, and uniqueness if he is to ever achieve the proper theatrical effects. Rapidity of pace is seen, then, as a means of compensating for the script's obvious insignificance. Plautus is praised as a farceur because of his ability to move from situation to situation, incident to incident, so fast that the audience never has the time to question the implausibiliy of what is taking place on the stage, nor to be bored by what is essentially only cotton-candy fluff. However, interspersed in the midst of all of this are numerous kind references to the author's earthy sense of humor and his boisterous animal spirits.

Such well-intentioned criticism could not be more wrong!

Farce is a surrealistic art. Like the fairy tale and the dream, it is an art of flat surfaces. It is also an art of images. Like a giant collage, it is composed of violent juxtapositions, short, bright flashes, and disparate patterns having no apparent continuity. As a result, through all the external hilarity, we become aware of the child-like truth of its nature and the mysterious quality of its means. Both in its techniques and in our responses to them, the dynamics of farce are much like those of the Punch-and-Judy shows. Since the laws of logical cause and effect do not exist in such a world, the facts of our daily existence are presented in what seems to be a distorted fashion. But, as Bentley has pointed out so persuasively, farce is "always faithful to the inner experience."

"That's the way it is; that's the way it *really* is!" So the saying goes, and so it goes in farce. We may never have literally experienced the trials and tribulations of the Brothers Menaechmus, but our most profound psychic dramas certainly includes an Erotium and a wife, an irate father-in-law and a Brush, and above all an alter ego among its cast of characters.

Farce, then, appeals directly to our senses and our psyche and not to our ratiocinative faculties. And this accounts for the unique rapidity of its pace. It is not a question of plausibility or implausibility; it has a quick tempo because in the world of fantasy the laws of logic have been suspended and everything that happens occurs more directly, and hence more quickly.

No other form of drama makes such great demands on the actor, and Plautus, being an actor, must have been well aware of it. This fact, probably more than any other, accounts for the great disparity which exists between the audience's enthusiastic response to farce and the scholar's general lack of regard for it. Its most important qualities cannot be gotten inside the covers of a book. Farce is always acted. For its effects it concentrates on the actor's body—on his facial expressions, his mimicries, and his physical gestures. (Bentley, to quote him yet again, put it beautifully when he wrote: "The dialogue of farce is sound and movement.") The critics' problem is to capture the physics of performance. This is next to impossible to do except through performance itself. But what the critics can do is to make directors and actors aware of the fact that the tempo of farce is not an external compensatory technique; it is not something a George Abbott can come in and impose upon a production that won't get off the ground. To do Plautus—or the plays of any farceur—well one must first enter into fantasy's magic realm; once there, the buoyant and violent spirit of that world will provide all the other necessary directions.

A FUNNY THING HAPPENED ON THE WAY TO THE FORUM

When *A Funny Thing Happened on the Way to the Forum,* starring Zero Mostel, opened on May 8, 1962, many people were surprised to learn that this successful musical was actually a pastiche of scenes from Plautine farce. How amazing, many of them thought, that the works of an old Roman could have such vitality and be so much fun. They shouldn't have been surprised, for the authors were doing little more than updating essentially Plautine techniques. In fact, Plautus is history's first known writer of musical comedy and it is no accident that count-less musicals (*Fanny, The Boys From Syracuse* and *A Funny Thing*, to name a few) have been based on his plays.

Because musical comedy is not generally respected in academic circles, most scholars have not paid much atten-tion to this aspect of Plautus's work. They do discuss his practice of *contamnatio* (the technique of stealing and piecing together scenes from several plays by the writers of the Greek New Comedy), and then go on to talk about the puns, racy obscenities, the many comic-coined words, and the general exuberance of his language. But the most significant aspects of Plautine theatre are the songs and the dance routines.

From the more than 130 plays which we know Plautus wrote, we have close to sixty songs still remaining. And it is clear from these texts that the typical Plautus play was composed of forty percent songs and another twenty per-cent was probably chanted or recited to a flute, *à la* Rex Harrison in *My Fair Lady*. (One play, *Epidicus*, was eighty percent musical.)

The clue to this is the great variety of meter to be found in any one of Plautus's plays. All Roman comedy was composed in verse, but no other playwright used so many different kinds of meter and, more important, used them in such wild combinations. Terence, for instance, almost always used regular iambic meters and only oc-casionally shifted to regular trochees. Plautus, on the other hand, used not only highly irregular iambic and trochaic meters, but the extremely colloquial proceleus-matic and the rarely used anapestic meters as well. Even the Roman critics tended to denigrate Plautus for such impurity. Quintillian considered Terence a better play-wright because he wrote with greater consistency of style rather than in the hodgepodge style of his predecessor. Horace complained of Plautus's fame, using many of the same arguments that the academic detractors of musical comedy use today. But at least one critic of great repute was on Plautus's side. At the playwright's death, Varro wrote in *De Poetis:*

> After the death of Plautus, comedy mourned, the stage was deserted, and laughter, sport, jest, and countless numbers all shed tears of sorrow.

The "countless numbers" *(numeri innumeri)* was a direct reference to both the songs and the polymetry of Plautine farce.

This raises a difficult question: it is generally believed that the source of Roman comedy was the Greek New Comedy, especially the plays of Menander. But polymetry is not a characteristic of Greek New Comedy. We find shifts of meter only in the choruses, and these follow a very consistent pattern. It is more likely that Plautus borrowed his plots from the Greeks and then infused them with the musical-comedy techniques of the Italian popular theatre, especially those of the Etruscan *satura* and the Fescenine verses of Etruria. Whatever the explanation, the medieval editor put it just right when he wrote on a Plautine manuscript, *"mutatis modis cantica."* (Songs in changing measures).

It is this quality which makes Plautus's plays so devilishly hard to translate. There are frequent elisions (or else hiatuses); synizesis—the running together of separate vowel sounds within a word to create a pun or other comic effects—is common; and the songs themselves are filled with unnatural accents, obviously necessary to create the proper rhythms of song. In short, only if approached as a musical text will a Plautine play make much sense.

So, in reading Plautus, we must realize that we are reading a musical-comedy script. Not much is there. This fact certainly explains why a literary playwright like Terence became more influential than Plautus in the Augustan period and also later on in both the Middle Ages and early Renaissance. But the Renaissance theatre of both England and Spain had no real vitality until its writers began to discover Plautus; or, if not Plautus himself, at least the buoyant spirit of musical comedy that dominates his plays.

THE BEGINNINGS OF THE COMMEDIA TRADITION

Probably the most penetrating, brief description of the peculiar genius of the Italian theatre can be found in Pirandello's essay, "Introduction to the Italian Theatre." [1] The

---

[1] "Introduzione al teatro italiano," translated by Anne Paulucci, in *The Genius of the Italian Theatre*, (N.Y.: Mentor Books) Eric Bentley, Editor.

great playwright writes about many aspects of his country's theatre, but he is at his best when he accounts for the development and describes the nature of the *Commedia dell'arte*. One passage in particular is worth noting here:

The *Commedia dell'arte* emerged, little by little, precisely from theatrical personalities . . . who, as actors, knew the pulse of the public and, as authors, also indulged their own personal tastes and ambitions. . . . But they were also well acquainted with the output of the *litterati*, and as producers took out options on those works, performing them with their own, or revising them to suit their purposes. It is absurd to imagine in this an accidental discovery of mere actors. Anyone having even the slightest acquaintance with the way an actor works on stage, with the precise directions he requires if he is to take a step to the right instead of the left, will readily see that the idea of improvising their performances could never have occurred to actors.

The *Commedia dell'arte* is born, on the contrary, out of authors who are so deeply involved in the Theatre, in the life of the Theatre, as to become, in fact, actors; who begin by writing the comedies they later perform, comedies at once more theatrical because not written in the isolated study of the man of letters but in the presence, as it were, of the warm breath of the public; who then take up the task of adapting for their own performance and that of their troupe the comedies of other authors, old and new, in order to supply the pressing need for repertory, constantly revising these adaptations, after having tried out on their audiences the effectiveness of certain flourishes added as an outlet and vehicle for the particular talents of some actor of the company. And as their fellow actors gradually become skilled in keeping up the already-familiar repartee of the middle episodes, they will write only the exits and the outline of the action.

In other words those authors must have lost all their serious artistic pretensions; the transitory, impassioned life of the Theatre must have taken such full possession of them that the only interest left to them was that of the spectacle itself—a complete absorption in the quality of the performance and communication with the audience.

They are no longer authors; but they are no longer even actors, in the true sense of the word.

What are they, then?

By now each one of them has become a *type*, with a completely defined stage life of its own; so that finally a theatrical convention is established whereby with ten of them, ten such types—no more, no less— a complex and varied spectacle can be put on that will provide full satisfaction for the audience—an audience already familiar with these conventions, with the rules of the game, and passionately interested in how their favorites carry on, how far each succeeds in giving prominence to his part.

Pirandello then goes on to point out that the *Commedia* is uniquely Italianate in spirit. There is no doubt he is right about this; the traditions of the *Commedia* are as old as Italy itself. But one might have wished that Pirandello had broadened his perspective a bit more, for no man of the Italian theatre embodied those traditions more fully than Titus Maccius Plautus. He even had a *Commedia* name.

The popular Italian theatre has always been imbued with the spirit of *Commedia* and the particular genius of Plautus is that he was the first to incorporate it into his plays. The first known theatrical performances in Italy were the *Fabulae Atellanae*, developed by the Oscans in the town of Atella in Campagna. The *Fabulae* were short (300 lines) satiric parodies of life in the country. They had such titles as "The Sick Boar" or "Daddy, the Farmer," and occasionally they were parodies of heroic figures, as can be gathered by a title like "Hercules, the Tax Collector." These sketches were filled with riddles and obscenities and were played by companies of touring actors. It is interesting to note that the actors played them *"planipes,"* with bare feet, and not in the *cothurni* of tragedy nor in the *socci* of comedy; indicating that, from the beginning, the *fabulae* were farcical in nature.

However, the most significant thing about them was the fact that their casts were composed entirely of the "stock" or type characters which Pirandello referred to in his essay. The first records tell us of only four characters

(Maccus, the clown; *Bucco,* the glutton or braggart; *Pappus,* the foolish old man; and *Dossemus,* the hunchback trickster), but this number was gradually increased, and by the middle of the third century B.C. there were at least eight. And all of them can be found in the plays of Plautus.

Plautus began as an actor, and from his name it is obvious that he played the clown. He was not the first known Roman dramatist (both Livius Andronicus and Gnaeus Naevius are known to have preceded him), but it is clear that he was the first to incorporate the native comic traditions of the *Fabulae* into the framework of the literary comedy which his predecessors had borrowed from the Greeks. And very soon Plautine farce came to dominate the Roman theatre.

The first thing one notices about Plautus's plays is how insignificant the plots are. In fact, the plot is usually revealed in the prologue. The audience was not concerned with what happened; their interest was in how things were worked out and the form of the performance itself. For this reason, type characters are ideally suited for Plautine drama. A type character is one who needs no explaining and whose future is predictable no matter what his situation might be. Such a character is, as Bentley describes him, a creature of habit, and he brings a great energy to the theatre. He has the characteristics essential for farce; these also happen to be the same qualities which Pirandello ascribed to the characters of *Commedia.*

No one, to my knowledge, has ever referred to Plautus as the father of the *Commedia dell'arte;* and one would probably be in error to do so now. But the *Commedia* did not come into being *de novis* either. Ruzzante and his colleagues may not have known it, but Titus the clown was out there on the platform with them.

Plautus:
THE MENAECHMI

———

Translated by Palmer Bovie

Characters	*Peniculus [Brush], a parasite*
	Menaechmus I, a young gentleman living in Epidamnus
	Menaechmus II [Sosicles], a young gentleman of Syracuse
	Désirée [Erotium], a courtesan
	Mixmaster [Cylindrus], her cook
	Messenio, slave of Menaechmus II [Sosicles]
	Maid, in the service of Désirée
	Wife, wife of Menaechmus I
	Old Man, father-in-law of Menaechmus I
	A Doctor
	Whipster I
	Whipster II

Prologus in Person

Ladies and gentlemen, and everybody else, I announce
  In the first fine foremost and friendly words I pronounce,
  Myself! How are you all out there? Do let me greet you.
  It's a particular pride and personal privilege to meet you,
  And present to you Plautus in person, that is as he looks
  When he speaks in his very own words; I don't mean
    in books
  When you read what he says, but here on the stage
    where he *is*.
  Won't you lend us your ears and put yourselves quite
    at ease,
  Tune in on our logic, and turn your minds to the plot
  I now go over in a very few words, not a lot?
        Oh yes . . . poets often insist, more often than not
  In their comedies, "It's an action in Athens," it takes
    place
  Where you're expected to find it most charming, in
    Greece. [*Irish pronunciation.*]
        But I'm not the underhanded sort who is willing
          to say
  It takes place somewhere it doesn't, or . . . anyway
  Nowhere except *when* it does occur there. And today
  While I grant that our play bubbles up through Greek
    grounds,
  It's distilled in Sicilian, not acted in Attic towns.
  So your Prologue expounds the preface to his foreword.
    He pounds
  In the plot now, not a little, but a lot; it's scoops of
    synopsis
  To ladle out. I'll shovel on now, and bury my worries,
  In view of the generous way you hear out our stories.
        A certain old man was a merchant in Syracuse.
  To him twin sons were born, identical youths

249

So alike in appearance the wet nurse could never get
used

To telling them apart when she popped up to offer her
breasts;

Their own mother didn't know which was which, she
just guessed.

Well . . . at least, that's what someone who saw these
boys once told me:

I don't want you thinking *I* went there and saw them,
you see.

Now one day when both boys were seven, their father
loaded up

A huge cargo ship full of goods to be sold, and toted up

One of the boys on the boat. Then off they went

To the market together being held in the town of
Tarentum;

The other son, of course, he left back home with the
mother.

And when they got to Tarentum, the father and the
other,

There was some sort of fair going on, with hundreds of
games,

And hundreds of people to watch them, which quickly
explains

How the boy wandered off in the crowd, away from his
dad.

A merchant from Epidamnus latched on to the lad

And snatched him off home. And then when the father
discovered

He'd lost his son, sick at heart, he never recovered

From the fatal depression that carried him right to his
grave

In Tarentum a few days later on. When the messenger
arrived

At Syracuse with this grisly news of how the father
lay dead

At Tarentum, and twin number one was completely
mislaid,

The affectionate grandfather promptly took it in his head

To rename the Syracuse son in honor of the other,

And call him Menaechmus from now on, after his
brother;

So dear to the grandfather's heart was that boy and
his name:

The grandfather's own, as a matter of fact, was the same.

I remember that name *Menaechmus* all right, all the better

Because I'm sure I've seen it stuck up somewhere in *Big Letters.*

Isn't that just like us? "Hmmm, *Menaechmus* . . ." we say,

Funny how it strikes us . . . "Haven't I seen that somewhere today?"

But, not to lead you astray,

I hereby officially announce, pronounce, and relay

The fact that both twins henceforth have identical names.

> Now, my feet must head Epidamnuswards, for the claims

Of this complicated plot I must measure by the foot; this explains,

I hope, how metricalloused my rhythmic diet may be.

To survey this plot I must personally run on and see

Where it happens to be ambling along itself, iambically.

And if any of you out there have something you'd like me to do

At Epidamnus for you, speak up and let me know.

Don't forget what things cost, though; I'll need some dough.

If you don't tip you're bound to be rooked, even though

When you do tip you'll also be had, for the money will flow

Even farther; the less you hold on to, the more you let go.

> Anyway, here I am back where I started. I stand as

I originally did when I came out and ran on. Epidamnus

Is the name of the place, you remember the merchant of which

Kidnaped the twin other brother. Being very rich,

But childless, he adopted the boy to add interest to his life,

And invested as well for his son in a suitable wife

With a juicy dowry, to marry, and arranged his whole life

By making Menaechmus his heir, when he passed away.

Not bad for a lad whose dad was a thief, wouldn't you say?

And curiously enough, that end came around rather
   soon;
For the merchant was out in the country, not far from
   town
On a day it had rained very hard, and started across
   a river.
Darned if that body-snatching sliver of a river didn't
   deliver
The kidnaper himself into the hands of his jailer forever,
And clap the chap off the scene in death's unseen trap.
Menaechmus promptly inherited a fortune; although
   kidnaped,
He is very well off in Epidamnus. He feels quite at ease
And at home with his funds. And guess now, just who
   would breeze
Into town just today with his slave on the run right
   behind him?
Menaechmus (you like this?) to search for his brother,
   and find him,
Perhaps . . . we'll see about that. *Twins Billed to Appear*
At Epidamnus today. Of course, they wouldn't be here
Not a bit of it, if our plot didn't admit of it, but *there*
Wherever the story demanded, and in that case I'd steer
You to the right destination and make the situation clear.
        In the acting profession things tend to change:
           the town
The play's in, the actor's part, the lines handed down
He has to say. That house front behind me, for instance,
Depends for its very existence on the playwright's
   insistence
In installing inside it the characters he would provide it
With, and let live a moment; not even reside, it
Appears, but multiply or divide there. Shifty as the
   truth,
It houses an oldster, kings, beggars, gangsters, a youth;
A sharp-witted bellyaching sponger, any kind of quack
You can think of, the real one, the fake. Our profession
   is kind,
And makes room for all. Like me, the actors will remind
You of the double dealings dwelling anon in our comedy.
I'm off and away now, just going down on one knee
To hope you'll applaud us: smile on poor Plautus
        And Not Frown on Me!

Act One

scene one

[PENICULUS.

Peniculus

The boys all call me Peniculus, which may sound
   ridiculous
But just means *Table Duster* and shows *How Able an
   Adjuster*
I am to dinner and meticulous in clearing off the table:
You can call me Soft Hairbrush: It seems to be my fate
To be famous as a famished feaster and wear such a tail
   plate.
   You know, some men chain down their captives,
      and they shackle
The legs of runaway slaves. I think *that's* ridiculous,
To load still worse weight on a badly enough burdened
   crate.
If you put pressure on him, the underdog *wants* to get up
And take off, and never do another stroke of work.
Somehow, they'll always wriggle loose, file off the link
Or knock the lock to bits with a rock. Are chains worth
   the pains?
If you'd like to rope someone in, so he doesn't feel
Like escaping, snare him with wine and a meal!
You're putting a ring through his nose when you take
   him to dinner.
And as long as you keep him well stocked with food
   and liquor,
Regularly and the way he likes it, he'll stick with you,
Even though he's under heavy sentence. He'll want to
   serve you;
As long as you're bound to give him food, he's bound
   to eat it.

The nets and meshes of food are remarkably strong
And elastic, and squeeze even tighter when they get
    long.
I'm off to Menaechmus' at the moment, where I've
    signed on
To appear for dinner. I volunteer gaily for a jail
Like his, especially at meals. He doesn't feed, he deals
With his guests, increasing their status; like a good
    restauranteur
He doesn't diagnose, he offers a cure. This sharp epicure
Puts out a very fine spread, he doesn't spare the courses;
He builds up skyscrapers of dishes—you see something
    delicious
And have to stand up on the couch and stretch out to
    reach it
Over all the other things that look nearly as luscious.
I've been out of commission for quite a long intermission,
Not in the preferred position at Menaechmus' house,
    but at home,
Domiciled and dominated by my own little sweetmeats.
    Those treats
I provide for myself and my near ones have proved
    dear ones,
Thanks to my expensive tastes—and they all go to waist.
So I'm drumming myself out of those ranks, not burning
    up money
Trooping in with food for the group. Instead, I'm turning
    tummy
To Menaechmus' place. He may just embrace my com-
    pany. Here he comes now
Flouncing out of the house—looks like they've had a row.

scene two

[PENICULUS *and* MENAECHMUS I.

Menaechmus I

If you weren't such a mean, prying snoop,
You stoop, you'd see that when I blow up
It's *your* fault. You'd better stop, or
I'll pack you right back to your papa,
Drooping out-of-doors, divorced, good and proper.
    Every time I go for a walk, you let go a squawk

And assault me with questions. Where am I going?
What's doing? Where? What's *that* I've got there?
I didn't bring home a wife, I brought home a hawk-
Eyed customs inspector, an unconscientious objector
To everything I do. One who makes me *declare*
Everything I've got in mind. Oh woemankind!
Personal effects, you defect detective. Oh, the heck
    with it!
I guess I've spoiled you with too much attention
And turned this into a house of detention.
From now on, things will be different. I'm here to
    mention
What I expect or else from your lie detector: shelves
    full of silence;
No more prying, my high-powered Highness; absolute,
    utter compliance.
I gave you money and clothes,
Robes and dresses, domestics;
I've been pretty good and elastic
In meeting your demands.
You keep your hands, and your nose,
Out of my business. That's the best trick
To play if you want to stay on good terms with me.
Why look over, inspect, and go right on shaking
The man who's made you a major in his own
    homemaking?
To prove that you can't fence me in, I've promised today
To take a girl out to dinner and reward you that way.

Peniculus

Taking it out on his wife? Taking that line
Won't ruin his wife but will leave me out on a limb.

Menaechmus I

Ah now, by God, and good show! I've finally told my
    wife where to go:
Inside, and to leave me alone. Now where are you
    uxorious types, all of you
Out there, you who ought to be oozing up front to
    shower your thanks
On me for fighting the good fight? And look what I've
    done, each and every one
Of you, my fellow sufferers. I've taken this delicate
    mantilla-dress

Out of my wife's most favorite chest, to present to
    my girl.
An excellent trick, don't you think, to reward the
    warden
By stealing something right from under her nose? I
    propose
A subject for congratulations: this beautifully planned,
Charming little crime, dutifully and well carried out:
Converting a legalized loss to a preferable self-ruination.
Diverting the loot from the foe's hands to those of our
    allies.

Peniculus
I say there, young fellow, what share in the prize can I
Hope to realize?

Menaechmus I
God! I've dropped into a trap!

Peniculus
Not at all, a fortified position.

Menaechmus I
                        Who in perdition
Are you?

Peniculus
Fine, thanks, who are you? I'm me, as a matter of fact.

Menaechmus I
Oh, you. My most modern convenience, you beautifully
    timed supergadget!

Peniculus
Greetings.

Menaechmus I
What are you doing at the moment?

Peniculus
                        Fervently latching
Onto the hand of my right-hand man.

Menaechmus I
                    You couldn't be stringing along
At a better time than this that's bringing you on into
    my orbit.

Peniculus
> That's how I usually time my launching forth in search
> of a luncheon.
> I've studied, got the thing down pat, I don't just play
> my hunches.

Menaechmus I
> Want to feast your eyes on a sparkling treat I've
> completed
> The arrangements for?

Peniculus
> It'll look less crooked to me when I see
> Who's cooked it up. If there's been any slip-up in
> preparing this fête
> I'll know when I see what's left untouched on the plate.

Menaechmus I
> Say, you've seen the famous painting plastered against
> a wall
> Showing the eagle ferrying off that handsome sort of
> fancy-bred boyfriend
> To his handler in the sky? Or the one that shows Venus'
> and Adonis'
> Bare . . . ?

Peniculus
> Kneeness? Sure, lots of times, but what do I care
> about art?

Menaechmus I
> Just look at me? Don't I do that part to perfection?

Peniculus
> Cahn't sigh I'm accustomed to a costume . . . what the
> hell is that you're wearing?

Menaechmus I
> Aren't I the apple of your eye, your Prince Charming?
> Come on, say it.

Peniculus
> Not until I know what time dinner is and whether
> I'm invited.

Menaechmus I
> Why not be so disarming as to admit what I ask you to?

Peniculus

All right, all right, Prince, you're charming.

Menaechmus I

Anything else

You'd like to add voluntarily?

Peniculus

Well, that's a fairly airily merrily
Wingspread you've got there.

Menaechmus I

More, more! Makes me *soar!*

Peniculus

Damned if I'll say any more, by God in heaven, until
I get some whiff
Of what my reward will be if. You've had a row with
your wife.
I'd better look out warily carefully, my life is in danger.

Menaechmus I

Incidentally, my wife hasn't a clue about where we're
going to do
The town today. We're going to set the hot spots on
fire.

Peniculus

Well, thank heavens, now you make sense. How soon
do I light the pyre?
The day's half used up already, dead down to the navel.

Menaechmus I

You're slowing up the show, interrupting with that
drivel.

Peniculus

Knock out my eye, Menaechmus, dig it into the ground,
bash it
Back and below till it comes out my ankle, if I ever
make a sound
From now on, except to say what you order me to.

Menaechmus I

Just step over here, away from my door.

Peniculus

How's this for size?

Menaechmus I

A little farther, please.

Peniculus

It's a breeze. How's this? Far enough?

Menaechmus I

Now, step out, like a man safe out of reach of the
lion's den.

Peniculus

By God in heaven, if you wouldn't make the best
jockey.

Menaechmus I

How come?

Peniculus

You keep looking back over your shoulder to see
If your wife isn't thudding up behind you.

Menaechmus I

You're telling me?

Peniculus

I'm telling you? Well, fellow, I'm not telling you
anything,
Let's get that clear; just what you want to hear, or
you don't.
That much I'll say, or I won't. I'm your best yes man yet.

Menaechmus I

All right, let's have a guess, then, at what you can
make of
This garment I'm exposing to your nose. What sort of
scent
Does it put you on the trail of . . . ? Why get pale
and shove it out of range?

Peniculus

Strange, it doesn't put me on the trail of, it pins me
to the tail of . . .
Look here, old boy, you know as well as I do, men
shouldn't try to
Imbibe the fragrance of feminine apparel except from
up near the top
Of same dainty. Down lower the unwashed part makes
you feel fainty.

Menaechmus I

> All right, Peniculus, try this part over here; tickle
> your nose
> With this wholesome whiff. Aha! Now you make like
> truffles.

Peniculus

> Sure, it suits my snuffles.

Menaechmus I

> Oh, puffle, come on and say,
> Say what it tells you. What sort of smells you deduce.

Peniculus

> Phew, what a naral escape! I'm glad to produce my
> solution.
> This is my diagnosis: You steal a *jeune fille* for a meal;
> You purloin a *fräulein* for some sirloin; you flirt with
> a skirt
> And alert your tastebuds to a smorgasbord; a distress
> And theft, and this dress is left for your mistress to
> drape round
> Her; gleaming napery; conjugal japery, all very vapory.
> The whole deal,
> From my point of view, leads straight toward an
> excellent meal, and I'm joining you.

Menaechmus I

> Don't! I'm not coming apart. But you've hit
> The female suggestion on the head, no question, and
> orated convincingly.
> For I've pretty winsomely sneaked this dress from
> my wife
> And am spiriting it off to the niftiest mistress of mine,
> Désirée. I'm ordering a banquet, this very day
> For you and me, a treat at her place.

Peniculus

> Oh, I say!

Menaechmus I

> We'll drink from now till tomorrow's morning star
> puts out
> This night so bibulous.

Peniculus

> I say, you *are* fabulous. Shall I knock
> At Désirée's door?

Menaechmus I

Sure, go ahead. No, better knock off.
Hold it! I said.

Peniculus

You're the one that's holding it: my head
Wants to get at that bottle, not back off a mile in the
distance.

Menaechmus I

Knock very gently.

Peniculus

The door, evidently, 's the consistency
Of papyrus.

Menaechmus I

Knock off, I insist, do desist! God in heaven!
Lay off or I'll knock your block off! And besides, rub
your eyes:
Can't you see? Here she comes out, herself, free and
easy. Her body
Eclipses the sun. An excellent exit, dancing
Into view like this; she wins more acclaim than the
flame
Of the sun. He goes quite blind, when I find her so
entrancing.

scene three

[DÉSIRÉE, PENICULUS, *and* MENAECHMUS I.

Désirée

Oh, my dear, *dear* Menaechmus, how *are* you today?

Peniculus

Hey, say!
What about me? Don't I rate a greeting?

Désirée

Zero, you cipher.

Peniculus

Well, a soldier has to get used to being a serial
number, I guess.

Menaechmus I

Now darling look here, I would love to have you go
and fix up . . .

Peniculus

Ohhh, fray can you see? Let's have us a mix-up: you
be the smorgas

And I'll come aboard you. We'll fight it out all day;
ohhh, I say . . .

Till the dawn's early light, which of us battlers is the
heavier weight

When it comes to hitting the bottle. Daisy, you can be
the general,

And feel free to choose which company you'll spend
the duration

Of this dark operation with. Let's hope your proper
ration is . . . me.

Menaechmus I

Sweet and lovely! How loathly my wife appears in
my eyes

When they light on you.

Peniculus

Meanwhile you put on her things
And wifey still clings to you.

Désirée

What in the world . . . ?

Menaechmus I

I'm unfurled.

My dear girl. Here's the dress I deprive my wife of
and provide

You with. You look better in her clothes than she does
without them,

My rose.

Désirée

Touché or not touché, I must say I must give way

To so super-sartorial an assault on my virtue. You win
the day.

Peniculus

Listen to the mistress whisper sweet somethings, as
long as

She sees he's bringing her that gay thing for nothing.
Now is

The time, if you love her, to have what you want of her
In the form of some toothsome kisses.

Menaechmus I

                            Oh, hang up, Brush Face.
I've only done just what I swore I would with this garment: placed
It on the altar of her grace.

Peniculus

                         By God in heaven, I give in!
Listen, *twist* in it, won't you? I can see you in the ballet, like a fine
Boy, a dear for the dance, with the veil trailing behind your tight pants.

Menaechmus I

Dance, me? By God in heaven, you're crazy.

Peniculus

                                Me, crazy?
I'd say, easy does it, *you* may be *that* way instead, in your head.

Désirée

If you're not going to wear it, take it off then. And stop saying
"By God in heaven!"

Menaechmus I

                        After all, I won this today by playing
A pretty dangerous game; I stole it.

Peniculus

                     On the whole, it's even more fraying
To the nerves than Hercules (or "heavenly God," if you please)
Swerving round those curves to steal Hippolyta's girdle and sneak off swaying.
I'd say you were in more mortal danger than that thievish stranger
Ever ran into, even though he was stronger.

Menaechmus I

                             I can no longer
Hold back this offer I proffer to you, Désirée. So do have it,
You wonderful girl, sole creature alive sympathetic to my wants.

Désirée
> This is the true-hearted sort of fervor nature should
> > always transplant
> In the souls of romancers whose desires are their
> > favorite haunts.

Peniculus
> Or at least sharp sparks going broke at full speed
> > chasing spooks.

Menaechmus I
> I bought it for my wife last year. $85.00.

Peniculus
> We can close the books on that sum and kiss it good-by.

Menaechmus I
> And now can you guess what I want to do?

Désirée
> > > > > Yes, I know
> And what's more, I'll do what you want.

Menaechmus I
> > > > Dinner for three,
> Chez Daisy. Order this done and I'll be pleased.

Peniculus
> > > > And say, see
> While you're at it that whoever goes to buy the food at
> > the forum
> Picks out something specially tasty; a perfect little
> > pork filet
> Or savory thin-sliced prosciutto, ham recherché,
> Like a succulent half-section head of a pig—let's do it
> > the big way,
> And have that ham so well cooked that I can pounce
> > on the table like a hawk
> Who knows what he likes, and then strikes. And let's
> > make it quick.

Désirée
> > > By Jiminy, yes! You're on!

Menaechmus I
> > > That's very nice, the way you didn't
> Say "By God in heaven." Me and old slothful here,
> > we're heading down-

Town to hang around the forum and see what's up.
    We'll be right back.
While dinner's cooking, we'll start with the drinking.

Désirée

Come on
Along whenever you want. Things will be ready.

Menaechmus I

But do get a steady move on.
Now let's go, and let's you keep up.

Peniculus

By God in heaven, how true!
I'll follow you all right and I'll slave for you too. If I
    lost you
Today and got all the wealth in heaven, I wouldn't
    break even.

[*Exeunt* MENAECHMUS I *and* PENICULUS.

Désirée

[*Alone.*]
    I wonder why they always say "God in heaven"?
    Where else could he be?
    You, girls in there! Call out Mixmaster, the head cook,
    And tell him to come outside here. I need him this
        minute.

[*Enter* MIXMASTER.]
    Take this shopping basket, my man, and, yes, here's
        some money;
    Let's see . . . $9.63.

Mixmaster

Right you are, miss.

Désirée

Now scoot, Sonny-boy
And get on with your catering. Buy enough for three
    people only,
No more, no less.

Mixmaster

Who's coming?

Désirée

Menaechmus, and that lonely
Crowd of his, Soft Hair, the never-to-be-brushed off,
    plus me.

Mixmaster

Well, Miss, that's three *times* three plus one, actually:
Peniculus eats enough for eight, and you both make
two.

Désirée

I've given out the guest list. The rest of this is up
to you.

Mixmaster

Right you are, Miss. The dinner is as good as all done.
You can all take your places. Won't you all please
sit down?

Désirée

Get going now, you fix-faster, and hurry right back
from town.

Mixmaster

I'll be back here so soon you won't even know I've
been gone.

Act Two

scene one

[MENAECHMUS II *and* MESSENIO.

Menaechmus II

Messenio, I tell you, there's no greater source of delight
For sailors than to look out across the deep water and
sight
The land they're heading for.

Messenio

                I couldn't be more
In agreement, provided the land you refer to is home.
Therefore,
Why in hell, I implore you, are *we* in Epidamnus?

Do you plan to act like the ocean and noisily slam us
Against every damned piece of land we can touch?

Menaechmus II

As much
As I need to cover to locate my own twin, my brother.

Messenio

But how much longer do we have to keep looking for
　　him?
It's six years now since we started. When we departed
You didn't say we'd try everywhere, moseying to
　　Marseilles,
Skirting around Spain, bounding back to menace Venice,
And do the whole coastal *bit* from Trieste to Dubrovnik
　　to Split,
Or skim the whole rim of Italy, littorally. As the sea
Goes, that's where we rows. My point is—a haystack
With the well-known needle in it . . . you'd have found
　　it. But we lack
The object to bring our search to a head. He's quite
　　dead,
The man you're after, while you ransack the land of
　　the living
If he were anywhere around you'd have found him.

Menaechmus II

I won't give in
Until I've found out for sure from someone I have to
　　believe in
Who'll say that he knows that my brother is dead. And
　　when that day
Arrives, our travels are over. But I *won't* stop pursuing
My other half, and I know what I'm doing: he means
Everything to me.

Messenio

You're looking for a knot in a marshmallow reed.
We won't go home until we've gone round the world,
　　then, as fellow
Travelers, and written a book about what it looks like?

Menaechmus II

I doubt it.
But see here, my boy, you just do as you're told; don't
　　be too bold;

Eat your food; be good; don't be a bother. It's not
your good
That matters in this expedition.

Messenio

Take that definition
Of a typical slave's condition. I know who I am now,
all right.
He couldn't have put a bigger proposition in many
fewer words,
Or in so clear a light. Still and all, I just can't keep
stalling
Around; I can't just stop talking. You listening,
Menaechmus?
My purse, I mean, our purse, now that I look at it,
Has too much vacation space; our wardrobe there looks
quite scanty,
Are we going in for summer sports? By God in heaven,
you'll groan,
Exhausted by the search for your twin, unless you turn
back home.
They'll *wham* us in Epidamnus, positive; Dubrovnik
us to clinkers.
The town's chock full of nuts, fast-living long-range
drinkers,
Go-between wheedlers, middlemen who take you, the
stinkers,
In to be cleaned and doused by the masters of the
house,
I mean mistresses, who whisper sweet slopniks to you,
And profit from your losses in the process. That's what
they do,
Damn us strangers in this town. No wonder it's called,
up and down,
Epidamnus; every damn one of us innocents in Greece
Gets introduced here to the golden fleece, before he's
released,
Enormously decreased in value.

Menaechmus II

Take it easy. Hand me that greasy
Wallet.

Messenio

What do you want with it?

Menaechmus II
Your speech has haunted
Me. I'm panicked by your frantic appeal to the facts
of life.

Messenio
Afraid, why afraid for me? . . .

Menaechmus II
You'll whammy us both in Epidamnus.
You're a great lady's man, Messenio: I know you. And I?
I'm a man of many moods, all of which prompt me
to fly
Off the handle in a hurry. And since I'm the furious sort,
And you the luxurious sport, always in pursuit of a skirt,
I'll manage both crises nicely, and simply divert
The money into my control. Then you won't waste the
whole
Thing on women; and I won't get mad when you do;
or even peeved.

Messenio
Take it and keep it then, do. I'm somewhat relieved.

scene two

[MIXMASTER, MENAECHMUS II, *and* MESSENIO.

Mixmaster
I've shopped very shrewdly and well, if I say so myself:
I'll spread a fine feast in front of these dauntless diners.
Oh, oh, Menaechmus, already! I'll bet I'm in for a
beating:
The guests have arrived and here I've just gotten back
From the market. They're walking around in front of
the house;
I'll go up and greet them. Menaechmus, good afternoon!

Menaechmus II
Best wishes, old chap, whoever you happen to be.

Mixmaster
Whoever I'm . . . ? You don't say, Menaechmus, you
don't know?

Menaechmus II
Oh God in heaven, you know I don't.

Mixmaster

But where
Are the rest of our guests?

Menaechmus II

What guests?

Mixmaster

Your parasite, for one.

Menaechmus II
My parasite? Obviously this fellow is quite off his nut.

Messenio
Didn't I tell you this town was lousy with scroungers?

Menaechmus II
Which parasite of mine did you mean, young man?

Mixmaster
Why that peachy little Peniculus, the fuzzy table duster.

Messenio
Oh *him*, peenie brush? He's safe all right, here in
    our bag.

Mixmaster
Menaechmus, you've come along a bit soon for dinner:
I'm just getting back from buying the food.

Menaechmus II
Listen here,
How much does a good box of sure-fire tranquilizers cost
In this town?

Mixmaster

$1.98 for the economy size.

Menaechmus II
Here's $3.96. Get yourself a double prescription.
I can see you're quite out of control, making trouble
    like this
For someone like me you don't even know, whoever
    you are.

Mixmaster
I'm Mixmaster: that's not complicated, and don't
    say you don't know it.

Menaechmus II
You can be Mixmaster, or Sizzling Ham Steak

With Cloves En Brochette,
I couldn't care less. I've never seen you before today
And now that I have, I'm not at all very pleased to
meet you.

Mixmaster
Your name's Menaechmus.

Menaechmus II
You seem to be talking sense
At the moment, since you call me by name, but where
did you learn
Who I am?

Mixmaster
Who you are? When I work for your mistress right
in this house?
Désirée?

Menaechmus II
By God, she's *not* my mistress and I *do not*
Know you.

Mixmaster
Don't know *me,* who pours you out drink after drink
when you come here
For dinner?

Messenio
I wish I could lay hands on something to bat this
nut with.

Menaechmus II
You mix drinks and pour them for *me,* for *me,*
Who never even came this way, much less saw
Epidamnus
Before today?

Mixmaster
Never even saw it, you say?

Menaechmus II
Yes; I mean *no,* dear God in heaven, so help
me, *no!*

Mixmaster
I suppose you don't really live in that house over
there?

Menaechmus II

May the gods cave the roof in hard on whoever
does!

Mixmaster

Stark, raving loony. Wishing himself such bad luck.
Can you hear me, Menaechmus?

Menaechmus II

Depends on what you're saying.

Mixmaster .

Now look, take my advice. Remember that $3.96
You offered to give me a minute ago for the pills?
Go spend it on yourself; you're the one who needs it
the most,
And the soonest, calling down curses, by God in
heaven,
On your very own head. You're just not *all there*,
Menaechmus.
If you've any brains left you'll send out at once for the
medicine;
There's a new triple-dose thing out, The Three Little
Big Tranquilizers,
Frightens off all kinds of weird wolves.

Menaechmus II

He sure talks a lot.

Mixmaster

Of course, Menaechmus always teases me, like this;
he's a joker
When his wife's not around. What's that you're saying
Menaechmus?

Menaechmus II

I beg your pardon, Mixmaster, did you say something?

Mixmaster

How does this stuff look? Like enough for dinner for
three?
Or shall I go out and buy more for the girlfriend
and you
And your parasite pal?

Menaechmus II

Women? Parasite? Pals? What
women, what parasites, pal?

Messenio

Look here, old boy, what terrible crime is weighing on
  your mind
And making you pester him so?

Mixmaster

Stranger boy, you stay out
Of my business; I'll conduct that with the person I know
And am talking to.

Messenio

Oh God in . . . I give up; except for the fact
That I'm sure as can be that this cook is completely
  cracked.

Mixmaster

Well, now, I'll just get busy with these things. I can
  promise you
Some succulent results, very soon. You'll stay around
  the house,
Menaechmus, I hope. Anything else you can think of?

Menaechmus II

I can think of you as one real upside-down cake.
  You're baked.

Mixmaster

Oh by God in . . . somewhere or other, I could swear
  it's you
Who are the mixed-up master. I wish you would go . . .
  lie down
Somewhere until you feel better, while I take this stuff
And commit it to the fire-breathing forces of Vulcan.
  I'll tell
Désirée you're out here. She'll want to ask you in, I
  feel sure.

[*Goes into the house.*

Menaechmus II

Gone, has he? God, how right I see your words were
When you talked about this place.

Messenio

Mark my words further.
One of those fast-working, loose-jointed women lives
  here, you can bet,

As sure as that crackpot cook who went in there said
she did.

Menaechmus II

I do wonder, though, how he came by my name?

Messenio

That's easy.
Why, that's a cinch. The women have it all worked out.
They send their slave boys or housemaids down to
the docks.
When a strange ship comes in, they ask the passenger's
name,
And find out where he's from. Later on, they pick him
up casually
And stick close to him. If their charms have the right
effect
They ship him back home plucked quite clean of his
money.[*Pointing to* DÉSIRÉE's *house.*]
And right over there rocks a fast little pirate sloop at
anchor:
We'd better look out for her, and look sharp,
Commander.

Menaechmus II

Damned if I don't think you're right.

Messenio

I'll know what you think
For sure when I see what preeeeecautions you're
taking.

Menaechmus II

Just a moment.
I hear the door swinging open; let's see who comes out.

Messenio

I'll drop our seabag right here. Heave ho, my bellboys!
You fleet runners, shift this gear into neutral for a while.

scene three

[DÉSIRÉE, MENAECHMUS II, *and* MESSENIO.

Désirée
[*Singing gaily.*]
Open the doors, open wide: I don't want them shut.

You in there, look to it, come here and do it,
What has to be done:
Couches to be hung with fine drapes;
Tables adorned; some incense burned;
Lights set blazing; the place made amazing.
To dazzle and delight your bright lover's heart
Is to play with skill your gay charming part,
And importune at his expense while you make your
    fortune.
           Where is he though? A moment ago, my cook
           said I'd find him standing
Around by the door . . . oh there he is, the one I adore
    when he's handing
His money over freely. I'll ask him in now for the meal
    he wanted made ready
And get him started on the drinks, to keep him from
    staying too steady.
I'll just slip over and speak to him first.
Oh my favorite fellow, my poor heart will burst
If you keep standing here outside
When the doors to our house are open wide
To take you in. It's much more your place,
This house, than your own home is, an embrace,
A bright smile on its face just for you, and a kiss
On that most generous of mouths. This really is your
    house.
And now all is prepared just the way you wanted
And shortly we'll serve you your dinner and pour out
    the wine. [*Pause.*]
I said, the meal's all in order, just as you commanded;
Whenever you're ready, come on in now, honey, any
    time.

Menaechmus II

Who in the world does this woman think she's talking to?

Désirée

To you, that's who.

Menaechmus II

                But what business have I with you
At present, or what have I ever had to do with you up
    to now?

Désirée

Heavens! It's you that Venus has inspired me to prize

Over all the others, and you've certainly turned out to
    be worth it.

Heavens above! You've set me up high enough with
    your generous gifts!

Menaechmus II

This woman is surely quite crazy or definitely drunk,
Messenio, talking such intimate stuff to me
A man she doesn't even know.

Messenio

                  I told you so!

And now, it's only the leaves that are falling, just wait;
Spend three more days in this town and the trees
    themselves
Will be crashing down down on your head. The women
    are biased,
Buy us this, buy us that, and buzzing around for your
    money.
But let me talk to her. Hey, sweetie, I'm speaking
    to you.

Désirée

You're what?

Messenio

No, I'm not, I'm who. And while I'm at it, just *where*
Did you get to know the man here who's with me
    so well?

Désirée

Why, right here in Epidamnus, where I've been for so
    long.

Messenio

Epidamnus? A place he never set foot in before today?

Désirée

A *delicious* joke, you rascal. Now, Menaechmus, darling,
Won't you come in? You'll feel much cozier and settled.

Menaechmus II

By God, the woman's quite right to call me by my
    own name.
Still I can't help wondering what's up.

Messenio

                She's got wind of your moneybag,

The one you relieved me of.

Menaechmus II
And damned if you didn't alert me
To that very thing. Here, you'd better take it. That way,
I can find out for sure whether she's after me, or my
money.

Désirée
Andiam', O caro bene! And we'll tuck right into that
meal;
Mangiamo, igitur, et cetera.

Menaechmus II
Music to my ears,
And you're very nice to sing it, my dear. I only regret
I cannot accept.

Désirée
But why in the world did you tell me, a short while ago,
To have dinner ready for you?

Menaechmus II
I told *you* to have dinner ready?

Désirée
Of course, dinner for three, you, your parasite, and me.

Menaechmus II
Oh hell, lady, what the hell is all this parasite stuff?
God, what a woman! She's crazy as can be once again.

Désirée
Cookie duster Peniculus, C. D. Peniculus, the crumb
devourer.

Menaechmus II
But I mean what kind of a peniculus? We all know
that's a soft hair
Brush, but I don't know anyone *named* that. You mean
my ridiculous
Little thing, the traveling shoebrush I carry for my suede
sandals,
The better to buff them with? What peniculus hangs so
close to me?

Désirée
You know I mean that local leech who just now came
by with you

When you brought me that sweet silk dress you stole
   from your wife.

Menaechmus II

I gave you a dress, did I? One I stole from my wife?
You're sure? I'd swear you were asleep, like a horse
   standing up.

Désirée

Oh gosh, what's the fun of making fun of me and
   denying
Everything you've done?

Menaechmus II

                              Just tell me what I'm denying.

Désirée

That you gave me today your wife's most expensive silk
   dress.

Menaechmus II

All right, I deny that. I'm not married. And I've never
   been married.
And I've never come near this port since the day I
   was born,
Much less set foot in it. I dined on board ship, dis-
   embarked,
And ran into you.

Désirée

   Some situation! I'm nearly a wreck. What's that ship
You're talking about?

Menaechmus II

                        Oh, an old prewar propeller job,
Wood and canvas, patched in a million places;
   transportation,
I guess, runs on force of habit. She's got so many pegs
Pounded in now, one right up against the next, she looks
   like the rack
You see in a fur-seller's store where the strips are hung
   all in a row.

Désirée

Oh, do stop now, please, making fun, and come on in
   with me.

Menaechmus II

My dear woman, you're looking for some other man,
not me.

Désirée

I don't know you, Menaechmus? the son of Moschus,
Born at Syracuse in Sicily, when Agathocles ruled,
And after him, Phintia; then Leporello passed on the
power
After his death to Hiero, so that Hiero is now the man
in control?

Menaechmus II

Well, that information seems certainly accurate, Miss.

Messenio

By God Himself! Is the woman *from* Syracuse to have
This all down so pat?

Menaechmus II

By the various gods, I don't see
How I can now really decline that offer she's making.

Messenio

Please do, I mean *don't* step over that doorstep!
You're gone if you do.

Menaechmus II

Pipe down. This is working out well.
I'll admit to anything she says, if I can just take
advantage
Of the good time in store. Mademoiselle, a moment ago
I was holding back on purpose, afraid that my wife
might hear
About the silk dress and our dinner date. I'm all set
Now, anytime you are.

Désirée

You won't wait for Soft Hair?

Menaechmus II

No, let's brush *him* off; I don't care a whisker if he
never, . . .
And besides, when he does, I don't want him let in.

Désirée

Heavens to Castor!

I'm more than happy to comply with that one. But now,
Just one thing, darling, you know what I'd like you
to do?

Menaechmus II
All you need do is name it.

Désirée
That sweet silk dress: send it over
To the Persian's place, the embroiderer's shop. I want
It taken in, and a pattern I've specially designed added
to it.

Menaechmus II
What a good idea! It won't look at all like the dress
I stole, if my wife should happen to meet you in town.

Désirée
Good. Take it with you, then, when you go.

Menaechmus II
Yes, of course.

Désirée
And now let's go on in.

Menaechmus II
Right away. I've just got to speak
To him for a minute. Hey, Messenio, hop over here!

Messenio
What's cooking?

Menaechmus II
Jump, boy.

Messenio
What's all the hurry?

Menaechmus II
We're all the hurry, that's what. I know what you'll say.

Messenio
You're a dope.

Menaechmus II
Nope, I'm a fiend. I've already stolen some loot.
Real loot. This is a big deal: Operation Mix-up.
And I'm one up already without even throwing up
earthworks.

Race off, fast as you can, and drape all those sea
  troops [*points to the sailors.*]
In the local bar, on the double. Stay where you are then,
Until just before sunset, when it's time to come pick
  me up.

Messenio

Really, Commander, you're not *on* to those call girls.

Menaechmus II

You manage your affairs, I'll handle mine, and you
Can hang up and stay there. If I get into trouble, it's me
Who'll suffer for it, not you. That girl isn't crazy, she's
  dumb
And doesn't know what's up, at least as far as I can see,
Or where could this high-priced, pretty little dress have
  come from?

[*Exit.*

Messenio

I give up. You've gone, have you? In there? You're
  gone,
And done for. The pirate ship's got the rowboat on
  the run,
And you'll end up in the drink, *Menaechmus on the
  rocks.*
But who. am I, a dumb slave, to try to outfox
That woman, with my hopes of showing Menaechmus
  the ropes?
He bought me to listen to him: I'm not in command.
Come on, kids, let's do what he says. But I'll be on hand
Later on, as he wanted, and drag him out to dry land.

Act Three

scene one

[PENICULUS.

Peniculus

In all my born days—and it's more than thirty years'
  worth—I've never

Pulled a boner like this, I'm a trecherous fiend, and
this time
I guess I've really transgressed. Imagine my missing
a meal!
And why? I got involved in listening to a public speech
And while I stood around gawking, all open mouth
and ears,
Menaechmus made his getaway and got back to his girl,
And didn't want *me* along, I suppose. May the heavenly
gods
Crack down on whoever it was that thought up public
speeches,
That invented this out-of-doors way to use up people's
good time
Who haven't any. Shouldn't the audience consist only
of those
With time on their hands? And shouldn't they perhaps
be fined
If they fail to attend those meetings where someone
gets up
In public and starts sounding off? There are people
enough
With nothing much to do, who eat only one meal a
day,
Never dine out, or have guests in, and it's to them
the duty
To show up at meetings or official functions should be
assigned.
If I hadn't stuck around today to listen, I wouldn't
Have lost out on the dinner Menaechmus invited
Me to come to—and I do think he meant it, as sure
as I can see
I'm alive. I'll show up, anyway, on the off-chance
There's still something left; the mere hope makes
my mouth water.
What's this I see? Menaechmus *leaving*, well looped?
That means *dinner's over:* by God, my timing is perfect.
I'll hide over here and watch a bit to see what he does
Before I go up to my host and give him a buzz.

scene two

[MENAECHMUS II *and* PENICULUS.

Menaechmus II

Calm down in there, woman! I'll bring the dress back
soon enough,
Expertly, so charmingly changed you won't even
know it.

Peniculus

Dinner's done, the wine's all gone, the parasite's lost,
And *he's* off to the couturier, with that dress in tow.
Is *that* so? I'm not who I am if I take this last bit
In my stride, lying down. Watch how I handle that
garment worker.

Menaechmus II

I thank you, immortal gods, each and all of you.
On whom have you ever showered so many good gifts
As you have on me today? And who could have hoped
for them less?
I've dined, I've wined, I've reclined, and at very close
quarters,
With one of the most delicious daughters . . . well, I've
had it in the best sense
Of that past tense. And here I am at present, still gifted
With a precious piece of silk. No one else will inherit
These convertible goods, much less wear it. How high
am I, its
Heir—O!

Peniculus

Hell, I can't hear from over here—did he say "hair,"
though?
That's my cue to brush in, isn't it, and sweep up my
share?
Hair today and bald tomorrow . . . Drink to me only
with mayonnaise . . .
I'll demand re-dressing . . . I'll scrape something out of
this mess yet.

Menaechmus II

She said I stole it from my wife and gave it to her.
When I realized how wrong she was, of course I began
To agree with everything she said, as if we agreed
On whatever it was we were doing. Need I say more?
I never had so good a time for so little money.

Peniculus

Here I go; I'm raring to get in my licks.

Menaechmus II

Well, well, who's this comes to see me?

Peniculus

What's that you say,
You featherhead, you worst of all possible, good-for-
    nothing . . . man?
Man? You're not even a mistake, you're a premeditated
    crime,
That's what you are, you shifty little good-for-nothing
    . . . I just said that . . .
So-and-so. And so you spirited yourself away
From me at the forum a while ago, and celebrated my
    funeral
At this cheerful dinner your friend just couldn't attend?
Some nerve, when you said I was invited to share it
    with you.

Menaechmus II

Look, kiddo, what's with it, with you and me, that
    can make
You curse out a man you don't even know? Would you
    like
A nice hole in the head in return for turning loose
    your lip?

Peniculus

God damn it to God damn. That hole's already in my
    stomach,
You gave my mouth the slip.

Menaechmus II

What's your name, kid,
Anyway? Spit that much out.

Peniculus

Still being funny,
As if you didn't know?

Menaechmus II

As far as I know, no.
God knows I never saw you before today, never knew
    you,

Whoever you are. I do know, though, if you don't
Get funny with me I won't make it hard for you.

Peniculus
For heck's sake, Menaechmus, wake up!

Menaechmus II
                                    For Hercules' sake,
I'm up and walking around. I'm completely convinced
    of it.

Peniculus
But you don't recognize me?

Menaechmus II
                        If I did, I wouldn't say I didn't.

Peniculus
You don't know your old parasite pal?

Menaechmus II
                            It's your old paralyzed dome
That's slipped, or cracked. You'd better have it patched
up and fixed.

Peniculus
All right. Here's a question for you. Did you, or did
    you not,
Sneak a dress out from under your own wife's nose
    today,
And give it to dear Désirée?

Menaechmus II
                        For Hercle's sake, no.
I don't happen to be married, and I didn't happen to
Give it to Désirée, and I didn't happen to fasten onto
A dress. Are you quite sure you've got it in the head,
    enough?

Peniculus
Well, that's that, I guess. *Caput! E pluribus* be none.
Of course I didn't meet you coming out of your house
    and wearing
The dress, just a while ago?

Menaechmus II
        Ohhhhh for *sex'* sake! [*Very effeminate sibilants.*]
You think we're all fairy fine fellows just because you're
    such

A *native* dancer, in a perfect fright at what's under our
    tights?
You say I put on a dress, and I wore it?

Peniculus
Could of swore it, on Hercules' head.

Menaechmus II
                           Don't bring him up,
He was a he-man, but you aren't even a me-man:
You don't even know who you are or I am, you
    absolute nut.
You'd better take the cure; you're asking for trouble
    from the gods.

Peniculus
Yeee gods, that's it! Now nobody's going to stop me
    from going
Straight to your wife to spill the beans about you and
    your schemes.
You've creamed me, and I'm whipped. But banquet boy,
    just you wait
Until this stuff starts coming back at you. That dinner
    you ate
And I never got to, is going to give you bad dreams.

Menaechmus II
What's going on around here? Is everyone I see
Planted here on purpose to make fun of me? And
    what for?
And here comes another, whoever it is, out that door.

scene three

[MENAECHMUS II *and* MAID.

Maid
Menaechmus, Désirée would like you to take
This bracelet to the jeweler's, as long as you're going
    downtown
With the dress, and have this piece of gold worked
    into it.

Menaechmus II
Oh, glad to take care of both things, of course, and
    anything

Else you want done along those lines; you only need
  mention it.

Maid

You remember the bracelet, don't you?

Menaechmus II

It's just a gold bracelet.

Maid

But this is the one you sneaked out of your wife's
  jewel box
And stole from her.

Menaechmus II

I don't do things like that, I'm damned sure.

Maid

Well, if you don't recognize it . . . look, you'd better
  give it back to me.

Menaechmus II

Hold on . . . I think I do remember it now. . . .
Yes, that's the one I gave her, that's it all right.
But where are the armlets I gave Désirée when I
  gave her
The bracelet?

Maid

You never gave her no armlets at all.

Menaechmus II

Oh yes, that's right, it was just the bracelet, come
  to think of it.

Maid

Can I tell her you'll have this fixed up?

Menaechmus II

Yes, I'll take care of it.

Maid

And look, be a dear, and have him design me some
  earrings,
Won't you, teardrop style, six dollars of gold work
  in each?
If you do, you'll be *persona* terribly *grata* to me, your
Obedient, co-operative servant, the next time you visit.

Menaechmus II

    Why of course. Just give me the gold, and I'll stand
the cost
    Of having it set.

Maid

            Oh, you furnish the gold, why don't you?
And I'll pay you back later.

Menaechmus II

               No, no, after you, my fair lady.
    You let me pay ypu back later, and I'll pay twice
as much.

Maid

    I don't have the gold at the moment.

Menaechmus II

               When you get it, I'll take it.

Maid

    Is there anything else, kind sir?

Menaechmus II

             No, just say I'll handle this.
[*Exit* MAID.]
    And make a quick turnover on the market value of
the stuff.
    She's gone in? Yes, I see she's closed the door.
    The gods must be on my side the way they're helping
me out,
    Enriching me, and doing me favors. But why hang
around
    When now is my chance to get away and out of reach
    Of these foxy and, I must say, sexy confidence women?
    Come on, Menaechmus, my boy, my own likeness, enjoy
    Your rapture; and pick up your feet, old chap, let those
sandals slap.
    Here goes the laurel lie for today [*throws it right*], but
I think I'll go this way,
    In case they come looking for me; they can follow
this lead
    In the wrong direction. I'll dash off and make enough
speed
    To head off my slave, I hope, and tell that good lad
    The good news about the goods we've acquired. Won't
he be glad?

Act Four

scene one

[WIFE *of* MENAECHMUS *and* PENICULUS.

Wife

I suppose I'm supposed to submit to total frustration
Because I married a man who steals everything in
the house
He can lay hands on and carts it off to his mistress?

Peniculus

Not so loud, please. You'll catch him with the goods,
I promise.
Come over here. Now look over there. He was taking
Your dress to the couturier; he was well looped and
weaving
Downtown with the same dress he snuck from your
closet today.
And look, there's the laurel loop he had on, lying on
the ground.
Now do you believe me? He must have gone in that
direction,
If you'd like to follow up his tracks. Hey, we're in luck:
Here he comes back, just this moment; but not with
the dress.

Wife

What should I do?

Peniculus

Oh, what you always do, start nagging,
Nag him to pieces; don't take it, let him have it, I say.
Meanwhile, let's duck over here on the sly and not
let him
See us. He'll tangle himself in the birdcatchers' net.

289

scene two

[WIFE, PENICULUS, *and* MENAECHMUS I.

Menaechmus 1

This is some social system we've got going here,
The troublesome custom of patrons and clients:
Bothersome clients, and jittery patrons, who fear
They may not have a big enough following. Compliance
And conformity to habit require even the best of us
To just make the most of it; and as for the rest of those
Trapped in place in the status race, let's face it,
They're coming at us, pushing forward from the ends
To swell out the middle. And it isn't *fides*, it's *res*
That matters in the clientele deal, which depends,
Not on the client's value as man and as friend,
But simply on his assets. Money is what he's worth
And you must amass it to show off less dearth
Of a deficit than the next aristocrat. You give a wide
     berth
To the poor man who needs you, however fine he may
     seem,
But if some rich bastard shows up and wants you to use
Your influence, you're ready to go to any extreme
To hang onto him. That's the scheme, and does it
     confuse
Us poor patrons with a gang of fast-breaking scofflaws
To stand up for in court? Thereby hang the loss
And the profits for us poor patricians. The clients'
     position
Is: pressure on the middle. He's got the money,
We've got the rank, we need his dough and he needs
     our thanks.
It's only lucky the prolies don't rate either of any;
Thank heavens, they're not powerful, just many.
          I'm from a good family and entitled to go into court
And represent as I wish some client who's short
Of the necessary social credentials. And, confidentially,
I say a lot that I wish I didn't have to. A lawyer can
     manage
To do this pretty well if he concentrates on it; and
     damages

Are his principal concern: to collect for, to sue for,
    to affirm
What is said to be false, and deny what is said to be
    true for.
On behalf of some client whose character makes him
    squirm
He will bribe the witnesses or rehearse them in what
    to do.
When the client's case comes up on the calendar, of
    course
That's a day we have to be on hand too, and be
    resourceful
In speaking up professionally in defense of his actions,
    awful
And impossible to defend though they are.
It's either a private hearing at the bar;
Or a public proceeding before a jury with people in
    the congregation;
Or a third form it takes is what you would call
    arbitration,
When a mediator is appointed to decide this special
    situation.
Well, today a client of mine had me right on the ropes;
His case came up as a private hearing, and my hopes
Of doing what I'd planned to today, and doing
It with the person I wanted to, have drooped and
    dropped near to ruin;
He kept me and kept me; there was angle after angle.
He was obviously at fault, with his wrong, tangled
Illegal action, and I knew it when I went in.
So in arguing the case I laid it on pretty thin,
And pleaded *extenuating circumstances;* that's a logical
    maze
And a judge's jungle, but a lawyer's paradise.
I summed up the case in the most complicated terms
I could summon up, overstating, sliding words like
    worms
Off the track, leaving a lot out when the need
Of the argument indicated, and the magistrate agreed
To drop the proceedings; he granted permission
For a settlement by *sponsio.*
There's a legal ounce for you, of the words we pronounce
    in due process,

Full of awful, responsible-sounding phrases like: I
promise
You this *sponsio* I owe you, et cetera. What it comes
down to
Is that a civil hearing can be brought to an end by
payment
Of a fixed fee known as a forfeit or *sponsio*, a defrayment
Of the expenses plus a sum added on: call it "costs
And considerations" if you will, in consideration for
the lost
Time and money involved. What happened today was
that I
Had worked hard and fast to convince the judge that my
Client should be allowed to settle for costs and
considerations.
The judge came around; and I was set to leave for
the celebration
Of a good time at Désirée's party, when what did my
other smarty party
Of a client pull but an "Oh, well . . . I don't know
about that *sponsio* . . .
I don't think I ought to flounce in with a lot of money
all at once
You know . . . I'm not so sure I've even got it. Are
you sure
That's the way we want it to go, the case, et cetera?"
The totally pure
Imbecile, caught redhanded, absolutely without a legal
leg to stand on
And three unimpeachable witnesses were waiting just to
get their hands on
Him and wring his neck! He nearly let it come up
for trial.
     And that's where I've been all this while.
          May the gods, all the gods, blast that fool
Who wrecked my beautiful day
And they might as well, while they're at it, lay
Into me for thinking I could steal
Off to town and look the forum over that way
Without being spotted and tapped for something dutiful.
No doubt, I've messed up a day
That promised to be quite alluring
From the moment I told Désirée
To set things up nicely for dinner. All during

The time I've been detained, she's been waiting for me
And here I am at last, the first instant I could break free.
If she's angry, I suppose she has some reason to be.
But perhaps the dress I purloined from my wife won't annoy her
In the least, and I'll win this one too, as my own lawyer.

Peniculus
What do you say to that?

Wife
                That I've made a bad marriage
With an unworthy husband.

Peniculus
            Can you hear well enough where you are?

Wife
All too well.

Menaechmus I
The smart thing for me is to go on in there
Where I can count on a pretty good time.

Peniculus
                    Just you wait,
Bad times are just around the corner.

Wife
[*Confronting him.*]
                  You think you got away
With it, do you? This time you'll pay up, with interest.

Peniculus
That's it, let him have it.

Wife
             Pulled a fast one on the sly, didn't you?

Menaechmus I
What fast one are you referring to, dear?

Wife
                You're asking me?

Menaechmus I
Should I ask him, instead?

Wife
             Take your paws off me.

Peniculus
That's the way!

Menaechmus I
      Why so cross?

Wife
          You ought to know.

Peniculus
He knows, all right, he's just faking.

Menaechmus I
        With reference to what?

Wife
To that dress, that's what.

Menaechmus I
        That dress that's what what?

Wife
A certain silk dress.

Peniculus
      Why is your face turning pale?

Menaechmus I
It isn't.

Peniculus
    Not much paler than a thin silk dress, it isn't.
And don't think you can go off and eat dinner behind
  my back.
Keep pitching into him.

Menaechmus I
        Won't you hang up for a moment?

Peniculus
God damn it, no, I won't. He's shaking his head
To warn me not to say anything.

Menaechmus I
          God damn it, yourself,
If I'm shaking my head, or winking or blinking or
  nodding.

Peniculus
Cool! Shakes his head to deny he was shaking his head.

Menaechmus I

I swear to you, wife, by Jupiter, and all the other gods—
I hope that's reinforced strong enough to satisfy you—
I did *not* nod at that nut.

Peniculus

Oh, she'll accept that
On good faith. Now let's return to the first case.

Menaechmus I

What first case?

Peniculus

The case of the costly couturier's place.
The dress-fixer's.

Menaechmus I

Dress? What dress?

Peniculus

Perhaps I'd better bow out.
After all, it's my client who's suing for redress of
grievance
And now she can't seem to remember a thing she
wanted to ask you.

Wife

Oh dear, I'm just a poor woman in trouble.

Menaechmus I

Come on, tell me,
What is it? One of the servant's upset you by answering
back?
You can tell me about it; I'll see that he's punished.

Wife

Don't be silly.

Menaechmus I

Really, you're *so* cross. I don't like you that way.

Wife

Don't be silly.

Menaechmus I

Obviously, it's one of the servants you're mad at?

Wife

Don't be silly.

Menaechmus I
You're not mad at me, are you?

Wife
                              Now you're not being so silly.

Menaechmus I
But, for God's sake, I haven't done anything.

Wife
                              Don't start being silly
All over again.

Menaechmus I
Come on, dear, what is it that's wrong
And upsets you so?

Peniculus
              Smooth husband, smooths everything over.

Menaechmus I
Oh, hang up, I didn't call you.

Wife
                              Please take your paw off me.

Peniculus
That's the way, lady, stick up for your rights. We'll
    teach him
To run off to dinner and not wait for me, and then
    stagger out
Afterwards and lurch around in front of the house still
    wearing
His wreath and having a good laugh on me.

Menaechmus I
                              Dear God in heaven,
If I've even eaten yet, much less gone into that house.

Peniculus
You don't say?

Menaechmus I
That's right, I don't say, you're damned right I don't.

Peniculus
God, that's some nerve. Didn't I see you over there
    just now,
In front of the house, standing there with a wreath
    on your head?

Didn't I hear you telling me I was way off my nut,
and insisting
You didn't know who I was, and were a stranger here
yourself?

Menaechmus I

But I left you some time ago, and I'm just getting back.

Peniculus

That's what you say. You didn't think I'd fight back,
did you?
Well, by God, I've spilled the whole thing to your wife.

Menaechmus I

Saying what?

Peniculus

How should I know? Ask her.

Menaechmus I

How about it, dear?
What all has this type told you? Come on, don't
repress it;
Won't you tell me what it is?

Wife

As if you didn't know,
You ask me.

Menaechmus I

If I knew, for God's sake, I wouldn't be asking.

Peniculus

This is really some man the way he fakes out. Look,
you can't
Keep it from her, she knows all about it. By God in
wherever he is,
I practically dictated it.

Menaechmus I

Dictated what?

Wife

All right. Since you seem not to have an ounce of
shame left,
And you won't own up, give me your undivided
attention.
This is why I'm upset and this is what he told me.
I repeat,

I'm not really "cross"; I'm double-crossed, and doubly
   upset.
Someone sneaked one of my very best dresses right out
   of my house.

Menaechmus I
A dress? Right out of my house?

Peniculus
                              Listen to that louse,
Trying to scratch his way into your affections. Look,
   Menaechmus,
We're not playing matched towels in the doctor's
   bathroom
Marked "Hisia" and "Hernia"; we're discussing a
   valuable dress,
And its *hers* not yours, and she's lost it, at least for the
   time being.
If *yours* were missing it would really be missing for
   good.

Menaechmus I
Will you please disappear? Now dear, what's your
   point of view?

Wife
The way I see it, one of my best silk dresses is not at
   home.

Menaechmus I
I wonder who might have taken it.

Wife
                              I'm pretty sure
I know a man who knows who took it, because he did.

Menaechmus I
Who dat?

Wife
   Welllll . . . I'd like us to think of a certain Menaechmus.

Menaechmus I
Some man, just like us! Isn't that the fancy one, that
   man?
But he's a mean man. And who the hell are all the
   men you mean
Named Menaechmus?

Wife

                  You, that's what I say, you.

Menaechmus I

  Who accuses me to you?

Wife

                  I do, for one.

Peniculus

  I do too. And I say you gave it to a dear little Daisy.

Menaechmus I

  I? Me? I'm that mean aechmus who . . .

Wife

                  Yes, you, that's who,

  You brute, *et tu.*

Peniculus

             You who too too too . . .

  What is this, the Owl Movement from the Bird

      Symphony?

  My ears are feeling the strain of that to-who refrain.

Menaechmus I

  I swear, wife, by Jupiter, and all other gods within

      hearing distance—

  And I hope that's a strongly enough reinforced religious

      insistence—

  That I did not *give* . . .

Peniculus

           But *we* can appeal to Hercules and he's

  Even stronger, that we're not exactly not telling the

      truth.

Menaechmus I

  That technically I did not *give* it, I only *conveyed* it

  To Daisy today; you see, she doesn't have it, she's just

      using it.

Wife

  I don't go around lending out your jacket or cloak.

  A woman ought to lend out women's clothes, a man

      men's.

  You'll bring back the dress?

Menaechmus I

                I'll see that that's done.

Wife

If you know what's good for you, you will, I'm here
  to assure you.
You won't get back in this house unless you're carrying
  that dress.
I'm going in.

Peniculus

What about me and my work?

Wife

I'll pay you back when something is stolen from your
  house.

Peniculus

Oh God, that means never. There's nothing in my place
  worth stealing.
Well, Husband and Wife, may the gods do their very
  worst for you both!
I'll run along now, to the forum. It's quite plain to see
I've lost out, and lost my touch, with this family.
  [*Exit; never returns.*

Menaechmus I

My wife thinks she's making life hard for me, shutting
  me out
Of the house. As if I didn't have a much more pleasant
  place
To go into. Fallen from your favor, have I? I imagine
I'll bear up under that and prove pleasing to an even
  more desirable
Favorite. Désirée won't lock me out, she'll lock me in.
I guess I'll go in there and ask her to *lend* back the dress
I *conveyed* to her this morning, and buy her something
  much better.
Hey, where's the doorman? Open up, somebody,
  and tell
Désirée to come out; there's someone to see her.

scene three

[DÉSIRÉE *and* MENAECHMUS I.

Désirée

Who's calling me?

Menaechmus I

A man who'd be his own enemy
Before he'd be yours.

Désirée

Menaechmus, *dahling,* come in!
Why stand out there?

Menaechmus I

I bet you can't guess why I'm here.

Désirée

Oh, yes I can. You want something sweet from your
honey,
And what's more you'll get it, you naughty little
tumblebee.

Menaechmus I

As a matter of fact, or thanks heavens, or something . . .
What I have to have is that silly dress back I gave you
This morning. My wife's found out all about it.
But I'll buy you one worth twice as much, whatever
kind you want,
So be a good girl and romp in there and get it, won't
you?

Désirée

But I just handed it over to you to take to the Persian's,
Just a while ago, and gave you that bracelet to take
to the jeweler
And have the gold added to it.

Menaechmus I

The dress and a bracelet?
I think you may find you did no such thing. I gave
The dress to you and then went to the forum, and here
I am looking at you for the first time again since I
left you.

Désirée

Don't look at me, I'll look at you. I see
Just what you're up to, and what I'm down to, for
that matter.
You take the stuff off my two trusting hands and then
Do me out of it and pocket the cash for yourself.

Menaechmus I

I'm not asking for it to cheat you out of it, I swear.

I tell you, my wife's cracked the case.

Désirée

Well, I didn't ask
For it in the first place. You brought it of your own free will,
And you gave it to me as a gift, you didn't *convey* it, you shyster.
Now you want it back. I give up. You can have the stuff;
Take it away, wear it yourself if you want,
Or let your wife wear it, or lock the loot in your safe.
You're not setting foot in my house from this moment on,
Don't kid yourself about that. I deserve better treatment
From you than being jerked around and laughed at like a clown.
I've been your friend, lover boy—but that's at an end.
From now on, it's strictly for cash, if and when.
Find some other doll to play with and then let her down.

Menaechmus I

God damn it, don't get so God damn mad. Hey, don't go
Off like that, wait a minute! Come back here. You won't?
Oh come on, Dee. Not even for me? You won't? So I see.
She's gone in and locked the door too. And I guess that makes me
Just about the most locked-out fellow in this town today,
Most unwanted man, most unlikely to get in, much less to say
Anything that a wife, or a mistress, might take to be true.
I'll go ask my friends what they think I ought to do.

Act Five

scene one

[MENAECHMUS II *and* WIFE OF MENAECHMUS I.

Menaechmus II
It was really pretty dumb of me to put that purseful
of money
In Messenio's hands, the way I did. He's probably
holed up
In some dive, drinking it down, and looking them over.

Wife
I think I'll just take a look and see how soon husband
Wends his way home. There he is now. And all's well
for me:
He's got the dress with him.

Menaechmus II
Where in hell has Messenio wandered off to?

Wife
I'll go up and welcome him now in the terms he
deserves.
Aren't you ashamed to show up in my sight, you mistake
Of a man . . . I mean, you deliberate premeditated
crime,
Tricked out with that fancy gown?

Menaechmus II
I don't get it, do I?
What's on your mind, my good woman?

Wife
How dare you address me?
How dare you utter a single slimy syllable, you snake?

Menaechmus II
What have I done that's so bad I don't dare address you?

303

Wife

You must have cast-iron nerves to inquire about that.

Menaechmus II

I don't know if you read much, lady, but Hecuba:
The Greeks always called her a bitch. I suppose you
    know why?

Wife

As a matter of fact, no. I don't.

Menaechmus II

                                    Because she acted the way
You're acting right now. She kept dumping insults and
    curses
On everyone she met, and snarling at, pitching into
    everyone
Her eyes lighted on. No wonder they called her a prime
    bitch.

Wife

I really can't take this kind of abuse any longer.
I'd much rather never have been married, than
    submit to
The kind of dirt you shovel on me the way you do now.

Menaechmus II

What's it to me whether you like being married or not,
Or want to leave your husband? Do all the people
    around here
Tell their stories to every new man that blows into
    town?

Wife

What stories? I simply won't take it any longer, I
    tell you.
I'd rather live all alone than put up with you.

Menaechmus II

For God's sake, then, live alone, as far as I care,
Or as long as Jupiter may decide to grant you the
    option.

Wife

A few moments ago you were insisting you hadn't
    sneaked off
That mantilla-dress of mine, but now you're waving it

In front of my eyes. Aren't you a tiny bit conscience-
stricken?

Menaechmus II

God only knows what kind of a squeeze play you're
pulling,
You whack, you brazen. . . . How dare you say I took
this,
When another woman gave it to me to take and have
altered?

Wife

By God (my God, this time), a statement like that
Makes me want to . . . and I'm going to send for my
father,
And tell him every single horrible thing you've done,
That's what I'll do. Hey, Decio, in there, come out,
And go find my father and ask him to come here
with you.
Tell him please to come quickly, I simply have to
see him.
I'll show him every single horrible thing you've done
to me.

Menaechmus II

Are you feeling all right? What single horrible thing?

Wife

You housebreaker-into! You steal my dress and my jewels
From my house and rob your wife of her goods to
throw at
The feet of or load in the arms of your girlfriend as loot.
Have I rehearsed the story accurately enough for your
ears to take in?

Menaechmus II

Lady, you ought to watch your prepositions; and while
you're at it
Could you mix me a sedative of half hemlock, half lime
juice?
You must have some hemlock around here. I must be
kept *quiet*
If I'm meant to sustain your attacks. I'm not sure I know
Exactly who you think I am. I may have known you
Long ago in the days of Hercules' father-in-law's father.

Wife

Laugh at me all you want, but your father-in-law

Won't stand for that. Here he comes now. Take a good look,

Won't you? Recognize somebody?

Menaechmus II

Oh, him? I may have known him . . .

Yes, I did . . . oh sure, I remember old George from the Trojan War:

He was our Chaplain, bless his old heart. No. I guess not.

I've never seen him before, just as I've never seen

You before either, either of you, before today.

Wife

You say, you don't know me, and you don't know my father?

Menaechmus II

You're right. And actually, if you produced your grandfather,

I'd say the same.

Wife

One joke after another. What a bother!

scene two

[OLD MAN, WIFE *and* MENAECHMUS II.

Old Man

Here I come, pushing one foot after the other,

As fast and as far as my age allows, and to meet

This crisis at my own pace, pushing these pedals, progressing

As best I can. Papa isn't planning to pretend,

Though, to anybody, that it's easy. He's not so spry any more.

I'm pretty darned pregnant with years, that's a fact; planted

With a crop of them, if you conceive of me carrying the burden

Of this body. And there's precious little power left. Oh, it's a bad deal,

This business of being old. We're stuck with the bulk

Of our unwanted goods. Maybe we get more than we
    bargained for
Out of life. Old age brings the most of the worst when
    it comes,
To the ones who want it the least. If I named every
    pain
It bestows on us oldsters, I'd be drawing up a long
    long list,
And you'd have too much to listen to.
                        I wonder why my daughter
Sent for me all of a sudden? It weighs on my mind
And tugs at my heart to know what's afoot that can
    bring me
Running over here to see her. She didn't say why she
    sent for me,
Or tell me what's up. I can figure it out pretty well,
Of course. A quarrel with her husband has sprung
    up, I bet.
That's the way wives behave who bring a big dowry,
Coming loaded into the marriage and expecting their
    husbands
To love, honor, and slave away for them. They can
    be rough.
Of course, the husbands are at fault themselves, every
    now and then.
But there's a point at which it's no longer dignified
For the husband to take it any longer. That dear
    daughter of mine,
Darn her, never sends for me unless they've both of them
    been doing
Something wrong and a quarrel has started or is
    definitely brewing.
Whatever it is, I'll find out. *Yup!* I'll get brought up on
    the news.
Here she is now in front of the house. I see how
    aroused
They both are. She must have lashed into him; he looks
Pretty dashed. *Yup!* Just as I thought. I'll go call to her.

Wife

I'll go greet father. Good afternoon, Dad. How are you?

Old Man

Fine, thank you dear, and you? I hope everything's all
    right.

You didn't send for me because you're in trouble? But
    you look
Pretty peaked. And why's he standing over there looking
    mad?
You both look as if you've been trading punches,
    exchanged a few blows
Just for size, to see how it goes. Fill me in on the facts.
Tell me who's to blame, and explain the whole situation.
But briefly, I implore you. Let's not have even one
    oration,
Much less two.

Wife

              I didn't do anything, Father,
Don't worry. But I can't live here any longer, I can't
Stick it out. Please take me back.

Old Man

                        How did this happen?

Wife

I've become someone just to be laughed at.

Old Man

                          By whom?

Wife

                          By him,
The man, the husband you conferred me on.

Old Man

                          A fight, eh?
That's it, eh? How many times have I told you both
    of you
To watch out you don't come whining to me with
    your troubles?

Wife

How could I watch out, Father dear?

Old Man

                        You really ask that?

Wife

Only if you don't mind my asking.

Old Man

                    How often have I told you

To put up with your husband? Don't watch where he
goes;
Don't see what he does; don't pry into what he's
engaged in.

Wife

But he's crazy about this daisy of a flower girl; and
she lives right next door.

Old Man

That's perfectly natural, and in view of the way you're
so busy
Keeping an eye on his business, he'll get even dizzier
about Daisy,
I just bet you.

Wife

But he goes over there for drinks all the time.

Old Man

What's it to you whether he drinks over there? If he
drinks,
He'll have to do it somewhere. And what's so terrible
about that?
You might as well ask him to stop having dinner in
town,
Or never bring anyone home for a meal. Are husbands
Supposed to take orders from you? Let them run the
house then,
And order the maids around, hand out wool to be
carded
And get on with their spinning and weaving.

Wife

But Father, I ask you
To represent *me*, not to be *his* lawyer in this case.
You're standing here on my side, but you're taking his.

Old Man

Of course, if he's misbehaved, I'll get after him as much
As I've lit into you, in fact more so. But he seems to
be taking
Pretty good care of you, giving you jewels, clothes,
Your servants, furnishing the food. You ought to take
a practical,
More sensible view of the thing.

Wife

> But he's rooked me by stealing
Jewels and dresses from my closet at home to sneak
>> off with,
My clothes, my jewels, to dress up that girl he calls
>> on on the sly with.

Old Man

That's some prep . . . I mean proposition, I mean some
>> imposition.
I mean, that's terrible if that's going on—if it isn't
Your supposition's as bad, putting an innocent man
>> under suspicion.

Wife

But Dad, he's got them there with him, the dress and
>> that *sweet*
Gold flexible bracelet. He took them to her
And now, since I've found out about it, he's bringing
>> them back.

Old Man

Well, now, we'll see about that. I'm going to find out
About that. I'm going right over there and ask him,
>> I am.
Oh say, Menaechmus, would you mind telling me, if
>> you don't
Mind, about the matter you've been . . . discussing
>> with her?
I'm curious to know. And why are you looking so down
In the mouth, old fellow? Why's my girl standing
>> over there
By herself, all alone, and so cross?

Menaechmus II

> I summon all the gods,
And Jupiter Himself Supreme, as they are my
>> witnesses. . . .
Old boy, whoever you are, whatever your name
May happen to be.

Old Man

> As they are your witnesses to what?
Why do you need such a cloud of high-ranking
>> witnesses?

Menaechmus II
> That I have not done anything wrong to this woman
> Who claims that I surreptitiously deprived her
> Of this dress and carried it off under suspicious
> circumstances.

Wife
> Well, that's a clear enough lie. He's perjured himself
> for sure.

Menaechmus II
> If I have ever even set foot inside her house
> May I be of all men the most terribly tremendously
> miserably.

Old Man
> That's not a very bright thing to wish for, is it? You
> don't say
> You've never set foot in the house there you live in,
> do you,
> You stupid goop?

Menaechmus II
> What's that you're saying about me
> Living in that house, you goofy duffer? I live *there?*

Old Man
> You deny it?

Menaechmus II
>   Oh for Hercle's sake, of course I deny it.

Old Man
> Oh for Hercle's sake right back, you lie if you do
> Say you don't, I mean deny it. Unless you moved out
> last night.
> Come here, Daughter, listen: You two haven't moved
> Recently, have you?

Wife
>   Heavens! Where to? Or why should we have?

Old Man
> Well, of course, I couldn't know about that.

Wife
>   Don't you *get* it?
> He's joking around with you.

Old Man

>   All right, Menaechmus, I've taken
> Enough of your joking now. Come on, boy, let's get
>   down to business.

Menaechmus II

> *Je vous en prie!* What the hell business have you got
>   with me?
> In the first place, who the hell are you? And in the
>   second place
> I don't owe you any money. Nor her, in the third
>   place.
> Who's giving me all this trouble, in the next few places?

Wife

> Look, do you notice how his eyes seem to be going
>   all green
> All of a sudden? And there's a green tinge developing
>   on the skin
> Around his temples and forehead. Look at his eyes
>   glowing red,
> Or is it green?

Menaechmus II

> I wonder if I'd better not pretend I *am* crazy
> And scare them away by throwing a fit? They're the
>   ones
> Who seem to be insisting on it.

Wife

>   His arms twitch, his jaw drops.
> Oh, Father, what shall I do?

Old Man

>   Come here to your father,
> My girl, stay as far away as you can from him.

Menaechmus II

> *Ho yo to yo! Tobacco Boy! Take me back to ya!*
> *I hear ya callin' me out to that happy hunting ground*
> *Deep down in desegregated Damnasia (that's in the*
>   *Near East),*
> *Callin' your boy to come on out huntin' with his hound*
>   *dogs!*
> *I hear ya, Bromie Boy, but I jes' cain come near ya.*
> *They won't let me loose from this toothpickin' witch-*
>   *huntin' northland.*

> *They's an old foam-covered bitch and she's keeping*
> *   watch*
> *On my left. And right behind me here they's a goat,*
> *An ole toothpickin' garlic-stinking but I mean old goat,*
> *Who's been buttin' down innocent citizens all of his life*
> *By bringing up things that ain't true against them*
> *And then rounding up people to come listen to them*
> *   refute them.*

Old Man

I'm afraid your mind's been affected.

Menaechmus II

I've just swallowed an oracle
Of Apollo that orders me instantly to start setting about
Finding two red-hot searchlights to put her eyes out
      with.

Wife

Goodness, what a prepositionous preposterous
      proposition,
Father. He's threatening to burn out my eyes in.

Menaechmus II

Touché, for me. They say I'm raving, but they
Are rather wild at the moment. The straitjacket's on the
      other foot.

Old Man

Oh, my poor girl.

Wife

Yes, Father?

Old Man

What shall we do?
Suppose I send for the slaves in a hurry; I'll go
And bring them myself, to take him away and chain him
Safely at home before he starts getting more destructive.

Menaechmus II

Trapped! Strung up by my own guitar! If I don't
Improvise something soon they'll come on and cart me
      away.
Yes I hear you, sugar Radiant Apollo! I'll follow through
With my fists (you insist?) and spare not the laying on
of hands.

Punch that woman in the jaw, you say, according to
   your law,
Unless she disappears from my view and gets herself
   gone
The holy hell and crucified crutch of a cross
Out of my way? Apollo, I'll do what you say!

Old Man

Scoot into the house, fast as poss, or he'll slug you.

Wife

                              Scoot I go,
Father, *ergo*, soon I'll be out of the way. But please,
   Father,
Keep stalling him, don't let him slip out of reach. Don't
   you agree,
I'm a most put-upon specimen of woman to put up
   with that?

Menaechmus II

I've got rid of her: not bad. Now for dad. You slob,
Listen, you baggy-bearded, quavering long-since-past
   father,
You shriveled old, dried-up grasshopper—and besides
   your voice's changed,
Singing your Glorias Swansong soprano in your second
   childhood.
What's that, Apollo? Thou sayest I should smashest
   his frame,
His bones, and the joints that hook them to same? I'm
   game.
Smashomin, you say, with his owncluboff? Use his cane?

Old Man

There'll be trouble for you if you lay a finger on me,
Or move any closer.

Menaechmus II

                Oh sir, Apollo? The following
Changes in wording? Take one each two-headed axe
And split right down through the frame, through the
   guts to the bones,
And hack his back to bits and make slivers of his liver
   and his
Whole intestinal tract, don't just cudgel the codger?

Roger to tower. Look at that geezer cower and run
for cover.

Old Man

I suppose I'd better look to my laurels, what's left of
them, withered

As an old man's may be. I'll look after me. He's a
menace,

That's clear enough. He just may decide to take it
out on my hide.

Menaechmus II

For god's sake, Apollo, what's this? Another message?
The traffic's

Getting heavy. *Take four wild bucking broncos and
hitch*

*Them up to a buckboard, and climb aboard and drive
them over*

This lion, this bearded biped, this antique toothless

Gumclicking biped with bad breath? Roger, I'm
mounted, oh joy

To Yoy, King Roy Apolloy. I'm holding that wagon's
reins

And flicking the whip already. Up there, you double
pair

Of quadruplets. Drum it out on the ground when you
trample him down.

Bend your knees, noble steeds, be nimble as the breeze.

Pound you there, pound.

Old Man

He's coming at me with two pairs

Of horses?

Menaechmus II

Whoa there! *Yes, Apollo, of course I hear you*

Telling me to launch my attack against him, yes, him

Over there, and murder him. Whoa there! Who's hauling
me back

By the hair, and pulling me out of the chariot? Who
does this

Reverses the very command and eeeeeeedict of Apollo.

Old Man

It's really this poor fellow who's having the attack,
I would say.

And he's really having one, the full-scale deluxe one
with nuts in it,
God save us all. Well, that's how it is, by God. Here's
a fellow
Completely crackers, and a minute ago he was perfectly
rational.
When that mad stuff hits you it lands hard all of a
sudden.
I'll go ask the doctor to get here as soon as he can.
[*Exit.*

Menaechmus II

[*Alone, faces audience and addresses them across the
stagefront.*]

Now I ask you, have those two at last gotten out of
my sight,
Who forced me to play this mad role, when, as *you*
know,
I'm perfectly well? This is my chance to pick up and go
Winging back to my ship, don't you think, quick as a
wink,
While I'm still safe and sound? Listen, if you're still
around
When the old man comes back, you won't tell—he'll
be in a rage—
Where I went when I left the stage? You won't say
where I can be found?
[*Exit.*

scene three

[OLD MAN *and* DOCTOR.

Old Man

My back's stiff with sitting, my eyes nearly worn out
with looking,
Hanging around waiting for God darn that darn
medicine man
To finish with his patients and meet this emergency.
Well *finally* he's pulled himself away—not much urgency
Either, from his victims. He's his own worst pain in
the neck!
Such a specialist, in name-dropping at least, of who's
on his list

Of big shots with big troubles only he can fix. When
  I insisted
He hike over here, he said "Right away," but first he
  must set
This broken leg, to the Greater Glory of Aesculapius,
And then put an arm back in place, On Behalf of Apollo.
Which half of Apollo beats the Belvedere out of me:
  but I see
Him racing over now, weaving down the track like
  an ant
With lumbago. It's just his ego slows him down, the
  hot airman.
Putting those pieces together! What is he, a repairman,
A tinker, a joiner at heart? Are his patients all coming
  apart?

Doctor

Now let us see, my man. . . . You described the case of
  the deseased
As *larvated, id est,* he sees actual, live, dead ghost
  spooks?
Or *cerebrated, id est,* perturbated footzled left lobar
  cavity?
Which is of course only a false hallucination and
  would show
Some degree of mental inquietude. Would you be
  so good
As to describe the condition again, so I can decide
What to prescribe or proscribe, indeed just how
  to proceed?
Did you mention a species of *Hibernating* coma, a
  kind of
Tendency to feel sleepy all the time? Or did you more
  plainly see
A subaqueous subcutaneous *slurpation,* like say, water
  on the knee?

Old Man

The reason I've brought you in on the case is to find out
From you just what's wrong and ask you to cure it.

Doctor

                                        How true,
And I'll do it to perfection, never fear; upon my
  profession

I assure you he'll be quite well again.

Old Man

You'll give him

The most careful attention?

Doctor

First-class care, rest assured.
My word, Deluxe! Private room; personal visits from me.
I'll see him daily and ponder him most thoughtfully,
Heave hundreds of luxury sighs. He'll rate a thrill
Being ill; and so will you when you see the bill.

Old Man

Shh. Here's our man. Let's watch and see what he does.

scene four

[OLD MAN, DOCTOR, *and* MENAECHMUS I.

Menaechmus I

By God in heaven, if this hasn't been the worst
Of all possible days for me! Everything's gone blooey.
What I planned to do on the sly, that particular parasite,
Peniculus, brought to light, and flooded me with shame
and remorse
In the process. Some Ulysses type, doping out this
dirty deal
For his own best protector and patron. Why that . . .
sure as I live,
I'll do him right out of his ensuing existence, I'll unroll
His scroll for him. *His* existence? I'm a fool
To call *his* what's actually mine. I'm the one who
brought him up
By wining and dining him. It was my subsistence he
lived on:
All he ever managed was coexistence. I'll snuff out
That half of his light by cutting off the supplies.
As for that mercenary Daisy, all I can say is she
Acted quite in keeping with the character of a kept
woman,
And I suppose that's human, if meretricious. A very
meretricious
And a happy new year to her. When in doubt, just
give money.
All I did was ask her for the dress to return to my wife

And she claimed she'd already handed it over. Turned
  it over,
I bet, to some dealer for cash. Crash! Oh God in heaven,
Did any man ever let himself in for this big a cave-in?

Old Man
You hear that?

Doctor
                    He says he's unhappy.

Old Man
                              Go on up to him.

Doctor
  Meeeeenaechmus, *ciao!* How are you? Why expose your
    arm
  That way? Exposure can aggravate your serious con-
    dition.

Menaechmus I
  Why don't you go hang up, yourself, on the nearest
    branch?

Old Man
  Notice anything peculiar?

Doctor
                        Anything? The whole thing,
  That's what I notice. This case couldn't be kept under
    control
  By a mountain of Miltowns. Menaechmus, just a word
    with you, please.

Menaechmus I
  What's up, Doc?

Doctor
                    You are. Answer a few questions, please,
  And take them in order. First, what color wine do
    you drink?
  White wine, or red?

Menaechmus I
                    Oh, my crucified crotch!
  What's that to you?

Doctor
                    I seem to detect a slight tendency
  To rave, here.

Menaechmus I

Why not color-quiz me on bread?

Do I take purple, cerise, or golden red? As a rule,

Do I eat fish with their feathers or birds with their scales and all?

Old Man

I win! Ill, eh? Pu! Can't you hear he's delirious? Hurry up

With that sedative, can't you? Why wait for the fit to come on?

Doctor

Just hold on a bit. I've a few more questions to ask.

Old Man

You'll finish him off with the questions you keep inventing.

Doctor

Do your eyes ever feel like they're starting out of your head?

Menaechmus I

What do you take me for, you seahorse doctor, a lobster?

Doctor

Do your bowels rumble powerfully, as far as you can tell?

Menaechmus I

They're perfectly still when I'm full; when hungry, they grumble.

Doctor

Well now, that's a perfectly straightforward, digestible answer,

Not the word of a nut. You sleep until dawn, and sleep well?

Menaechmus I

I sleep right through, if I've paid all my bills. Listen, you

Special investigator, I wish to heaven the gods would crack down on you.

Doctor

Ah, now, to judge from that statement, he's being irrational.

Old Man

Oh no, that's a wise saying, worthy of Nestor, compared
To what he was saying a while back, when he called
    his own wife
A stark raving bitch.

Menaechmus I

What's that you say I said?

Old Man

You're out of your head, that's what I say.

Menaechmus I

Who's out of what? Me?

Old Man

Yes, you, that's who. Boo! Threatening to flatten me out
With a four-horsepower chariot. I can swear to it.
I saw you with my own eyes. I charge you with it.

Menaechmus I

Ah, but here's what I know about you. You purloined
    the crown
Of Jupiter, his sacred crown, and were locked up in jail.
That's what I know about you. And when they let
    you out,
It was to put you under the yoke and whip you in public,
With birch rods. That's what I know about you. And
    then, too,
You killed your own father and sold off your mother
    as a slave,
That's what I know about you. Don't you think that
    might possibly do
As a reasonably sound reply to the charges you're
    letting fly?

Old Man

Oh hurry up, Doctor, for Hercle's sake, and do what
    you ought to.
Can't you see, the man's *off?*

Doctor

You know what I think is best?
Have him brought over to my place.

Old Man

You're sure?

Doctor

Sure, why not?
I'll be able to treat him there by the very latest methods.

Old Man
Good. You know best.

Doctor

I assure you, Menaechmus, you'll lap up
Super tranquilizers for twenty days.

Menaechmus I

Is that medicine
Your madness? I'll gore you, hanging there, for thirty days.

Doctor
[*Aside.*]
Go call the help, to carry him over to my house.

Old Man
[*Aside.*]
How many men do we need?

Doctor
[*Aside.*]

At least four, to judge
From the way he's raving at present.

Old Man
[*Aside.*]

They're practically here.
I'll go run and get them. You stay right here, Doctor, do,
And keep a close eye on him.

Doctor
[*Aside.*]

No. As a matter of fact,
I think I'll be off for home, and make the preparations
To receive him. There's quite a lot to do. You go get
      the help;
Have them bring him to me.

Old Man
[*Aside.*]

He's as good as carried there already.

Doctor
I'm off.

Old Man
>So am I.

Menaechmus I
>>>Now I'm alone. That father-in-law
>And that doctor have gone, somewhere or other. But
>>what in God's name
>Makes these men insist I'm insane? I've never been sick
>A day in my life, and I'm not ailing now. I don't start
>>fights,
>Or dispute everything that comes up. I wish others well
>When I meet them, quite calmly, I recognize people
>>I know,
>And speak to them civilly enough. I wonder if they,
>Who absurdly declare that I'm mad, since they're in
>>the wrong,
>Aren't in fact crazy themselves? I wish I knew what
>>to do.
>I'd like to go home, but my wife won't allow it—as for
>>that place [*points to* DÉSIRÉE's *house*]
>No one will let me in there, Well, it's all worked out
>All right; worked me out of house and home. So I guess
>I'll stick around here. I imagine, by the time night comes
>I'll be welcome to enter the right one of these two homes.

scene five

[MESSENIO.
Messenio
>God slave the king!
>And of me I sing.
>Or rather, the slave's the thing
>I present and I represent.
>The good slave, intent
>On making his master content,
>Looks after his master's affairs.
>Arranging and planning, he never spares
>Any effort in lavishing cares
>On everything that needs being done.
>When the master's away, he handles all alone
>Problems that keep coming up, and he solves them
>As well as the boss could, himself, all of them;
>And sometimes manages the whole business better
>>than master.

You need a good sense of balance, to fend off disaster
From your legs and your back. And you've got to
  remember
That your throat and your stomach are not the most vital
  members.
If you go off guzzling and eating, instead of performing,
When you come back you're in for a beating and a
  good body-warming.
      May I remind all the shiftless delinquents who
        keep hanging back
From doing their work, of the price all masters exact
From good-for-nothings, men they can't count on,
  in fact?
      Lashes, and chains;
      Turning those wheels at the mill
      Until you begin to feel
      Your brains churning loose and writhing
        like eels.
      You'll be starved and left out to sleep in the
        cold open fields.
      That's the wages of laziness.
      Not to fear earning that would be the worst
        sort of craziness.
Therefore, I've decided, for once and for all, to be good
And not bad. I'd rather be lashed by the tongue than
  the wood.
As for meal, I find it more pleasant to eat than to
  grind it.
Therefore, I always comply with the will of my lord
Calmly, and well I preserve it; and I can afford
To deserve whatever I get by way of reward.
Let others look after their interests; they'll find a good
  way.
But this is how to serve your man best. That's what
  I say.
Let me always be careful, and pretty darn prayerful
Not to get in any trouble, so that I'll always be there, full
Of energy, coming in on the double where he needs
  me most,
His assistant host. Slaves who keep themselves good
  and scared
When they're not in the wrong usually find that they
  are declared

Highly usable by their owners. The fearless ones are
the goners;
When it comes time to face the music, these singsongers
Will be cheeping like jailbords and wishing they weren't
such gone-wrongers.
But I don't have to worry much longer, not me.
The time's almost here now when he promised to set
me free.
That's how I slave and work well, and how I decide
To do the best thing and take the best care of my hide.
Sooooo . . . now that I've seen all the baggage and
the porters in their bedding
In the tavern downtown, as Menaechmus instructed,
I'm heading
Back to meet him. Guess I'll knock on the door
So he'll know I'm out here and get up off the floor
Or at least let me pull him outside
From this den of iniquity, now that he's tried
To have a good time, and probably found out the cost.
I hope I'm not too late and that the battle's not already
lost.

scene six

[OLD MAN, WHIPSTERS, MESSENIO, *and* MENAECHMUS I

Old Man

Now I tell you, by all that's human or holy, make sure
You carry out my orders just right as I ordered you to
And order you now. You're to heft that man on your
shoulders
And hustle him off to the clinic, if you don't want
your legs
And your back pounded in. And don't pay the least
attention,
Any one of you, to anything he says. Well, don't just
stand there.
What are you waiting for? You ought to be after him,
lifting him.
I'll trot on over to the doctor's and be there when you
pull in.

Menaechmus I

Well I'll be *God* damned! What's on the schedule now?

Why are these men rushing at me, what in the name
of . . . ?

What do you guys want? What's all the racket about?

Why are you closing in on me all of a sudden? What's
the hurry?

Where we going? Some rumble. Creepers! They're
giving me the tumble.

God *damn* us! Citizens all, of Epidamnus! To the rescue!

Save me, my fellow men! Help! Let go me, you
whipster bastards.

Messenio

Holy smoke! Creepers! What's this bunch of gypsters
think

They're gonna get away with? My master? Why those
hijacking lifters,

They've got him on their shoulders. Let's see who gets
the most blisters.

Menaechmus I

Won't *anyone* lend me a hand?

Messenio

                    I will sir, at your command:

You brave Captain. Boy, this is gonna give Epidamnus
a black eye,

A mugging like this, right out in the open. *Epidam-
nee-ee-ee-I!*

My master's being towed away in broad daylight, a
free man

Who came to your city in peace, attacked on the
street. *Can*

Anybody help us? Stay off, you lugs. Lay off.

Menaechmus I

Hey, for God's sake, whoever you are, help me out,

Won't you? Don't let them get away with murder. You
can see

I'm in the right.

Messenio

                    Quite. Of course I'll pitch in

And come to your defense and stand by you with all
my might.

I'd never let you go under, Commander, I'd sink first.

Now you sink your fist in that guy's eye . . . No, not
    that one,
The one who's got you by the shoulder. That's it. Now
    a bolder
Swipe at the ball, gouge it out for him. I'll start
    distributing
A crack in the puss here, a sock in the jaw there. I'm
    at liberty
To do so? By the heavyweight Hercules, you thugs
    are gonna lug
Him away like a carload of lead, today. You'll pay by
    the ounce
When you feel my fists bounce all over your faces. Let
    go his grace.

Menaechmus I
I've got this guy's eye.

Messenio
               Make like it's just a hole in his head.
You're a bunch of bums, you body snatching, loot-latch-
    ing whipsters.

Whipster I
Hey, this wasn't what the doctor ordered, was it, or
    the old mister?

Whipster II
They didn't say we'd be on the receiving end, did
    they . . . ouch!
Gee Hercules, Jerkules, that hurt!

Messenio
               Well, let him loose, then.

Menaechmus I
How dare this ape lay hands on me? Bongo him,
    jungle boy.

Messenio
Here we go, kids, you too; take off, fade out, monkey
    face;
Get the crucified cross of a holy hell and gone out of
    here.
You too, take that, you vandal. Get a lift from my
    sandal.
You're the last one, might as well get what's left behind.

Well . . . Phew . . . ! Say, I made it, didn't I? Just about
in time.

Menaechmus I

Young man, whoever you are, may the gods always
shine
On your face. If it hadn't been for you I wouldn't have
lasted
Through sunset today.

Messenio

By all that's holy, if you wanted
To reward me, oh Master, you could free me.

Menaechmus I

Me liberate you?
I'm afraid I don't follow, young fellow. Aren't you
making some mistake?

Messenio

Me make a mistake?

Menaechmus I

By our father Jupiter, I swear
I am not your master.

Messenio

Don't talk that way.

Menaechmus I

I'm not lying.
No slave of mine ever helped me as you did today.

Messenio

Well, then, let me go free, even if you say you don't
know me.
Then I won't be yours.

Menaechmus I

But of course! Far as I'm concerned,
Thou art henceforth free—and thou mayest go wherever
thou wantest to.

Messenio

You say that officially?

Menaechmus I

Hercules, yes. In my official capacity,
Insofar as that governs you.

Messenio

> Thanks very much.
> And greetings, dear patron! Now that I'm free to be
> your client
> And depend on you on equal terms. [*Turns to audience.*]

> *Gaudete! He's free today!*
> *Good show for Messenio!*
> *Aren't you all glad he's let go?*

[*Audience cheers and applauds—and that is some stage
direction.*]
[*Still to audience.*]

> Well, I guess I'll accept it from you; thanks for the
> congratulations.
> You've all given me quite a hand. I feel *man you mitted.*
> But, Menaechmus, my patron, I'm just as much at your
> service
> As I was when I used to be your slave. I want to stay
> by you.
> And when you go home I want to go with you too.

Menaechmus I
[*Aside.*]

> God, no! Not another client.

Messenio

> I'll ankle downtown
> To the tavern and bring back the baggage and cash.
> That purse
> I hid away and locked in the trunk with the traveler's
> checks.
> I'll go get it now and deliver it all back to you.

Menaechmus I

> Oh yes, do bring that.

Messenio

> I'll bring it all back intact
> Just as you handed it over. You wait here for me.
[*Exit.*

Menaechmus I

> There's a bumper crop of miracles manifesting marvels
> by the millions

Around here today: some people saying I'm not who
    I am

And keeping me out from where I belong; then comes
    along

This slave who says he belongs to me, whom I've just
    set free.

Now he says he'll go bring me back a purseful of cash;

And if he does that I'll insist he feel perfectly free

To take leave of me and go where he wants, just in case

When he comes to his senses he begins asking back for
    the dough.

The doctor and my father-in-law, though, claim I'm
    out of my head.

At least, that's what they said. It's all very hard to get
    hold of,

Like a dream you dream you're having or are just being
    told of.

        Oh well, I'll go on in here to visit my mistress,
        even though

She's provoked at me, and do my best to prevail

On her to give back the dress. I can certainly use it
    as bail

To get off the street and into my house, *id est*, my jail.

scene seven

[MENAECHMUS II *and* MESSENIO.

Menaechmus II

You have the nerve to be telling me you reported back
    to me

Since the time I sent you away and told you to meet
    me?

Messenio

Exactly. Only a moment ago I saved you from de-
    struction

At the hands of those four whipsters hoisting you on
    their shoulders

And carting you off, right in front of this house. You
    were letting out

Loud shouts, calling on all the gods and on men,

When I roared in and pulled you loose by sheer brute
    strength

And knocked the block off them all, much to their
surprise.
And for the service I rendered in saving you, you set
me free.
Then I told you I'd go get the baggage and our cash—
and then *you*
Doubled round the corner as fast as you could, to
meet me
And deny the whole thing.

Menaechmus II

I told you you could be free?

Messenio
Positive.

Menaechmus II
I'm more positive still that before I'd see
You turned free man I'd turn into a slave, yes me, man.

scene eight

[MESSENIO, MENAECHMUS I, *and* MENAECHMUS II.

Menaechmus I
[*Comes out of* DÉSIRÉE's *house.*]
You can swear by your two jaundiced eyes if you want,
that won't
Make it any more true that I took away the dress and
bracelet today,
You whole bunch of blue-eyed, organized man-eaters
for pay.

Messenio
Heavens to . . . let's see . . . What's this I see?

Menaechmus II
So, what
Do you see?

Messenio
You're looking glass, boss.

Menaechmus II
You mean to say what?

Messenio

I say I see your reflection over there. I could swear
It's your face exactly.

Menaechmus II

God, if it isn't like me,
When I stop to consider how I look.

Menaechmus I

Oh boy, there, whoever you are,
You saved my life. Glad to see you.

Messenio

Young man, I wonder
If you'd mind telling me what your name is, by God
in heaven?

Menaechmus I

Heavenly God, no, of course I don't mind. The favor
You did me rates in return my nonreluctant behavior:
After all, you're my savior. I go by the name of
Menaechmus.

Menaechmus II

So do I, for God's sake.

Menaechmus I

I'm Sicilian, from Syracuse.

Menaechmus II

And my native city is the same.

Menaechmus I

What's that you claim?

Menaechmus II

Only what's the truth.

Messenio

I can tell you which is which easily.
I'm his slave [*points to* MENAECHMUS I], but I thought
all along I was his.
And I thought you were him. That's why I talked back
that way.
Please excuse me if I've spoken too stupidly for words
to you.

Menaechmus II

You're raving right now. Think back. Remember how

You got off the ship with me today?

Messenio

A fair enough question.
I'll change my mind. You're my master and I am your
slave.
So long, you. Good afternoon, again, to you. And I
mean you.
I say, this one's Menaechmus.

Menaechmus I

I say that's me.

Menaechmus II
What's the story, you? Menaechmus?

Menaechmus I

Yep. Menaechmus. Son of Moschus.

Menaechmus II
You're my father's son?

Menaechmus I

No, fellow, *my* father's. I'm not
After yours. I don't want to hop on yours and take him
from you.

Messenio
By all the gods, all over heaven, can my mind
Be sure of what it hopes for so desperately? *I've got 'em
untwined:*
These men are the two twins who separately now are
combined
To recall the same father and fatherland they shared
in their likeness.
I'll speak to my master. Ahoy there, Menaechmus.

Menaechmus I and Menaechmus II
[*Together.*]
What is it?

Messenio
No, no, not both. I only want my shipmate.

Menaechmus I
Not me.

Menaechmus II
But me.

Messenio

You're the one I must talk to. Come here.

Menaechmus II
Here I am. What's up?

Messenio

That man's either your absolute brother
Or an absolute fake. I never saw one man look more like
    another.
Water's no more like water, or milk more like milk
Than you two drops of the same identical ilk.
Besides, he cites the same fatherland and father.
Don't you think investigating further might be worth
    the bother?

Menaechmus II
Say, that's very good advice you're giving me.
Thanks very much.
Keep boring in, I implore you, by Hercules' knee.
If you come up with my brother, I fully intend to see
That *thou shalt go free*.

Messenio

I hope I come out right in the end.

Menaechmus II
I hope the same thing for you.

Messenio
[To MENAECHMUS I.]
Now, fellow, what do you say?
Menaechmus, I believe that is what you said you were
    called.

Menaechmus I
Right you are.

Messenio
Now this fellow here has the name of Menaechmus,
Just like you, and you said you were born at Syracuse.
So was he. Now both of you pay close attention to me,
And see if what I work out doesn't prove well worth it.

Menaechmus I
You've already earned the right to whatever you want
From me. You've only to ask and you'll gain it. If
    it's money

You want I'm ready to supply it. Just ask. I won't
deny it.

Messenio

I am hopeful at the moment of setting about to discover
The fact that you two are twins, born for each other
And on the same day to the very same father and
mother.

Menaechmus I

That sounds miraculous. I wish you could keep that
promise.

Messenio

I'll come through all right. Now listen here, each one
of you
To just what I say. And answer my questions in turn.

Menaechmus I

Ask what you will. I'll answer and never keep back
Anything I know.

Messenio

    Is your name Menaechmus?

Menaechmus I

            I admit it.

Messenio

Is that your name too?

Menaechmus II

      So it is.

Messenio

      You say that your father
Was Moschus?

Menaechmus I

So I do.

Menaechmus II

   Me too.

Messenio

    You're from Syracuse?

Menaechmus I

That I am.

Messenio

How about you?

Menaechmus II

Naturally, me too.

Messenio

So far, it all checks perfectly. Now let's forge ahead.
Tell me, how far back do you remember having been
in your country?

Menaechmus I

Well, I remember the day I went to Tarentum, to
the fair
And wandered off away from my father among some
men who took me
And brought me here.

Menaechmus II

Jupiter One and Supreme, that can only mean . . . !

Messenio

What's all the racket? Can't you pipe down? Now,
how old
Were you when your father took you with him from
Sicily?

Menaechmus I

Seven. I was just beginning to lose my first teeth,
And I never saw my father again.

Messenio

Here's another question:
How many sons did your father have?

Menaechmus I

Two, to my knowledge.

Messenio

Were you the older, or was the other?

Menaechmus I

Both the same age.

Messenio

That's impossible.

Menaechmus I

I mean, we were twins.

Menaechmus II

The gods are on my side.

Messenio
If you keep interrupting, I'll stop.

Menaechmus II

No, no. I'll be quiet.

Messenio
Tell me, did you both have the same name?

Menaechmus I

Not at all. I had
The name I have now, Menaechmus. They called him
Sosicles.

Menaechmus II
The lid's off! I just can't keep from hugging him hard.
My own twin brother, *ciao!* It's me: Sosicles!

Menaechmus I
How come you changed your name to Menaechmus?

Menaechmus II
After they told us how you had been taken away
From our father, and carried off by strangers, and
father died,
Our grandfather gave me your name. He made the
changes.

Menaechmus I
I bet that's just how it happened. But tell me something.

Menaechmus II
Ask me something.

Menaechmus I

What was our dear mother's name?

Menaechmus II
Henrietta Battleship.

Menaechmus I

That's it, all right. Never on a diet.
Oh, *brother*, this is a riot. I just *cain't* keep quiet.
Imagine meeting you here after all these years, I mean
I never thought I'd ever lay eyes on you again, much less

Wring your neck, you old numero *uno,* I mean *duo.*

Menaechmus II

Oh, you big beautiful brute you. *Et ego et tu.* You know
How long I've been hunting for you, and how much
trouble
I've gone to to locate my double! I'm glad to be
here, lad.

Messenio

You see, boss, that's why that mercenary much of a
wench in there
Called you by his name. She thought he was you when
she hauled
You in to dinner.

Menaechmus I

As a matter of heavenly fact, I did order dinner set up
Behind my wife's back, right here today, and sneaked
out a dress,
And gave it to Désirée.

Menaechmus II

Wouldn't be this dress, brother,
Would it?

Menaechmus I

That's it, brother. But how did you happen to come
by it?

Menaechmus II

I just happened to come by and the girlfriend pulled
me in to dinner
And said I'd given her the dress. I dined very well,
I wined like a lord, I reclined with my refined escort.
Then I took away the dress, and this gold bracelet too.

Menaechmus I

Good for you,
Old boy. Because of me, you've at least enjoyed
Your day in Epidamnus. I'm glad of that. Now, when she
Called you in, she of course, thought sure you were me.

Messenio

Ahem! Need I wait much longer to be free as you
commanded?

Menaechmus I
Brother, he's asking for only what is his just due.
Just do it
For my sake, won't you?

Menaechmus II
Thou art henceforth free.

Menaechmus I
> *Gaudete! He's free today!*
> *Good show for Messenio!*
> *Aren't you all glad he's let go?*

Messenio
Congratulations are all very fine, but perhaps something
    more *exchangeable*
Like, say, money, will make a free future not only
    assured but *manageable*.

Menaechmus II
Now, brother, everything's finally worked out so well,
Let's both go back to our homeland.

Menaechmus I
                    I'll do anything you wish,
Brother. I'll have a big auction here and sell all I own.
Meanwhile, temporarily, here we go home rejoicing.

Menaechmus II
I'm with you.

Messenio
        I've a favor to ask.

Menaechmus I
            Don't hesitate.

Messenio
Appoint me auctioneer.

Menaechmus I
        Sold! To the former slave!

Messenio
Well, shall I announce the sale then?

Menaechmus I
        Sure, for a week from today.

Messenio

[*To audience.*]

    Big auction at Menaechmus' house a week from today!
Must sell slaves, furniture, town house, country estate!
Everything's going, everything, for whatever you
        can pay!
He'll even sell the wife to any buyer willing to try her.
We'll make a million dollars and we may even go higher
If you count my commission. All invited! It ought to
        be great!
—But, oh, wait, Spectators! Don't forget the theater's
        laws.
We'll leave you first, on a burst of good loud applause!

V

Introduction
by Palmer Bovie

The *Mostellaria* has always been one of Plautus' more popular comedies, valued as an amusing and tightly constructed play. It influenced English and European playwrights in the seventeenth and eighteenth centuries, and with the *Menaechmi, Amphitryo, Rudens,* and *Miles Gloriosus* belongs to the group of Roman comedies most often read and appreciated by students of Latin and by the general reader today.

Shakespeare, who had read the play in Latin, (as he had others of Plautus) named two waiting-men in *The Taming of the Shrew* Grumio and Tranio, after two characters in the *Mostellaria,* and assigned a similar role to his Tranio, the mischievous accomplice and ostensible guardian of Lucentio. Although not directly indebted to this play, the musical comedy *A Funny Thing Happened on the Way to the Forum* (1962) by Shevelove and Sondheim provided one of the most accomplished actors on our stage with a superb comic role as the leading character, in the role of the manipulating slave Pseudolus. Like Tranio, he controlled the crazy crises of his drama with gigantic aplomb, and brazen inventions drawn from different plot elements in Plautus and Terence. The marvelous performance of Zero Mostel in the main part has been the best evidence our stage has yet seen of what Plautus was capable of creating 2200 years ago when he defined this type of role. For one of the very successful features of the *Mostellaria* is the masterful daring of its star. Tranio begins, continues, and ends as the master of the situation. Of course he is its lock as well as its key, a heady developer of difficulties and a compounder of intricate maneuvers that would trip up any but the most accomplished escape artist.

When the father of the young man Tranio has been assigned to protect and guide suddenly appears at the harbor after three years' absence, the son Philolaches is frantic. As a young man about town he has lavished money sumptuously on feasting and entertainment and borrowed heavily to buy the freedom of his mistress slavegirl Philematium. The first act of the *Mostellaria* arrays the characters so as to give a candid but sympathetic exposition of this state of affairs, from the ferocious opening debate between Grumio the good country slave and Tranio the bad town slave, through the soliloquy of Philolaches on his abandonment to pleasure, and the worldly scene between Philematium and her older attendant Scapha, to the romantic encounter between Philolaches and Philematium and the subsequent beginning of another of their never-ending round of parties. As their friends appear to join in the festivities, and the stage is set once more in this last scene of the first act for a cheerful day of pleasure, we see how this whole first act is virtually a play before the play, a brightly sketched view of how the young people acted in the absence of the censorious father. It sparkles with joyous abandon, but at intervening moments, like the soliloquy of the young man, or Scapha's worldly interview with her young charge, expresses worry and self-criticism and betrays a haunting concern with the perishability of pleasure.

When the hour of reckoning arrives, it provides Tranio with an opportunity to show what a lightning calculator he is. He takes command and begins to invent the "plot" from which the play is named, the "mostellaria fabula" or "little monster" story (*mostellaria* is the diminutive adjective formed from *monstrum*). Hiding the nervous Philolaches and his group in the house behind barred and locked doors, Tranio boldly greets the father Theopropides with the news that his house is haunted. They discovered the ghost, oh, some six or seven months ago, and of course no one lives there now. Has Theopropides by any chance disturbed the spooky spirit on the premises, the ghost of a murdered man, by rattling at the doors and pounding on them for admission? Horrors! Theopropides is quickly enough persuaded to withdraw from the scene with his head covered up in his cloak.

The remainder of the second act and the third are built on a series of natural, unpredictable interruptions that keep Tranio hopping as a master improviser. A moneylender appears to ask about the interest on his loan; Theopropides returns from his interview with the former owner of the "haunted house." Hearing snatches of the argument between Tranio and the moneylender, Theopropides asks Tranio what the money was for and what it amounts to. Tranio names the sum promptly and says that Philolaches used it to buy another house. Theopropides is pleased that his son was capable of investing the money so wisely. "Going into business, is he?" Theopropides remarks delightedly, "He takes after his father!" (*Patrissat*). The second invention of Tranio has explained the money very neatly: and it rids the stage of the moneylender whose demands Theopropides promises to satisfy on the following day. The inevitable question "What house?" now makes Tranio take the third step in his creative thinking. "This house right here, next door to ours," he decides, as the next natural interruption in the form of the neighbor himself, Simo, is seen coming out the front door of the house in question.

Here in the third act in the central scenes of the play Tranio's wits are doubly sharpened by the need to play Theopropides and Simo off against one another. Approaching Simo on the pretext of asking permission to look over the house, he wins a promise from his new victim not to tell Theopropides about Philolaches' reckless behavior and then gains the permission sought on the pretext that Theopropides wants to use Simo's house as a model for some building plans of his own. Bringing the two oldsters together Tranio insulates the conversation dexterously and has a little fun of his own at their expense. The act ends with Tranio triumphantly escorting Theopropides over the threshold of the new house, stepping briskly over a sleeping dog, while Simo strolls off to the Forum.

The stage is now clear for the entrance of two slaves of Philolaches' friend Callidamates who have come to escort their master home from the party. Finding the "haunted house" locked and apparently unoccupied they flutter about discussing the predicaments of good and bad slaves in general and of themselves in particular. Soon Theopropides and Tranio reappear from the inspection of Simo's house and Tranio is dispatched to bring Philolaches from the country to receive his father's congratulations. Theopropides then sees the slaves at the other side of the stage and accosts them. Without revealing his identity he soon has more answers to his questions than he had anticipated, for they spill the beans by recounting what has been going on in the "haunted house" these many months. When they leave to search for Callidamates elsewhere, Theopropides is reeling under the new information but is still not aware of how utterly he has been the dupe of Tranio until Simo returns from the Forum in the next scene and disposes of the story of the alleged purchase of the house. Theopropides asks him for the loan of a pair of heavy-handed slaves to help in subduing Tranio.

At the beginning of the fifth act Tranio blithely saunters back, meditating on how to stave off still further the inevitable, for now Philolaches has had enough of his help and wants to confess all to Theopropides. Overhearing Theopropides' instructions to the strong-arm slaves (the Latin designation for them is simply *Lorarii*, "Floggers"), Tranio confronts the father, who asks him to account for Simo's denial of the house purchase. The dialogue continues as Theopropides stalls, waiting for the right moment to order the *lorarii* to pounce on the intractable Tranio, but Tranio meanwhile has edged nearer and nearer the altar standing in front of Simo's house. Suddenly he reaches it and vaults up onto it. Here where he is immune from violent seizure, Tranio holds up his end of the dire conversation with Theopropides in a fine, fresh, supremely self-confident vein. The last scene of the play brings in Callidamates, who successfully pleads with the father to pardon Philolaches' youthful excesses, and promises to defray the total cost of their extravagance. He proceeds to ask for forgiveness for Tranio. At first Theopropides stubbornly refuses to spare Tranio, but ultimately he yields to Callidamates'. appeal, reminded at the end by Tranio that tomorrow will find the slave in just as much trouble, some other trouble. So why not wait and punish him then for both times together?

Like all of Plautus' works this comedy was drawn from a Greek original, the *Phasma*, or *Ghost*, perhaps of Philemon. It is a translation into Latin verse of the Greek version, one which doubtless represents an extensive reworking and adaptation. Certainly it has its own style and character, and sounds like Plautus at the height of his powers, agile and confident in the expression of its lively and lilting Latin verses, robust in situation, sly and occasionally arresting in thought. Against the fundamental currents of spoken verse in long lines of iambic or trochaic measures are set the lyric measures variously contained in the monologue passages (Philolaches' entering song, Callidamates' stagger scene, Simo's lament, Phaniscus' soliloquy). The jokes, turns, buffets, thrusts, ripostes are there for all to see and hear with their appropriate sound effects.

In translating the *Mostellaria* I have used long iambic and anapestic lines to reflect the fundamental meters of the dialogue, generally in an iambic scheme. For the lyrics I have changed the meter and introduced more definite rhyme patterns, to set these *cantica* in the niches where they separately belong. Throughout I have tried to incorporate alliteration, assonance, and rhyme freely enough to convey in English the equivalent effect of Plautus' love of alliteration and his abundant interest in words, and the sounds ideas make when they are tossed around on the stage.

Plautus:
MOSTELLARIA
(The Haunted House)

Translated by Palmer Bovie

CHARACTERS

TRANIO,
GRUMIO, } Slaves of Theopropides

PHILOLACHES, Son of Theopropides

PHILEMATIUM, Mistress of Philolaches

SCAPHA, Her maid

CALLIDAMATES, A young man, friend of Philolaches

DELPHIUM, Mistress of Callidamates

SPHAERIO, Slave of Theopropides

THEOPROPIDES, Father of Philolaches

MISARGYRIDES, A money-lender

   DANISTA

SIMO, An old man

PHANISCUS,
PINACIUM, } Slave escort of Callidamates

LORARII, Whipsters

Porters

Attendants

The action takes place on a street in Athens. The houses of THEOPRO-PIDES *and* SIMO *at either end of the stage in the rear are separated by a narrow back street. The side entrances lead (left) to the harbor and (right) to the Forum or countryside.*

ACT I[1]

Scene 1

GRUMIO: Come out of the kitchen! Out here, you miserable mutt!
  Giving me the smart side of your smooth tongue in the middle of those
    saucepans.
  Out of the house, you wreck of your master's existence!
  I'll pay you back in the country with interest, for sure.
  Out of the pantry, you stinker.[2] Why hide in there?
TRANIO: What's all this noise out in front of the house? What's cooking?
  Think you're out in the sticks? Lay off the town house,
  You hick! Off to the field with you; stop thrashing around
  On our threshold. (*Cuffs* GRUMIO.) That what you thought you had
    coming?
GRUMIO: Ouch! That hurt! Why throw those punches at me?   10
TRANIO: Because you're alive, that's why.
GRUMIO: All right. I'll endure
  It a little while longer. But just let the master come back,
  Just let him come back home safe, the one you're devouring
  In his absence.
TRANIO: That's illogical as well as unlikely, to speak of devouring
  Someone who's not there.
GRUMIO: Smooth-talking bum about town,

---

[1] Divisions into acts were made by Renaissance Italian editors when the plays were
first printed, and have been conventionally followed. Originally the comedies of
Plautus and Terence consisted of a succession of scenes with occasionally a musical
interlude. In the opening scene Grumio, the loyal "conservative" country slave of
Theopropides has come into the city to get new supplies of provender for the cattle.
His slanging-match with Tranio, the profligate town slave not only is a noisy quarrel
in itself but exposes the problem or argument of the play.

[2] *sauce pans . . . pantry . . . stinker* (i.e., reeking of cooking oil): the many
references to cooking and eating in this scene show Grumio's scorn for the self-indulgent city spendthrifts who live to eat.

Oh, they love you in Athens![3] And you throw the country at me?
But I think I know why: in the back of your mind you're aware
You're headed straight for the mill,[4] to slave away there.
Time's almost up, season's finished, old Tranio;[5]
You'll soon be a countryman too, rural yokels union of iron[6]—
Workers, slaves who clank chains and grind daily bread in the mills.

[3] *they love you in Athens*: literally, "favorite of the people" (*deliciae popli*), momentarily popular celebrity.

[4] *headed for the mill*: the hard labor of grinding wheat into flour was a punishment akin to torture for the slaves forced to perform it.

[5] *finished, old Tranio*: Grumio repeats Tranio's name twice in this passage in a threatening manner that Sonnenschein (upon whose standard edition of the Latin text I have drawn extensively) compares to the entreating repetitions in the first scene of *The Taming of the Shrew*:

> LUC.: But see, while idly I stood looking on,
> I found the effect of love in idleness,
> And now in plainness do confess to thee,
> That art to me as secret and as dear
> As Anna to the Queen of Carthage was,
> Tranio, I burn, I pine, I perish, Tranio,
> If I achieve not this young modest girl.
> Counsel me, Tranio, for I know thou canst;
> Assist me, Tranio, for I know thou wilt.   (I.1. 153–161)

I think this is quite typical of Shakespeare's associative memory of his Latin texts. Without attempting to "prove" that Shakespeare used this or that Latin author definitively, we can see here that he associates love with Vergil's Dido and the person the victim of love confides in with Dido's sister, as in the *Aeneid*. But the confidant is also the young man's servant, so Lucentio confides in his closest companion, the servant Tranio. Also, Tranio's advice in the lines immediately following, rounded off with a Latin quotation from Terence, is both like Anna's (admit your passion—don't try to expel it from your heart by scolding—) and like a more worldly attitude that the Tranio of the *Mostellaria* would manifest, were he to be consulted on the subject, or like Philolaches' estimate of his actual situation in the next scene—you ought to redeem yourself from this captivity at the least possible additional expense:

> TRA.: Master, it is no time to chide you now:
> Affection is not rated from the heart:
> If love have touched you, nought remains but so:
> *Redime te captum quam queas minimo.*   (I.1. 162–165)

Shakespeare's editors tell us that he remembered this line of Terence (*Eunuch* I.1.29) from its citation in Lily's Latin grammar.

[6] *rural yokels union of iron*: literally, "you will add one to the number of country people, an iron race": *augebis ruri numerum, genus ferratile*. A further reference to forced labor by slaves in the country, chained together in gangs.

Make hay in town while the sun shines, my boy: drink and spend,   20
Ruin that wonderful lad with your dissolute ways;
Drink day and night, live for pleasure like a Greek;[7]
Buy up the girls, set them free, buy the meals
For your free-loading friends, spend like a god let loose
On earth with a credit card. Were those the instructions our master
Left, when he left? Is this how he told you act
As the person in charge of affairs? Do you think that a slave
Has a duty to go through his master's estate
And ruin his son? And it's *ruin* what he's busy doing:
A lad who up to this time was the best you could find
In all Attica,[8] thrifty and self-contained—   30
But now takes the prize[9] for excellence in self-indulgence,

---

[7] *like a Greek: pergraecari*, i.e., dissipate. Not what a Greek would say, but one of the Roman elements introduced by Plautus.

[8] *Attica*: the Greek region of which Athens was the "Capitol."

[9] *takes the prize*: literally "bears the palm for the precise opposite." *Is nunc in aliam partem palmam possidet* Sonnenschein notes the percussive alliteration here, which is very typical of Plautus. The many instances of the plosive alliteration, in the *Mostellaria* alone, show Plautus' fondness for the device:

Latin line

111	parietes perpluont
143	pectus permanavit, permadefecit
164	pectus perpluit . . . optigere possum
245	pendere prae Philolache (pr. *Pil.*)
312	praedam participes petunt
353	peregre: periit
536	perii plane in perpetuom
550	perpetuo perierint
963	Pergam porro percontarier
976	postquam . . . pater . . . profectus peregre, perpotasse
1171	pessumis pessum premam

Happily, this sound also coincides with that of the applause Plautus might expect to hear at his plays. Examples of alliteration based on other letters are given by Sonnenschein, e.g.:

Latin line

41	canem capra commixtam
135	cum immigravi ingenium in meum
170	Scapha, sapit scelesta

Thanks to your teaching and superb abandoned example.

TRANIO: Why should you care about me or what I do,
Potato-face? You've got cattle to tend in the country.
I like to drink and make love and go out with girls
And I risk my own back in living it up, not yours.

GRUMIO: Cool! I say "you're a fool," yours drooly, Grumio.

TRANIO: Why don't you go up in smoke?[10] I'll see you inhale first,
You halitosis garlic-green rotten excuse for a rustic
Retreat, with goat-goo on your feet. I repeat: 40
You whiff of damp air, what's it like down there in your pig-sty?
Whew! What a combination of nanny goat and mongrel bitch!

GRUMIO: Oh, does your highness object? What did he expect?
We can't all reek of Greek perfoom, though God knows you do—
Whew—We can't all sit above the lord at the head of the table,
Or live in the elegant style apparently you're able.
I'll take my food cooked in garlic. You can have your pigeons
En casserole, your fish and your fricasseed thrush.
No thanks, very mush. You're very well off; I'm poor;
And, ah, these things we must *endure*, at least till the day
Of RE-TRI-BU-TION: the wages of sin then will pay
You off with interest in evil, but decency won't leave me at bay.   50

TRANIO: All very moral, I must say. But Grumio, I assume you are
Holding it against me that I'm in good shape and you're not.
That's all very normal. It suits me, this passionate life
With lasses to love at my liking. You're good at milking
And mucking around in the mire. I live rather higher,
You rather lower; my desires are gratified your cows are satisfied.

GRUMIO: Oh, you crucified crookshanks,[11] as I believe you will be!
How the crucifiers will drill you as you carry your cross
At the side of the road, when old master comes home again.

---

218   scelestam stimulatricem
352   mali maeroris montem maxumum ad portum modo
753   oppido occidimus omnes

[10] *drooly, up in smoke, etc.*: Grumio punctuates his remarks with a *fue!* exhaling a
gust of redolent breath.

[11] *crucified crookshanks*: i.e., candidate for crucifixion. Plautus often refers to this
punishment as the exaggerated "fate" of unruly slaves. In mock horror Tranio later on
envisages a twice-crucified victim.

TRANIO: How do you know that won't happen to you before me?

GRUMIO: For the simple reason that I've never deserved it, and don't
Deserve it at present; you always have and you do.   60

TRANIO: Oh, save your hot air for some future inflation, deposit it—
If you don't want your ribs in the red from the ruin I'll rain on you.

GRUMIO: Anything further? How about the fodder for my cattle?
If you're handing it over, come across; if you're not, just keep going
The way you've started; keep slinking around like a Greek[12]
And drinking and stuffing your gluttonous sackful of guts.

TRANIO: Oh, hang up and head for the sticks. I'm off to the harbor[13]
To find some nice fresh fish for our suppertime dish.
Tomorrow I'll have someone fetch that vetch fodder further
Out to the villa. What are you staring at, jailbird?[14]

GRUMIO: That pen name will suit you sooner than me, that's what I think.

70

TRANIO: "Sooner," who cares, when the present's so particularly pleasant?

GRUMIO: Is *that* so? Here's one thing *you* ought to know: the bad
Comes along much sooner than you wish it had.

TRANIO: Well, let's not you be my bad news at present, you goose:
Flap off to your pen, get out from under my feet.
I repeat: SHOOO!
(*Exit.*)

GRUMIO: What? Whoosh! Well, he's beat a hasty retreat.
And he doesn't seem to care one frit[15] for all that I've said.
Oh ye immortal gods, I'll apply then, instead,
To your holy powers. Bring my master back home from abroad
As soon as you can, perhaps even sooner, while the lord
Still has a home and a farm to be lord of. Three years
He's been gone and what's left of his property here   80
Will last about three more months at the most.
I'm off to the country. Here comes our host,
The master's son, once by far the best

---

12 *like a Greek*: the second usage of *pergraecari.*
13 *to the harbor*: Tranio says "to Piraeus" (the harbor of Athens).
14 *jailbird*: literally "yoke-bearer", *furcifer*, a victim bound by his arms to the stocks.
15 *one frit*: literally not worth a *floccus*, single strand of wool, i.e., insignificant.
For *frit* see note to p. 114.

Of all young men, now as ruined as the rest.
(*Exit.*)

Scene 2[16]

Enter PHILOLACHES.

PHILOLACHES: I have thought about this, and pondered it deep in my
    heart:
What is a man? And what is he like from the start?
And I think I've discovered the answer—so let me disguise
Man's likeness in an image you're likely to recognize.   90
From the moment he's born, a man is just like a house!
And I'll prove this, for once and for all, so conclusively
That all of you listening out there will agree inclusively
As soon as you've heard my words. "Why, of course,"
You'll admit, "that's it, to a *T*. That's us."
So listen closely as I set about proving my case:
I want you as cleverly informed by the portrait I trace   100
As I am. When the house is finished and ready for its residents
Beautifully built and cannily constructed, a precedent's
Established in other people's minds. They envy the establishment
And congratulate the carpenter.[17] Ambitious for such embellishments,
They take this house for a model and spare no labor or cost
To create a copy of the house they admire the most.

16 *Scene 2:* marked by the entrance of Philolaches who sings his *canticum* in lyric
meters, accompanied by the flute. The soliloquy is intricately proportioned in four
parts each alternating in rhythms predominantly bacchiac (parts 1 and 3) and cretic
(parts 2 and 4) e.g., line 85, the first line of the first section, bacchiac: $\cup - -$
$\cup - - \cup \quad - - \quad \cup - - \cup -$
Recordatus multum et diu cogitavi
line 105, the first line of the second section, cretic: $- \cup -$
$- \quad \cup - \quad - \cup - \quad - \cup \quad - \cup -$
Atque ubi illo inmigrat nequam homo indiligens.
17 *congratulate the carpenter:* literally "praise the builder," *laudant fabrum.*
Throughout Philolaches uses *faber* (joiner, smith, carpenter, mason, builder, maker),
which I have translated variously. Later on, Tranio uses the word *architecton*, architect or masterbuilder.

And then the new owner moves in, with his whole sloppy family
And is lazy and disorderly and shiftless and worthless and shambly.
So the house develops flaws because a good place is badly looked after.
And what often happens? A high wind exposes a rafter
By tearing some tiles from the roof or gouging the gutters
While the unindustrious lord and master hardly flutters   110
To replace the tiles or plug the holes. Then it rains cats and dogs
And the walls are lashed by the downpour and then waterlogged.
The wet rots the beams and undoes the intricate schemes
Of the carpenter-architect-maker. There go his dreams
Of a dwelling that's useful and good. Damp, rotten wood.
The place, much the worse for wear, becomes of less use.
Of course it's not the builder's fault. But there's no excuse
For the way owners generally act in a crisis like this.
They could patch the damage for a drachma but they will insist
On stalling around, not getting to it: they don't do it,
Until finally the walls come falling down to the ground
And the whole building has to be built up all over again.
Well, this is the case I've constructed for buildings. Now then,
I want you to think how like are these dwellings and men.   120

The children are the parents' building:[18] as its architect,
The parents lay the foundation and on it erect
The framework, firm on a stable, reliable base.
They don't count the cost of materials, or in fact
Feel apprehensive because it's expensive to build a child
Who will grow to be useful and good and present a fine face
To the world. They are eager to drive other parents wild
With the wish to produce children exactly like those.
When the boys enlist in the army[19] along with them goes
An older cousin or uncle to see them through the first throes
Of being on their own. Just so far are they allowed to stray
From the builders' hands. Duty done, they collect one year's pay   130

[18] *parents' building*: literally "in the first place, the parents are the *fabri* of their children": *primumdum parentes fabri liberum sunt* (bacchiac).
[19] *enlist in the army*: a reference to the year of compulsory military service.

And go free. And this is the time to inspect the sample to see
What kind of a combination
Comes of all this edification.

Well, for a sample
Just look at me, the perfect example.
Up until the time my military service was ended
I was as good as could be, while I still depended
On the power of my makers. I was worthy and wise.
But then I moved into the house of my natural guise
And wrecked the builders' work from the roof to the ground.
Laziness dropped in: this was my high wind, I found,
When it tore off my self-control and innate sense of shame.   140
It unroofed them, but I was the one most to blame
For not replacing those tiles. I put it off too long.
And soon enough, like the rain love came along,
Drenching my body and seeping down into my chest
And soaking my heart through and through. Dispossessed
Am I now of money and credit and reputation, all of them fled,
Like my good character and sense of honor: they've left me for dead.
No Excuse: Worse for Wear, I've Become of Less Use.
Lord! How these timbers are crumbling with rot! I'll never
Be able to prop up my house. It'll tumble right over
Since the dampness has seeped inside. And no one outside
Can help me stave off this inner collapse, my soul-slide.

How my heart aches to think of myself, so far gone
In ruin from the young man I was, the paragon   150
Of young animals. With a healthy interest in strength
And sports, I lived for the daily delight of more length
With the discus, or javelin; in footrace, in parries and feints
With the broadsword; in gymnastics, in horsemanship trials,
I was a lesson to others in the manly art of self-denial
And austerity. All the best young men were inspired
By the example I set. And now, when I've virtually expired,
And dwindled down to nothing, I've learned to make sense
Of the truth by the simple exercise of my own intelligence.

Scene 3[20]

Enter PHILEMATIUM, SCAPHA. PHILOLACHES *withdraws to far right of stage.*

PHILEMATIUM: Heavens![21] That lovely cold bath was marvelous.

I've never felt better inside and out, Scapha dear,

So clean and fresh.

SCAPHA: With some end in view,

I do hope, some successful solution from all these ablutions.

After all, there's been a very happy harvest this year.

PHILEMATIUM: But what has a harvest to do with my taking a bath?   160

SCAPHA: Nothing more than your bathing has to do with a harvest, my dear.

PHILOLACHES (*Aside.*): Lovely Love Herself![22] That's my heavenly hurricane,

Who unroofed the top from the whole sphere of self-control

I'd been housed in. Exposed as I was and then doused

When love and desire rained down hard and flooded my heart,

I can never put the roof on again. The walls of my heart

Are all soaking wet. My dwelling is falling apart.

PHILEMATIUM: Tell me now, Scapha, my love: Does this dress do me justice?

I want to look nice for the apple of my eye, that wonderful guy

Who possesses me, my dear Philolaches.

SCAPHA: Really, Philematium

You're superbly presentable, you with your adorable ways,

Just because you're so lovely. Men in love aren't in love

---

[20] *Scene 3:* the meter changes back to iambics and then to trochaics in long units of six to eight feet. This is the usual style for the *diverbia*, or dialogue passages, as distinct from the *cantica* or lyric passages.

[21] *Heavens:* literally "By Castor," an oath invoked exclusively by women.

[22] *Lovely love: Venus venusta. Venustas*, the noun, is the Latin word for charm, loveliness, elegance. (Cf., Italian *garbo*, manner, but especially a graceful and elegant manner.)

With what their women wear but with what they find there.

PHILOLACHES (*Aside.*): Ye gods! That Scapha knows lovers inside out,   170
  How they really feel, and just what they're thinking about.

PHILEMATIUM: Now how's this?

SCAPHA: How's what?

PHILEMATIUM: Oh, please, take a look
  And tell me now how you like this on me.

SCAPHA: It so happens,
  Thanks to the fact that you're very beautiful, anything
  Looks good on you.

PHILOLACHES (*Aside.*): For these kind words, Scapha you scamp,
  I'll see that you're given a generous . . . something or other
  Today. That is, it won't be gratis or complimentary
  That you are gracious to this girl who is so very dear to me.

PHILEMATIUM: Oh but I don't agree.

SCAPHA: Come now, how dumb can the lady
  be?
  You wouldn't rather have me criticize you falsely than praise
  You honestly, would you? I'd rather be praised unduly
  Than be criticized truly or have others laugh at my looks.   180

PHILEMATIUM: I cherish the truth and I want you to tell me the truth.
  I can't abide lying.

SCAPHA: Well, so help me then, and on a stack of drachmas,
  Philolaches adores you, as much as you are adorable.

PHILOLACHES (*Aside.*): What's that you say, you devil? How did that oath
  go?
  I adore her? And how about the "she loves me"
  Other part of it, why wasn't that added on? I promised
  You a gift, but you've lost it: you just tossed it
  Away, and I hereby declare that good deed undone.

SCAPHA: But I must say, heavens knows, I simply cannot imagine
  How a clever, intelligent, worldly young woman like you
  Can act like a stupid little silly.

PHILEMATIUM: Am I doing something wrong?
  Do tell me, please, if I am.

SCAPHA: Heaven's name, doing wrong!
  Going wrong, that's the way you're headed, as sure as my name

Means skoal,[23] bottoms up or, in Greek, the Devoted Souse.
You are wandering, dear, by setting your cup, I mean cap
For one man alone. You wait hand and foot upon him
And refuse to see all the other interested callers.
It's playing the role of a wife, not using your wiles
As a woman of the world, to yield to one man alone.   190

PHILOLACHES (*Aside.*): Super Jupiter! A snake, nourished at my own
   domestic bosom!
May all the gods, and goddesses too, while I'm at it,
Bring the whole world down on my head if I'm not the man
To kill off that hag by exposure, and hunger, and thirst.

PHILEMATIUM: Now, Scapha, no naughty advice!

SCAPHA: He'll leave you stranded,
I warn you right now, when your youth and beauty are ended[24]
And his pleasure palls at repetition. To think of the current condition
Of his friendship and generous behavior as lasting forever
Is to be monumentally dumb.

PHILEMATIUM: Well, I hope not.

SCAPHA: Reality consists for the most part of things unhoped for.
If you're quite incapable of being persuaded by words
To believe what I say is true, just estimate the facts
On the basis of my experience. You see, for instance, my face,
As it is now, and you remember how I used to look.
No less than you I once was loved and adored   200
By a person I exclusively chose for my master and lord.
When a few years went by and the hair on my head changed its color
I was abandoned, left stranded. That's your future with this fellow.

PHILOLACHES (*Aside.*): I can hardly keep my fingers from flying at that
   vixen's eyes.

PHILEMATIUM: I still think I ought to accommodate this man alone.
It was he who set me free, after all, to have for his own.

PHILOLACHES (*Aside.*): Gods, what a woman! Intelligent and modest and
   charming.

---

23 *skoal, etc.*: I have introduced the play on Scapha's name.
24 *stranded . . . ended*: There is a rhyme sound in the Latin here, "he will desert
you because of age and surfeitage" . . . *te ille deseret aetate et satietate.*

Hercules,[25] no joke: for her I'm glad to go broke!

SCAPHA: But heavens, girl, you don't seem to know yourself.

PHILEMATIUM: Because . . .

SCAPHA: You're so busy

Making sure he'll like you.

PHILEMATIUM: Why shouldn't I want him to like me?

SCAPHA: Because you're free. You have what you wanted and what can he
do   210

But keep right on loving you? Otherwise he's bound to lose

Both you and the whole heap of silver he paid for your head.

PHILOLACHES (Aside.): Hercules I'll be a bum if I don't tear her limb from
limb.

She's ruining my wonderful girl plying her with advice

Of the kind a procuress would use to bid up the price.

PHILEMATIUM: I'll never be able to repay the kindness he has shown

In the measure he fully deserves. So don't make me think

Any less of him. Anyway, that's impossible.

SCAPHA: But the plausible

Thing to think of is this: if you're a slave to him only at present

As a pretty young thing, your old age will be unpleasantly lonely.

PHILOLACHES (Aside.): I wish I could turn into quinsy, angina of the
voice box,

And throttle the poisonous jaws of that sinful old fox.

PHILEMATIUM: Well, I think I ought to behave the same way toward him
                                                                          220

When I've got what I wanted as when I was wheedling it out of him.

PHILOLACHES (Aside.): Let the gods do whatever they will with me, for
better or for worse

If I don't set her free all over again, fair Philematium

As a reward for that noble oration—as for Scapha,

I'm planning to bash in her skull for once and for all.

SCAPHA: If you're perfectly sure in your mind that this lover of yours

Will be yours alone for the rest of your life, and provide

For you unfailingly, you should sleep with this man

---

25 *Hercules*: The references are no doubt to Hercules in his capacity as guardian
of hidden treasure.

And only with him, and braid your hair[26] like a bride.

PHILEMATIUM: If a person's a good credit risk he can always get a loan;
   If I have a good reputation I'm wealthy enough.

PHILOLACHES (*Aside.*): By Hercules if my father had to be sold
   Into slavery, I'd sell him outright, long before you
   Ever went in need or were forced to beg for a thing,   230
   So long as I lived.

SCAPHA: But what about your other admirers?

PHILEMATIUM: They'll admire me even more when they see how grateful
   I am
   To the one who deserves my best thanks.

PHILOLACHES (*Aside.*):   I wish the news
   Of my father's death were announced to me this very minute
   So I could disinherit myself and confer upon her
   The claim as heiress to all my goods and possessions.

SCAPHA: But his money is practically gone: the lavish dinner parties
   And drinking bouts lasting all day and most of the night
   Show how little he knows about how to put money aside.
   The pile of provisions in the larder is flat as a pancake.

PHILOLACHES (*Aside.*): By Hercules I'll prove how closefisted I can be,
   Beginning right now with you: your ration of food and drink
   For the next ten days at our house will be cut down to none.

PHILEMATIUM: If you care to say something pleasant about Philolaches
   You'll be listened to gladly. If you keep lacing into him, though,
   By Castor, your nasty remarks will get you a beating.   240

PHILOLACHES (*Aside.*): Hooray for the house of Pollux! If I'd written a
   check
   To Jupiter on High in the amount I paid out for her
   It still would have been nowhere nearly so sound an investment
   It's obvious how very much she loves me down deep in her heart
   What a masterstroke that was to set free my future patron
   In the form of this lovely lawyer to plead a case for her client.

SCAPHA: I see that all other men come to nothing for you
   When compared to Philolaches. And I don't want a beating for my
   pains

---

[26] *braid your hair:* "At marriage the hair of a Roman maiden was divided into six plaits" (*crines*) by means of a small spear-shaped iron pin (Sonnenschein, p. 89).

So I'll be the cheerful chorus to your lovelorn refrains.

PHILEMATIUM: Will you hand me the mirror and my jewelry box, Scapha?
I want to look my best when my favorite person comes home.

SCAPHA: A woman who can't trust herself or her looks has a use for a
    mirror.   250
What need have you for a mirror, when any mirror would prize,[27]
Above anything else, a chance to gaze in your eyes?

PHILOLACHES (*Aside*.): Those fair words, Scapha, I assure you, won't go
    unrewarded.
And to make sure I'll draw something out of my privates account
And present it this very day to you, Philematium darling.

PHILEMATIUM: Am I all in order? Do have a look at my hair, and tell me
If it's staying prettily in place.

SCAPHA: You are so well disposed
As you are, that your hair couldn't fail to be neatly arranged.

PHILOLACHES (*Aside*.): Ugh! Can you think of anything lower than a
    woman like that?
A moment ago all scowls, and now all wreathed in smiles.

PHILEMATIUM: That jar of face powder.

SCAPHA: Face powder? Whatever for?

PHILEMATIUM: To touch up my cheeks.

SCAPHA: You might just as well expect
To whiten the shade of ivory by applying some lampblack.

PHILOLACHES (*Aside*.): Oh, very well said, Scapha. I must applaud that
    remark   260
About improving on ivory by blackening it.

PHILEMATIUM: Well, then, the rouge, please.

SCAPHA: No, I refuse. That's not at all clever of you
Do you want to daub over a beautiful work of art
With streaks of new paint? No false colors should touch
Your exquisite youth, no powder, paint, or cosmetics
There, take the mirror.

PHILOLACHES (*Aside*.):   Oh dear, oh me, missing this!

---

[27] *mirror would prize*: A positively Shakespearian conceit: literally "you yourself
are the best looking glass for a looking glass," . . . *quae tute speculo speculum es
maxumum*. There is a further play two lines following on the sound of *peculi*, echoing the slighted "s" of speculum; *peculi*, "something from my own private funds" is
lightly off-color.

She's giving the mirror a kiss! If I had a stone
I'd bash in the silver face of that mirror.
SCAPHA: Now, use a linen cloth to wipe your hands clean.
PHILEMATIUM: But whatever for?
SCAPHA: You've held the mirror in your hands
I don't want the smell of silver clinging to your fingers.
PHILOLACHES (*Aside.*): I haven't seen a shrewder procuress anywhere
around.   270
Astonishingly astute, that thought about the mirror on her hands.
PHILEMATIUM: I could do with the delicate gloss of this fragrant scent,
Don't you think?
SCAPHA: Not a drop, not a dab.
PHILEMATIUM: Oh? Why not?
SCAPHA: A woman smells best when she doesn't smell in the slightest.
Think of those old gals constantly refinishing their surfaces,
Lavishing lotions on their skins: they're shriveled and toothless,
But, concealing their bodily blemishes, they're dyeing to take you in.
When the sweat mixes in with the grease and lotion and cream
Well, it's like a cook making one sauce by concocting several;
What it smells like you can't say precisely but you do know it smells.
PHILOLACHES (*Aside.*): She certainly has it all doped out: there's no
higher learning
Than this learned lady displays. (*To Audience.*) And it's perfectly true
280

As most of you husbands know who have old wives at home
Who put down a dowry for the privilege of marrying you.
PHILEMATIUM: Tell me if my robe and jewels are becoming to me.
SCAPHA: That's none of my business.
PHILEMATIUM: Well, whose is it then?
SCAPHA: It's his,
Philolaches'. He shouldn't buy anything unless he's sure
It's something you want. The lover purchases the favors
Of his mistress by showering her with jewelry and expensive clothes.
And it isn't the presents he wants, so theres' no use parading
The gifts before his eyes. Expensive clothes
Disguise old age and gold is for the ugly duck.
A beautiful girl without a stitch on her back outshines
A woman well wrapped in the latest costliest cloth.

For if she is pretty, she is well enough dressed as is.   290

PHILOLACHES (*Aside.*): I've kept out of this long enough.

(*Comes forward.*)   What are you

two up to?

PHILEMATIUM: I'm dressing up—I want to look nice for you.

PHILOLACHES: Whatever you wear looks wonderful just with you in it.

Scapha, you may go, and take this stuff away, too.

But Philematium, darling, I'm longing to stretch out here

And have a drink with you.

PHILEMATIUM: Heaven knows I want

To be with you. Whatever your heart desires

I want just as much as you do, my dearest darling.

PHILOLACHES: That remark is worth $500[28] cash.

PHILEMATIUM: Oh, take it

For $250. You deserve a remarkable bargain.

PHILOLACHES: The $250 is in your bank right now. And balance the account:

I paid $750 for you.

PHILEMATIUM (*Dismayed.*): Oh, must you remind me?   300

PHILOLACHES: Me remind you? When I'm hoping others will insist

On reminding me of it? It's been an awfully long time

Since I made such a handsome investment.

PHILEMATIUM: I'm perfectly sure

I could not have better employed my heart than by falling

In love with you.

PHILOLACHES: Then our books do balance precisely;

Expenses against receipts—you really do love me

And I love you and each thinks that's how it should be.

PHILEMATIUM: Now come balance me here on the couch. Slaveboy, some water

At once, for our hands! And bring us a table. Find the dice.

(*To* PHILOLACHES.)

Some perfume?

PHILOLACHES: I've no need of that with Fragrance herself

---

28 *$500*: literally 20 *minae*. I am calculating the *mina* at the rate of $25. (One silver *mina* equals 100 drachmas, so the drachma equals 25 cents.) *$250*, literally 10 *minae*. *$750*, literally 30 *minae*.

Breathing sweetly beside me. Oh, look someone's coming there:
Isn't that my friend bearing down on us, with his girl?   310
Yes, it's Callidamates, with his girl friend to boot:
So here come our comrades-in-arms for a share in the loot.

Scene 4[29]

CALLIDAMATES, DELPHIUM, PHILOLACHES, PHILEMATIUM, PHANISCUS, PINACIUM.

CALLIDAMATES (To PINACIUM, slave attendant.): Now boy, you call for me on time
    At Philolaches' house. Get that? Oof!
    (Swings at him but misses.)
    There! That'll make you do what you're told, you goof.
    That fellow whose house I was at
    What a D-R-I-P drip!
    No wonder I gave him the slip
    And the conversation? Even drippier.
    So, I thought I'd skip over here
    Where I'm sure to be so much hippier.
    I mean happier, I mean Philolaches
    He's a tickler, he's no stickler . . .
    Say Delphium, old Sybil syllable

---

[29] Scene 4: This is the second canticum, in the following meters: (1) Solo of Callidamates, bacchiac; (2) duet of Delphium and Callidamates, a variety of cretic, anapestic, trochaic, and iambic rhythms; (3) quartet of Delphium, Callidamates, Philematium, Philolaches, predominantly cretic. I mention these patterns to remind the reader of the intricate and inventive musical texture of the cantica in the Mostellaria. They manifest Plautus' buoyant interest in lyrical song. Their structure within this one play alone is evidence of the rich vein in Plautus of "the immense variety of ways in which the different units are mixed together to form the so-called mutatis modis cantica." (Martin Ostwald, in The Meters of Greek and Latin Poetry, by Rosenmeyer, Halporn, and Ostwald [New York: Bobbs-Merrill, 1963], p. 110.) Of this scene Sonnenschein (p. 98) says, ". . . a very effective passage, full of life and humour (duet of Callidamates and Delphium) . . . Altogether this scene must be regarded as one of the most vigorous in Plautus."

Do I sound pickled?[30] I mean Philolaches
He's as jolly as he's . . . *hic* . . . *haec* . . . *hoc.*
That's an old Greek joke, put it in your tripod and smoke on it
With laurel sauce on it. He's no drip he's free as a faucet!

DELPHIUM: Steady, old chap. We ought to be heading *that* way.   320
(*steers him around toward* PHILOLACHES' *house.*)

CALLIDAMATES: Les pray on each other, whadda ya say?
You and me, me and you?
(*Embraces her intricately.*)

DELPHIUM: Sure thing, heartbeat. I'm your clinging vine.

CALLIDAMATES: You're so charmin' I want go arm in arm in arm in cetera
Oh be my guide eight times, octopussy mine.

DELPHIUM: Whoops! You nearly gave me the slip.
Watch it there! Atten-SHUN

CALLIDAMATES (*Hums.*): Oh, when the iris of my eye is smiling
I'm your bosomy boy, honey bee
(*Weaving and buzzing.*)

DELPHIUM: Look out! You'll be stretching out here on the street
Before we make it to the rather more strategic retreat
Prepared for us at Philolaches' headquarters. Don't shilly, Calli.

CALLIDAMATES: I can't wait to recline in comfort somewhere.
Feel like declining and falling right here
By this wall. I'm all in. A sleep.
Lemme go. Drop right here in a heap.

DELPHIUM: All right. Look out, BELOW!

CALLIDAMATES: Oh no, you don't; not without what I'm holding
Here in my hands I'm not folding
(*Laces his arms around her.*)
United we falls, divided we stands.

DELPHIUM: If you do fall, you won't unless I go down too.

CALLIDAMATES: Well, some pasherby will pick us both up later on.   330

DELPHIUM: This man is most mashed.

CALLIDIMATES: Whom? M-m-me? M-m-mashed, you
shaid?

---

[30] *Do I sound pickled:* Callidamates stammers on the Latin word for "to be drunk" *ma-m-ma-madere.*

DELPHIUM: There, now. Give me your hand. I don't want you smashing
Your head on anything hard.

CALLIDAMATES: There you are

DELPHIUM: Ready now, all together

CALLIDAMATES: Say, where'm I headed?

DELPHIUM: You mean you don't know?

CALLIDAMATES: Oh yes, it just came back to me:
I'm going home to have a drink.

DELPHIUM: No, no. To this house over here.
(*Points to* PHILOLACHES'.)

CALLIDAMATES: Of coursh, that place. Now I've got it straight.

PHILOLACHES (*To* PHILEMATIUM.): I think I ought to step out and greet
him, don't you?
He's my very best friend in the world. I'll be back right away.

PHILEMATIUM: That "right away" has already lasted too long for me.

CALLIDAMATES: Hello, there. Anyone at home?

PHILOLACHES (*Coming forward.*): Yes, anyone is.

CALLIDAMATES: Hey, Philolaches, Philolaches, old best friend in the world!

340

PHILOLACHES: Gods bless you, boy. Come right in here and join us
Where have you been?

CALLIDAMATES: Where a man can get mashed first clash.

PHILEMATIUM: Come sit beside us here, Delphium, dear.

PHILOLACHES: Do pour old Calli a drink.

CALLIDAMATES (*Pushes it away.*):   No thanks, I feel sort
of sleep . . .
(*Sinks to the floor and dozes off.*)

PHILOLACHES: There's nothing very new or different about his condition.

DELPHIUM: What shall I do with him now, Philematium dear?

PHILEMATIUM: Oh you might as well leave him alone.

PHILOLACHES (*To slave.*):   Hey there, boy!
Come pass the wine around. Delphium first,
Then us. So we all can satisfy our thirst.

ACT II

Scene 1[31]

TRANIO, PHILOLACHES, CALLIDAMATES, DELPHIUM, PHILEMATIUM,
SPHAERIO.

TRANIO: Jupiter Almighty, his eagle eye fixed on Philolaches,
    The master's son, and on me, is putting every ounce of effort
    And money he can into annihilating us. Our hopes
    Are gone. No steady place is left for self-confidence   350
    To take a stand. Salvation Herself couldn't save us
    Even if she wished to. At the harbor I clamped my eyes
    On the mightiest mountain[32] of monstrous misery imaginable.
    The master is back home from abroad. Anyone here
    Want to make some quick cash? Where are all you tough guys?
    Heroes tattooed with chain gang insignia, or rangers
    Ready to assault the enemy ramparts for practically
    Nothing a month? I'll offer a thousand to the first man
    Who volunteers to carry my cross. But on this condition:
    That he climb up there twice and let both arms and legs   360
    Be nailed to the wood two times. When the second time shows
    That he really means business, he has only to apply
    In person for the money. It'll be ready and waiting for him.
    As it is, I'm not so well off, am I? Shouldn't I
    Be loping off to my own little home at full tilt?
PHILOLACHES: The provender for the festive board! Here's Tranio back
    From the harbor.
TRANIO: Philolaches!

---

    [31] *Act II, Scene 1:* Tranio races in from the Forum. The meter for the ensuing
diverbia from here to the next *canticum* (entrance of Simo) is, first trochaic (lines
348–407), then iambic (lines 408–609).
    [32] *mightiest mountain:* a tidal wave of alliteration: *Ita mali maeroris montem
maxumum ad portum modo.*

PHILOLACHES: What's up?

TRANIO: You and I.

PHILOLACHES: You and I what?

TRANIO: We're up, that's what. We're done for.

PHILOLACHES: Why so?

TRANIO: Your father is coming.

PHILOLACHES: What's that I hear?

TRANIO: We've been swept away: your father's coming, I say.

PHILOLACHES: Where is he?

TRANIO: Down at the harbor right now.

PHILOLACHES: Who says so?

  Who saw him?

TRANIO: Well, I say I'm the one who saw him.

PHILOLACHES: Oh me, oh my . . . father. What am I supposed to do?

TRANIO: Why ask me? You're supposed to be sitting at table.

PHILOLACHES: Did you see him yourself?

TRANIO: I'll say I saw him myself.

PHILOLACHES: Are you sure?

TRANIO: Sure I'm sure.

PHILOLACHES: I'm done for if that's the truth.

370

TRANIO: What good would it do me to lie?

PHILOLACHES: What can I do now?

TRANIO: Have all this stuff removed. Who's that asleep?

PHILOLACHES: Callidamates. Wake him up, Delphium.

DELPHIUM: Callidamates!

  Wake up, Callidamates!

CALLIDAMATES: I'm awake. Hand me a drink.

DELPHIUM: Wake up! Philolaches' father has just come home

  From abroad.

CALLIDAMATES: Goodbye, father.

PHILOLACHES: It's hello to him,

  And he's fine, thank you. I'm the one you can kiss goodbye

  After I show you inside.

CALLIDAMATES: Show who suicide?[33] At my age?

<hr />

[33] *Show who suicide:* When Philolaches says dis*perii* "I'm utterly done for," Callidamates says bis*peristi?* "Did you perish twice? How's that possible?"

DELPHIUM: Come on, for heaven's sake, get up! His father's coming.

CALLIDAMATES (*To* PHILOLACHES.): You father? Coming. T-t-t-tell him t-t-t-to

G-g-go away ag-g-g-gain. What business does he have coming back here?

PHILOLACHES: What will I do? My father's going to come here and catch me

Drunk, the house full of guests and girls. What's the use

Of digging a well[34] when you're already dying of thirst?

That's how much chance I see for my own survival   380

Now that I'm faced head on with my father's arrival.

TRANIO: Look! He laid his head down and gone to sleep again

Revive him.

PHILOLACHES: Won't you wake up? My father'll be here

Any moment, I tell you.

CALLIDAMATES: Your father, you say? Well, hand me

My shoes, I want to get dressed for battle. By god,

I'll run him through, that father.

PHILOLACHES: Yes and ruin us all.

DELPHIUM: Quiet, honey child.

TRANIO (*To attendants.*):   Get your hands on him, you two, and hustle

Him inside, right away.

CALLIDAMATES (*To attendants.*): I gotta go and I'll use you

For a pot if you don't bring me one.

(*Staggers off with them.*)

PHILOLACHES: It's the end of me.

TRANIO: Now cheer up. I've got just the medicine for your fears.

PHILOLACHES: I'm finished and done for.

TRANIO: Shhhhh. I'm thinking of a scheme

To crack the case. Is it all right with you if I manage to make

Your father, when he comes, not only not enter the house

But run away as far as he can? Now all of you get inside   390

And clear away this stuff, but fast.

PHILOLACHES: And where will I be?

TRANIO: Where you like it best, right next to her, and to her?

(*Points to* PHILEMATIUM *and* DELPHIUM.)

---

[34] *digging a well:* This sounds like a homemade proverb: *Miserumst opus. Igitur demum fodere puteum, ubi sitis fauces tenet.*

DELPHIUM: Don't you think we ought to get away from here?

TRANIO: No farther
Than that, Delphium
(*Indicates a tiny distance with his thumb and forefinger.*)
Keep the party going inside the house
Just as if this slight rearrangement had never occurred.

PHILOLACHES: I'm soaking wet with sweat just thinking how hot
Those cool words of his will turn out to be for me.

TRANIO: Can't you be still and do what I tell you?

PHILOLACHES: Yes I can.

TRANIO: Now Philematium and Delphium you go in first please.

DELPHIUM: At your service, sir.
(*Exeunt.*)

TRANIO: I rather wish you were.
Now, you pay attention to what I want you to do.
First of all, you're to close the house and shut it up tight: 400
Don't let a soul make the slightest sound inside, not a whisper.

PHILOLACHES: Right.

TRANIO: As if there wasn't a living thing[35] inside.

PHILOLACHES: Count on me.

TRANIO: When the old man raps on the door, don't answer.

PHILOLACHES: And what else?

TRANIO: Tell them to bring out the front door key
To me here. I'll lock the house up from outside.

PHILOLACHES: To your safekeeping I entrust myself and my hopes.

TRANIO (*Strolling about looking confident.*): A feather of a difference it
makes if a man
Is in charge of, or in the charge of another,
If he isn't daring at heart. 410
Anyone at all, the best or the worst,
Can easily hatch a plot in a burst
Of inspiration and get things off to a bad start fast.
But the mark of a man of genius is seen
When he steers the complicated mess
On through its mischievous confusion
To a calm and innocent conclusion

---

[35] *a living thing*: literally "no mortal creature," *natus nemo.*

And suffers no punishment, not even deep embarrassment.
And I propose to handle what's at hand,
And has gotten a bit out of hand at present,
So as to bring our rollicking ship to land:
Clear weather after the storm is always pleasant.
I don't want events upsetting our noble band.

Hey, Sphaerio, how dare you drift out of there?

SPHAERIO: The key, sir.   420

TRANIO: Oh yes of course, the key. You're obeying my orders
  Precisely.

SPHAERIO: Himself says please sir, please to ask
  You to frighten his father somehow, so he don't come in
  And catch him.

TRANIO: You tell him this for me, do you hear?
  The old man won't even dare to look at the house:
  He'll take to his heels with his head wrapped up in his cloak
  In an absolute panic—that's how I mean to manage it.
  Now give me the key, and get in there and bar the door
  While I lock it outside, here.
                      Now let the old master appear!
  I'll put on a play[36] right now before his eyes
  That will cost him so much he won't have a cent when he dies
  To pay for the funeral games. So let him enjoy

36 *I'll put on a play: ludos faciam. Ludos facere* is the usual expression for "entertain, divert, put on a show for." Funeral games (*ludi*) often included dramatic entertainment, paid for by the dead man's family. Philolaches has spent so much of his father's money that Theopropides might as well enjoy his "games" while he's still alive, so Tranio proceeds to put on his play. The idea is accented again by the pointed remarks in the final scene, ending, "Tell them (two famous Greek playwrights) how your slave had such fun with you and you will have provided them with the perfect example they need for portraying frustration in their comedies.":
  Dicito eis quo pacto tuos te servus ludificaverit
  Optumas frustrationes dederis in comoediis.
Taken together with this passage at the other end of the play-within-a-play parenthesis, Tranio seems to register Plautus' own engaging interest in his artistic business. Finally, Roman plays were performed at festivals called *Ludi*, specifically the *Ludi Romani* (in September), *Ludi Plebeii* (in November), *Ludi Apollinares* (in July), *Ludi Megalenses* (in April). (Cf., G. E. Duckworth, *The Nature of Roman Comedy* [Princeton, 1952], pp. 76 ff.)

The festivities while he's alive. I'll dive over here,
Away from the house and take up my station, so when
He comes in soon and heads for his home destination
I can make him the comic hero of this situation.   430

Scene 2

THEOPROPIDES *and* TRANIO.

THEOPROPIDES (*Drily offering thanks to Neptune in a satisfied grumble.*):
Neptune, I suppose I owe you a great debt of thanks
For letting me out of your clutches at least long enough
To come back home still alive. If ever again
You hear that I've ventured so much as a foot from the shore,
You have my permission to do to me then what you tried
This time. Get thee behind me,[37] thou Saline Tempter!
And begone henceforth forevermore, starting now.
Whatever I intended to entrust to your hands, I have.

TRANIO (*Aside.*): Good lord, Neptune, you've made a ghastly mistake,
Letting an opportunity like that slip through your fingers.

THEOPROPIDES: After three years I've finally come home from Egypt,   440
Eagerly awaited, no doubt, I'll walk in on the household.

TRANIO (*Aside.*): The messenger bringing news of your death would
enjoy
A more enthusiastic welcome at the hands of your family.

THEOPROPIDES: What's this? Here's the front door closed in broad daylight.
I'll knock. Hey there! Anyone in? Will you open the door?

TRANIO (*Coming forward.*): Who's that man walking up to the front door
of our house?

THEOPROPIDES: Oh, here's my slave himself, Tranio.

TRANIO: Theopropides!
My old master! Ciao! I'm delighted to see you back safe
And sound. You *are* in sound health?

THEOPROPIDES: Why of course. You can see
I'm fine.

[37] *Get thee behind me: Apage.* I have translated this word whenever it appears as
it is rendered in the Authorized Version of the New Testament.

TRANIO: Gee, sir, that's great.

THEOPROPIDES: Listen, what are you,
Some kind of a nut?

TRANIO: Nut?

THEOPROPIDES: Yes, nut. Strolling   450
Around in the street, and not a soul in the house
Looking after things, no one to open the doors,
No one to answer my knock. I almost knocked a hole
In those darned double doors with my pounding.

TRANIO: You mean, you
touched them?

THEOPROPIDES: Yes, I touched them and knocked good and hard.

TRANIO: Wow!

THEOPROPIDES: What's wrong?

TRANIO: You did something awful.

THEOPROPIDES: What's this "wow-
ful" business
You're giving me?

TRANIO: I can't tell you how horrible the thing is
You've done, master, how disastrous.

THEOPROPIDES: What horrible thing?   460

TRANIO: Get away from the house, I beg and beseech you, clear off.
Come over here this way, toward me. You touched those doors?

THEOPROPIDES: How do you think I could knock on the door without
touching it?

TRANIO: Oh Lord, you've murdered . . .

THEOPROPIDES: Murdered who?

TRANIO: The members of
this family.

THEOPROPIDES: For a crack like that may the gods slap your fresh face.

TRANIO (Musing.): I don't think you can do anything to make up for this.

THEOPROPIDES: Why not? Or are you trying to change the subject?

TRANIO: Just stay over here, keep well away from the house
And tell those two gigantic attendants to back off.

THEOPROPIDES: All right. Back off, you two gigantic attendants!

TRANIO (To slaves.): And don't touch the house. Now touch the ground
three times over here.

THEOPROPIDES: In the name of the gods will you kindly explain what's
    Going . . .

TRANIO: On? It's been seven months since any soul planted a foot   470
    Inside that house, from the day we all moved out.

THEOPROPIDES: Would you explain just why you did that?

TRANIO: Give a look around
    Is there anyone near who might overhear what we're saying?

THEOPROPIDES: No, the coast is clear.

TRANIO: Take another look.

THEOPROPIDES: No one, continue.

TRANIO: A capital crime was consummated . . .

THEOPROPIDES: I don't understand you.

TRANIO: I say, a hell of a murder was committed a long time ago.

THEOPROPIDES: A long time ago?

TRANIO: But we just found out about it recently.

THEOPROPIDES: What murder? Who did it? Tell me more.

TRANIO: The host in the house
    Killed his guest with his own bare hands. The same guy,
    I'm sure, who sold us the house.   480

THEOPROPIDES: Murdered him, did he?

TRANIO: And stripped the guest of his gold, and buried the body
    Of the guest himself right here underneath the house.

THEOPROPIDES: What made you begin to suspect it?

TRANIO: I'll explain: you listen.
    Your son had gone out for dinner and come home late
    From the party; we all went to bed and were soon fast asleep.
    Suddenly he let out a bloodcurdling cry of fear.

THEOPROPIDES: Who let out? My son?

TRANIO: Quiet, please. Shhhhh.
    Just listen. He said that the dead man had appeared in a dream.   490

THEOPROPIDES: In a dream? Are you sure?

TRANIO: Yes, I am. And listen to this:
    He said that the dead man had spoken to him as follows:

THEOPROPIDES: In a dream? Are you sure?

TRANIO: Look, you wouldn't want him walking around
    And talking in broad daylight, when the whole live world was up,
    Would you? A man who was murdered sixty years ago?
    At times, Theopropides, you are positively obtusely stupid.

THEOPROPIDES: I'll keep quiet.

TRANIO: So the dead man said to your son in his sleep:
"I am a guest in this house from across the sea.
My name is Mudd D. Waters. I live in this house.
The dwelling has been duly given and granted to me.
Orcus, the king of the dead, has had to refuse
Me passage across Acheron to the land of the dead
Because I died prematurely. I was foully deceived   500
When I trusted my host, who killed me here in my bed,
And dug a deep hole underneath the house, and heaved
Me into it when no one was looking. Devoid of burial,
Down in the hole he dumped me, that hell of a host, and he stole
All me gold. Now young man, get out of here, and carry all
Your household possessions along. This house is unholy,
A hell of a place. It's hexed, and you will be next."
Gosh, it'd take me a year to describe the manifestations
This dead man demonstrated: we were almost delirious
At what he said and did, this guest his host
Mysteriously murdered and monstered[38] into a ghost.
(*A muffled noise is heard from inside the house.*)
Psst

THEOPROPIDES: Oh god, what was that?

TRANIO (*To ghost.*):   He was the one
Who rattled the doors, not me. It was he who knocked!

THEOPROPIDES: I'm drained. I haven't a drop of blood in my veins.
The dead are coming to take me to Acheron alive.

TRANIO (*Aside.*): I'm done for. Those creeps inside the house will wreck
    the plot   510
Of my play right now. And I just made it up. I'm panicked
For fear he'll catch me in the act with my plans down.

THEOPROPIDES: Why are you talking to yourself?

TRANIO: Back away from the door.
Take to your heels, in Hercules' name.

THEOPROPIDES: Where to?
Hadn't you better get going too?

---

[38] *manifestations . . . monstered:* literally "what horrible apparitions there were
here" *Quae hic monstra fiunt.* From this line about the *monstra,* "ghosts," the play
derives its title *mostellaria* (*fabula*) "the little ghost story."

TRANIO: Ohhhhh no, not me,
I've nothing to fear. I've made my peace with the dead.
(*Muffled call from within*—Choo-choo! Tranio!)
TRANIO: Don't call me, I'll call you.
I didn't do it! I didn't pound on the doors.
THEOPROPIDES: Say . . .
TRANIO: Shhhh . . . not so loud.
THEOPROPIDES: Why do you keep on
Breaking off our conversation?
TRANIO: Thou senile Tempter! Get thee behind me!
THEOPROPIDES: What's got hold of you,
Tranio, anyway? Whom are you mumbling that stuff to?
TRANIO: Oh! (*Much relieved.*) Was it you that called? As the gods love
    me,   520
I thought it was old dead and downcast bawling me out
In a flap because you pounded the door of his flophouse.
(*Laughs weakly.*)
But you're still standing there? Not following instructions?
THEOPROPIDES: What should I do?
TRANIO: Be careful not to look back,
And run away, with your neck covered up in your cloak.
THEOPROPIDES: Why don't you run away?
TRANIO: I've made my peace
With the dead.
THEOPROPIDES: I heard you the first time you said that. But what
I don't get at the moment is why you acted so scared.
TRANIO: Don't bother your head about me, I can take good care
Of myself. But go on as you started, take to your heels
As fast as you can. And pray to Hercules for help.
THEOPROPIDES: Hercules![39] This is no joke! Your help I hereby invoke.
TRANIO: Me too,[40] Hercules! Grant me with all your might
(*Exit* THEOPROPIDES.)
The power to make this old man a prey to stage fright.
And in the name of the immortal gods, I think I can say   530
I've cooked up a pot of terrible trouble today!

[39] *Hercules*: An apotropaic invocation.
[40] *Me too*: But Tranio invokes Hercules *against* Theopropides.

ACT III

Scene 1

DANISTA, TRANIO, THEOPROPIDES.

DANISTA (*Soliloquizing.*): I've never seen a worse year than this one for
   lending out money.
I work the Forum from dawn to dark, but I can't
Seem to interest a soul in borrowing a bit of cash.

TRANIO (*Aside.*): Well, this is it, pure and simple from now on perdition.
Here's the moneylender who loaned us the cash at interest
We bought the girl and staged our parties by means of.
We're caught in the act if I can't come up with a plan
To keep the old man from knowing. I'll intercept him.
But here's Theopropides back home again too soon.
I'm afraid he's heard something more than I saw fit to tell him.
I'll go up and intercept *him*. Oh, what a rogue   540
And peasant slave am I! And scared to death.
There's no worse ill the flesh is heir to than conscience,
Especially a guilty conscience.[41] And I've got a beaut!
But however it all turns out, I plan to proceed
To continue to confuse things as chaotically as I can:
That looks like what they demand.
   (*To* THEOPROPIDES.) Where have you been?

THEOPROPIDES: Oh, I met the man I bought this house from

TRANIO: And told him—
Of course about what I had said to you?

THEOPROPIDES: Every word.

TRANIO (*Aside.*): I'm out of luck now, Poor Io! My beautiful schemes
   Are scheduled for the scrapheap one by one, I have the feeling.   550

THEOPROPIDES: What's that you're saying to yourself?

---

[41] *guilty conscience*: a gnomic line: *Nihil est miserius quam animus hominis con-
scius.*

TRANIO: Who? Me? Oh, nothing.

THEOPROPIDES: Well, I told the whole story just as you unrolled it to me.

TRANIO: And he confessed to the ghost of the guest?

THEOPROPIDES: Denied it completely.

TRANIO: He did?

THEOPROPIDES: He most certainly did.

TRANIO: Now, just think back a bit:
He did *not* admit it, you say?

THEOPROPIDES: I'd admit it, if he did.
What do you think I should do?

TRANIO: I? Think? Do?
Sue him. And insist on an honest judge, a good man
Who will trust my testimony. That way, you'll win the case
As easily and neatly as a fox can pilfer a pear.

DANISTA: Ah, Philolaches' man, Tranio. And they haven't paid a thing   560
On their loan, either principal or interest.

THEOPROPIDES (*As* TRANIO *starts off.*): Where are you going?

TRANIO: Me? Oh, nowhere. I was just practicing. (*Aside.*) How negative
Can you get? The gods must have frowned the day I was born.
That moneylender will soon be right here, talking to the master.
I'm so *measly!* They'll give me the business both ways.
I'll try and intercept him.

DANISTA: Ah, he's heading my way.
I'm in luck. There's a slight whiff of cash in the air.

TRANIO: He's in a good mood. Wait till he comes to his senses.
Ah, greetings, Silverdespiser.[42] I *trust* you are well.

DANISTA: Greetings! Can you make a payment?

TRANIO: Get off it, you beast.
You walk up and start right in hitting me over the head.   570

DANISTA: You empty-handed, empty-headed fool.

TRANIO: And you're a mind reader?
No doubt. Or is it a pickpocket?

DANISTA: Why not relax
From the funny business somewhat?

TRANIO: Some what is it you want?

---

[42] *Silverdespiser:* The *danista* (moneylender) is here, and once only, addressed by
Tranio by his "other" name, *Misargyrides.*

DANISTA: Where's Philolaches?

TRANIO: Say, you couldn't have come
At a better time than you did.

DANISTA: Oh, really?

TRANIO (*Motions him aside.*): Rally over here.

DANISTA (*In a loud voice.*): How about the interest payment that's coming
to me?

TRANIO: I know you've got a good voice, you don't have to shout.

DANISTA: I'll clamor like a commercial.

TRANIO: Oh come on, be nice!

DANISTA: How can I be nice to you?

TRANIO: Go on back home.

DANISTA: Leave now?

TRANIO: Come back around noon.

DANISTA: And the interest
That's coming to me?

TRANIO: It'll be ready then. Now go. 580

DANISTA: Why should I wear myself out and waste time going home
And coming back again? I'll just hang around until noon.

TRANIO: No, go on home. Look, I mean it, kid. Scoot on home.

DANISTA: I don't want to until my interest . . .

TRANIO: Get under way,
Slowpoke.

DANISTA: Why don't you pay me my interest? This negative
Kick is making me sick.

TRANIO: That's nothing to the way
You nauseate me. Listen, run along home.

DANISTA: Just for that I'll call your master, PHILOLA . . .

TRANIO (*Interrupting.*): Good voice there. Feel better, now that you're
shouting?

DANISTA: I'm only asking for what is mine. You've been putting
Me off for days. If I'm a bother to you,
Hand over the cash. I'll go. And you can be rid 590
Of all these question and answers by redeeming one word.

TRANIO: What word's that?

DANISTA: Pay up.

TRANIO: That's two words at least.

DANISTA: Well, it's one thing, like principal and interest. Pay up what's
    due.

TRANIO: Say, how about if we pay the principal?

DANISTA (*Loud.*):   NO NO, I'M DUE
    THE INTEREST FIRST!

TRANIO: Did you come here to practice your scales,
    You bull-throated auctioneer? Stop moaning for your money,
    You materialist. Make all the musical fuss you must,
    You still won't get a sniff of your note from my master.
    He doesn't owe you a dime.

DANISTA: Doesn't owe . . . ?

TRANIO: Not one bit
    Richer will you leave this place. You won't get a *frit*.[43]

DANISTA: What's a *frit*?

TRANIO: The unformed granule at the top of an ear of wheat.

DANISTA: Thanks very much.

TRANIO: Well I mean it's the principle of the thing.
    You refuse payment of the principal. And you think my master
    Will sneak out of town into exile because of the interest
    Due to a banker who's unwilling to accept the principal?

DANISTA: I don't want the whole sum paid, necessarily, now.
    What I do want is the interest that's due on the whole amount.   600

TRANIO: Don't be a pain. No one's going to give it to you,
    Whatever you do. You're not the only man in town
    Who loans money out at interest.

DANISTA: Give me my interest,
    Pay back that interest, hand over the interest, you two.
    Will you both be so kind as to pay back my interest at once?
    Will the interest now be paid to me?

TRANIO: Interest here,
    Interest there, interest everywhere.
    An interesting subject to our speaker, apparently; it's all
    He's interested in discussing. Personally, I find it disgusting.
    Get thee behind me, thou loud percentage of a beast.
    You're rude and unattractive.

[43] *frit*: I have let Tranio offer the technical definition of this agricultural term signifying "particle."

DANISTA: Sticks and stones
May bruise my bones, but tones can't touch my loans.

THEOPROPIDES: Things are getting warm. I can feel the heat
Even way over here. Now what can the interest be,   610
I wonder, the fellow's after with such a vengeance?

TRANIO: All right, here's Philolaches' father just back from abroad.
He landed today. He'll pay off the interest and principal
Both, so you don't try to take us for more. You'll see
If he keeps you waiting.

DANISTA: I suppose I should take what I can get.

THEOPROPIDES: What's going on?

TRANIO: I beg your pardon?

THEOPROPIDES: Who is that,
And what is he after? Why is he shouting the name
Of my son and starting this brawl with you? Do you owe
Him some money?

TRANIO: Ah, splash the cash in his face, the fish—
Shove it down the filthy shark's throat. That's an order.

THEOPROPIDES: That's a what?

TRANIO: No it is not a what, it's an order, for money.
Plaster the fish in the face with a fist full of cash.   620

DANISTA: A wonderful way to go.

TRANIO: You heard that didn't you?
A typical moneylender: no sense of shame.

THEOPROPIDES: I don't care about the man's professional status
Or what names you call him. I want to be told, and by you,
What this cash debt is that Philolaches owes.

TRANIO: Oh, a trifle.

THEOPROPIDES: How big a trifle?

TRANIO: One thousand bucks.
You don't mean to say you think that's a big amount?

THEOPROPIDES: What's your definition of a trifle?

TRANIO: A lot less than a lot.

THEOPROPIDES: Thanks very much. Now, I seem to have heard that credit
Has also been advanced in the amount of the interest.

TRANIO: Well, that's forty *minae* [*pronounced miney.*] plus four. Eeeny,
meeny, miney   630
And one mo', well, let's see that's about 1100 chunks,

More or less, the principal and the interest.

DANISTA: That's right.

That's the sum of it. That's all I'm after.

TRANIO: I dare you

To ask for a half-as more.[44] We could sue and you know it.

Tell him you'll pay it, so he'll go away.

THEOPROPIDES: Tell him

I'll *pay* it? I never carry more than two and a half asses

In cash.

TRANIO: Yes, you tell him you'll pay it

THEOPROPIDES: *I'll* pay it?

TRANIO: Yes, your very own sweet little self. Now just tell him.

Listen to me. Promise him you'll pay, go on now,

That's an order.

THEOPROPIDES: Oh I get it, a money order. Answer me this.

What have you done with the money you borrowed?

TRANIO: It's safe,

Perfectly safe. An investment.

THEOPROPIDES: If the money's intact,

You people can pay back the loan.

TRANIO: Your son bought a house.

THEOPROPIDES: A house?

TRANIO: A house.

THEOPROPIDES: Well, good for Philolaches!

Looks like he's filial; taking after his father, becoming

A good business man.

TRANIO: When this house turned out to be haunted,

As I told you, he went out and bought another at a bargain.   640

THEOPROPIDES: Bought a house, did he?

TRANIO: A house. And you can imagine

What a property, too!

[44] *I dare you/To ask for a half-as more: Velim quidem hercle ut uno nummo plus peto* "I wish you would ask for just a nickel more." I have given the lowest Roman denomination, the *as* for *nummus* here, literally a *sestertius*, or 2½ *asses*, about five cents. Sonnenschein's note (p. 117) on the demand for anything more than the exact amount reads, in part: "This reference to the *plus petitio* is a thoroughly Roman touch: if the plaintiff in an action demanded more than he had a right to, he was liable to be cast in his suit (*causa cadere, causam perdere*). Four kinds of *plus petitio* were recognized . . ." etc.

THEOPROPIDES: I don't quite see how I can.

TRANIO: Wow, what a place!

THEOPROPIDES: What kind of a place?

TRANIO: Don't ask.

THEOPROPIDES: Why not?

TRANIO: A phenomenal buy. A marvelous place!

THEOPROPIDES: Sounds like a good deal. How much did it cost?

TRANIO: Two talents:[45] Me plus you, 3000 bills.
But he paid down the forty miney, or 1000 bills.
Do I make myself clear?   650

THEOPROPIDES: Sounds like a very good deal.

DANISTA: Gentlemen, it's noon. (*Flourishing his hourglass.*)

TRANIO: Pay the guy, to stop his puking.

THEOPROPIDES: Just apply to me for the miney, I mean money.

DANISTA: You?

THEOPROPIDES: Come see me tomorrow.

DANISTA: I'll go, and suffer no sorrow
If I'm going to get it tomorrow.
(*Exit.*)

TRANIO: Procrastinator!
May all the gods (and goddesses too, while I'm at it)
Do him in promptly for his "Borrow today, pay later."
There's no more repulsive a race of men than these bankers,
Always hankering to get back their money. They're unreasonable.

THEOPROPIDES: Where is the house located, the one my son bought?

TRANIO (*Aside.*): Here I go down for the fourth time.

THEOPROPIDES: Will you answer my query?
660

TRANIO: Yes, that's some query. I'm trying to think of the name
Of the owner.

THEOPROPIDES: Well, think . . . or thwim (ah, chuck, chuck, chuck).

TRANIO (*Aside.*): Going down for the fifth.
I can't think. Oh, buoy! I've come up with it! Next door neighbor!
Why not call that the house his son has acquired?
They say the lie you have just cooked up and serve

---

[45] *Two talents:* literally *Talentis magnis totidem quot ego et tu sumus.* The *talentum magnum,* the Attic silver talent equals 60 *minae* or $1500.

While still piping hot, is the best. What *has* to be said
It is perfectly proper to say.

THEOPROPIDES: How about it? Remember?

TRANIO: Damn the man! I mean *that* one.

(*To audience, pointing to* THEOPROPIDES.)

Our next door neighbor
It was whose house your son acquired. 670

THEOPROPIDES: A good buy?

TRANIO: If you make the loan good, a very good buy, if you won't
It's goodbye to us. You'll admit the *location* [*French pronunciation.*]
is good.

THEOPROPIDES: *À merveille!* I'd love to go have a look.
Rap on the door and call someone out, Tranio.

TRANIO (*Aside.*): I'm in for some hard knocks. I'm dashed if I know
What to say at this point. The waves are washing me back
All over again, and dashing me on the same rocks.

THEOPROPIDES: What's holding you up?

TRANIO (*Aside.*): You are, you pirate. I'm stranded.
I can't figure out what to do. I'm caught barehanded.

THEOPROPIDES: Go ask at the door for someone to show us around.
Come on, get a move on.

TRANIO: Don't you know there are ladies present? 680
We'll have to inquire if they're willing, or not so willing.

THEOPROPIDES: Well, that's a sound suggestion. Go over and request it.
I'll wait outside right here while you go in.

TRANIO (*Aside.*): May all the gods (and goddesses too, while I'm at it)
Do you in for once and for all, old *chap*, from now on.
Your resistance meets my attacks at every turn.
Hoo-oo-l-y Smoke! Just in the nic-o-tine!
The owner of the house is coming out: yes, it's Simo,
And he's going for a stroll. I wonder, will the stroll get away?
I'll duck over here for a moment and plan what to say:
I'll summon the senate of my mind to congress today
And then prime Simo in the part I want him to play!

Scene 2

SIMO, TRANIO, THEOPROPIDES.

SIMO (*Soliloquizing.*): I haven't had so good a time all year[46]   690
At home, or a meal that pleased me more.
My wife prepared a banquet here,
And she's hauling me off to bed. I swore
I'd go, but oh *no*, you don't. Enough is enough!
I knew there was some ulterior motive
In setting that marvelous meal before me:
She wanted to lure me to bed like a votive
Lamb to the slaughter in the sheets. I tore free.
Anyone knows it's bad for the health
To go to bed after eating. Myself,
I refuse, Get thee behind me, old girl of the ruffled fluff!
So I sneaked out the door, and the coast is clear.
Inside the house my old woman is fully aroused,
With fury at me, I fear. Let the fur fly, you overused stuff.

TRANIO (*Aside.*): But there's something unpleasant in store for the old
rod tonight.   700
Neither dinner nor bed will deliver him much delight.

SIMO (*Continues the* canticum.): The more I ponder the problem
The fonder I become of my conclusion:
You marry an older woman for her money,
You *don't* have a lot of sleep breathing down your neck.
Funny: Husbands with rich old wives do not adore them.
Rather than curl up in bed they head for the Forum
Where the non-uxorious form a formidable quorum.
Of course I don't know how the wives of you husbands out there
Behave, but considering how mine always raises the roof
With me, I'm in bad enough. After this I'll be even worse off!

---

[46] The third *canticum* is a recitative by Simo in cretic rhythm, with asides from
Tranio, who is eavesdropping, until he comes forward to greet the *senex*.

TRANIO: Well old fellow, if your getaway gets you in trouble   710
  At least there won't be one of the gods to blame.
  You can only in all due fairness indict yourself.
  Now it's time I went up and had a few words with my victim.
  He's had it! I've thought of how to deceive the master:
  A masterstroke, in brief, that will keep my grief at bay.
  I'll approach the man now. May the gods shine on you, Simo.

SIMO: Good health, Tranio.

TRANIO: You're fine?

SIMO: Not bad.
  What's on?

TRANIO: I'm on, to you, taking the hand
  Of the finest of fellows.

SIMO: Well, aren't we the friendliest?   720
  Handing out compliments!

TRANIO: It's only gladhanding a man
  Who deserves it.

SIMO: But I'm not holding a worthwhile slave
  By the hand, Herc knows.

TRANIO: Whose Herc?

THEOPROPIDES (*From across stage.*):   You jerk,
  Snap back to me!

TRANIO (*Yells.*): I'll whip right over.

SIMO: I say,
  Now, how much longer . . .

TRANIO: What's that you say you say?

SIMO: Do you think you can keep on like this?

TRANIO: What's that you say
  You say?

SIMO: You know quite well what I'm talking about.
  Life is short and you're succeeding in making it sweet.

TRANIO: What's that? Oh, yes . . . Er . . . I really wasn't aware
  You were discussing us particularly.

SIMO: It's got some *style*,
  The way you map your menus like a gourmet   730
  And choose choice wines and snare your seafood fresh
  At the fanciest prices. Ah, that's the life to be living!

TRANIO: That is the life we used to be living till now.

At this point our pleasures have positively petered out and pancaked.

SIMO: Ah, soooo? (*Rising inflection.*)

TRANIO: We're torn down, Simo, down to the ground.

SIMO: Nonsense, boy! Everything has gone just right

For you both so far.

TRANIO: I won't deny those words.

We've lived the way we wanted and lapped up the luxury.

But, Simo, now the wind has dropped and left

Our ship becalmed.

SIMO: Ah, sooooo? How so?   740

TRANIO: Well, not so so-so. It couldn't be worse.

SIMO: But the ship

Was safe, high and dry on land.

TRANIO: Don't remind me of landings!

SIMO: Why not?

TRANIO: Someone landed, all right, and landed on us.

SIMO: Ah, sooooo?

TRANIO (*Prose interruption.*): Look, cut out that "ah, sooo" stuff will

You? This is supposed to be a *Roman* comedy.

            Some ship, a master vessel, could be,

Could it not? crashed into and crushed our yacht.

SIMO: I sympathize with you, my boy. What happened exactly?

TRANIO: I'll tell you: the master came home today from abroad.

SIMO: From abroad? He did? Well the old past master! I predict:

One: Your hide is in for a good bit of stretching;

Two: The chain gang will see that you're all right for ironing;

Three: You'll be crucified, later.

TRANIO: Sway now, die later!

Procrastinator! Look, Simo, you won't tell on us?

SIMO: He won't learn a thing from me, don't you worry your head.

TRANIO: Oh, new-found patron, your client salutes you!

SIMO: Client?

I can't use a client like you.

TRANIO: About the business

My master sent me to see you about . . .

SIMO: Tell me first,

How much does he know of the way you've been carrying on?

TRANIO: Not a *frit*.

SIMO: Not a what? He isn't one whit annoyed   750
   With his son?

TRANIO: Oh no, the weather is clear, as sunny
   And fine as weather can be. Halcyon days,
   When the kingfisher plans for his fledglings on calm waves.
   Now my master urgently asks that he be allowed
   To come and look at your house.

SIMO: It isn't for sale.

TRANIO: I know that. But my old man wants to build an addition
   To his own place, quarters for women, with baths,
   A cloister and walk.

SIMO: So? What is he dreaming of?

TRANIO: I can tell you. He wants his son to marry a wife
   As soon as it can be arranged. And that's the reason
   He wants a new women's wing. Some architect told him,   760
   He says, that your house was a gem of model construction.
   So he now wants to use your place as a model for his,
   And particularly wants the advantages of your design
   For trapping the maximum shade—yours is superb,
   Or so we've heard—no matter how bright the day.

SIMO: By god, I can tell you, when there's a good shade everywhere else
   The sun is hitting my house from dawn to dusk
   Like a salesman at the front door. There's never any shade
   Anywhere on my place, except in the shaft of the well.

TRANIO: If you haven't got some colored shade[47] to serve as umbrella,
   Perhaps you've got a nice light *jade*, a kind of high yellow?   770

SIMO: Oh, very funny: but that's how it is.

TRANIO: All the same,
   He wants to look around.

SIMO: Let him look around,
   If he likes. If he likes what he sees, he can build
   Himself something on those lines.

TRANIO: Shall I go call him, then?

---

[47] *colored shade: Quid? Sarsinatis ecquast si Umbram non habes?* "*Umbram*, a pun
on *umbra*: 'If you don't keep any *shade*, perhaps you keep a *jade* from Sarsina?' Sarsina, a town in Umbria, was the birthplace of Plautus." (Sonnenschein, p. 123.)

SIMO: Go call him, you're vocal enough!

TRANIO (*Monologue as he crosses the stage.*): Vocal? I'm a local
   Leonardo!
   And proudly lay claim to my fame! Single-handed, I frame
   These fiendish designs that will live on to future times
   And make me remembered as one who, like Alexander,
   Was Great, or like Agathocles,[48] the noble but late
   King of Sicily. These two old men I have busily
   Saddled with bags, my bundle of tricks. Each one
   Is now carrying out his share of my plan. What fun
   To get them to work for me! And I think I've found
   A new source of income, too. Mule drivers pound
   Their mules along the road loaded down with freight,   780
   But I have men to shoulder and move the weight.
   Of my bundles of tricks. And as if it were their fate,
   Men are strong and patient and capable of carrying on,
   No matter how much or how long they're imposed upon! (*Beat.*)
   I'm not quite sure whether to . . . yes, I'll go
   And speak to him. (*Clears his throat.*) Ahem! Theopropides!

THEOPROPIDES (*Clears his throat.*): Harumph! Who's that calling me by
   name?[49]

TRANIO: A slave who serves his master in the most amazing
   Manner.

THEOPROPIDES: Ah, so? Where in the hell have you been?

TRANIO: Where you sent me. I beg to report, sir: mission accomplished.

THEOPROPIDES: Does it take all day to tender a simple request?

TRANIO: The old man wasn't free, so I waited around.

THEOPROPIDES: Up to your same old tricks. Taking an olive break,
   I bet.

TRANIO: Now listen, sir, take this saying to heart: 790
   "You can't blow on your soup and slurp it simultaneously."
   That's from Euripides' fragments, Theopropides.
   I couldn't be there and here at the same time, could I?

THEOPROPIDES: And what now?

---

   [48] *Agathocles*: a famous King of Sicily, d. 289 B.C.
   [49] The dialogue exchange between Theopropides and Tranio is a *canticum* in
bacchiacs.

TRANIO: Come and look, just as much as you wish.

THEOPROPIDES: All right, escort me.

TRANIO: Shall I follow you over?

THEOPROPIDES: No, I'll follow you.

TRANIO: Ah, here's the owner himself.
Waiting in front of the door for you, downcast
Because he's sold the house.

THEOPROPIDES: What's that to me?

TRANIO: He's asked me to ask Philolaches, please
To sell it back to him.

THEOPROPIDES: I should *say* not.
Every man must mow his own field. If we'd bought the house
At an unfair price we'd have no right to return it. 800
Money in hand is better than beating around the bush.
The quality of mercy should not be strained
To apply to money matters.

TRANIO: Stop dragging your feet,
And dragging in those famous quotations. Keep up with me.

THEOPROPIDES: Coming, slave, coming.

TRANIO (*To* THEOPROPIDES.): Here he is.
(*To* SIMO.) Ahem! I present my master, Simo.

SIMO: Theopropides!
Welcome home from so long a time overseas
How are you?

THEOPROPIDES: Fine, thanks, how are you?

SIMO: He says
You'd like to look around my domicile.

THEOPROPIDES: If it's not too much trouble.

SIMO: No trouble at all. Enter!
Look around!

THEOPROPIDES: But the ladies . . .

SIMO: The hell with the ladies,
God bless 'em! No woman's worth her weight in feathers.
Just walk around, as if you owned the place.

THEOPROPIDES: "As if?" 810

TRANIO: Now don't rub it in. Can't you see how sick
He feels about your buying the place? It's written
All over his face.

THEOPROPIDES: I can read it.

TRANIO: So don't make a show
  Of being content with the bargain, or terribly cheerful.
THEOPROPIDES: I quite understand. I think the point's well taken
  And shows a considerate and truly human nature[50]
  On your part, my lad. (*To* SIMO.) And now?
SIMO: Why not walk in
  And look around at your leisure? Make yourself at home.
THEOPROPIDES: Thanks so much. You're being terribly kind.
SIMO: I want you to do as you wish.
TRANIO: See the front entrance
  Here, and the walk it affords along the gallery;
  Isn't that lovely?
THEOPROPIDES: Absolutely, a marvelous feature.
TRANIO (*Pointing slyly at* THEOPROPIDES *and* SIMO.): And cast your eyes
                    Over these two great big uprights—
  Aren't they terrifically thick, and dense, and wooden?
THEOPROPIDES: I've never laid eyes on such beautiful blocks of timber 820
SIMO: And they cost me a pretty price, by god, originally.
TRANIO: Did you hear that "originally"? He can hardly contain
  His tears.
THEOPROPIDES: How much, originally?
SIMO: Seventy-four dollars
  And fifteen cents, f.o.b., for the pair.
THEOPROPIDES: I'll be darned
  If they don't look a lot more faulty than I felt at first.
TRANIO: Really, how so?
THEOPROPIDES: Termites. They've been bored into
  Darned deep.
TRANIO: Cut down out of season, no doubt,
  With worms still in them. But that's all that's wrong with them
  They'll be perfectly good if they're coated all over with pitch
  No oatmeal-eating Roman[51] crucifix carpenter

---

[50] *considerate . . . human nature*: . . . *esse existumo humani ingeni*. "This is the
only passage in Plautus in which *humanus* has the ethical sense, 'humane,' 'considerate' . . . The sense, however, is common enough in Terence . . ." (Sonnenschein,
p. 125).

[51] *No oatmeal-eating Roman*: *Non enim haec pultifagus opufex opera fecit barbarus.*
"In this passage *barbarus* probably denotes Roman, as so often in Plautus . . ."
(Sonnenschein, p. 126).

Put this house together. Look at those two blockheads
At the door joints? You see they're fast asleep?

THEOPROPIDES: You mean, they're sleepers? 830

TRANIO: Yes, the way they stick together:
Impenetrable, nothing could ever get through them

THEOPROPIDES: The more I see, the better I like the place.

TRANIO: And oh, look at that! It's a mural showing a crow[52]
Tearing two vultures[53] apart.

THEOPROPIDES: Afraid I don't see it.

TRANIO: But I do. The crow is standing behind two old buzzards
And nipping his beak in one, ducking back and doing
The same to the other.

THEOPROPIDES: Sounds like a pretty fast picture.

TRANIO: Look in my direction: perhaps you can pick out the crow?

THEOPROPIDES: I can't see a sign of a thing that looks like a crow.

TRANIO: Train your eyes in the direction of yourself and Simo;
If you can't spot the crow, perhaps you can see the vultures.

THEOPROPIDES: Oh never mind the art lesson now. I can't see a thing
That looks like a painted bird anywhere around.

TRANIO: Oh all right. Skip it. I can't blame you, at your age, 840
If your eyes are not up to scratch.

THEOPROPIDES: Well, what I do see
Certainly pleases me very much, I must say.

SIMO: But you haven't seen half of it yet, just wait for the rest.

THEOPROPIDES: Yes of course how true.

SIMO: Ho, houseboy! Here!
Conduct this gentleman around the house: let him see
All the rooms, I'd take you in myself, and around,
But I'm expected down at the Forum on a matter of business.

THEOPROPIDES: (Good-humoredly.): Oh that doesn't matter. But I don't
want to be *taken in*.[54]
Get this leader behind me! I don't need conductors
To tell me where to get off. Misleading advice
Won't help. I prefer to go astray by myself.

---

[52] *crow*: the type for sagacity.
[53] *vultures*: the type for rapacity.
[54] *taken in*: Theopropides makes this pun.

SIMO: I meant, take you into the house.

THEOPROPIDES: I'll just walk on in,
And do without the conductor.

SIMO: Of course, as you wish.

THEOPROPIDES: So here I go.

TRANIO: Wait just a minute! I want to see
If a watchdog . . .

THEOPROPIDES: Take a quick look

TRANIO: SSSST! WOOF!
Get going, you mutt! Go find the nearest tree.   850
Come on, lope! Still lying there, you son of a dogma?
Make tracks! Follow your nose!

SIMO: She's not dangerous.
You can walk right up and she won't do a thing but lie there
Like any other pregnant bitch. Just go on in
And march right past her. I must be off to the Forum.

THEOPROPIDES: Have a nice walk downtown. You've been very kind.

(*Exit* SIMO.)
Tranio, make someone take that hound away
Even if she isn't dangerous.

TRANIO: Can't you see
How peacefully she's lying there? What's wrong
With you? Are you nervous?

THEOPROPIDES: All right, all right, all right!
Follow me in here, will you?

TRANIO: Will I? I'll dog
Your tracks, unshakable off. That's a fact.
I wouldn't want anyone getting into my act.

ACT IV

Scene 1

PHANISCUS, PHANIUM.

PHANISCUS: Slaves who are easily cowed,[55]
    Even when not to blame,
    Are useful to the master.
    But those who are saucy and proud   860
    Cause trouble, and then proclaim
    Innocence in the teeth of disaster.
    They get good exercise
    By running away, but caught,
    They pay a heavy price
    For the mischief they have wrought.
They ought not to act this way.
    When they follow their own advice
    Instead of fearing the worst,
    They get chased and then chastised.
    Had they been timid first,
They'd burst before acting that way.
    I've long since come to prefer
Keeping my skin intact, unbeaten, unbruised.
    And by making my body defer   870
To my wishes I have a roof of sorts, to be used
    To protect me from the rain
When troubles descend on all the rest of the crew.
    The master, I maintain,
Reacts in the way his servants most want him to:
    If they're good, he behaves,

[55] The fifth *canticum* is in two parts, the solo of Phaniscus and the duet of Phaniscus and Pinacium, in a variety of meters.

If they act wicked, he turns into a fiend.
  Now at our place all the slaves
Are the worst kind of rascals and wastrels born to be beaned.
  They're lazy, inclined to say "No!"
When told to meet the master. "I can't be bothered"
  They chant, "I just *Won't Go!*
New fields to conquer, eh? Something further to be fathered
  In greener pastures, eh, master mule?
I'm staying right here. You go ahead and roam!"
  So I left them there—after all, I'm no fool—
And came on the errand to escort my master home.
In that whole bunch of slaves, there's only me   880
With enough get-up-and-go to meet him here.
Tomorrow when the master comes to see
What's happened, they'll be whipped with cowhide gear.
In short, I value my back more than theirs.
They can do wholesale business in cowhides, who cares?
I'd rather see all the leather used up on their rears
Than do any business myself in whips and tears.
  (*Enter* PINACIUM.)
PINACIUM: Wait, up, Phaniscus! Hey, you with the whiskers!
  Can't you hold it a minute?
PHANISCUS: Don't be a pain
  In the neck, you inner limit.
PINACIUM: Well, watch Phaniscus
  Whisk us away, with a sweep of his tail, oh joy!
  Hold it! Wait for me parasite boy!
PHANISCUS: Parasite am I?
PINACIUM: That's right, dusty: anyone
  Can lead you around as long as it ends in dinner.
PHANISCUS: It's my own business if I happen to like to eat
  What difference does it make to you?
PINACIUM: Oh, aren't we *tough!*
  And master simply dotes on us.
PHANISCUS: If dotes
  Is all he does on me that's not too bad.
  Ow! My eyes are watering!   890

PINACIUM: Oh, does the eyes
  Hurt the poor little fellow, does they smart?
  I wonder why?
PHANISCUS: The general effect of gas
  Created when you're in range.
PINACIUM: Your jokes are as current
  As counterfeit money.
PHANISCUS: Well, stupid, I refuse
  To stoop to your level of insult and besides, I enjoy
  The master's confidence.
PINACIUM: Aren't we just making our bed
  And aren't we just lying in it?
PHANISCUS: If only you weren't
  So gassed you wouldn't be so crude and rude in your thoughts.
PINACIUM: Why should I play up to you when you won't play up to me?
PHANISCUS: Oh, come on with me, you pessimist, go in and call
  Callidamates and tell him we're here.
  And for god's sake, lay off the disgusting talk.
PINACIUM: All right, I'll go right up and pound on the door.
  Hey there! Anyone at home in there to protect these doors
  From assault and battery? Somebody, open the door!   900
  Well, not a soul who dares to venture outdoors;
  Understandably, since they're all out cold
  Inside: but all the more reason not to be too bold:
  Some one of these grumpy grouches might slouch out
  With a hangover and clout me right on the snout.

                        Scene 2[56]

TRANIO, THEOPROPIDES, PHANISCUS, PINACIUM.

TRANIO: Look like a good buy to you?
THEOPROPIDES: I'm utterly delighted!
TRANIO: You don't think it's too expensive?

[56] *Scene 2*: From here on the meter is iambic and trochaic.

THEOPROPIDES: If I've ever seen a house
Thrown away, it's this one.

TRANIO: And so, you do like it?

THEOPROPIDES: Like it?
I love it.

TRANIO: How about the women's quarters, and cloister,
That colonnade, I mean?

THEOPROPIDES: T-rific, it's larger
Than any portico[57] you'll find anywhere in the street.

TRANIO: As a matter of fact, we compared the dimensions with those   910
Of all the others in town, Philolaches and I.

THEOPROPIDES: How did they stack up?

TRANIO: Ours is longer by a long shot.

THEOPROPIDES: What a heavenly buy! If some one offered me cash
And three times as much, I'd never part with the place.

TRANIO: And if you wanted to sell, I wouldn't let you.

THEOPROPIDES: Our money is well invested in a house like this
At a price like that.

TRANIO: And thanks to me, for *insisting*,
And urging your son on to drive a good hard bargain—
I forced him to borrow the cash we needed at interest
To make the down payment.

THEOPROPIDES: Then you certainly saved the ship.
And we now owe 80 *minae*? 2000 more?

TRANIO: And *no* change.

THEOPROPIDES: He shall have it today.

TRANIO: A good idea. That way,
The lender won't have any cause to sue.   920
Or, I tell you, count the money out now, to me:
I'll count it out and pay it over to him.

THEOPROPIDES: I'm not completely convinced there wouldn't be a catch
Somewhere along the line if I paid you.

TRANIO: Have I ever, in word or deed, been false to you,
Even as a kind of practical joke?

THEOPROPIDES: Have I ever

---

[57] *portico:* This passage has led C. H. Buck to suggest a topical allusion to the porticoes built by Aemilius Lepidus and Aemilius Paulus in 193 B.C. The date would then be a *terminus post quem* for the composition of the *Mostellaria*.

Dropped my guard long enough to trust you an inch?
TRANIO: That's because after I became your slave, I never
   Gave you a bit of trouble.
THEOPROPIDES: Because I took care
   To see that you couldn't.
TRANIO: For that you have me to thank,
   And my good character.
THEOPROPIDES: Don't drag in some character:
   It's all I can do to keep a sharp eye out for you.
TRANIO: I'm with you there.
THEOPROPIDES: Now, off to the country with you.
   And tell my son I've arrived.
TRANIO: Just as you say, sir.
THEOPROPIDES: Tell him to come right back into town with you.   930
TRANIO: Yes, sir! (*Aside.*) I'll go around back and call a meeting
   Of my colleagues, reporting this situation all quiet,
   Then bring the son to this destination. Isn't this a riot?
   (*Exit* TRANIO.)
PHANISCUS: Strange! I don't hear the usual sounds emanating
   From the party in progress, the girl on flute,
   Or anyone else, doing anything at all, in fact.
THEOPROPIDES: What in the world's going on? Why are those men
   Hanging around my door? What can they want?
   Why are they looking in?
PINACIUM: I'll try pounding.
   Hey, unlock the place! Hey, Tranio! Open up!
THEOPROPIDES: What kind of a comedy is this?
PINACIUM: Hey, you
   In there! Come and open up! We're here
   To pick up our master Callidamates.
THEOPROPIDES: Hey, you boys! What do you think you're doing?
   Why are you battering down that building, tell me!
PHANISCUS: Hey yourself, Pop! Why are you prying into   940
   Something that has nothing to do with you.
THEOPROPIDES: Nothing to do with me?
PHANISCUS: Oh perhaps you're the mayor
   Just been elected to office, prowling around

Prying into other peoples' business, asking them questions,
Eavesdropping.

THEOPROPIDES: It's not other peoples' business
That house isn't, it's mine.

PHANISCUS: Oh really? Philolaches
Sold it, did he? Or Pop's making fun of us.

THEOPROPIDES: I'm telling you the truth—but what about you?
What's your business here?

PHANISCUS: The explanation
Is simple: our master is in there having drinks.

THEOPROPIDES: Your master is in there having drinks?

PHANISCUS: I explained
All that to you.

THEOPROPIDES: Aren't you the fancy one!

PHANISCUS: We've come to pick him up.

THEOPROPIDES: Pick whom up?

PHANISCUS: Not whom, him, the master: how many times
Do I have to tell you whom?

THEOPROPIDES: But listen, lad,
No one lives there. I'm sure you mean well, but . . .

PHANISCUS: Young Philolaches doesn't dwell in that domicile?   950

THEOPROPIDES: He used to, but he moved out, long ago.

PINACIUM: I'm afraid the old jar's cracked.

PHANISCUS: You're quite wrong, Pop.

THEOPROPIDES: Stop calling me Pop . . .

PHANISCUS: Unless of course yesterday
Or today was his moving day. I happen to know
As a matter of actual, that this is where young Phil lives.

THEOPROPIDES: For six months now, no one has lived in that house.

PHANISCUS and PINACIUM: WAKE UP!

THEOPROPIDES: Whom? Me?

PINACIUM: Yes'm, youm.

THEOPROPIDES (To PINACIUM.):   Don't horn in, you.
Let me talk to the boy. (To PHANISCUS.) No one's living there.

PHANISCUS: Oh yes, someone is, and yesterday, and the day
Before, that's three; and the fourth and fifth and sixth
And so forth: every day since his father left.

And they haven't let three days in a row go by
Without a drinking session.

THEOPROPIDES: I'm not sure I'm hearing
Things right.

PHANISCUS: I said, they haven't let three days go by
Without a party's getting started, drinks, and eats,
And girls, and conducting themselves like Greeks,[58] and music,   960
And girls to play the music, and . . .

THEOPROPIDES: And who was in charge?

PHANISCUS: Philolaches.

THEOPROPIDES: Philolaches who?

PHANISCUS: The son of Theopropides.

THEOPROPIDES: Oof! I'm done for if what you say is true
But I must insist on persisting in investigating.
Philolaches formed the habit, you say, of holding
Wild parties with your master, right here?

PHANISCUS: Yes, right in that house.

THEOPROPIDES: I'm afraid you're a good deal dumber than I first realized,
Young fellow. You must have stopped somewhere on the way
And tossed off a few too many.

PHANISCUS: What makes you think so?

THEOPROPIDES: Because you've obviously wound up at the wrong house.

PHANISCUS: But I know where I'm supposed to be: I recognize the place
I left not so long ago. Here liveth Philolaches   970
Whose father iseth Theopropides, and lefteth
To go overseath on busineth, so Philolaches
Setteth free a lovely young lady on the premiseth.

THEOPROPIDES: Premises? Philolaches?
Is that who you mean?

PHANISCUS: That's the very exact same person, and the pretty young woman
Who is now about his closest relation, that is "Philematium."

THEOPROPIDES: Uhh, how much did it cost to buy her freedom?

PHANISCUS: Sixteen . . .

THEOPROPIDES: Sixty?!

PHANISCUS: Heavens, *nein!*[59] I mean 16 miney.

58 *like Greeks: pergraecari* for the third time.
59 *Heavens, nein:* Phaniscus swears in Greek "By Apollo!"

THEOPROPIDES: He bought her freedom, you say?

PHANISCUS: That's what he bought.
And it cost him 16 *minae*.

THEOPROPIDES: Now let's see, you say
Philolaches acquired a mistress, that was at a cost
To him of 16 *minae*?

PHANISCUS: So I say.

THEOPROPIDES: And he manumitted the girl?

PHANISCUS: So I say.

THEOPROPIDES: And after his father went overseas
He drank a good deal in the company of your master?

PHANISCUS: So I say.

THEOPROPIDES: And what do you say about this: he bought
The house next door?

PHANISCUS: No I *don't* say.

THEOPROPIDES: And paid 40 *minae* down to the owner?

PHANISCUS: No I *don't* say.

THEOPROPIDES: It's absolute ruin.

PHANISCUS: What the young man has done
In fact is ruin his father.

THEOPROPIDES: How true a tune
You're singing now!

PHANISCUS: I wish it were slightly off key.
Perhaps you're some kind of friend of his father?   980

THEOPROPIDES: I must say, I feel sorry for the man whose ruin
You're describing so definitively.

PHANISCUS: But *her* price was *nothing*,
A mere 16 miney, compared to the cost of the feed
And wine for those fabulous parties and the entertainment.

THEOPROPIDES: Financially, then, his father's a failure.

PHANISCUS: And of course there's
that slave,
Tranio's his name, an absolute fiend of a spender,
A sieve with money. He could spend Hercules' whole hoard
Overnight, if he had it. Heavens, how I sympathize
With Philolaches' father! When he finds out what's happened
Searing sorrow will scorch his heart and reduce it
To a cardiac cinder.

THEOPROPIDES: Of course, if you're telling the truth.
PHANISCUS: But why should I lie? I've nothing to hide.
PINACIUM: Hey, kids!
   Won't someone please open up the door?
PHANISCUS: Don't pound
   Anymore, there's nobody home. They've probably gone
   To somebody else's place to continue the action.
   So let's be off . . .
THEOPROPIDES: Hey, lad . . .   990
PHANISCUS: And keep on looking,
   Wherever they are. Keep up with me.
PINACIUM: I coming.
THEOPROPIDES: Oh, lad, are you leaving?
PHANISCUS: Freedom is a good thick cloak
   For *your* back, sir, and you have that to wear.
   But I am only a slave, with a master to fear
   And to care for, and so of course I crave his protection.
   If I'm slack nothing can save my back from detection.

Scene 3

THEOPROPIDES, SIMO.

THEOPROPIDES: This is the finish of me. Why even discuss it?
   From what I hear, I would say I did not depart
   On a trip to Egypt: I went to the ends of the earth
   And traveled to the outermost rims of the world.
   Where I am now I don't really know for sure,
   But I'll find out, perhaps, for here comes the man
   My son bought the house from. Ah, hello, how goes it?
SIMO: It goes back home from the Forum.
THEOPROPIDES: Oh, anything new
   Turn up at the Forum today?   1000
SIMO: Yes, one little thing.
THEOPROPIDES: Oh yes? What was that?

SIMO: They were hauling a dead man away.

THEOPROPIDES: Ugh! That doesn't strike me precisely as new.

SIMO: Well, I saw them lugging this recent corpse outside.

He had been alive a moment ago, they were saying.

THEOPROPIDES: So that's what turned up! I didn't mean it quite that way.

SIMO: Have you nothing to do but stand around listening to news?

THEOPROPIDES: I've only returned from abroad today.

SIMO: I'm sorry,

But I can't ask you to dinner. I'm promised elsewhere.

THEOPROPIDES: Oh, I wasn't expecting you to.

SIMO: But tomorrow, let's see . . .

Yes . . . I'll be free to come to your house.

THEOPROPIDES: Actually,

I wasn't planning on that, either. Do you have a minute?

There's something I wanted to ask you about.

SIMO: Why, of course.

THEOPROPIDES: So far as I know, you received from Philolaches   1010

A payment of 40 *minae?*

SIMO: So far as I know,

I never received a cent.

THEOPROPIDES: From Tranio, then?

SIMO: From *him?* I received even less, a more negative nothing.

THEOPROPIDES: And this was a down payment?

SIMO: What are you dreaming about?

THEOPROPIDES: Me? You're the dreamer, to think you can hoodwink me

And nullify the deal by claiming to know nothing of it.

SIMO: What deal?

THEOPROPIDES: The transaction my son completed with you

While I was away.

SIMO: To think that I would conclude

Some sort of business with him while you were away!

What in the world for? And on what date was it done?

THEOPROPIDES: Look, I owe you the sum of 80 *minae* in silver.   1020

SIMO: Look, you *don't.* Of course, if you do owe me that

You can hand it right over. A promise to pay must be honored.

I wouldn't want you to think that you could deny it.

THEOPROPIDES: Well, I don't deny it. I owe and will pay you this money.

SIMO: Now wait just a minute.[60] I've got a few things to ask you.
   What is this about the money your son and the slave
   Supposedly paid out to me? And this big transaction
   Supposedly sealed and signed while you were away?

THEOPROPIDES: Tranio says they paid half the sum in advance
   As a binder, to you when you sold your house to him.

SIMO: To whom? Philolaches? But I still live there,
   As you saw for yourself. And I don't intend to move out.

THEOPROPIDES: But the money . . .

SIMO: Don't be funny. Not a ghost of a shadow of a cent
   Has passed between me and Philolaches. How could it?
   My house was never for sale.

THEOPROPIDES: He didn't buy it?

SIMO: Either that or I didn't sell it. You take your choice.

THEOPROPIDES: But the money that's owed to the banker . . . Oh, lord . . .

SIMO: What the hell
   Does your son need two houses for?

THEOPROPIDES: Well, this one is haunted,
   So they moved out, six months ago.

SIMO: Oh, they've been moving
   All right, they've been moving along pretty fast ever since
   You first left for Egypt. They've been hosts to some lively ghosts
   If you ask me. Nobody ever seems to sleep in there,
   It sounds like a wake to me. They didn't move out,
   But they sure moved around, and moved in a gaggle of girls.

THEOPROPIDES: But Tranio said . . .

SIMO (Imperturbably.):   He told me you wanted to see
   The inside of my place . . .

THEOPROPIDES: When he said that we were the owners,
   Naturally, I was curious . . .

SIMO: Especially the women's quarters . . .

THEOPROPIDES: I'll quarter those women after I get my hands on that slave.

SIMO (Still imperturbably.): Because, he said, you wanted your son to
      marry
   And wanted to build an addition, as quarters for the women,
   There in your house in time for the wedding, he said.

THEOPROPIDES: I wanted to build an addition?

---

60 *Now wait just a minute:* There is a gap in the manuscript here of twenty-one
lines.

SIMO: That's what he said.

THEOPROPIDES: It's all up with me (*Gulp!*). I haven't a thing to say,
Or voice left to say it except these three little verbs: 1030
I lived. I died. I was buried.

SIMO: Has Tranio perhaps
Created some kind of catastrophe?

THEOPROPIDES: Just complete chaos,
That's all, and he's made ridiculous fools today
Of you and me.

SIMO: You mean the joke's on us?

THEOPROPIDES: More or less—less on you, more on me. I see it now.
He's made an absolute fool of me today,
And as far as I can see, in the visible future.
Now look, would you help me plan some means of revenge?

SIMO: What would you like me to do?

THEOPROPIDES: Come along with me.

SIMO: I coming.

THEOPROPIDES: Lend me a couple of slaves, with whips.

SIMO: Take them from my supply; I've plenty of both.

THEOPROPIDES: And while we plan the revenge I mean to have
I'll give you more examples of the way
That rascal made a fool of me today. 1040

ACT V

Scene 1

TRANIO.

TRANIO: The man who is faint and fearful in a crisis
Is just not worth his salt, he is "as naught."
But what that means, "as naught," I have no notion.
Now after the master packed me off to the country
To summon his son, I veered back through this alley
To our garden, secretly, and opened the little gate

That leads from behind our house into the alley.
I led forth my legions, masculine and feminine.
Right now I'm having a conference with myself
About calling a congress of some clever cronies of mine.
For I had called a meeting of the senate of my friends   1050
In there. but they refused to let me come to it!
I realized I was being taken advantage of, so
I got busy immediately getting ready to do
What any intelligent, strong-minded person would do
In my situation so fraught with peril and confusion.
Create even more confusion, surely that's the solution!
Keep it all moving around and around. I'll be found
Out, of course, the old man can hardly be kept from knowing
Much longer, but I can still hope to get to him first,
And head them off and make some sort of a deal.   1060
I haven't any time to waste. But listen, the door
Of the neighbor's house is rattling, yes they're coming this way
I'll hide in this corner and hear what they have to say.

Scene 2

TRANIO, THEOPROPIDES, WHIPSTERS.

THEOPROPIDES: You men, stand back inside the doorway; be ready
    When I call, to jump out and slap the handcuffs on him.
    I'll wait in front of the house for my funny man.
    His skin will feel even funnier by the end of the day.
TRANIO: The cat's out, Tranio. You'd better see what there is
    You can do about it now.
THEOPROPIDES: Now I want to be subtle in getting him into my net
    When he shows up. I won't let him see the hook,   1070
    Just the bait, while I reel in the line. I'll pretend I don't know
    Anything about what's going on.
TRANIO: You clever man!
    No one in Athens is any wiser than you.
    It's as hard to take advantage of you as it is

To get a rise from a rock. Now watch me approach
This masterful man and proceed to get his attention.
THEOPROPIDES: I wish the fish would show his head.
TRANIO: The catcher
Is looking for me awry, and I'm standing by.
THEOPROPIDES: Oh there, good old Tranio! What's the news?
TRANIO: The rustics are returning from the . . . uh . . . sticks.
Philolaches will soon be here.
THEOPROPIDES: Well, you've arrived
In the nick of time for me. Good lord, that neighbor
Of ours has his cheek, wise guy.
TRANIO: Because why?
THEOPROPIDES: He denies that he's had any dealings with you.
TRANIO: Denies it?
THEOPROPIDES: And says you haven't paid him a blessed cent.   1080
TRANIO: Oh come on, you're kidding! I can't believe he says that.
THEOPROPIDES: Why not?
TRANIO: I know, you're just having a joke on me.
I can't quite believe he'd say anything like that.
THEOPROPIDES: Well, he does say precisely that, meaning no,
And denies that he sold his house to Philolaches,
TRANIO: And also denies he was given the money?
THEOPROPIDES: Denies it?
He's willing to affirm under oath, if I want him to,
That he did not sell the house, that he never received
Any money.
TRANIO: When we bought it, and paid the cash down?
THEOPROPIDES: That's just what I told him.
TRANIO: And what did he say?
THEOPROPIDES: He offered to hand his slaves over to me
For questioning under torture.
TRANIO: He's faking; he won't.
THEOPROPIDES: Yes he will, right away.
TRANIO: Well, summon him to court.
I'll dash over now and put the finger on him.
(*Heads for the altar*[61] *in front of* SIMO's *house.*)

[61] *Heads for the altar*: where he would be immune from violent seizure.

THEOPROPIDES: No wait here. I've decided to check up on him.   1090
TRANIO: Just you leave him to me. Or better, challenge him
   To contest the legal possession of that property.
THEOPROPIDES: But first I want to put his slaves on the rack
TRANIO: By all means.
THEOPROPIDES: So now I'll have them brought out here.
TRANIO: By all means. Meanwhile, I'll take a seat on this altar.
THEOPROPIDES: Oh no. Why do that?
TRANIO: You're so darned dumb.
   To keep the slaves from having this as a refuge
   When they come out to be questioned. I'll preside over things,
   To make sure the investigation proceeds properly.
THEOPROPIDES: Oh, come off it! I mean climb down from the altar.
TRANIO: En oh.
THEOPROPIDES: Come on now, I'm asking you not to take over that altar.
TRANIO: Why not?
THEOPROPIDES: Because that's what I *want* them to do,
   Take refuge there. So let them. It'll be clear evidence
   Before any judge, and a means of getting him fined.
TRANIO: Look you're going to do something; all right: do it.   1100
   Why confuse the issue? You just don't know
   How involved these matters are when you take them to court.
THEOPROPIDES: Come down from there, over here to me. There's something
     thing
   I need to consult you about.
TRANIO: I dispense advice
   Very well from a sitting position. I seem to know more
   When I'm seated. From the holy seats of the gods, after all,
   The counsels are all the more binding.
THEOPROPIDES: Don't fool around.
   Come down. Just look at me: You have nothing to fear,
   You see.
TRANIO: I'm looking.
THEOPROPIDES: You see?
TRANIO: Ah, I see you there!
   If a third person tried to come between us two,
   He'd die of starvation.
THEOPROPIDES: How come?

TRANIO: No source of income:
We're both so *close!*

THEOPROPIDES: Oh good god dammit to hell.

TRANIO: Is something bothering you?

THEOPROPIDES: No; nothing but you.

TRANIO: Poor little defenseless me?

THEOPROPIDES: You've wiped me out.

TRANIO: I had to, your nose was running. It runs in the family.

THEOPROPIDES: You've wiped out my whole set of brains and taken my
head   1110
To the cleaners. For now I've finally gotten to the bottom
Of your *clever,* frantic antics. I've dug down deep
And gotten to the root of the trouble. I've even uprooted
The radical region 'way down beneath the root.[62]

TRANIO: Well, in that case I shan't arise from my heavenly seat
This day at all, except with a promise of safety.

THEOPROPIDES: Get up! I'll have some dry kindling brought out here
And a roaring fire started up underneath your bottom.

TRANIO: Better not: I taste much better boiled than roasted.

THEOPROPIDES: I'll make an example of you.

TRANIO: To be held up to others?
That shows how highly regarded I am.

THEOPROPIDES: Tell me this:
In what condition was my son when I left him?

TRANIO: Let's see, he has feet and hands, two each, with fingers
And toes, two ears, two eyes, and two Dutch flowers.

THEOPROPIDES: I was asking about something other than his physical
status.

TRANIO: I was answering in another vein from your quizzical status.
But look, here comes your son's best friend and companion,
That charming Callidamates. See what you can do   1120
With me in his presence, a man who's loyal and true.

---

[62] *beneath the root:* exradicitus, "a humorous compound, forming a climax after
radicitus. The word is quoted by Fronto in a letter to Marcus Aurelius as *Plautino-
taton.*" (Sonnenschein, pp. 141–142.)

Scene 3

CALLIDAMATES, THEOPROPIDES, TRANIO.

CALLIDAMATES: I buried myself in sleep—(*Stretches and yawns.*) that was
    a good deep one—
And slept off the effects of the wine. I'm feeling fine.
Now Philolaches has told me how his father has come
Back home from abroad and how the slave had his fun
Misleading the new arrival, or leading him on,
Or leading him away anyway, from the true situation.
He has asked me to make a diplomatic approach
And plead his case and make his peace with his father.
Ah, there he is, just the man I was looking for.
Greetings, Theopropides! I'm glad you are back
And looking so well. Have dinner with me this evening.
Please do accept.
THEOPROPIDES: Good day, Callidamates.   1130
And thanks all the same for inviting me to dinner.
I'm sorry I must decline.
CALLIDAMATES: Oh please, do come.
TRANIO: Say you will. Or shall I go in your place?
THEOPROPIDES: You knothead, actually laughing?
TRANIO: You mean because
I swear I'll go to dinner instead of you?
THEOPROPIDES: You *won't.* I'll have you carried to the cross:
That's where you ought to be hanging out.
CALLIDAMATES: Never mind
The slave, Theopropides. Promise you'll come
To my house for dinner? Why not simply say yes?
And tell me, (*To* TRANIO.) blockhead, what's gotten into you,
To make you take refuge on the top of the altar?
TRANIO: The new arrival scared the wits out of me.
Advise me what to do. For you are here

And like a judge can listen to both sides,
So let us try the case.
THEOPROPIDES: I say that you
Have led my son astray.
TRANIO: But now hear me:
I admit he misbehaved while you were away
And bought his mistress' freedom with money borrowed
From a moneylender, and the money is all used up,   1140
I'll say that loud and clear. But is it MIS-
Behavior, I ask you? Or is it standard conduct,
When the sons of all great families act that way?
THEOPROPIDES: I'll have to watch my words debating you:
You're pretty shrewd when it comes to the orations.
CALLIDAMATES: Now let me rule on that point. Dislodge yourself,
Tranio. I'll sit up there and preside over things.
TRANIO: It's a trap! No, Callidamates, you must first
Assure me I won't be grabbed the moment I leave
My perch of immunity. Then you can have my place.
THEOPROPIDES: Back to the argument: I don't hold it against you,
My son's misbehavior, half as much as the means
(Or is it extremes?) you've gone to in making a fool
Out of me and making me look like a dope.
TRANIO: Serves you right, sir—a jolly good show.
These are things a man of your age should know.
THEOPROPIDES: Now that I know how a white-haired man can be fooled
By people he takes for granted, what do I do
With the new-found knowledge?
TRANIO: Offer it to the comic poets.
If you're a friend of the writers Diphilus and Philemon   1150
Tell them how your slave made a comic character
Out of you. That's good frustration material for them
To use in their comedies.
CALLIDAMATES: Quiet, there on the altar!
It's my turn to say a few words. Listen, for a change.
THEOPROPIDES: Hear, hear!
CALLIDAMATES: First of all, you know I'm a very good friend
Of your son. He's come to me—he's ashamed, you see,

To show his face or let himself in your sight
Because he knows that you know what he's done.
So I appeal to you—please pardon the boy
For his childish foolishness. He's your son, after all.
You know how lads of his age love to lark around
And live it up. And I was as bad as he was:
I joined in it all. We're both completely at fault.
As for the money, the principal, the interest, the cash
He used up, the girl he bought, every bit he spent,
I will have it paid back and the expenses all made good   1160
From my own funds and my friends', not yours.

THEOPROPIDES: No more effective
A speaker than you could present this case before me.
I'm no longer angry at him, nor do I bear
Any kind of a grudge. Let him follow his heart; make love,
Enjoy his wine, and count on my friendly indulgence.
If he's genuinely sorry he's wasted all this money,
That's punishment enough for me.

CALLIDAMATES: He's abjectly sorry.

TRANIO: In the spirit of that indulgence, what fate is in store
For me?

THEOPROPIDES: The lash, you slab of mud, and then
Stringing up, for further flaying and jabbing.

TRANIO: Even if I'm genuinely sorry?

THEOPROPIDES: As I live and breathe,
You'll choke and die.

CALLIDAMATES: Why not make a clean slate
Of all your pardons, and forgive Tranio his sins,
For my sake?

THEOPROPIDES: I would gladly grant your request   1170
For anything else, *except that* I refrain
From cracking down on this nut, to prove to him
He's not so tough as he's cracked up to be.

CALLIDAMATES: Come now, do let him off.

THEOPROPIDES: LET HIM OFF!!!
Look at him, grinning! Nonchalant; couldn't care less.

CALLIDAMATES: If you had any sense, Tranio, you'd leave off acting
So fresh and let things subside.

THEOPROPIDES: You can leave off asking
  Any sort of favor for him, I'll make him subside
  With a tattoo of bright body blows bounced off his outside.
CALLIDAMATES: Oh come now, let yourself be persuaded by me.
THEOPROPIDES: I don't want you to persuade me.
CALLIDAMATES: Oh please give in.
THEOPROPIDES: I tell you I don't want you to talk me into it.
CALLIDAMATES: It's no good your not wanting me to when I want to!
  Forgive Tranio his sins, just this once, for my sake.
TRANIO: Why be so reluctant? As if tomorrow
  I won't cause you just as much trouble as I'm doing today!
  Then you can take revenge on me for both times.
CALLIDAMATES: Do let me convince you . . .
THEOPROPIDES: Oh *all right, then:*
  You fiend, go free! But thanks to *him* not *me!*
ALL: Spectators, our play is over, and in this cause
  We ask you now for handfuls of applause!

VI

Fathers hope their sons will stay on good terms with them and behave properly. Sons grow up to be young men who fall in love and begin to get ideas of their own. Mothers move about, rather unobtrusively, trying to bring reason to bear on the conflicts that develop. There can be a collision of wills, and a generous share of misunderstanding. Helped, often inspired and impelled by, the trusted family servant, the sons act out schemes for circumventing their fathers. The action does not save the sons, but can stave off the inevitable showdown when everyone gets caught up in the truth. Then the fathers discover things they didn't expect to, and the sons can be lured into conforming to their fathers' wishes. The servant is spared punishment, for another day, and cheerfully contemplates the wreckage of his improvised plans.

As one of the sons in *The Self-Tormentor* expresses the predicament: "Fathers are not good judges of young men. . . . They think we should be born old. . . . They govern as their passion now dictates, not as it was then."

CLITIPHO: *Quam iniqui sunt patres in omnis adulescentes iudices!*
Qui aequom esse censent nos a pueris ilico nasci senes. . . .
Lubidine ex sua moderantur nunc quae est non quae olim fuit.
(ll. 213–216)

On the spot Clitipho promises himself that if he ever has a son he will treat the young man indulgently, remember what it is to be young, and understand his son.

A bit later on in the play Clitipho's father is equally sure of himself and his insistence on strict control:

413

We are all made worse by self-indulgent freedom.
He'll want whatever pops into his mind
And won't stop to consider whether it
Is right or wrong, but just go after it.

CHREMES: *Nam deteriores omnes sumus licentia.*
Quod quoique quomque inciderit in mentem volet
Neque id putabit pravum an rectum sit: petet.

(ll. 483–485)

The difference between Chremes and his son Clitipho forms the second plot of the play. Its first plot unfolds in the opening scene on Menedemus' farm adjoining Chremes, a few miles outside of Athens. Menedemus had quarreled with his son Clinia over Clinia's love affair with a young woman of unidentified origins, brought to Athens from Corinth by a woman supposed to be her mother. The father scolded his son and pointed out that when he was young he was poor and had no time or money for such affairs. Instead, he had enlisted in the army as a mercenary in the service of an Asian king, winning glory and wealth for his efforts. As Menedemus continued to criticise him in this vein, Clinia took the lesson to heart and left his home in Athens to serve in an army in Asia Minor. Menedemus felt lost and guilty, sold his house and possessions in Athens, and bought the farmhouse and land next to Chremes'. This all took place some three months before the time of the play, which begins with Chremes coming out to find Menedemus hard at work on his land, raking and hoeing. Chremes cannot keep from asking Menedemus why he torments himself with such hard work. Menedemus suggests that this is none of Chremes' business but Chremes answers with Terence's most often quoted line:

homo sum: nil humani alienum mihi puto

I am a man and I consider nothing human foreign to me.

(l. 77)

Chremes further argues that if Menedemus' course is the right one he can learn a lesson from it; if not, Menedemus can learn from him how a father ought to manage his life. Menedemus consents to the conversation, during which the background story of the separation of Menedemus and Clinia is told. Chremes observes that Clinia's instincts are good and indicate an underlying regard for his father. But a good father, he insists, must show his son that he trusts him. Chremes then invites Menedemus to join in a dinner party at his house that day, the Feast of Dionysus, but Menedemus declines, and continues with his self-inflicted hard labor.

In the next scene Clitipho brings Chremes the surprising news that Clinia has returned from abroad and is already at their house. The two young men have long been friends and Clinia is as yet unwilling to face Menedemus, being more than ever in love with the mysterious young woman over whom they originally quarreled. Clitipho tells his father how mean and strict Menedemus is, but Chremes does not trust his son far enough to reveal what he has already learned of Menedemus' true character. He seems to use the conflict as a kind of object lesson, and delivers a short lecture on how sons should restrain themselves in deference to their fathers' wishes.

The second act opens with Clitipho's soliloquy on fathers' unfair judgments of their sons and proceeds to a scene of dialogue between him and Clinia, waiting for their young women to appear for the dinner party. Clinia's anxiety about his mistress' behavior in his absence is put to rest by the servants' account of arriving at her house unexpectedly and finding her to be a model of decorum. The young woman, Antiphila, was overwhelmingly happy to learn that Clinia had come back. Clitipho also has a mistress, Bacchis—an affair his father does not know about—but she is a hardened mercenary and has already cost Clitipho a good deal of money to maintain. Currently he owes her an additional sum that he and the family slave Syrus are trying to acquire by some means without Chremes' knowing of it. In view of Clinia's return, Syrus improvises a scheme for getting around Chremes by passing off Bacchis as Clinia's mistress and sequestering Antiphila with Clitipho's mother in the women's quarters.

The two women make their appearance, Bacchis praising Antiphila for her single-minded devotion to Clinia, and contrasting it with the unevenness of her own existence as a prey to the transitory male. For a brief moment, Antiphila and Clinia are happily reunited.

The third act begins early in the morning after the dinner party. Chremes is on his way to bring Menedemus the news of Clinia's return. When Menedemus expresses unqualified joy Chremes again cautions restraint. Mistakenly supposing Bacchis to be Clinia's mistress, Chremes regales Menedemus with an account of her fastidious expensive tastes and demanding ways as displayed at the dinner party. Chremes envisages Menedemus' unguarded welcoming of Clinia and his alleged mistress as financially ruinous. He also suspects the young men and Syrus of being up to something and suggests that he and Menedemus play along with whatever develops. Even if it involves some cash, outwitting their outwitters might be a better investment than unguarded indulgence of Clinia's least desire. Menedemus consents, thinking that Chremes sees his situation more clearly than he himself can.

In the ensuing scenes of Act III Syrus allows Chremes to talk him into pursuing the schemes he has in mind; Clitipho almost gives the truth away by fondling Bacchis and being observed by Chremes; Syrus pretends to be outraged by Clitipho's behavior and sends him off on a long walk; Syrus devises a plan for getting the money promised to Bacchis. He tells Chremes that Antiphila was left as a pledge in security for a loan to Bacchis by the old woman supposed to be her mother. The old woman died and Bacchis now has Antiphila as a servant in exchange for the money. Furthermore, she is hounding Clinia for the money and will not give up Antiphila until she gets it. Syrus proposes that they offer Antiphila to Menedemus as a captive of war who could be sold back for a great profit. When Chremes opposes this move on the ground that Menedemus is not in the market for bargains, Syrus airily says that that is quite all right because Menedemus will not really need to buy her. Chremes is left in the dark about what Syrus actually means.

The fourth act brings a third plot into view when Sostrata, Chremes' wife, informs him that Antiphila wears the very ring she had left with their infant daughter, exposed soon after her birth. Prompted by superstition, Sostrata says, she had given the child to another woman to expose but had also taken the ring from her own finger, to be left with the child. This way, should the child chance to survive and grow up she would not have been totally disinherited. Antiphila is, of course, discovered to be the daughter of Chremes and Sostrata. Both parents are now happy to have back their lost child.

But Syrus is in a dither because now that Antiphila is recognized as a free-born Athenian citizen she cannot be held as the alleged security for a debt he claimed she was. Wondering how to keep Chremes from learning that Bacchis is in fact Clitipho's mistress and also how to lay hands on the money promised to her, Syrus invents a new plan of action. He is rather impatient with Clinia's rapture at the discovery of Antiphila's true status, and proudly advances his new scheme for outwitting both fathers by simply telling the truth. He wants Clinia to return to Menedemus and take Bacchis with him, and simply tell Menedemus that she is Clitipho's mistress. Clinia can also of course ask for Antiphila's hand in marriage. Syrus assures Clinia, over his protests that this will interfere with his marriage, that they only need to maneuver long enough to get the money in question, and he will be helping Clitipho momentarily, and Clinia finally consents. Bacchis also, after giving Syrus a jolt by threatening to leave entirely, falls in with the new scheme for producing the money.

Chremes can only pity Menedemus for having Bacchis as well as Clinia move in. When Syrus tells Chremes that Clinia had told Menedemus that Bacchis was in fact Clitipho's mistress, Chremes nimbly concludes that Clinia has not only said this but also asked for Antiphila in marriage to raise the money (as expenses for the proposed wedding) promised to Bacchis. When Chremes refuses to be party to such a scheme Syrus suggests that he at least recompense Bacchis outright for the loss of her servant Antiphila and Chremes agrees. Clitipho returns from his long walk and is given the bag of money to take to Bacchis.

Now Menedemus appears on stage to ask formally for Antiphila's hand in marriage to his son and inform Chremes of the truth that Bacchis is actually Clitipho's mistress. Chremes' strong disbelief of this hard fact even dissuades Menedemus for the moment; he respects the force of Chremes' argument and ruefully admits to the possibility, but still asks for the betrothal of Antiphila to his son, to satisfy Clinia's ardent wishes. And Chremes consents on the grounds that only this way can Menedemus see the light and discover just what and just how much his son is demanding of him.

In the last act the truth comes out. Chremes is crestfallen when regaled by Menedemus with a description of the bedroom scene at his house enacted by Bacchis and Clitipho. He is furious and determined to read his son the riot act. Menedemus responds by urging Chremes to consider more suitable ways of managing his son:

> MENEDEMUS: Let your son realize
> That you're his father. Let him have the courage
> To trust you every way, to ask for things,
> To seek your help, and not go looking out
> For some other support, and desert you.
>
> (ll. 925–927)

But Chremes is bent on revenge, on knocking sense into Clitipho's head, and tells him that he has been disinherited in favor of his sister Antiphila. At this penultimate crisis Syrus makes Clitipho believe that it sounds as if he is not their son after all, and Clitipho confronts his parents with the question of whether he really is. Chremes now reads Clitipho the riot act, a simple bill of particulars on his recent behavior as an idler and a cheat. Clitipho is genuinely sorry when he sees himself in this light. As Menedemus appears to intercede for Clitipho and calm down Chremes' anger, Chremes agrees to forgive Clitipho on condition that he now take a wife. Clitipho is reluctant to accept the condition but gives in, strenuously refusing the red-head his mother first offers and substituting as his choice a young woman he's had his eye on for some time. Clitipho also asks that Syrus be pardoned, not punished, and Chremes lets the slave off. So both sons are launched on the path of marriage and parenthood.

From Menander's original single-plot version of the *Heautontimorumenos* Terence has fashioned an intricate story of emotional gambits and moral pressures, of fathers hoping in very different ways to make good men of their sons without losing their companionship and respect. In the young men infatuation and genuine affections struggle for recognition and survival. The two fathers well represent the permissive and authoritarian species of this genus. If Menedemus' winning desire to cherish and honor his son dominates the atmosphere of this play in a noble and affectionate spirit, Chremes' hard-fisted standards and correctives also succeed in transforming Clitipho's behavior from the acrobatics of anxiety into a straight walk along the road to responsibility. Bacchis is once more left to her own resources, but they seem to be ample. Antiphila and Clinia were right all along in their devotion to one another, not only a sound instinct, but now even socially respectable. The emotional and moral behavior of both parents and children is seen to have many overtones.

All of this Terence has converted to use in steady, simple Latin poetry, straightforward in diction, sparing in imagery. Hardly ever is the voice raised. The lines of action are as complex and at times mystifying as the words are simple and unadorned. But Terence's art, like all good poetry, is "the clear expression of mixed feelings."

Terence:
THE SELF-TORMENTOR

Translated by Palmer Bovie

CHARACTERS

CHREMES, an old Athenian
MENEDEMUS, an old man, neighbor of Chremes
CLITIPHO, son of Chremes
CLINIA, son of Menedemus
SYRUS, a slave of Chremes
DROMO, a slave of Menedemus
BACCHIS, a courtesan, mistress of Clitipho
ANTIPHILA, a girl, loved by Clinia
SOSTRATA, wife of Chremes
PHRYGIA, a servant of Bacchis
CANTHARA, a nurse, servant of Sostrata

SCENE: *The adjoining farms of Menedemus and Chremes, a few miles outside of Athens.*

PROLOGUE *

In case you may be wondering just why
The poet gave the Prologue to an old man
When a young man usually delivers it,
Let me tell you why I'm out here.
                                    Today
I do the comedy *The Self-Tormentor,*
With its double plot, fashioned by Terence
From the original single-plot version.
I've told you what it is, and that it's new.
I'd tell you, too, who wrote the Greek version,
But most of you, I know, already know.

I'll tell you why I learned the Prologue's role.   10
Terence wanted me to plead a case for him,
Not speak a prologue. He leaves the verdict
Entirely in your hands. I hope that I,
The advocate, can happily devise
And fluently present the speech he wrote.

Some ill-willed critics have been handing out
Rumors that Terence tacked together plays
From several Greek originals, and made
A few Latin plays from them. And he did!
He doesn't say he didn't. He's not sorry
For it. He means to go right on doing it.
He has good writers as his precedent   20
And thinks he's quite entitled to practise
Their methods. As for what a mean old poet
Keeps saying, that Terence is a parvenu
And got into dramatic poetry
With no formal training, by leaning on
The talents of such friends as Scipio,

* Spoken by L. Ambivius Turpio.

423

Not on his own ability—only
Your judgment and decision can resolve.
I therefore want to appeal to all of you
So that the arguments of enemies
Are balanced by the arguments of friends.
Be fair to us, and let those have a chance
Who give you chances to witness new plays,   30
I mean good plays, of course,

                    not Luscius' recent effort
To thrill his audience by letting a slave run wild
In the street. Why should the populace
Be at a madman's mercy? Terence will tell
You more about old Luscius' aberrations
When he writes more new plays; UNLESS he makes
An end of pointing out the flaws in Terence.
   So, be at hand with equanimity,
And let me act a quiet play for you,
So that The Running Slave, or The Old Grouch,
Or Greedy Parasite, or Sharp Con Man,
Or Pimp, do not have to be played by me
At the top of my voice and height of energy.   40
For my sake, tell yourselves my case is just,
So that my work can be lightened somewhat.
The men who write new plays have no mercy
On an old man like me. They have a script
That calls for lots of action—right away,
They come to me with it. But if it's light
And frothy, they engage another troupe.
   In this play Terence has a good clean style.
So make a test of what my powers are
In both directions, the fast action play,
Or here, the quiet one. I never have
Set too greedy a price on my own skill.
I think that I derive the greatest gain
By bringing you pleasure. Let me stand for that.   50
And let young actors have it in their hearts
To please you, rather than indulge themselves.

ACT I

Scene 1

CHREMES, MENEDEMUS

CHREMES: Although our acquaintance is so recent,
Dating from when you bought this land next door
To mine, and we have had little to do
With each other—still, your manliness,
Or your being my neighbor, which I regard
As bordering on friendship, makes me bold
To talk to you on familiar terms.
It seems to me that you are acting out
Of keeping with your years, and quite beyond   60
What your status requires. By all the faith
Of men and gods, what do you want of yourself?
What are you after? Sixty years ago,
Or more than that, I'd say, was your birthday.
In these parts no one has a better piece
Of property or one worth more. You own
Some slaves. But you do all the work yourself
As if you hadn't one. I never leave
In the morning or come back home at night
Without seeing you digging in your land,
Or ploughing, or lugging something around.
You never take time off, or take it easy   70
On yourself. I'm sure this is no pleasure
For you. "Well, I'm not satisfied at all
With the work being done here." Still, if you
Put in the time you spend doing the work
On making them do it, you'd get more done.
MENEDEMUS: Chremes, are you so much at your leisure
From your business that you can look after
Others' business, foreign to your interests?
CHREMES: I am a man: nothing that is human
Is foreign to my interests. So, suppose
I want to offer you advice, or be
Advised by you of what goes on. If what
You do is right, then I should do the same,
If not, I might persuade you to desist.
MENEDEMUS: I have to act this way. You go ahead   80

And act as you have to.

CHREMES: But must a man
Torment himself?

MENEDEMUS: I must.

CHREMES: Well, if you have
Some troubles, I could wish you didn't have them.
But what is your distress? Tell me just what
Has made you feel so guilty?

MENEDEMUS: Oh lord, lord!

CHREMES: Don't cry, but let me in on what it is.
Don't keep silent; don't be afraid; trust me.
I'll help you out, with money, or advice,
Or sympathy.

MENEDEMUS: You really want to know?

CHREMES: But that's the reason I've spoken to you.

MENEDEMUS: Well, then, I'll tell you.

CHREMES: Meanwhile, as we talk,
Put those rakes down, won't you? Don't keep working.

MENEDEMUS: I will not.

CHREMES: Why won't you?

MENEDEMUS: Don't let me give
Myself a moment off.   90

CHREMES: I refuse you that.

MENEDEMUS: Ah, that's unfair of you.

CHREMES: With a rake like that?
God, it's heavy.

MENEDEMUS: And just what I deserve.

CHREMES: Now tell me about it.

MENEDEMUS: I have one son,
A young man. "I have?" I meant, "I had."
Whether I've still got him or not, Chremes,
I don't quite know.

CHREMES: Why don't you know?

MENEDEMUS: You'll know.
An elderly woman came here from Corinth,
In reduced circumstances, and my son
Began to love her daughter to distraction.
It was as if he had her for his wife.
And all this started up unknown to me.
When I found out about it, I began

To treat my ailing son quite unkindly   100
As ill suited his case, violently,
The way fathers will act. I railed at him
Day in, day out. "I suppose you hope
You'll be allowed to carry on like this,
With your father alive and well, and have
A mistress in the place of a real wife?
You're wrong if you think that and, Clinia,
You don't know me. I want you for a son
Only as long as you conduct yourself
In a worthy manner. If you don't do that,
I'll find some way of dealing with your case.
This sort of behavior could not exist
Except for too much leisure. Why, when I   110
Was your age, I did not invest my time
In love affairs. For I was poor. And so,
I left for Asia, and out there I found
Money and reputation in the army." [1]
So it came down to this: the young fellow
Was won over by hearing, so often,
The same remorseless speech. He thought that I,
Through age and wisdom, knew more than he did.
He left for Asia, for army service
Under some satrap, [2] Chremes.

CHREMES: Well, I must say!

MENEDEMUS: He went without my knowing it, and now
    It's been three months.

CHREMES: You're both at fault,
    But his initiative remains the sign
    Of a respectful, far from lazy spirit.   120

MENEDEMUS: When I found out about it from his friends
    I came back home depressed, nearly frantic
    And sick at heart, upset, and bewildered.
    I sat down, slaves ran in, took off my shoes.
    I saw others hurrying to set the table
    And get dinner ready, doing what each one could
    To lighten my sadness. When I saw that

---

[1] *in the army:* that is, as a mercenary in the army of a ruler of a kingdom in the Near East.

[2] *Under some satrap:* Clinia follows his father's example.

I started thinking, "So many of them,
Worried for me alone, all so concerned
To care for me alone? All these housemaids 130
To see to my clothing? Ought I alone
To lay out so much money on my house?
And my son, who could equally make use
Of these things, or enjoy them even more,
At whose age it is only right for things
Like this to be available, I sent
Away from here in an unhappy state.
A sheer injustice! I'd think myself willing
To do whatever evil you could name
If I went on living in luxury.
As long as he leads such a life of need
And lacks a native land, because of my
Wrongdoing, so long will I slave for him."
I went ahead, left nothing in the house, 140
No furniture, no finery: I swept
It all away, the maids, and all the slaves
But those who could repay their own expense
By working on the farmland readily.
I put them all together and sold them.
I advertised the house immediately
For sale, and got some fifteen thousand [3] for it,
With which I bought this piece of land, and here
Is where I work. I had concluded, Chremes,
That I would be that much less in the wrong
By being a poor man for my son's sake;
That it was not right for me to enjoy
Any pleasure unless he came back here,
Safe and sound, to share in it with me. 150
CHREMES: I think you have a kind heart for your child,
And he is utterly agreeable
If handled properly and sensibly.
But you did not know your son well enough,
And he did not know you. When this is so,

---

[3] *fifteen thousand:* fifteen talents in Greek silver, equivalent to $30,000 or more.

It's hard to live aright. You never showed
How much you valued him; he didn't dare
Believe in you the way a son should trust
His father. But if that had been the case,
These things would never have happened to you.

MENEDEMUS: It's like that, I admit. But I'm the one
Who's most at fault.

CHREMES: Menedemus, I hope
That things will be all right. And I am sure
That he will be here, safe and sound, quite soon.   160

MENEDEMUS: Would god it were that way!

CHREMES: Well, it will be.
If it suits you, please be my dinner guest
This very day. It's Dionysus Day.

MENEDEMUS: I cannot.

CHREMES: Why not? Spare yourself a bit,
I beg you. And your absent son would want
The same for you.

MENEDEMUS: It's not fitting for me,
Who drove him out to work, to take myself
Away from hardship.

CHREMES: Your mind is made up?

MENEDEMUS: It is.

CHREMES: Farewell, then.

MENEDEMUS: And the same to you. (*Exit*)

CHREMES: He brings me to the verge of tears, I feel
So sorry for him. But it's time today,
Time to remind my next door neighbor here,
Phania, to be my guest at dinner. I'll go   170
See whether he's at home. (*Exits and returns immediately*)
                     I didn't need
To remind them. They say they've already gone
To my house. So I keep my guests waiting.
I'll go right in. But why, I wonder now,
Are my doors creaking open? Who's coming out?
I'll just step over here and listen in.

Scene 2

CLITIPHO, CHREMES

CLITIPHO (*Calling back inside*): No need to worry, Clinia. They
  won't be long.
  I know she'll be with you right here today
  As soon as she gets the message. Dismiss
  The needless worry that's tormenting you,
  Right now.
CHREMES (*Aside*): Who can my son be talking to?
CLITIPHO (*Seeing him*): Oh, there's my father. I wanted him.
    Father,
  You're here in the nick of time.
CHREMES: Why is that?   180
CLITIPHO: You know our neighbor here, Menedemus?
CHREMES: Rather.
CLITIPHO: You know he has a son?
CHREMES: I heard
  He had. In Asia.
CLITIPHO: No, he isn't, father.
  He's here, at our house.
CHREMES: Well, I declare.
CLITIPHO: I caught
  Him disembarking, brought him from the ship
  Right off to dinner here. He's always been
  One of my best friends, from our childhood days.
CHREMES: You bring me pleasant news. I only wish
  I'd urged Menedemus to be with us
  More strongly, so I could be the first one
  To spring this unexpected happiness
  On him in my own home. But there's still time.
CLITIPHO: No: don't do that. It wouldn't work, father.
CHREMES: Why not?

CLITIPHO: Because Clinia's not at all sure
  What he might do. He's only just arrived,
  Afraid of everything, his father's wrath,
  The way he feels toward his girl. He loves
  Her to distraction, and on her account
  There was a row, and Clinia left.
CHREMES: I know.   190
CLITIPHO: He sent his slave to find her in the city,
  I sent our Syrus too.
CHREMES: How does he feel?
CLITIPHO: Clinia? He says that he's upset.
CHREMES: Upset?
  Could anyone be less so? What is lacking
  For him to have but what are called good things
  For a man to have? Parents, countryland,
  Friends, family, relations, affluence, all
  Intact? Such things, of course, depend upon
  Their owner's state of mind. For him who knows
  How to use them, they are good things; for him
  Who misuses them, they're a disadvantage.
CLITIPHO: His father always was a mean old grouch
  And I'm afraid now more than ever, father,
  He'll be angry at him more than he ought.
CHREMES (Aside): That man? But I'll restrain myself. It helps
  If Clinia is still a little fearful.
CLITIPHO: What's that you're saying to yourself?
CHREMES: I'll say.   200
  However things were going, Clinia
  Should have stayed at home. Perhaps his father
  Was a bit too hard on him for his passion.
  He should have put up with it. For who can he
  Put up with if he can't bear his own father?
  Was Clinia to live in his father's style,
  Or his father in his? He says he's hard on him.
  That's wrong. Fathers' anger is almost always
  Uniform; fathers, I mean, who are
  Reasonable men. They want their sons not to
  Be always after women, out for parties,

And give them small allowances. It all
Makes for good conduct. Once the mind is trapped
In sinful appetites, it cannot help
Following in its misguided footsteps.
It's wise to learn from the trials of others.
What is of use to you.   210

CLITIPHO: I'm sure it is.

CHREMES: I'll go in now and see what's for dinner
And seeing now what time of day it is,
Be sure you don't go too far from the house.

ACT II

Scene 1

CLITIPHO

CLITIPHO: What unjust judges fathers are of all
Young men! They think it only right that we
Should be born old men, instantly, as boys,
Not privy to what adolescence brings.
They govern as their passion now dictates,
Not as it used to be. If I ever do have
A son, he'll have an easygoing father,
I swear; allowance made for his straying,
An understanding of it, and forgiveness.
Not like my father, who points out to me
His own views through another. And, oh my god,   220
When he's had a little to drink, how he
Goes on about his own goings-on! And now
He says, "Take your example of what's useful
From others' trials." Shrewd! He just has no

Notion how deaf an ear I give his story.
My mistress' words move me much more, when she
Says, "Give me this," or "Get me that," but I
Have nothing to reply. I can't. No one
Is worse off than I am. For even Clinia,
Who has enough to deal with on his own,
Still has a nice, well-educated girl,
Unconscious of the courtesan's merry tricks.
There's no controlling mine: lady loverly's chatter!
She's so stuck-up, expensive, proud, a show-off.
As to what I might give her, I can say
Only, "Oh, certainly." I haven't nerve
To tell her I have nothing to draw from.
I've just got into the mess recently
As yet my father doesn't know about it.

Scene 2

CLINIA, CLITIPHO

CLINIA: If my affair was in all that good shape   230
   I know they'd have arrived by now. I fear
   That in my absence my woman has been
   Corrupted here. And many things fit in
   To strengthen that opinion in my mind:
   The place, the opportunities; her age;
   Her being subject to a scheming mother,
   Whose sweetest thoughts are those that tell of cash.
CLITIPHO: Clinia!
CLINIA: I feel so sorry for myself!
CLITIPHO: Won't you be careful not to let someone
   From your father's house see you coming out here?
CLINIA: All right. It's just that I sense some trouble
   In store for me.

CLITIPHO: Won't you keep from predicting
Before you know the truth?

CLINIA: If it weren't bad,
They'd have been here long since.

CLITIPHO: They will be here
Quite soon.

CLINIA: But when will that "quite soon" be "now"?

CLITIPHO: Didn't you think how far it is from here?
And you know women. While they're getting ready,   240
Fussing around and starting to start out,
It takes a year.

CLINIA: Oh, Clitipho, I'm afraid.

CLITIPHO: Breathe in, breathe out. Oh look there's Dromo now
And Syrus with him. They're here now, for you.

Scene 3

SYRUS, DROMO, CLINIA, CLITIPHO

SYRUS (*Enters from far right*): That's it?

DROMO: That's it. Meantime,
while we carved out
Our sentences, the women got lost in transit.

CLITIPHO (*Seeing them in the distance*): Your woman's here, you
hear that, Clinia?

CLINIA: I hear, at last, I see; I feel quite well.

DROMO (*To* SYRUS): No wonder, they're so loaded down, bringing
That flock of maids with them.

CLINIA: Her maids? From where?

CLITIPHO: You're asking me?

SYRUS: It was wrong to leave them.
What stuff they're lugging with them!

CLINIA: Oh dear, oh dear!

SYRUS: Gold trinkets, clothes. And now it's getting dark
And they don't know the way. Stupid of us

To go ahead. Go back to meet them, Dromo.
Get a move on, don't stand there.

CLINIA: Oh dear me!   250
What a let-down!

CLITIPHO: Why so? What is it now
What torments you?

CLINIA: You're asking me? that question?
The maids, the jewels, clothes. When I left here
She had one servant girl. Where do you think she got
The rest of that stuff?

CLITIPHO: Oh, at last I get it.

SYRUS: God, what a mob! I know this house of ours
Will hardly hold them all. And will they eat!
And will they drink! Could anything be worse
For our old man? But there come the young men.
I wanted to see them.

CLINIA: What of our trust?
Oh Jupiter! While I, because of you,
Strayed off, half-mad, in exile from my land
You made yourself well-off, Antiphila;
You left me in the lurch, in great distress,
For whose sake I incurred the greatest blame
And disobeyed my father. Now I'm sorry
For him. I feel guilty. He used to harp
On such women's habits, to warn me off   260
In vain; he never could drive me away
From this one. But I'll do it now. But when
It would have been gracious of me, I couldn't.
No one could be worse off than me.

SYRUS (Aside):   I see:
He went astray because of what he heard
Us saying over there. (To CLINIA) Clinia, your girl
Is quite different from what you are thinking.
Her life is the same, her idea of you
The same it was, as far as we can judge
From first-hand evidence.

CLINIA: And what is it?

I'd rather think, more than anything, that I
Suspected her wrongly.

SYRUS: So you can know
Each point in turn: the old woman, alleged
To be her mother formerly, was not.   270
And she is dead. I heard Antiphila
Telling the other girl so, on the way
To our house, just by chance.

CLITIPHO: What other girl?

SYRUS: Wait, Clitipho. I'll get to that after
I've finished telling what I started to.

CLITIPHO: Well, hurry up.

SYRUS: Well, when we first arrived
At their house, Dromo knocked hard at the door.
An old woman came up and opened it
And he burst in. And I was right behind him.
The old woman bolted the door again
And went back to her wool. So, in this way,
If in no other, Clinia, you'd know
How carefully she looked after her life   280
In your absence. When you suddenly break
In on a woman who doesn't expect you
You have a good chance then to estimate
The way of life daily habit prescribes
For almost everyone's behavior.
We found her working hard at her weaving,
Modestly clad in black, and I suppose
That old woman's death was the reason:
No jewels; gotten up in the manner
One dresses for oneself, no fancy garb
Of the sort women wear to lead you on,
Her hair let down and tossed back carelessly   290
Around her head. But that's enough of that

CLINIA: Syrus, go on. Don't leave me in suspense
About my happiness.

SYRUS: Well, the old woman
Was working at her loom. One servant girl

Was working there beside her, clothed in rags,
Untidy, unlooked after.

CLITIPHO: If all this
Is true, as I believe it is, Clinia,
Can anyone be luckier than you?
That girl, you know, he said was so untidy,
Unlooked after? That's a good indication
Of how beyond reproach your mistress is,
Whose go-betweens are handled carelessly.
The system is for those who would approach   300
The mistresses to pay out money first
To their attendants.

CLINIA: Go on, please. But don't
You try to get in good with me. What did
She say when you mentioned my name to her?

SYRUS: When we said you were back and wanted her
To come to you, your mistress stopped her weaving
At once, her face became flooded with tears.
It happened, rest assured, for love of you.

CLINIA: I'm so happy, I don't know where I am.
The gods love me. And I was so afraid.

CLITIPHO: I told you it was nothing, Clinia.
But now it's my turn, Syrus. What about
The other girl?

SYRUS: We've brought Bacchis along.   310

CLITIPHO: You have? Brought Bacchis? Brought her where,
You character?

SYRUS: Where else, but to our house?

CLITIPHO: My father's?

SYRUS: One and the same.

CLITIPHO: You've got some nerve.

SYRUS: Well, after all, no daring deed is done,
No great move made, without taking some risks.

CLITIPHO: But look here, you devil, are you looking
For fame by throwing my life in the balance?
You make the slightest slip, and I'm done for.
(To CLINIA) What would you do to him?

SYRUS: I meant . . .

CLITIPHO: Meant what?

SYRUS: I'll tell you if I get a chance.

CLINIA: Give him the chance.

CLITIPHO: All right, Syrus, go on.

SYRUS: As the situation now stands, it's rather as if . . .

CLITIPHO: What's this long story he's starting out now
To tell me? Hell with that.

CLINIA: He's right, Syrus.
Lay off. Get to the point.

SYRUS: But really, I   320
Can't keep quiet, you're so unfair to me,
Clitipho, in so many ways; you're hard
To get along with.

CLINIA (To CLITIPHO): We ought to hear him out,
By Hercules, so just be still a moment.

SYRUS: You want to be in love, you want to get
Your girl, you want the money you give her
To be made up. You don't want to take risks
To get her. You're not wise foolishly,
Of course, if it is wise to want something
That cannot be. You either take the risks
Along with the blessings, or let the blessings go,
And with them the pitfalls. So, take a look
At which of these alternatives you want.
But still, I know the plan I found is right,
And a safe one. For at your father's house
You have the chance to be with your mistress
Without worry. The money you promised her [*]
I'll find the same way I planned to at first.
You've made me deaf in both ears asking me   330
To bring it off. Can you want something else?

CLITIPHO: If only this works out.

SYRUS: "If only"? Try it:
Then you'll see.

---

[*] *The money you promised her:* Syrus keeps trying to find means of helping Clitipho get this sum, equivalent to $1,000, to smooth the course of his relationship with Bacchis. If Clitipho can't get the money he will lose her.

CLITIPHO: All right, now: let's have your plan
    What is it?
SYRUS: We pretend that your mistress
    Is Clinia's.
CLITIPHO: Oh, great! So what will he
    Do with his own? Will she be called his too,
    As if the one were not disgrace enough?
SYRUS: Oh no, she'll be whisked off to your mother.
CLITIPHO: Why there?
SYRUS: It's a long story, Clitipho,
    If I tell you why I want to do that.
    I have a good reason.
CLITIPHO: Oh, what nonsense!
    It's not solid enough for me to think
    I won't be nervous.
SYRUS: Wait. If you're nervous—
    I have another scheme you'll both admit
    Is not risky.
CLITIPHO: I wish you could hit on
    Something like that.
SYRUS: Exactly. I'll meet Bacchis
    And tell her to go right back home.   340
CLITIPHO: I meant . . .
    What did you say?
SYRUS: I'll see that your worries
    Are all removed and you can sleep soundly
    On either ear.
CLITIPHO: Let's see. What shall I do?
CLINIA: You do? When something good . . .
CLITIPHO: Syrus, just tell me . . .
SYRUS: Just do what I tell you, or you will wish
    You had, too late, today, and hopelessly.
CLINIA: . . . is offered, take the pleasure while you can.
    You can't tell . . .
CLITIPHO: Syrus, I mean . . .
SYRUS: You may mean,
    But I intend to do it.

CLINIA: . . . when a chance
　Like this will come your way again, if ever.

CLITIPHO: By Hercules, you're right. Syrus! Hey, Syrus!
　I mean, don't go.

SYRUS (Aside): He's warming up. (To CLITIPHO) Did you want
　something?

CLITIPHO: Want something? Hey! Syrus, come back, come back,
　Come back!

SYRUS: I'm right here. Tell me what you want.
　You'll soon say you don't like this plan, either.   350

CLITIPHO: Oh no, Syrus. I trust you with myself,
　My love, and my good name. You be the judge.
　But don't do something I will be blamed for.

SYRUS: It's foolish, Clitipho, to caution me
　On that subject, as if my own interests
　Were less at stake than yours. If things go wrong
　Somehow, for you there are hard words in store,
　But for this man, hard blows. So this affair
　Is not one I intend to take lightly.
　But ask him to pretend that she is his.

CLINIA: Of course I'll do that. What it comes down to
　Is that we have to.

CLITIPHO: No wonder I like you,   360
　Clinia.

CLINIA: But don't let her spill the beans.

SYRUS: She's too clever for that.

CLITIPHO: I'm quite amazed
　At how you could get her to come along
　With you so nicely. She handles her lovers
　Firmly: what lovers, too.

SYRUS: I got to her
　At the right time, which is of first importance.
　I came across an army officer
　There, begging her to spend the night with him,
　Beside himself with longing. She was handling
　The fellow skillfully, and put him off
　To keep his eager heart flaming, and earn
　Your thanks for her efforts. But watch it, you,

And don't do something rash. You know how quick
Your father is to catch on to these things.   370
And I know how impetuous you are.
Suppress those sighs, those looks over the shoulder,
Those double-meaning phrases, those throat-clearings
And come-on coughs, and those giveaway smiles.

CLITIPHO: You'll praise my conduct.

SYRUS: See that you deserve it.

CLITIPHO: You'll marvel at me, you yourself.

SYRUS: How fast
The women are in following us here.

CLITIPHO: Where are they! Why are you holding me back?

SYRUS: She's not yours any longer.

CLITIPHO: Yes, I know,
As soon as she is in my father's house,
But meanwhile, now . . .

SYRUS: And no more now.

CLITIPHO: Give in.

SYRUS: I won't give in.

CLITIPHO: A tiny bit.

SYRUS: I forbid it.

CLITIPHO: Oh, just to say hello.

SYRUS: If you're smart, you'll depart.

CLITIPHO: I'm off. But what
About him?

SYRUS: He'll stay.

CLITIPHO: Lucky man!

SYRUS: Start walking.   380

Scene 4

BACCHIS, ANTIPHILA, CLINIA, SYRUS

BACCHIS: My dear Antiphila, by Pollux, I
Can only praise you and find you well advised

To see that your good habits compare well
With your good looks. I'm not at all surprised,
As the gods love me, that every man in town
Wants you for his. Your character is shown
In what you were saying, and how you think.
When I reflect in my heart on your life,
And on all of you women who steer clear
Of taking on the common mob of lovers,
It's not so strange you are the way you are,
And we the way we are. It suits you right
To be upright. As circumstances are,
They don't give us that choice. Drawn by our looks,
Our lovers cultivate our company.
When beauty starts to fade, they turn their minds   390
To someone else. Unless, meanwhile, we have
Some further prospect, we live quite alone.
But for you, once you've chosen to go on
Living with some man whose conduct most suits
Your own, lovers like those will stick with you.
In this way, you are good for one another
And truly bound together by each other,
So no disaster can fall on your love.
ANTIPHILA: I don't know about other women, but
I do know that I've always tried to make
My own desires match his exclusively.
CLINIA (Aside): Oh my Antiphila, that's just the way
Only you bring me back to my country.
When I was not with you all my troubles
Were ones I took lightly except for one,
Having to be without you.
SYRUS (Aside):   I agree.   400
CLINIA: Syrus, I can hardly stand it, not being
Allowed to make the most of my treasure
In my own way.
SYRUS: But from what I have seen
Of your father's reputation, he'll give
You a hard role to play for some time still.
BACCHIS: Who's that young man watching us over there?

ANTIPHILA: Oh, catch me, please!

BACCHIS: What is it, darling?

ANTIPHILA: I'm dying, dying!

BACCHIS: What's come over you?

CLINIA: Antiphila!

ANTIPHILA: Do I see Clinia,
  Or don't I?

BACCHIS: Who is it you see?

CLINIA: Hello,
  Darling.

ANTIPHILA: My darling Clinia, hello.

CLINIA: How are you?

ANTIPHILA: Happy that you are back home safe.

CLINIA: May I hold you, Antiphila? Oh you,
  The one my heart most wanted!

SYRUS: Go in. Chremes
  Has been waiting for you for some time now.

ACT III
(The next morning)

Scene 1

CHREMES, MENEDEMUS

CHREMES: It's getting light already. Shall I knock   410
  On my neighbor's door to let him know, first
  From me, his son is back? I realize
  His son would rather I didn't. But when
  I see how much his poor father suffers
  Because he went away, can I conceal
  So unhoped for a joy? I can't do that.

I'll help the old man any way I can.
I see my son ready to serve a friend
Of the same age, and to be his ally
In his affairs. It's only right for us,
As older men, to be of service to
Our fellow older men.

MENEDEMUS (*Enters*):   Either by nature I   420
Was born with a gift for unhappiness
Or the remark I hear so often made
Is not true, that time takes away the pain
And sorrow men have felt. Mine keeps growing
Larger each day, my sorrow for my son.
The longer he's away, the more I want
Him back, the more I long for him.

CHREMES: Oh, there
He is, coming outdoors. I'll go and speak to him.
Menedemus, greetings. I bring you news
You most want to be in on.

MENEDEMUS: You haven't heard
Something about my son, Chremes, have you?

CHREMES: Alive and well he is.

MENEDEMUS: Where is he, though?   430

CHREMES: At my house.

MENEDEMUS: My son?

CHREMES: Yes.

MENEDEMUS: He has come back?

CHREMES: Indeed he has.

MENEDEMUS: My Clinia is back?

CHREMES: That's what I said.

MENEDEMUS: Let's go. Take me to him,
I beg you.

CHREMES: He doesn't want you to know, yet,
He's back here, wants to keep out of your sight.
He's still afraid because of his misconduct
That your former severity may have
Grown even worse.

MENEDEMUS: But didn't you tell him
How I felt?

CHREMES: No.

MENEDEMUS: Why didn't you, Chremes?

CHREMES: Because it would be the worst thing for you,
And for him too, if you showed so contrite
And soft a heart.

MENEDEMUS: I can't be unbending.
I've had enough of being a strict father,
Quite enough.

CHREMES: Oh there you go, Menedemus,
Impulsive either way, too generous,   440
Or too stingy. You'll let yourself in for
The same mischief, the one way or the other.
Before, you scared your son away from here
Rather than let him traffic with a mistress
Who was quite happy, then, with small favors,
And pleased with anything. Soon afterwards,
Forced into it against her will, she started
Pursuing profits in the common way.
And now, when she cannot be held on to
Without a huge outlay, you're eager to
Give anything. To give you some idea
Of how nicely set up she is at present   450
To make a killing, first: she brought with her
More than ten maids, loaded with clothes and jewels.
If she had some Persian prince as her lover
He'd never manage to meet her expenses.
Much less can you.

MENEDEMUS: Is she inside there now?

CHREMES: Is she, you ask? I've felt it, I tell you.
I've given one dinner just now, for her
And her companions. If I had to give
Another, I'd be done. To skip the rest:
The wine alone she ran through, tasting, sipping it!
"Oh, father," she'd say, "this is just so-so.
And this, a little on the bitter side.
See if you haven't something a bit smoother."
I unsealed all the jars, and all the flasks.   460
She had us all worried, and, mind you, that

Was only one night's feast. How will it be
For you, do you suppose, when they devour
You day after day? So help me god if I
Don't pity you, Menedemus, for your
Good luck.
MENEDEMUS: He's free to do just as he wants.
Let him have, use up, and exhaust my resources.
I'm quite determined to put up with anything
So long as I can have him here with me.
CHREMES: If you're set on that course, I think it is
Important not to let him know that you
Are giving him the money for his needs.
MENEDEMUS: How can I manage that?
CHREMES: Oh, any way
Except the one you're thinking of. Make use
Of anyone else, even if it means   470
Being tricked by some slave's clever dodges.
I know they were up to something, from the way
They acted on the sly at dinner, whispering
Together, Syrus and that slave of yours,
Advising the young men. For you it's worth
Losing a talent this way,[5] rather than
A mina your way. It's not so much, now,
A question of money as one of how
We give it to a young man with the least
Risk all around. Once your son understands
Your willingness to give away your life
And all your money rather than lose him,   480
Well, lord, how large a window you've opened
On idleness! How unpleasant for you
It would be then to live. For, all of us
Are made much worse by self-indulgent freedom.
He'll want whatever pops into his mind,

[5] *a talent this way, rather than/A mina your way:* Chremes is more money-conscious than Menedemus, perhaps because Menedemus was originally more well off, or has come to see that the value of money is nothing when compared to having a son. The mina is equivalent to a sixtieth of a talent, i.e., somewhat more than $25.

And won't stop to consider whether it
Is right or wrong, but just go after it.
Then you will not be able to endure
Both your money and him going to ruin;
And so you'll say you won't provide. Then, the issue
Will come to what he knows you most value,
And he will threaten to leave you again.

MENEDEMUS: You see it truly, and state it as it is.   490

CHREMES: By Hercules, I didn't close my eyes
In sleep last night, searching for some idea
Of how best to hand back your son to you.

MENEDEMUS: Here's my right hand, Chremes, I hope that you
Will offer me the same.

CHREMES: I'm with you there.

MENEDEMUS: You know what I would like you to do now?

CHREMES: Tell me.

MENEDEMUS: Since you have realized the slaves
Are starting to trick me, see to it that
They speed it up. I'm eager to give him
What he desires, and eager to see him.

CHREMES: I'll take the job. I have a little business
On hand that interferes. Our neighbors here,
Simus and Crito, are having a dispute
Over their boundaries, and they've asked me
To judge the case. I'll go to them right now   500
And tell them I can't help them out today
As I had said I would. I'll be right back.

MENEDEMUS: Please do. (*Exit* CHREMES) Oh, I could swear it by
    the gods!
How much better prepared by nature are
All men to see another's situation
And judge it than they are to see their own!
Is this because in our affairs we are
Too much wrapped up in our own happiness
Or in our sorrow? How much more this man
Knows of my case than I know by myself!

CHREMES (*Returning*): I've begged off, so I'm free to lend you
    help.

I'll have to catch Syrus and talk to him.
Oh, someone's coming out of my house now.
Let's step over toward your house a bit   510
So they don't think we've put our heads together.

Scene 2

SYRUS, CHREMES

SYRUS: Let's go, this way and that: in spite of all,
   We'll have to find money, and set a trap
   For his father.
CHREMES (*Aside*): It wasn't me, was it
   That they were setting their trap for? I guess
   Clinia's slave was too late getting here,
   And so the job was given to our man.
SYRUS: Who's talking over there? I'm done for now:
   Suppose he heard me!
CHREMES: Syrus!
SYRUS: Oh . . . er . . . ah.
CHREMES: What are you up to?
SYRUS: Oh quite up to scratch,
   Thank you. But I'm amazed, Chremes, to see
   You out so early. You drank so late last night.
CHREMES: Oh, nothing in excess.
SYRUS: You call that "nothing"?   520
   To me you're like one who, as they say,
   Has the constitution of an old eagle.
CHREMES: Now, never mind.
SYRUS: That woman's awfully nice,
   His mistress, quite polite.
CHREMES: Yes, I suppose so.
   She's awfully good-looking; that's the main thing.
SYRUS: Well, not good-looking as women once were,
   But as the style is now, I guess she'll do.

I'm not at all surprised that Clinia
Is crazy over her. He's got some father,
A frightful miser, terribly stingy,
Our neighbor here. You know him? As if he
Weren't dripping with money, his son decamped
For lack of means. Did you know that happened
As I say?

CHREMES: Why should I not know of it?
The man deserves the mill!   530

SYRUS: What man?

CHREMES: I meant
The young man's slave . . .

SYRUS (*Aside*):   Syrus, I was afraid
For you, for a moment there.

CHREMES: . . . who let it happen.

SYRUS: What could he do?

CHREMES: You ask? Somehow, he'd find
The wherewithal, invent some strategy
By which the boy could be given his girl
And keep his harsh father, against his will.

SYRUS: You're joking.

CHREMES: Syrus, that's what he should do.

SYRUS: But you're not praising those who fool their masters?

CHREMES: At the right time, I praise them.

SYRUS: You're right there.

CHREMES: In the sense that such tactics often are
A cure for much distress. For instance, here:
His only son would have stayed right at home.   540

SYRUS (*Aside*): I can't tell whether he's saying these things
In earnest, or joking. I only know
He gives me heart to feel better about
My plan.

CHREMES: And what's he waiting for, Syrus?
The boy to go away again because
His father won't put up with his expenses?
Isn't he inventing some clever plan
Regarding the old man?

SYRUS: He's much too dumb.

CHREMES: You ought to help him out for the young man's sake.

SYRUS: Oh, I can do that easily, if you
   Tell me to. I'm in close touch with how
   Business like that gets done.
CHREMES: So much the better, then,
   By Hercules.
SYRUS: Of course, it's not like me
   To be telling lies.
CHREMES: But do it anyway.   550
SYRUS: And you might make a point of remembering,
   If something else like this happens by chance:
   It's only human, if your son should act
   Along these lines.
CHREMES: There'll be no need, I hope.
SYRUS: I hope so, too. But I did not say that
   Because I'd noticed him planning something
   Along those lines. It's just that, if he does,
   I hope you won't be hard on him. You see
   How young he is. Of course, I have no doubt
   That, should occasion call for it, I could
   Handle you nobly, Chremes.
CHREMES: Well, as to that,
   Should need arise, we'll see what's to be done.
   Now get busy. (*Exit* CHREMES)
SYRUS: I never, ever, heard
   My master speaking more to my advantage,
   Or heard him offer such an invitation
   To me to outwit him and run less risk.   560
   But who's this coming out from our place now?

Scene 3

CHREMES, CLITIPHO, SYRUS

CHREMES: How dare you? How can you behave like that,
   Clitipho? Is that any way to act?
CLITIPHO: What did I do?

CHREMES: I saw you put your hand
  On that woman's breasts just now, didn't I,
  That courtesan's?
SYRUS (*Aside*): It's all over now. I'm done for.
CLITIPHO: Me?
CHREMES: With my own eyes, don't you dare deny it.
  You offer such an insult to Clinia
  If you don't keep your hands off her. Some gall,
  You've got, to invite a friend home with you
  And toy with his mistress. And last night, too,
  Over the wine, you were so shameless.
SYRUS (*Aside*): That's right.
CHREMES: So ill behaved! I worried endlessly
  About what might happen, so help me god.
  I know what lovers are. They take notice
  Of things you wouldn't think they were observing. 570
CLITIPHO: Believe me, father, I would never do
  A thing like that to Clinia.
CHREMES: May be.
  But I suggest you come out here, at least,
  Some distance off, not stick so close to them.
  Their passion packs a punch, but your presence
  Keeps them from doing what it tells them to.
  I speak from experience. There's not a friend
  Among those I call mine, in whose presence
  I'd dare reveal my secret thoughts, Clitipho.
  In another's presence, his rank deters me.
  I feel ashamed, in front of someone else,
  Of doing something that would make me look
  Awkward or brash. And you can rest assured
  This is the case with him. We, for our part,
  Are to respect the other's attitude
  And where and how we must fit in with it.
SYRUS (*Aside*): How he goes on!
CLITIPHO (*Aside*): I'm done for.
SYRUS: Clitipho,
  Is this how I instructed you? You play
  The role of sensible and self-controlled . . . 580

CLITIPHO: Oh shut up.

SYRUS: . . . gentleman, to perfection.

CHREMES: Syrus, I'm ashamed of him.

SYRUS: I can believe it.
You have good cause. It even worries me.

CLITIPHO: You're wrecking my chances.

SYRUS: I only speak
The truth as I see it.

CLITIPHO: Then I'm not to
Go near them?

CHREMES: I ask you, is there one way
To go near them?

SYRUS (*Aside*): It's finished. Clitipho
Will give himself away before I've managed
To get the money. (*To* CHREMES) Chremes, would you care
To listen to a dumb bunny like me?

CHREMES: What should I do?

SYRUS: Tell him to go away,
Somewhere away from here.

CLITIPHO: Go away where?

SYRUS: Wherever you want. Make some room for them.
Go take a walk.

CLITIPHO: A walk? A walk to where?

SYRUS: God, it's not as if there wasn't any place.
Just go out there somewhere, anywhere you want.

CHREMES: He's talking sense, I think.

CLITIPHO: May the gods wreck you,
Syrus, for pushing me away from here!

SYRUS: And after this, you keep your hands to yourself! 590
(*Exit* CLITIPHO)
You do think so? What do you think he'd do
If you did not chastise, control, and warn him
As much as the gods give you means to do so?

CHREMES: I mean to tend to that.

SYRUS: He must be, now,
Controlled by you, master.

CHREMES: It will be done.

SYRUS: That's a wise course. For he listens to me
 These days, less and less.

CHREMES: Have you managed anything
 About what I was speaking to you of
 A while ago, Syrus? Hit on something
 You like, or not?

SYRUS: Some scheme, you mean? Oh yes,
 I've just come up with something.

CHREMES: Good fellow.
 Tell me, what is it?

SYRUS: I'll lay it out now,
 But logically, as one thing falls in place
 After another.

CHREMES: Why do it that way, Syrus?

SYRUS: The courtesan's a shrewd number.

CHREMES: It seems so.

SYRUS: Ah, if you only knew! God, look at how
 She starts her scheming. There was an old woman   600
 From Corinth here. Bacchis had given her
 A loan of one thousand silver drachmas.

CHREMES: What then?

SYRUS: The old woman died, and left
 Her young daughter to Bacchis as a pledge,
 In security for the debt.

CHREMES: Oh, now I see.

SYRUS: Bacchis brought that girl here, and she's the one
 Who's with your wife now.

CHREMES: What then?

SYRUS: And so, then,
 She now insists that Clinia pay over
 The money right away, and says she won't
 Give her to him until she does. Insists
 On getting one thousand nummi for the deal.

CHREMES: Insists, does she?

SYRUS: God yes, no doubt about it.
 I took it just that way.

CHREMES: What have you in mind
 To do now?

SYRUS: Me? I'll go to Menedemus
And tell him she's a captive from Caria,
A wealthy, well-born girl. If he buys her,
There's plenty of profit in the bargain.

CHREMES: You're wrong there.

SYRUS: How so?

CHREMES: I now answer you   610
As if I were Menedemus: "No sale.
I'm not buying." How do you answer that?

SYRUS: Precisely what I wanted him to say.

CHREMES: How's that?

SYRUS: He need not buy her.

CHREMES: He need not?

SYRUS: Lord, no.

CHREMES: How's that, I wonder?

SYRUS: You'll find out soon enough.
But wait a moment. Why is our door opening
With such a noisy creaking of those hinges?

ACT IV

Scene 1

SOSTRATA, CHREMES, CANTHARA (Nurse), SYRUS

SOSTRATA: Unless my mind is fooling me, this ring
Is the same one, I do believe I left
Beside my daughter when she was exposed.

CHREMES (Aside): Now what's the drift of this announcement,
Syrus?

SOSTRATA: What do you say? Does it look like it to you?

CANTHARA: I said as much myself, the very moment
 You showed me it. That's it.
SOSTRATA: But do make sure
 You've looked at it closely enough, my dear.
CANTHARA: I really have.
SOSTRATA: Then go back in and tell me
 When she's finished bathing. (*Exit* CANTHARA) I'll wait out here,
 Meanwhile, for my husband.
SYRUS (*To* CHREMES): It's you she wants.
 See what she wants. She seems rather upset. 620
 And not for nothing. I'm a little worried.
CHREMES: She took great pains to speak a lot of nonsense.
SOSTRATA (*Seeing* CHREMES): Oh, there, my husband.
CHREMES: Oh yes,
 good wife.
SOSTRATA: You were
 The very one I wanted.
CHREMES: Do tell me
 What you wanted to say.
SOSTRATA: I ask you, first,
 Not to believe I dared do anything
 Against your strict instructions.
CHREMES: You want me
 To believe that of you, when there can be
 No shadow of a doubt? Well, I believe you.
SYRUS (*Aside*): An apology like this implies some guilt.
SOSTRATA: You will remember once when I was pregnant
 How strongly you insisted that if I
 Gave birth to a girl you were unwilling
 To acknowledge the child?
CHREMES: I know what you did:
 You had the child and raised her.
SYRUS (*Aside*): So she did.
 I've gained a lady boss, he's gained a loss.
SOSTRATA: Oh, not at all. There was a woman here
 From Corinth, a trustworthy older woman.
 I gave the child to her to be exposed.
CHREMES: Dear god, how could you have been so naive? 630

SOSTRATA: Too bad for me! What did I do?
CHREMES: You ask?
SOSTRATA: If I did something wrong, Chremes, I did it
    Unintentionally. I'm sure of that.
CHREMES: What I'm sure of, even if you deny it,
    Is that you speak and act very unwisely
    In everything you do. Just look, for instance,
    At the great number of mistakes you made
    In this affair. First, had you wanted to
    Abide by my instructions, you should have
    Let the child die, not say that she was dead
    In words, but in reality extend
    Hope for her life. I won't dwell on that. Granted,
    There is mercy, there are maternal instincts.
    But think how little thought you put into
    The consequences! It's quite obvious
    Your daughter was entrusted to that woman,
    For all you cared, to make her life one day
    As a courtesan, or to be sold off   640
    As a slave on the market. And I suppose
    You thought to yourself, "What matter, so long
    As she is kept alive?" But, why have dealings
    With people who know nothing of the law
    And have no care for what is just and right?
    Whether it's better, worse, advantageous
    Or inexpedient, they have no regard
    For anything but their own interests.
SOSTRATA: Chremes, I did the wrong thing. I'm convinced.
    I now ask this of you, that in so far
    As your nature is more severe, you be
    The more forgiving. Then, your sense of justice
    Will give protection to my foolishness.
CHREMES: Of course I'll overlook what you have done.
    But, Sostrata, my quickness to comply
    Teaches you much that isn't really right.
    Now come, what started you talking to me
    About this matter?

SOSTRATA: Since we are all so prone
   To silly superstitions, when I gave
   Our daughter to that woman to expose
   I took a ring from my finger [6] and told   650
   Her to leave it beside the exposed child.
   If she had died she still would not have been
   Cut off from her inheritance by us.

CHREMES: That was well done. You saved yourself and her.

SOSTRATA: And here's the ring.

CHREMES: Where did you get it?

SOSTRATA: The young girl Bacchis brought along with her . . .

SYRUS (Aside): Good lord, what's she saying?

SOSTRATA:
                                      . . . went in to bathe
   And gave it to me for safekeeping. At first
   I didn't notice anything, but afterwards,
   As soon as I saw what it was, right then
   I ran to you.

CHREMES: What do you make of her,
   Or suppose, now?

SOSTRATA: I don't know what to think.
   You might ask her where she came by that ring,
   If that could be found out.

SYRUS (Aside):   That does me in.
   I see more hope than I want to. If she's   660
   The one, she's ours.

CHREMES: The woman's still alive
   You gave our daughter to?

SOSTRATA: I wouldn't know.

CHREMES: At the time, what did she say she'd done?

SOSTRATA: That she'd obeyed my orders.

CHREMES: Her name, then?
   So she can be looked for.

SOSTRATA: Her name? Philtera.

SYRUS (Aside): The very one. Antiphila is saved,
   And I'm destroyed. No doubt about that fact.

   _____

   [6] *a ring from my finger:* the primarily Greek custom of exposing an unwanted
child is hedged about by scruples—in this case Sostrata did not want her daughter
to be thought of as disinherited, utterly without resources.

CHREMES: Come inside here with me now, Sostrata.
SOSTRATA: This has worked out beyond my wildest hopes.
  I was so terribly afraid, Chremes,
  That you would be as dead set in your mind
  Today, as when you acknowledged [7] the child.
CHREMES: A man often can't be the way he wants,
  If circumstance prevents. And at this point
  I want a daughter. Years ago, I didn't.

Scene 2

SYRUS

SYRUS: Unless my mind is fooling me a lot,
  Disaster is not very far from me:
  So hard pressed are my troops, entrapped
  In a narrow pass. If I don't see some way   670
  To keep the old man from discovering
  That she's his son's mistress. As for my hopes
  Of getting the money, or thinking that
  I could fool him, they've come down to nothing.
  If I can just get off, without exposing
  My flank, it's a triumph. And what a pain,
  To have so juicy a morsel snatched off
  So suddenly, when my mouth was watering.
  So what to do, to think up? My whole plan
  Will have to be replanned. Nothing's so hard
  It can't be worked out with a little planning.
  Shall I begin this way? No, not this way.
  Then this? It comes to the same thing.

[7] acknowledged: tollere, "to acknowledge." According to a custom prevalent among both Greeks and Romans, the father of a new-born infant was called upon to decide whether it should be raised or exposed to death. If he decided upon the former course he formally raised (tollere) the child from the ground or other place where it had been laid for the purpose. Hence the Latin expression liberos tollere, which means "to bring up." Otherwise the child was exposed.

Ah, here's one. No: that's just not possible.
Oh, wait. Here's a good one. Oh, excellent!
I've got it just right, now. By Hercules,
I think I'll drag that runaway money
Back here to my side, yet, and still and all.

Scene 3

CLINIA, SYRUS

CLINIA: After this nothing could happen to me
  That could bring sorrow. Untold happiness
  Has started up for me. I give in now   680
  To my father, a much more model son
  Than even he might want.
SYRUS (*Aside*):   I wasn't fooled:
  She has been recognized, from what I hear.
  (*To* CLINIA) I'm happy that this has happened to you
  Just as you might have wanted it.
CLINIA: Syrus,
  Old boy, you heard about it?
SYRUS: How could I
  Not have when I was present all the time?
CLINIA: Have you ever heard of something so perfect
  Happening to anyone?
SYRUS: No, I have not.
CLINIA: So help me god if I'm not more happy
  For her sake than for mine. She is well worth
  Whatever recognition there may be.
SYRUS: I think so too. But come now, Clinia,
  And take turns listening. We have to see
  That your friend's situation is secure
  And his father does not find out about
  His mistress.
CLINIA: Jupiter! What joy!
SYRUS: Quiet!   690

CLINIA: Antiphila, my girl, will marry me!

SYRUS: Will you keep on interrupting like this?

CLINIA: What can I do? Oh, Syrus, I'm so happy:
Put up with me.

SYRUS: I'm putting up with you.

CLINIA: We've entered on a life of the gods.

SYRUS: I guess
I'm just wasting my time.

CLINIA: Now speak to me:
I'm listening.

SYRUS: But not paying attention.

CLINIA: I will.

SYRUS: I said that now we have to see
That your friend's situation is secure.
If you leave us now and leave Bacchis here
Our old man will know she's his son's mistress.
But if you take her with you, the secret
Will be as well kept as it has been so far.

CLINIA: But, Syrus, nothing could work more against my marriage.
What face can I put on before my father? You see   700
What I'm saying?

SYRUS: Why not face up to him?

CLINIA: But what to say? What excuse can I make?

SYRUS: I don't want you to lie. Just tell it plain,
The way things are.

CLINIA: What's this you say?

SYRUS: I tell you:
Say that you love Antiphila, and want
Her as your wife, and that the other girl
Is Clitipho's.

CLINIA: A reasonable request,
A just command, an easy thing to do!
And I suppose you then want me to ask
My father to keep this from your old man?

SYRUS: Oh no. He tells it straight the way it is.

CLINIA: Are you sober, or in your right senses?
You're wrecking his chances, clearly. Tell me:
How can his situation be secure?

SYRUS: I think my plan deserves to take first prize.
  I take great pride in my capacities,   710
  My mighty cleverness, to fool them both
  By telling them the truth. When your old man
  Tells ours that Bacchis is his son's mistress,
  He still will not believe him.
CLINIA: But in this way
  You once again deprive me of all hope
  For my marriage. So long as Chremes thinks
  She's my mistress he won't give me his daughter.
  Perhaps you don't care what happens to me,
  So long as you look out for Clitipho.
SYRUS: How long the hell of a time do you think
  I mean for you to keep up this pretense?
  One day: until I've gotten the money.
  Just keep quiet that long; that's all I ask.
CLINIA: Is that enough? But what if his father
  Finds out about it? What will we do then?
SYRUS: Suppose I mention those who say "Suppose
  The sky fell in?"
CLINIA: I'm scared to do it.
SYRUS: Scared?   720
  As if you didn't have it in your power
  To clear yourself whenever you want to
  And bring the whole thing out into the open.
CLINIA: All right. Have Bacchis move over to our place.
SYRUS: That's fine. Here she comes, out of our place.

Scene 4

BACCHIS, CLINIA, SYRUS, DROMO, PHRYGIA

BACCHIS (*Pretends not to see* SYRUS *and* CLINIA):
  How nice of Syrus, enticing me out here
  With promises to lend me ten minae.

But if he stands me up, he'll ask me out
Again as often as he wants to come
And not find me. Or, when I've said I will,
And fixed the time, and he's told Clitipho,
Who's dangling in suspense, I won't show up.
Syrus will get paid back with a bruised back.

CLINIA (*Aside*): That's quite a shrewd promise she's making you.

SYRUS (*Aside*): You think she's only joking? She'll make good
On it, if I'm not careful.

BACCHIS (*Aside*):   Still asleep.   730
I'll wake them up. (*Louder*) Oh, Phrygia, dear, you heard
About the country villa of Charinus
That man was pointing out to us just now?

PHRYGIA: Yes, I did hear.

BACCHIS: He said it was next door
To Chremes' farm, on the right side?

PHRYGIA: Yes, I remember.

BACCHIS: Well, run right over there, fast as you can.
An officer is helping him enjoy
The Feast of Dionysus.

SYRUS (*Aside*):   What's she up to?

BACCHIS: Tell him I've been detained unwillingly
And am still here. But I'll work out some way
To give them all the slip and slip away
To join him there.

SYRUS (*Aside*):   That does us in. (*Aloud*) Wait, Bacchis,
   wait.
Where are you sending that girl, for heaven's sake?
Tell her to wait.

BACCHIS (*To* PHRYGIA): You'd better keep going.

SYRUS: I say the money's here and waiting.

BACCHIS: Well, then,
   I'll wait.

SYRUS: And then, you'll have it very soon.

BACCHIS: When you please. I'm not rushing you, am I?

SYRUS: I want you to do something for me, first.

BACCHIS: What?

SYRUS: You must move to Menedemus' house
And take your train of servants and baggage. 740

BACCHIS: What are you up to now, you poor excuse?

SYRUS: Me? Forging money to give you.

BACCHIS: Am I
Someone you think worth playing your tricks on?

SYRUS: I have my reasons.

BACCHIS: What business have I
With you in that house?

SYRUS: None at all.
I'm only giving you back what is yours.

BACCHIS: Well, let's be on our way, then.

CLINIA: Follow me. (*They go
into* MENEDEMUS' *house*)

SYRUS: Hey, Dromo!

DROMO (*Coming out of* MENEDEMUS' *house*): Who wants
me?

SYRUS: Syrus.

DROMO: What's up now?

SYRUS: Take all of Bacchis's maids and all her stuff
Over to your house, right away.

DROMO: Sure. Why?

SYRUS: Don't ask questions. Let them take along
Whatever stuff they brought with them to our place.
Our old man's going to hope his expenses
Are going down when they all go away.
He doesn't realize how great a loss
This gain will net him. You'll be smart, Dromo,
If you don't know a bit of what you know.

DROMO: You'll be saying I've lost the power of speech.

Scene 5

CHREMES, SYRUS

CHREMES: So help me if it isn't my turn now
  To pity Menedemus; so much trouble   750
  Has come his way. He has to play the host
  To that woman and all her retinue.
  Of course I know he won't feel anything
  For some days yet, it means so much to him
  To have his son back home. But when he sees
  How much it costs him every day at home,
  With no end to it, he'll wish that his son
  Would go away again. But here's Syrus:
  Just when I wanted him.

SYRUS (Aside):   Shall I go up
  To him?

CHREMES: Oh, Syrus!

SYRUS: Oh yes, there you are.

CHREMES: How are things?

SYRUS: I'd hoped I'd bump into you.

CHREMES: You seem to have transacted some business
  With old Menedemus.

SYRUS: What we talked of
  A while ago? No sooner said than done,   760
  That's my report.

CHREMES: You're sure?

SYRUS: Well sure, I'm sure.

CHREMES: I can't resist patting your head for that.
  So come here, Syrus. I'll do something for you
  For that good deed, and do it with pleasure.

SYRUS: If you knew how good a notion I had!

CHREMES: Oh come now, you're not boasting just because
  It came out as you wanted?

SYRUS: No, not boasting,
Just telling you the truth.

CHREMES: Tell me what's up.

SYRUS: Well, Clinia told Menedemus that Bacchis
Was the mistress of your son Clitipho,
And he had only brought her to their house
To keep you from finding out about it.

CHREMES: A smart move.

SYRUS: What's that? How do you like it?

CHREMES: Almost too good.

SYRUS: You ought to know how good. 770
But listen to the next moves we must make.
Clinia says that he has seen your daughter;
Her beauty won him to her at first sight.
He wants her as his wife.

CHREMES: You mean my girl
Who's just been found?

SYRUS: The same. And he intends
To ask that you be asked for her in marriage.

CHREMES: But why, Syrus? I don't quite follow that.

SYRUS: Oh, you're too slow.

CHREMES: May be.

SYRUS: He'll get money
To use for expenses, for clothes and jewels . . .
You follow that?

CHREMES: You mean, to buy things with?

SYRUS: Precisely.

CHREMES: But I won't give her to him.
I don't promise her to him in marriage.

SYRUS: You don't? Why not?

CHREMES: Why not? You ask me that? 780
To someone who . . .

SYRUS: As you please. I didn't mean
You ought to give her up for once and all,
But just pretend you would.

CHREMES: It's not my style,
To make pretenses. Tangle up your schemes
But don't entangle me in them. Would I

Promise my daughter to a man I don't
Intend to give her to?
SYRUS: I thought you might.
CHREMES: Not in the least.
SYRUS: It could have been worked out
Quite cleverly. I started this because,
Some time ago, you urged me to so much.
CHREMES: I know.
SYRUS: As to the rest of what you say,
Chremes, I acquiesce.
CHREMES: But still and all,
I very much want you to do your best
To bring it off, but in some other way.
SYRUS: It will get done. I'll find a way somehow.   790
As I told you, the money your daughter
Owes Bacchis will still have to be paid back.
And you of course won't try to get out of it
By saying, "What has that to do with me?
I didn't borrow it, did I? Did I
Issue orders? Did she have any right
To mortgage my daughter against my will?"
You know they say, "The letter of the law
Often obliterates the right decision."
CHREMES: I won't do that, of course.
SYRUS: Oh, others might,
But not you. They all think you're plenty rich,
And well set up.
CHREMES: I'll take her the money
Myself, in fact.
SYRUS: No. Better tell your son   800
To do it.
CHREMES: Why?
SYRUS: Because he's now the one
Suspected of being in love with her.
CHREMES: So what?
SYRUS: So: it will look more natural
For him to give it to her. I can get

What I want then that much more easily.
Oh, here he is. Bring the money.

CHREMES: I'll bring it.

Scene 6

CLITIPHO, SYRUS

CLITIPHO: There's nothing so easy it isn't hard
When you don't want to do it. This walk, now,
Was not tiring, but I got tired of it.
There's nothing I fear more than once again
Being pushed off somewhere away from here
And left without a chance of seeing Bacchis.
I hope the gods and goddesses, all of them,   810
Destroy you, Syrus, with that crackpot scheme
You hatched. You're always thinking something up
Like this, to use to put the screws on me.
SYRUS: Get out, won't you, and go where you belong?
Your charging in here almost ruined me.
CLITIPHO: I wish it had, by god. You deserve it.
SYRUS: Deserve it? Why? I'm glad I heard you say that
Before you got the money I was going
To give you.
CLITIPHO: But what would you have me say
To you? You pulled my leg. You brought my mistress
Here, but I can't lay my hands on her.
SYRUS: Well, I've cooled down a bit. But do you know   820
Where your Bacchis is now?
CLITIPHO: She's at our house.
SYRUS: No.
CLITIPHO: Where, then?
SYRUS: She's at Clinia's.
CLITIPHO: I'm done for.

SYRUS: Cheer up. You'll soon be taking
Her the money that you had promised her.
CLITIPHO: You're kidding. Where from?
SYRUS: From your own father.
CLITIPHO: You wouldn't kid me, would you?
SYRUS: You'll find out,
When it happens.
CLITIPHO: I'm such a lucky fellow!
You're great, Syrus!
SYRUS: Your father's coming out.
Don't act surprised by whatever he does.
Just go along with him. Don't say too much.

Scene 7

CHREMES, CLITIPHO, SYRUS

CHREMES: Where's Clitipho?
SYRUS (To CLITIPHO):   Say "Here I am."
CLITIPHO: Oh, here
He is, father.
CHREMES (To SYRUS): Have you told him what's on?
SYRUS: I told him nearly everything.   830
CHREMES (To CLITIPHO):   Take this money
And carry it.
SYRUS (To CLITIPHO): Go on, blockhead. Don't stand there.
Why don't you take it?
CLITIPHO: All right. Hand it over.
SYRUS: Come with me quickly, this way. (To CHREMES) You wait
here
Until we come out. We won't be there long. (They go out)
CHREMES: My daughter now has ten minae from me
I think of as paid out for her support.
Another ten will follow these for clothes;
And then they ask two talents for the dowry.

Our customs cost us more than is quite fair.
And now I'll have to let my business go
And look for someone, like a son-in-law,   840
To give the property I worked to own.

Scene 8

MENEDEMUS, CHREMES

MENEDEMUS (*Calling back inside to* CLINIA):
My son, I think I'm a very lucky man,
Knowing that you've come back to your senses.
CHREMES (*Aside*): How wrong he is!
MENEDEMUS: Chremes, I wanted you.
Help me hang on to my son and myself
And family, in so far as you can.
CHREMES: Tell me, what is it you want me to do?
MENEDEMUS: Today you found a daughter.
CHREMES: What of it?
MENEDEMUS: Clinia wants her given as his wife.
CHREMES: What kind of person are you?
MENEDEMUS: Person? I?
CHREMES: Have you forgotten already what we
Discussed about the scheme, the smart method
They'd use to get some money out of you?   850
MENEDEMUS: I remember.
CHREMES: That's what they're up to now.
MENEDEMUS: What's your story, Chremes? There is no doubt
That it's Clitipho's mistress at my house.
They say so.
CHREMES: And what's more you believe it.
They also say that your son wants a wife,
So when I have consented you will give
Money to buy clothes for her, and jewels,
And other things needed.

MENEDEMUS: That's it, of course:
  The money's for the mistress.

CHREMES: She's the one
  Who'll get it.

MENEDEMUS: Poor me, then! It did no good
  Being happy. But I'd do anything
  To keep from losing him. What can I say
  You said, Chremes, to keep him from knowing
  I found out, and holding a grudge against me?   860

CHREMES: A grudge? You're too easy on him, Menedemus.

MENEDEMUS: Let me go on as I've begun, Chremes,
  And see me through it.

CHREMES: Say that we've conferred,
  And taken up the matter of the marriage.

MENEDEMUS: I'll say that. And then what?

CHREMES: That I'll do it,
  That I approve the choice of son-in-law;
  And even go so far, if you want to,
  As saying that I offer him her hand.

MENEDEMUS: Well now, I'd hoped for that.

CHREMES: Then he can ask
  For what he wants from you the more quickly
  And you give him what he wants even sooner.

MENEDEMUS: That's what I want.

CHREMES: It won't be long before,
  In my view, you'll have had enough of him.
  No matter what, though, if you have good sense,
  You'll give with care, a little at a time.   870

MENEDEMUS: I'll do that.

CHREMES: Go inside. See what he wants.
  I'll be at home if you want anything
  Of me.

MENEDEMUS: I will want you. I'll want to let
  You know whatever it is I've been doing.

ACT V

Scene 1

MENEDEMUS, CHREMES

MENEDEMUS: I know I'm not so shrewd, so perceptive;
  But this stage-manager, prompter, director,
  Chremes, outdoes me. Any name you want
  That fits a fool applies to me: jackass,
  Lead-head, blockhead, dead log. But there's no name
  For him. His density outdoes them all.
CHREMES (*Calling back inside to* SOSTRATA):
  Oh, do desist from deafening the gods,
  Dear wife, by thanking them because your daughter
  Has been discovered. Unless, of course, you judge
  Them by your own standards, and think that they   880
  Don't understand a thing until it's said
  A hundred times over. I wonder now
  Why my son's been in there so long with Syrus?
MENEDEMUS: Who are those men you say are lingering
  Inside there, Chremes?
CHREMES: Oh, Menedemus,
  You're here. Tell me: did you tell Clinia
  What I told you?
MENEDEMUS: Yes, all.
CHREMES: What did he say?
MENEDEMUS: He started acting happy, like people
  Who want to marry.
CHREMES: Ho, ho! That's a good one!
MENEDEMUS: What makes you laugh?

CHREMES: I was thinking of my slave,
The so resourceful Syrus.

MENEDEMUS: Why think of him?

CHREMES: He even shapes the looks on men's faces,
The fiend.

MENEDEMUS: You mean, my son was just pretending
To be happy?

CHREMES: Quite so.

MENEDEMUS: The same idea
Occurred to me.

CHREMES: He's an old hand.

MENEDEMUS: You'd think so
All the more if you knew more about it.

CHREMES: Is that so?

MENEDEMUS: Would you like to hear the rest?   890

CHREMES: Wait. First I want to know how much you lost.
For when you told your son the girl was his
Dromo, of course, dropped hints about the need
For clothes, jewels, and servants for the bride,
So you'd give them the money.

MENEDEMUS: No.

CHREMES: What? No?

MENEDEMUS: Yes. No.

CHREMES: Your son didn't?

MENEDEMUS: No. Not at all,
Chremes. He only pressed me more for one thing:
To celebrate the wedding rites today.

CHREMES: You tell a strange story. And my Syrus,
He did something?

MENEDEMUS: Nothing.

CHREMES: I can't see why.

MENEDEMUS: That's strange, when you see all the other things
So clearly. But then, it's that same Syrus
Who shaped your son's behavior so shrewdly
As to leave not the slightest doubt that she
Was Clinia's mistress.

CHREMES (*Aside*):   What's going on?   900

MENEDEMUS: I won't mention the kissing and hugging:
That doesn't count.

CHREMES: What more could their pretense
Call for?

MENEDEMUS: Oh, really!

CHREMES: What else? Oh, really?

MENEDEMUS: Just listen. There's a room way at the back
Inside the house. A bed was put in there
And made up.

CHREMES: Then what happened after that?

MENEDEMUS: No sooner said than done, your Clitipho
Went right in there.

CHREMES: Alone?

MENEDEMUS: Yes, quite alone.

CHREMES: I'm worried now.

MENEDEMUS: And right away, Bacchis
Followed him there.

CHREMES: Alone?

MENEDEMUS: Yes, all alone.

CHREMES: I'm done in now.

MENEDEMUS: When they were in the room
They shut the door.

CHREMES: Did your Clinia see
This going on?

MENEDEMUS: How could he not see it?
He was right there with me.

CHREMES: So, Bacchis is
My son's mistress. I'm ruined, Menedemus.

MENEDEMUS: How so?

CHREMES: I've hardly cash for ten more days.

MENEDEMUS: Not worried are you, just because your son
Does a favor for his friend?

CHREMES: For his girl-friend.   910

MENEDEMUS: If he does favor her.

CHREMES: Can you doubt it?
You don't think any man's so easygoing
And docile as to let his own mistress,
Before his eyes . . . ?

MENEDEMUS: Why not? That's how they might
Put one over on me more easily.

CHREMES: You're justified in making fun of me.
I'm vexed at myself now. So many things
Gave hints I could have understood completely,
Had I not been a blockhead. What I saw!
I'm really in a mess. But, believe me,
They won't get away with it unpunished,
While I'm alive. Right now, I'm going to . . .

MENEDEMUS: Control yourself. Don't lose your self-respect.
Am I not enough of a lesson to you?

CHREMES: For anger, Menedemus, I'm not myself,   920

MENEDEMUS: For you to talk like that! Isn't it shameful
To give others advice, be wise in public,
And yet not be able to help yourself?

CHREMES: What shall I do?

MENEDEMUS: What you told me I did
Too little of. Let your son realize
That you're his father. Let him have the courage
To trust you every way, to ask for things,
To seek your help, and not go looking out
For some other support, and desert you.

CHREMES: Oh, no! I'd rather he went anywhere
In the world than by self-indulgence here
Drive his father to need. If I keep on
Paying his costly bills, Menedemus,   930
My resources will soon reach the level
Of garden rakes.

MENEDEMUS: But then you'll just create
More trouble for yourself, if you're not careful.
You'll show how strict you are, but later on
You'll still forgive him and get no thanks for it.

CHREMES: You don't know how upset I am.

MENEDEMUS: Oh, well,
Have it your way. But what about my wish
To have your daughter married to my son?
Or do you have some other preference?

CHREMES: Oh no. The son-in-law and the connection
Appeal to me.

MENEDEMUS: What dowry shall I tell
My son you offered? . . . Why are you so still?
CHREMES: Dowry?
MENEDEMUS: That's what I said.
CHREMES: Oh. I . . .
MENEDEMUS: Chremes, don't worry if it's less than usual.
CHREMES: The dowry doesn't bother me at all.
I thought two talents might do well enough,   940
In view of my income. But if you want
To safeguard me, my money, and my son,
You'll have to say that I've made over all
My property to set up that dowry.
MENEDEMUS: What are you up to there?
CHREMES: Pretend that you
Are taken by surprise. Ask Clitipho
The reason I'd do it.
MENEDEMUS: In fact, I can't
See the reason you should do such a thing.
CHREMES: Why do it? To make a dent in his mind
That's flowed over into extravagance
And self-indulgence: bring him to the point
Where he no longer knows which way to turn.
MENEDEMUS: What's on your mind?
CHREMES: Leave me with it. Let me
Behave the way I want in this affair.
MENEDEMUS: I won't press you. You do want it this way?
CHREMES: I do.
MENEDEMUS: It will be done.
CHREMES: Now, have your son
Prepare to have his bride summoned to him. (Exit MENEDEMUS)
My Clitipho will get his dressing down
In words, as suits children. But, as I live,
I'll dress up that Syrus with blows, not clothes.   950
And hand him over so well combed and groomed
He'll remember me all his life. He thinks
I'm someone to laugh at, to have fun with.
He wouldn't dare do what he's done to me
To a defenseless woman, so help me god.

Scene 2

CLITIPHO, MENEDEMUS, CHREMES, SYRUS

CLITIPHO: Can it be really so, Menedemus?
In so short a time has he rid himself
Of all his natural feelings as a father?
For what misdeed? What horrible offense
Have I committed, to my sorrow? Young men
Normally act the way I did.

MENEDEMUS: I'm aware
Of how this hurts more, is much harsher
To, the person it lands on. But I too
Take it as hard. I cannot understand
How it can be. I don't grasp the reason.
I only wish you well, with all my heart.

CLITIPHO: You said my father was waiting out here.

MENEDEMUS: And here he comes. (*Enter* CHREMES, *exit* MENE-
DEMUS)

CHREMES: Why blame me, Clitipho? 960
I took this action with a view to you
And your shortsightedness. For when I saw
How wrapped up in the pleasure of the present
You were, with no thought for the length of time in store,
I formed a plan so you would not be left
In need, and yet could not waste all I have,
This property. Then when your conduct made
It wrong for me to hand it on to you,
Who were entitled to first claim on it,
I chose your nearest relative, and made
It all over to him, to be his trust.
There'll always be protection, Clitipho,
For your folly with him, food and shelter,
A roof over your head.

CLITIPHO: I'm out of luck!
CHREMES: This is much better than with you as heir
  For Bacchis to possess my property.
SYRUS (*Aside*): Well, I'm completely out of luck. Stupid!
  It's criminal the way I've messed it up
  For everyone, without intending to.   970
CLITIPHO: I might as well be dead.
CHREMES: You might as well
  Learn first what living means. When you know that,
  If life still leaves you cold, try the other.
SYRUS: Master, may I?
CHREMES: Speak up.
SYRUS: But in safety?
CHREMES: Speak up.
SYRUS: What sort of craziness is this?
  It makes no sense to take it out on him
  When all the fault is mine.
CHREMES: The meeting's over.
  No one's accusing you, Syrus. Don't you
  Get mixed up in it. You won't need an altar
  As a refuge, or some kind intercessor
  To speak for you.
SYRUS: But what are you up to?
CHREMES: I'm not angry, either at you, or you;
  And it's not right for you to be angry
  At me for what I do. (*Exit* CHREMES)

Scene 3

CLITIPHO, SYRUS

SYRUS: He's gone away?
  And I wanted to ask him . . .
CLITIPHO: What?
SYRUS: Where to look

For food. He's cut us off so completely.
I know there's some for you at your sister's.

CLITIPHO: It's come to such a pass, then, Syrus, has it,   980
That I'm even in danger of starving?

SYRUS: As long as we're alive, there's still some hope . . .

CLITIPHO: Of what?

SYRUS: Of being hungry, both of us.

CLITIPHO: You laugh in this crisis, and don't help me
One bit with your advice?

SYRUS: No, I was thinking
About it while your father was talking,
And I'm thinking right now. So far as I
Can work it out . . .

CLITIPHO: What out?

SYRUS: Our plan.
It's not far off.

CLITIPHO: What is it, then?

SYRUS: Just this:
You're not their son at all. That's what I think.

CLITIPHO: How's that, Syrus? Are you in your right mind?

SYRUS: I'll tell you what's come to my mind, and you
Decide that for yourself. So long as they
Had only you and no other pleasure
To bring them more delight, they fawned on you,
They gave you everything. Now, a daughter
Has been discovered, and a good excuse,
In fact, for them to disinherit you.

CLITIPHO: That is quite probable.

SYRUS: You don't think he's   990
Angry at you because you misbehaved?

CLITIPHO: I don't think so.

SYRUS: And look at something else.
All mothers normally take the son's side
To help him in trouble and lend support
Against the father's strictness. That's not so
For you.

CLITIPHO: You speak the truth. What shall I do
Then, Syrus?

SYRUS: Raise this question with your parents;
  Bring it up openly. If it's not true,
  You'll soon evoke the sympathy of both,
  Or know whose son you are.

CLITIPHO: That's good advice.
  I'll take it. (*Exit* CLITIPHO)

SYRUS: I'm lucky this came to mind.
  The more he finds his suspicions groundless,
  The easier will he make peace with his father
  On his own terms. He just might take a wife.
  I can't tell yet. No thanks to Syrus, though.
  But what's this? Chremes coming out again.
  I'm taking off. For what I've done so far,   1000
  It's strange he hasn't ordered me hauled off.
  I'll take refuge in Menedemus' house
  And ask him to be my intercessor.
  I don't put any trust in our old man.

Scene 4

SOSTRATA, CHREMES

SOSTRATA: If you're not careful, my dear man, you'll do
  Our son real harm. I find it very strange
  That so foolish a notion could enter
  Your mind, my dear husband.

CHREMES: Will you persist
  In being a woman? Did I ever
  Want anything in my whole life, without
  Your contradicting me in it, Sostrata?
  But if I ask where I am in the wrong,
  Or why you act this way, you don't know why
  You take so strong a stand against me, foolish one.

SOSTRATA: I don't know why?

CHREMES: Well, yes. You do know why.

Let's not have the whole discussion once again. 1010
SOSTRATA: Oh, you're not reasonable to think that I'll
Keep still on a matter of this importance.
CHREMES: I don't ask that. Say what you want. But still,
I'll go ahead with it.
SOSTRATA: You'll go ahead?
CHREMES: I will.
SOSTRATA: Don't you see how much trouble you create
That way? He thinks he's a foundling.
CHREMES: Foundling,
You say?
SOSTRATA: It's so, and will be so, my husband.
CHREMES: Admit it, then.
SOSTRATA: Oh come now, I beg you.
That's something for our enemies to say.
Shall I say he's not my son, when he is?
CHREMES: You're not afraid, are you, that when you want
You can't prove he's your son?
SOSTRATA: You mean, because
Our daughter has been found?
CHREMES: I don't mean that.
I mean something that must win quick belief,
The fact that he behaves the way you do.
You'll prove he is your child quite easily: 1020
He's just like you. There's not a fault in him
That isn't matched in you. And furthermore,
No one but you could have a son like that.
Well, here he comes out, now. Ah, how straightfaced
He looks! So straightlaced, if you stop and think
Of what he's been up to, for some time now!

Scene 5

CLITIPHO, SOSTRATA, CHREMES

CLITIPHO: If there was ever any time, mother,
When I gave you pleasure, was called your son,
When both of you were willing to say so,
I beg you to remember it and now
Take pity on me in my time of need.
I beg, implore you. Show me my parents.

SOSTRATA: Really, my son, you must think no such thought:
You could not be another person's child.

CLITIPHO: I am.

SOSTRATA: Poor me! (*To* CHREMES) I suppose that this
Is what you were after. (*To* CLITIPHO) I assure you,
You are the son born to me and this man.   1030
And please, if you love me, don't let me hear
Such talk from you again.

CHREMES: And I tell you,
If you fear me, don't let me see you acting
The way you have been.

CLITIPHO: What way?

CHREMES: Well, if you want
To know, I'll tell you: indulging yourself
In guzzling, idling, wasting good money
On parties, food and drink. Believe me, now?
Believe, then, that you can be our true son.

CLITIPHO: Those aren't a parent's words.

CHREMES: Had you been born
From my forehead, like Minerva from Jove's
(They say), I would not let you, Clitipho,
Any the more make me suffer disgrace
Because of your contemptible behavior.

SOSTRATA: May all the gods prevent it!

CHREMES: I don't know
   About the gods. I only know that I
   Will do whatever I can to prevent it.
   You're looking for what you possess: parents;
   Not looking for what you don't have as yet:
   A way to comply with your father's wishes
   And look after what his hard work has earned.   1040
   To fool me, and bring right before my eyes
   That—I'm ashamed to use so vile a word
   In this woman's presence; but you were not
   At all ashamed to go ahead and do it.

CLITIPHO (*Aside*): Lord! How completely fed up with myself
   I am right now! And how ashamed I am!
   I don't know where to start to placate him.

Scene 6

MENEDEMUS, CHREMES, SOSTRATA, CLITIPHO

MENEDEMUS: Surely Chremes is tormenting the boy
   Too harshly, too inhumanly. So I
   Am coming out to make peace between them.
   Oh, good! I see them there.

CHREMES: Menedemus,
   Ah, why aren't you having my daughter called for
   And coming to agreement on the sum
   I offered for the dowry?

SOSTRATA: My dear husband,
   I beg you, don't do it.

CLITIPHO: I ask forgiveness,
   Father.

MENEDEMUS: Forgive him, Chremes. Let yourself
   Be won over by them.

CHREMES: And consciously

Make a gift of my property to Bacchis?   1050
I won't do that.

MENEDEMUS: And we won't let you do it.

CLITIPHO: If you want me to go on living, father,
Forgive me.

SOSTRATA: Do, dear Chremes.

MENEDEMUS: Come, Chremes,
I beg you to: don't be so obstinate.

CHREMES: What to do now? I see I can't go on
As I began.

MENEDEMUS: That's much more like yourself.

CHREMES: I give in, then, but on this one condition:
He does what I think right for him to do.

CLITIPHO: Command me, father: I'll do anything.

CHREMES: You'll take a wife.

CLITIPHO: But, father . . .

CHREMES: I hear nothing.

SOSTRATA: I'll vouch for him: he'll do it.

CHREMES: I hear nothing
From him, as yet.

CLITIPHO (*Aside*): Done for!

SOSTRATA: You hesitate,
Clitipho?

CHREMES: No. Let him choose for himself
Between the two.

SOSTRATA: He'll see it all right through.

MENEDEMUS (*To* CLITIPHO): At first, of course, it will seem hard
to you,
While you're still unfamiliar with it all,
But when you've gotten used to it, easy.

CLITIPHO: All right, father. I'll do as you command.

SOSTRATA: Oh, my dear son, I know a charming girl   1060
For you—you'll find her very nice—the daughter
Of our neighbor Phanocrates.

CLITIPHO: That redhead?
The girl with the cat's eyes? The freckle-face
With the turned-up nose? I can't do that, father.

CHREMES: He's so choosy! You'd think he'd thought and thought
About it for some time.

SOSTRATA: I know another.

CLITIPHO: No, look: since I'm the one who's getting married,
I know someone I might just like to have.

CHREMES: That's more like it. Good work, my son.

CLITIPHO: I mean
The daughter of our friend Archonides.

SOSTRATA: She's a nice girl.

CLITIPHO: But father, there's one thing.

CHREMES: What is it?

CLITIPHO: I wish you'd excuse Syrus
For what he did for me.

CHREMES: All right, I'll let him off.

(AMBIVIUS *reappears*)
And we'll let you off now,
Because,
You see, that's how it was!
Do we hear your applause?

ELIZABETHAN DRAMA
Eight Plays
Edited and with Introductions by
John Gassner and William Green

Boisterous and unrestrained like the age itself, the Elizabethan theatre has long defended its place at the apex of English dramatic history. Shakespeare was but the brightest star in this extraordinary galaxy of playwrights. Led by a group of young playwrights dubbed "the university wits," the Elizabethan popular stage was imbued with a dynamic force never since equalled. The stage boasted a rich and varied repertoire from courtly and romantic comedy to domestic and high tragedy, melodrama, farce, and histories. The Gassner-Green anthology revives the whole range of this universal stage, offering us the unbounded theatrical inventiveness of the age.

Arden of Feversham, **Anonymous**

The Spanish Tragedy, by **Thomas Kyd**

Friar Bacon and Friar Bungay, by **Robert Greene**

Doctor Faustus, by **Christopher Marlowe**

Edward II, by **Christopher Marlowe**

Everyman in His Humour, by **Ben Jonson**

The Shoemaker's Holiday, by **Thomas Dekker**

A Woman Killed with Kindness, by **Thomas Heywood**

paper • ISBN: 1-55783-028-2

CLASSICAL TRAGEDY:

edited by

"*Essential plays in highly readable translations ... useful in any course whose goal is to acquaint students with the masterpieces of Greece and Rome.*" **Harold Nichols**
Author, *The Status of Theatre Research*
Kansas State University

"*Outstanding essays ... with the right plays ... I am recommending them for our own Freshman Studies Program.*"
E. Peter Sargent
Associate Dean, Webster University

"*Each play is preceded by an insightful introduction ... carefully compiled anthologies.*" **Jed H. Davis**
Editor, *Theatre Education: Mandate for Tomorrow*
Dean, College of Fellows of the American Theater

"*Compelling ... offers a rich variety of translation-voices. ... The essays are unerringly chosen for their variety of critical approaches, accessibility, and potential to stimulate discussion and further reflection.*" **Felicia Londré**
Author, *Tennessee Williams*
University of Missouri

"*Corrigan remains one of our most visionary critics of dramatic literature ... [He] demonstrates his genius ... for finding the right critical commentaries to encourage students to discover the true classic nature of these plays.*"

Douglas C. Sprigg
Chair of Theatre & Film Dept.
Middlebury College

Paper • ISBN: 1-55783-046-0

GREEK AND ROMAN

Robert W. Corrigan

"The price is right! ... provides serious depth ... excellent choice of plays ... greatly enhanced by critical essays."

Phillip G. Hill
Editor, Our Dramatic Heritage
Furman University

"I know of no other collection of Greek and Roman plays ... as valuable to college and university theatre departments."

James M. Symons
Chair, Theatre Dept, University of Colorado
President, Association for Theatre in Higher Education

"An excellent selection of exciting translations ..."

Arthur W. Bloom
Dean, College of Communication
Loyola Marymount University

"Top of the line! Top notch! Corrigan has done it again! An excellent introduction to Greek and Roman drama."

Christian H. Moe
Chair, Theatre Dept.
Southern Illinois University

"Excellent addition to any freshman humanities syllabus. ... solid foundation for an introductory theatre course."

W.B. Worthen
Dept. of English, University of Texas-Austin

"Splendidly useful...up to Corrigan's usual high standards."

Robert Benedetti
California Institute of Arts
Author, *Actor at Work* (4th Ed.)

Paper • ISBN: 1-55783-098-3

MEDIEVAL AND TUDOR DRAMA
TWENTY-FOUR PLAYS
Edited and with Introductions
by John Gassner

The rich tapestry of medieval belief, morality and manners shines through this comprehensive anthology of the twenty-four major plays that bridge the dramatic worlds of medieval and Tudor England. Here are the plays that paved the way to the Renaissance and Shakespeare. In John Gassner's extensively annotated collection, the plays regain their timeless appeal and display their truly international character and influence.

Medieval and Tudor Drama remains the indispensable chronicle of a dramatic heritage — the classical plays of Hrotsvitha, folk and ritual drama, the passion play, the great morality play *Everyman*, the Interlude, Tudor comedies *Ralph Roister Doister* and *Gammer Gurton's Needle,* and the most famous of Tudor tragedies, *Gorboduc.* The texts have been modernized for today's readers and those composed in Latin have been translated into English.

paper • ISBN: 0-936839-84-8

THE LIFE OF THE DRAMA
by Eric Bentley

" ... Eric Bentley's radical new look at the grammar of theatre ... is a work of exceptional virtue, and readers who find more in it to disagree with than I do will still, I think, want to call it central, indispensable. ... The book justifies its title by being precisely about the ways in which life manifests itself in the theatre. ... If you see any crucial interest in such topics as the death of Cordelia, Godot's non-arrival ... this is a book to be read and read again."
—**Frank Kermode**
THE NEW YORK REVIEW OF BOOKS

"*The Life of the Drama* ... is a remarkable exploration of the roots and bases of dramatic art, the most far-reaching and revelatory we have had."
—**Richard Gilman**
BOOK WEEK

"*The Life of the Drama* is Eric Bentley's magnum opus or to put it more modestly his best book. I might call it an esthetic of the drama, but this again sounds ponderous; the book is eminently lucid and often helpfully epigrammatic. Everyone genuinely interested in the theatre should read it. It is full of remarkable insights into many of the most important plays ever written."
—**Harold Clurman**

paper • ISBN: 1-55783-110-6

SEEDS OF MODERN DRAMA

Introduced and Edited
by Norris Houghton

Five great forces—Chekhov, Hauptmann, Ibsen, Strindberg, and Zola—dramatists whose works define, embrace and transcend the trends and genres of the modern stage, meet here in this extraordinary exhibition of their sustained and sustaining power in today's theatre.

The ideal text for any course venturing into modern drama, Norris Houghton's volume boasts five landmark plays in distinguished modern translations.

THERESE RAQUIN
Zola

AN ENEMY OF THE PEOPLE
Ibsen

MISS JULIE
Strindberg

THE WEAVERS
Hauptmann

THE SEA GULL
Chekhov

Paper • ISBN: 0-936839-15-5